CUSTOMS VIOLATION

ALSO BY JANICE WEBER
The Secret Life of Eva Hathaway

CUSTOMS VIOLATION

by
Janice Weber

DONALD I. FINE, INC.
New York

For A. P.

Switzerland

"Of course women are the superior gender, Rhoda dear. Example? I defy you to name one man who can urinate and tie his shoelaces at the same time."

"Brilliant, Harriet."

"Thank you. It came to me one morning as I was late for my squashball lesson. I say, Fräulein Moser, what is this we're eating?"

"Zat is Sviss sausage. It likes you?"

"Delicious. But it must be just loaded with calories."

"Nein, zat is caravay seed."

"Harriet, forget about a few calories. In these mountains you'll walk them all off."

"That's no joke, honey. You see where they planted the school? On top of the friggin' Matterhorn! We're gonna hafta walk up that thing every morning for three weeks! I already checked, there are zero buses and one taxi which only runs in the afternoon. The driver milks his cows in the morning, his wife says. You think my boss told me about this? 'Breeze,' he says like Mr. Santa Claus, 'we're sending you to Switzerland. You're going to learn all about cooking from the best chef in the business! When you come back, you'll really be able to run the corporate cafeteria. It's our way of thanking you for coming to work for us.'"

"Vhat a nice man."

"Think again, Fräulein. My boss sent me here so he wouldn't lose his affirmative action subsidies. I wasn't even his first choice. None of the Hispanic employees wanted to go for a month without salsa radio stations. So he shipped me over and got double points. I'm not only female but half Cheyenne Indian."

"You're an Indian?!"

"Don't let the blond hair fool you, Rhoda. My first husband preferred blonds and I got used to myself that way."

7

"A typical male fantasy, unfortunately."

"Yeah, he was a real asshole. Sorry, Fräulein, I'll try not to say such words in your pension. I don't want to create a bad impression in front of the other ladies."

"Zat vould be apprissiated."

"Fräulein Moser, you don't know how thrilled I am to be staying in this pension. In the United States we have very few places for women only."

"Vhat? No kitchens?"

"I was referring to places of social interchange. You see how little progress we have made in twenty years of women's liberation. Society is as male-dominated as ever. It's quite discouraging, considering how well we started out."

"Yeah, just look at us old bags. We're not only wearing bras again but now we sag to boot. No offense, Froy. You're really in excellent shape."

"Zank you."

"How wonderful to be in a purely female environment, free of the sexual pressures which males so insidiously foist upon us. Isn't it, girls?"

"Definitely."

"Yeah, what the hell. I can let my roots show."

"Ze Indian roots?"

"No, the roots of my hair. They're black."

"Wonderful sausage. Why don't you eat yours before it gets cold, Breeze? As I was saying, Fräulein Moser, we're not here to impress men. We are here to learn. Ms. Squawfoot, for example, will be able to run a corporate dining room. Ms. Carlton will operate a new restaurant in Brooklyn."

"Vhat about you? You come to lose veight?"

"I am a food critic, as you may know. Harriet Swallow. Eating is my profession."

"Jeeeesus Christ, you're Harriet Swallow? You write *Piecemeal?* Listen, Froy, you'd better tell your cook to get on the ball. Harriet is merciless when it comes to food. Her column runs in every newspaper in the country, like *Peanuts*. Chefs commit suicide because of her."

"You kill my chef?"

"Of course not! Please sit down! How preposterous! Would you mind controlling yourself, Squawfoot? I have no intention of killing anything. I am here to write a bit of an exposé, if you must know."

"Sounds exciting, Harriet. What's it about?"

"I assume you will not babble this beyond our table. Have you noticed that most of our chefs are men? Why aren't more chefs women, I ask you?"

"Because those stupid hats wreck your hairdo."

"Why is it that women slave all day long in the kitchens of the world but men—once again—steal the limelight and every last cent in the end? What sex is Chef Boy-Ar-Dee? Why don't we have any Burger Queens? Did you ever hear of *coquilles St. Jacqueline?*"

"What about Aunt Jemima?"

"I hope you realize this only proves my point."

"I think you're really on to something here, Harriet."

"Of course I am, dear. I haven't fought my way to the top of my profession simply by eating cream puffs."

"Krim puffs? What is zat?"

"Profiteroles, Fräulein Moser."

"Ah ja! But ve do not eat zem here. My chef, he makes no dessert."

"You employ a chef? A man? In a pension for women?"

"Of course, vhy not? He is a fine fellow. He came just last week. My old chef, he got married."

"Where does this fellow sleep, Froy? Near our rooms?"

"Zat is ridiculous."

"Sorry, sorry, forget I mentioned it. I'm used to cohabitation."

"You'll be seeing enough men in school, dear. The instructors are all male. So is the rest of the class."

"We're the only women? Hot dog!"

"Squawfoot, may I tell you a few things before you embarrass us all?"

"Be my guest."

"This is an extremely exclusive culinary school. Only ten pupils are accepted at a time and each of them pays dearly for the privilege of studying with Chef Eggli. Perhaps had you financed this course yourself, you would think of it as something other than a sophomoric sex camp."

"Who said anything about sex? Did you, Rhoda?"

"Believe me, the last thing I'm interested in is men."

"Not even Italians?"

"Don't make me puke. My ex-husband was an Italian."

"Let's not digress, ladies. The point is, Rhoda and I are here to study. We take our careers very seriously."

"I know you do. You're both wearing business suits and sneakers."

"We're also very aware of being ambassadorpersons."

"Representing what? The U.S. Olympic Committee?"

"Women."

"Oh ja? Vhich vimmen, Frau Svallow?"

"The new women. We have husbands, children, jobs, houses, money, and brains."

"Zis is not possibell."

"Of course it is. Our European sisters are somewhat behind in this regard. But they are catching up, I assure you. Just wait a few years."

"Make sure you stock up on aspirin, Froy. I also recommend you check the local alimony laws with your lawyer. Is your name on all the titles?"

"I am not married."

"She's just joking. Squawfoot, what the hell is the matter with you?"

"Nothing, Rho, just a little fallout. Let's forget it. We're in the mountains now. Clean air, cows, cheese . . ."

"It certainly is quiet here. How far is Emwald from Montreux, Fräulein Moser?"

"Zirty kilometres."

"How convenient of us to arrive just in time for lunch. What a nice welcome present this sausage was."

"Tvelve Sviss francs I charge you."

"Well, well, you're quite a sharp businesswoman, aren't you?"

"Zank you. Now ve go. Bring ze dishes to ze little door, please. My cook vill clean zem."

"Don't we get to see the guy, Froy? Thank him for lunch or something?"

"No. You do not never look behind ze little door or I vill make you leave. I cannot have zis in my pension."

"My God, where are your manners, Squawfoot?"

"I was just being friendly."

"Sometimes Americans are too friendly. Like ze cowboys."

"That's a terrible thing to say to an Indian, Froy."

"Will you get away from that counter? Cripes! If you want a chef, wait until tomorrow!"

"Froy, can we at least shout through this little sliding door? Toodle-ooo, cookie! Keep peeling those potatoes!"

"Nice sausages, whoever you are. Go a little easier on the garlic next time."

"Girls, get away from there, will you? The man probably doesn't even speak English! He's not listening anyway. Can't you hear him banging his pots and pans?"

"I zink you have made him angry."

"How come? We ate everything!"

"Breeze, just shut up. You've strained enough diplomacy for one day."

"I show you your rooms. Zis vay, please."

1

One had merely to observe the tenscore wretches sagging like condemned tenements around the Swissair baggage carousel to realize that flying came naturally only to witches, fairies, and Clark Kent. Human eyeballs, forced upon shiny magazines, G-rated movies, paperback bilge, and the garishly tinted faces of the flight crew for eight hours running, usually rebelled after a shift in the ozone layer. Most of them grew red, haplessly snuggling into their swollen lids like hibernating amphibians; others just went into a coma, registering nothing. Hair was another part of the anatomy which could never finesse transatlantic flight. No matter how much or how little of it a traveler possessed, one half always became flattened against the scalp while the other half, acraze with voltage, stubbornly tried to re-launch itself into space. Aviation made the skin itch and it left the inner ear soaring at thirty-three thousand feet two days after the outer ear had landed. It leadened the brain and dehydrated the vital organs. Nevertheless, hoarding hours like priceless icons, all humanity flew in airplanes and called the Wright brothers geniuses for having invented jet lag, modernity's improvement upon sea sickness and saddle sores.

Still operating on European time, the bladders of passengers on Swissair Flight 309, Geneva to New York, distended woefully as inches away, stomachs already whimpered for more of those chocolate cigars with the kirsch insides. Four hundred feet swelled two sizes larger than the shoes which contained them. No matter that outside the sun dazzled the roses, enraptured the breeze: A battalion of biosystems yearned to shut down immediately. But it was only two o'clock in the afternoon, eons from bedtime in Manhattan. Everyone would have to remain mobile indefinitely; before expiring upon that Meccan pillowcase, the weary would have to deal with not only a clogged expressway, but a prying, inimical customs agent as well. Praying that their suitcases had followed them home, the dull crowd gazed at the motionless baggage wheel. Those with great faith in baggage handlers chatted softly. Those with wider experience, or cheaper suitcases, drooped over their carts as if awaiting judgment. A half dozen children, activated by light rather than the hands of a clock, scrambled amid the thicket of adults, who ignored them: Once beyond puberty, the human body preferred thirty-hour nights to thirty-hour days.

U.S. Customs Inspector Floyd Beck stood at his station checking out the still life: businessmen, several dips from the UN, but mostly tourists again. The average Americans were always easiest to pick out. They looked like slobs. Why was that, Floyd wondered. Plenty of Germans had pot bellies; all Japanese wore shorts and baseball caps. Sneakers reeked beneath the soles of all races. But stand the crudest Balkan goatherd in jeans and tee shirt next to an American wearing the identical outfit, and still the American would look like a slob. It had to do with a certain lack of deceit in the posture. The result of too wide oceans? Too easy wars? Too much English Spoken Here? Too many hogs in Iowa? Floyd shook his head as a woman, size eighteen stripped and shaved, bent to retie her sandal. She had probably worn that little pink tennis outfit into half the banks and all the confisseries in Geneva. What about that fop standing next to her with the white trousers and fifteen gold chains around his neck? How many times had he ordered a Miller Lite in the heart of Bavaria? Floyd didn't know which type did more harm to international fraternity, ignoramuses like these, or the overfriendly Texans who left twenty-percent tips when service was already included in the cost of dinner. Did they really have to wear those cowboy hats to the Swiss Alps? Floyd sighed. It didn't matter. They were home now, perhaps wiser than when they had left.

Two businessmen stepped back from the baggage wheel to light cigarettes, revealing a woman in a red hat who had been standing behind them. Floyd's eyes flew immediately towards the speck of color in the somber terminal and lingered for some moments upon the form beneath it. This was definitely a European woman. American ladies didn't wear high heels like that any more. Hurt the feet, they said. And they didn't wear fantastically tight skirts like that, either. They thought their behinds were too big. They were usually right. And they certainly didn't wear hats any more; didn't fit in with the life style. Floyd stared at the poppies adorning the woman's slender hatband. Did American females have any idea what hats did to a male's imagination? Of course they did. That's why they didn't wear them any more. The woman brushed something from the front of her blouse and Floyd wished he had moved back to Europe fifteen years ago, after Vietnam, before this liberation chimera had estranged the women of America from the gentlemen they shared bathrooms with. He would have set himself up in a little butcher shop near a great concert hall, made bratwurst by day, listened to Brahms by night, and flown to Sweden on weekends; women over there had better things to do on Saturday than stomp in demonstrations. Instead Floyd had finished his degree in criminology at NYU and joined the Customs Service. In those days four tourists out of five were carrying narcotics; as never before, his country needed him. That's what the recruiter had said, anyway. He knew a kamikaze patriot when he saw one.

Humming, the baggage wheel twirled slowly to life. Floyd watched the woman in the red hat shift weight from left to right foot, subtly amplifying the curve of her rear end. Then the two men stepped in front of her again. Suitcases began plopping onto the wheel, energizing the crowd; in a few moments the first of them would be passing by his station. Floyd punched a few keys on the terminal before him. Yesterday the computer had caught a French cocaine dealer who was stupid enough to use a U.S. passport with the same number as Jimmy Carter's. Some Colombian had probably framed him. *Ready;* flashed the screen.

Carrying one small suitcase, the woman in the red hat stopped in front of Floyd: Italian passport, Spanish name. She wore jewelry normally seen only after sundown and smiled as if she knew he had been looking at her. "Hello," he said, comparing her face with the picture on the passport. He preferred her life-size. "Are you visiting the United States for business or pleasure?"

"Business."

Was that a wink? A phantom smirk? Damn! Women who wore red hats and red lipstick after three thousand miles in the air still obliterated his concentration. There were so few of them nowadays that Floyd had no practice repressing his outmoded swinish reactions. She smiled an iota too slowly. "Open your briefcase, please."

Half the attaché case contained folders crammed with documents. She was a lawyer. Wondering what she wore to court, Floyd snapped open the partition.

There beside a pair of black silk stockings lay a gorgeous purple negligee with ribbons, feathers, and yards and yards of nothing. For one tiny moment, head to toe, Floyd petrified, and in the next moment melted back to flesh again: Sight had tripped memory had tripped darkness had tripped anger had tripped survival. Although swift, like the conversion of matter into energy, the process was hardly economical. "For emairgencies," the woman said.

"Thank you, ma'am." Inspector Beck quietly shut the briefcase. She was clean; he regretted that a little. "Next," he called, turning broadside, imagining her legs inside those dappled black stockings, pliant, warm . . . was he out of his mind? Tonight he'd be asking another woman to marry him! "Passport, please." The lady in the red hat left but her perfume lingered and spread like a coastal sunset.

Up the conveyor belt chugged a pink suitcase. Its owner, Doraleen-Sue Jones, would perhaps blossom in another life: in this one, she would winter beneath thirty excess pounds and designer eyeglasses with grotesquely convoluted bows. They were supposed to look elegant from the side. Doraleen? It sounded like something administered to either end of a rebellious digestive tract. "How long have you been away?" asked Inspector Beck, scanning her passport.

"Five weeks."

In Liechtenstein? Maybe she had tried to hitchhike. "Business or pleasure?"

"A funeral."

"Thank you," he said, waving her on. A browse through Doraleen's underwear would reveal nothing even subliminally confiscatory.

Now two plaid Hartmann bags halted in front of him. Their owner, Sydelle Chu, looked anything but Asian. Must have married one. She had probably divorced one, too, and was now dispensing her alimony on facelifts and tourism. She should not have been wearing a heavy shawl in July. Floyd watched her eyes. "Current address?"

Sydelle Chu scowled impatiently. "Fifth and Eighty-third. It's all on the passport." She leaned over to point. Then Floyd understood.

"Do you have anything else to declare?"

"No."

Naughty girl, Sydelle. "Take everything to that booth back there, please."

"What's the meaning of this? Where's the manager? What's your name? This is outrageous!"

Floyd impassively beckoned to a woman in uniform who accompanied Sydelle to one of the body search areas. There she'd find a contraband watch on Sydelle's upper arm.

Inspector Beck checked through an Italian family en route to a Bronx christening, six semidrunk Swiss businessmen, a few grandmas, and a huge Dane attired head to foot in black leather who asked him directions to Times Square. None of these resembled the shadowy courier Treasury had told them to watch for.

When the lines had finally thinned, Floyd's supervisor Albert McPhee approached. "Beck, take a break. We've got four 747s landing at 4:30."

"What happened this time?"

"What the hell didn't? An epileptic fit on Sabena, a coffin mistaken for an MX on El Al, hailstorms in Istanbul . . . now Lufthansa has to come in on schedule." McPhee munched a few expletives. "We won't get out of here til eight, count on it."

"We?"

"Yeah, you, me, the whole gang goes overtime tonight. I'm short-handed. Schmidt's got a migraine and Kwiesinski's pulled maternity leave again. I told her the next time she does this to me in high season I'm busting her to the piers."

"What about Diorello?"

"No windpipe for another two weeks." Diorello had been strangled by a Corsican who had not liked strangers rummaging through his shaving kit. "Come on, Beck, don't you need the cash? Young women cost money." McPhee coughed intently. "Old women even more."

"I've got to leave at six, Al, got a date with Portia. She's counting on me."

"For what? A lift to the dog pound?" Portia was a veterinarian, specialty canine therapy. She had irritated McPhee from the day he learned she still made house calls.

Floyd watched a sole tennis racket whirl lazily around the luggage wheel. "Maybe."

"Listen," his supervisor said after a moment, "I'll recheck the schedule. Don't go away." McPhee paused. "See anything intense on that flight?"

Floyd thought of a black silk stocking dissolving in air two seconds beyond a barrister's knee. "No."

"Idiot informer. Hash will be ripshit."

Special Agent George Hash was investigating the simultaneous disappearance of one government witness, ten bags of heroin, and fifty machine guns from various repositories in New York City. Everything had happened on Easter Sunday as Hash was intercepting a drop of Taiwanese telephones behind the Statue of Liberty: Both criminals and law enforcement agents worked overtime on holidays. Although Hash doubted these events were related, one of his most garrulous plants, a Korean greengrocer in Harlem, had told him that someone known only as Prong would be passing through JFK today. Prong knew more about international drug traffic than did fifty rock stars and was supposed to be carrying a pound or two of cocaine in from Europe. Customs agents were to be on the lookout for anyone with a pointed skull.

Floyd stepped over to the water fountain. Behind him the immigration terminal loomed ominously still, awaiting the 4:30 debacle.

"Hey Floyd! You bagged another Piaget!" Inspector Molly Fiske, known to her colleagues as Frisk, finished drinking and stood back. If skin-tight uniforms were unhealthy, Frisk would not outlive the week. Perhaps for this reason, McPhee had hired her from a brackish pool of female candidates several years ago. "Know what that dame tried to tell me? Her watch was a designer pacemaker! Dumb broad. For that I made her strip. Can you beat this? She was wearing a girdle! Remember those rigs that look like a rain barrel with fenders?" Frisk tucked her blouse another millimeter into her pants as her belt wheezed in agony. "How unnatural!" She tweezed a pad from her rear pocket. "Anyhow, nice going on the Piaget. That brings you up to twelve thousand in watches . . . four thousand in cameras . . . four in electronics . . . you're going to win the pot again if you keep this up." Frisk was running a little contraband contest among the customs inspectors. "McPhee should pay you a commission. Noses like yours are a freak of nature."

"Tell him yourself. Here he comes."

Inspector Fiske hastily fluffed her bangs. Years after her gender had rediscovered permanent waves, she still used a curling iron; she also spent many hours plucking eyebrows and buffing fingernails. Women with bodies like Fiske's could afford to be a little archaic. "What does the old fart want now?"

McPhee strolled to the water fountain. "Good afternoon! Run your hands over anything ticklish today, Tinkerbell?"

She looked disdainfully at him. "I was just complimenting Floyd on his latest haul. A six-thousand-buck Piaget."

"Nice work, Floyd. You're sharper than three bloodhounds and an atom smasher."

"Customs inspectors should get a ten-percent commission," Frisk said. "Incentive. So we don't join the forces of evil, you know?"

"Cut it out! You two stiffs love playing Wyatt Earp!" For a few moments Frisk and McPhee glared at each other with hatred. Floyd knew at once that they hadn't slept together in days. "That reminds me, Beck," said McPhee, spinning around, "how much does Portia charge for rabies shots? Jones got himself bitten by a monkey in a cargo hold yesterday."

"I'll ask her tonight."

"She still dragging you to those Lesbian History lectures?" cried Frisk.

They had ended last month. Still, Floyd was offended. "No, we're going out to dinner. It's our anniversary."

Frisk and McPhee fell thunderously silent. They had been lovers for three murky years so marriage was a sore point with them. "Great," said Frisk, stalking away. McPhee's eyes leapt after her. His body, prisoner of reason, held still.

"Wonder what she meant by that," he tried to chuckle after a moment. Floyd shrugged sympathetically; everyone in the terminal knew there was no way McPhee's wife would ever give him a divorce. He had made her miserable for twenty years, so now it was her turn. "Fiske!" the supervisor suddenly shouted after her. "You're on duty tonight! No commissions either! And take that scarf off, it's not part of your uniform!" He had given it to her for Valentine's Day.

Without slowing, Inspector Fiske entered the office. At once three men rushed to help her open the file cabinet. McPhee watched it all through the glass. "Beck," he said, face brick, voice stone, "you're on too. Sorry." He left.

Floyd glanced at his watch: twenty minutes ere typhoon. He walked briskly to a telephone at the far end of the terminal. Already hundreds of reception committees, their initial goodwill eroded by a three-hour delay, milled testily about the airport shops, eating chocolate, sniffing perfume, cursing aviation, and wondering why they had brought cranky children into the world. Behind every phone stood a helpless adult, one palm over one ear, explaining to a distant individual that nothing had landed yet. For many minutes Floyd stood behind a Greek gentleman spurting syllables faster than a dot matrix printer. Finally out of change, the man hung up and headed for the rest rooms.

Floyd lifted the overheated receiver and dialed a number. "Therapy," snapped a voice after one ring. His girlfriend, Dr. Portia Clemens, rehabilitated disturbed canines of all breeds. There were plenty of them in New York City apartments.

"Hi, honey," he said. "What's up?"

"Floyd, you know I hypnotize Barbetta every Wednesday," Portia sighed. A crazed yipping in the background indicated that today's session had not edulcorated the poodle's neuroses. "Anything wrong?"

"Oh, a few bombs, epilepsy, hailstorms, terrorists . . . now McPhee hit me with four 747s."

"So is dinner off?" Portia did not sound hurt. That hurt Floyd.

"No!" This was Wednesday night. The vixen would gladly attend another of her Female Awareness meetings. "Just later! Ten o'clock." He lowered his voice. "We have a lot to talk about." Floyd suddenly imagined Portia in a diaphanous purple negligee, calling softly to him.

"Barbetta," cooed Portia, "come down off the windowsill! Barbehhh-hta!"

"Hello?"

"Ooooooodle poodle. Nooooodle poodle. Goooood dog."

A loudspeaker behind Floyd pronounced the arrival of the Istanbul flight. "Gotta go. See you at ten."

Sounding almost human, Barbetta began to cry. Ever since those pooper scooper laws had gone into effect, the poodle had become fitful and depressed. Floyd hung up, irritated with the beast, irritated with Portia, who had stopped wearing negligees after her first Female Awareness meeting years ago. For a second Floyd wondered if tonight was the proper time to ask her to marry him. If Barbetta jumped out the window, no. Maybe never.

He swept back to the customs check-in amid a maelstrom of knees. The flagging multitudes had revived as the objects of their affections landed at last, perhaps with an expensive bottle of duty-free cognac. Who would ever enbosom him at an airport? Portia? Only if her patients' tails wagged. Floyd's lips compressed ever so slightly; even after myriad reason-rotten discussions with his girlfriend, he still found this disturbing.

Floyd trotted to his station as the first luggage wheel slowly ground into action. Five hundred tourists, still dusty from the Istanbul bazaar, lunged forward. Out plopped a knapsack which was immediately yanked by two right hands. Out came a pair of skis. Then there was nothing. Meanwhile, at the Lufthansa carousel, piece after piece slid onto the shiny steel plates.

"Now what's the holdup?" said Frisk, watching the crowd from the station next to Floyd. She had taken the fuschia-and-green scarf off. "They're going to riot in another minute." She reclasped a few loose curls beneath a pink barrette. It was against regulations but she did it to goad McPhee. "Gad, I hate tourists."

"Hey Floyd," said a voice behind them. "Hello, Frisky."

Floyd turned. "Any luck with Prong?"

Special Agent George Hash stood contemplating the front of Frisk's blouse. Should she sneeze and pop the buttons off, someone could be blinded. One day, when she gave up on McPhee, Hash would like to overtake Miss Fiske on a busy sidewalk. "Nope." He stared into the melee. "We're probably looking at him."

"How are we supposed to find a pointed head in this mess," muttered Frisk. "Half the men are wearing turbans anyhow."

"Those are fezzes, my dear," said Hash. "And the pointed head was only a clue, perhaps not to be taken literally. 'Prong' could mean something else entirely." He let that innuendo titillate Frisk's imagination a moment. "So just keep your eyes open. Everywhere." Hash stepped away.

Hundreds of American tourists again flooded by, proud to be back in a country where the plumbing worked, where they were not categorically taken for buffoons: Their travel agents had not told them that screens and air conditioners, unlike tobacco, were not global commodities, nor had they been forewarned that fine restaurants did not admit adult males wearing Bermuda shorts and Hawaiian shirts. But that was the whole point of tourism, to make them appreciate how superior America was to these other backward countries. Three out of four wayfarers were now attempting to slide watches, shoes, handbags, bracelets, and other foreign products into their native land without the blessing of its Treasury Department: Instead of dysentery or smallpox, tourists nowadays fell prey to a mysterious amnesia, variant of the strain which struck taxpayers around April fifteenth, which caused them to forget what had happened to their dollars overseas. The disease worsened in direct proportion to the exchange rate. Floyd and his colleagues detained only the most odious offenders; customs agents would be there til three in the morning if they started nickel-and-diming everyone. Besides, the average tourist had neither the guts nor the acumen to smuggle in a cache of drugs or NATO secrets. Those types flew the Concorde.

Floyd worked for three stifling hours before finally a well-dressed woman joined his line. Her perfume hit him like a gutful of amphetamines. Through her blouse he could see a lacy brassiere . . . he stared at it for a half second, almost smiling, reminded of something he had lost. "Gooodd' ahftaihrnoon."

Charming, but the mouths of French females were better rehearsed than a ballerina's legs. Plus they smoked more heavily than did whores on Christmas morning. "How long will you be in the United States," asked Inspector Beck.

"Wone monze." Her earrings dangled as she spoke. Prongs? Hollow, stuffed with cocaine? With diamonds? Uranium?

Floyd looked closely at her eyes and saw that tonight, wearing a stark silk blouse, she'd be in an East Side bar, *oo-la-la*ing herself silly. Before midnight she'd leave with the stockbroker who spoke the worst French. He closed her passport. "Enjoy your trip."

"Great ass," whispered someone very softly after she had gone.

"Bad teeth," Floyd muttered back.

Special Agent Hash remained behind Floyd for ten minutes, his saturnine demeanor frightening the fainthearted into spontaneous confessions. By now it was apparent that Prong had either planed his head or entered Manhattan by submarine: He was definitely not among the few dozen stragglers somnambulating aside the baggage wheels.

Hash's beeper cheeped. "Blew this one," he said to Floyd, receding like a sullen cloud.

Around eight o'clock Albert McPhee came by. He always became gloomy at this time of night, knowing he'd soon have to return home to a mammal other people called his wife. "Okay Beck, you can close up now." He glanced toward Inspector Fiske, frustration tweaking his eyes. "Minnie Mouse'll take the rest of them."

Frisk pretended not to have heard. She withdrew a ferruginous, stubby cylinder from a pink hatbox. "And what's this?" she asked the woman standing in front of her.

"Salammi. Eh maka mizelf forra mi boy Rinaldo. E live in Bracklyn."

"Sorry, you can't bring this into the country."

"Noa salammi? Eh no possibeel!" The woman tried to take it back.

Frisk signaled irritatedly to the Agriculture Inspector. "Blustein! Get over here!"

A wondrous fragrance of garlic and fennel floated over to Floyd. He stared at the sausage as if it were Baba Yaga beckoning seductively to him. Instantly he became a child again, running through his father's butcher store on a warm spring afternoon; he could almost smell the clean sawdust clinging to his shoes. Even after thirty years, if his past ambushed him at a dull moment, it could sweep him away to the rim of a giant volcano and dangle him just far enough over the edge to get singed. It was nature's way of reminding him he was too young to give up yet too old to hope for total victory.

"Floyd," said McPhee, pressing his arm, "go home." Unable to move, Floyd watched as Blustein took the sausage away, destination incinerator. "Beat it, I said," McPhee snapped. "You've got a candlelight dinner tonight, remember?" Last time McPhee had tried to take Frisk to a quiet little bistro, his wife's bridge partner had walked in. Since then, they had nourished themselves upon anger and room service. "You've got the second shift tomorrow. Sleep late."

"Portia gets up at five. Thanks anyway."

McPhee swore disgustedly. That bitchy little feminist had emasculated his best agent. She probably wouldn't give up until she turned him into a raving homosexual. Poor Beck! His future promised nothing but dishpan hands and Sunday morning analysis sessions with other earnest, hyper-*Weltschmerz*ed couples. Perhaps the boy suspected it; no one had heard him laugh at an ethnic joke in months. Suddenly disconsolate, McPhee gazed at the taut seam scaling Frisk's backside. Thank God she wasn't one of those rancid liberation wackos. They didn't know the meaning of the word fellatio. "Have a swell night."

Floyd padded subduedly into the locker room. His nervous system could not withstand rococo brassieres, homemade salami, a quartet of 747s, and foredoomed proposals of marriage all in one day. He had to pull himself together before he saw Portia.

Shaving, Hash leaned over a sink. On the shelf in front of him lay a bottle of aspirin. Floyd helped himself to six. "Heavy date, George?"

Hash's razor continued plowing deftly through shaving cream. He was fanatical about personal grooming and particularly about hair, the length and location of which emblematized not only a man's political philosophy but his libido as well. Thus, maintaining the dichotomous image of a swinging law officer required Hash's constant attention. "Some date. Two thousand fake Cabbage Patch dolls on a Liberian barge. I'm tempted to sink it, just for laughs."

"Sorry about Prong."

"We tried." Hash toweled himself dry. "Hitting a new bar in Teaneck afterward. Want to come along? The women are supposed to be dynamite."

"Thanks. I'm seeing Portia."

"Where're you going? A lecture on premenstrual syndrome?"

"No, dinner," Floyd said, trying to guffaw. "It's our third anniversary."

Hash yanked on a holster. "You been putting up with that crap for three years?"

What crap? Feminism, like jogging, had become part of Portia's modus operandi. After all these months, Floyd no longer noticed such quiddities. "I thought I might ask her to marry me tonight."

Hash's jaw momentarily sank. "You serious?"

"Of course I am!"

Hash froze, tongue pinned to the floor of his mouth like some malevolent slug. "That's terrific," he stuttered finally. "Congratulations."

"Thank you," snapped Floyd. Hash left, perhaps slamming the door.

Upset, Floyd walked to his car. He didn't mind when terminal machos like McPhee made fun of him and Portia, but when close friends like Hash persisted, even in the face of the inevitable, he got a little nervous. Perhaps he should forget this marriage fixation. Portia had repeatedly told him that enforced fidelity had caused more carnage than had the bubonic plague. What was a piece of paper anyway? She'd still sleep with him whenever mutually convenient. She'd still meet him for brunch Sundays at one. Why get smothered under an "I do" and its tacit million "You don'ts"? Portia had no intention of giving up her apartment next to the ASPCA. She would never wear another negligee. Children? She'd rather adopt a spare Nicaraguan.

Unlocking the door of his '64 Falcon station wagon, Floyd stepped aside as a pillow of heat still redolent of Beelzebub, an Irish setter who had voided himself upon the back seat, wafted by. Over the years this vehicle had sped many depraved dogs to Portia's clinic in the deep of the night; now, on hot days, after the sun had baked the Falcon for twelve hours, the effluvia of these departed creatures arose from the seats and floorboards, acrid as the day they had first gasified. Floyd slid into the front seat and headed toward the Van Wyck Expressway. Within four miles he counted eight neo-defunct engines along the wayside ditches. Half had already been stripped by capitalistic drug addicts, the only people with any ambition tonight. The rest of humanity preferred to sag in front of the tube, watch baseball, guzzle beer, and pray that Con Ed had enough juice to keep a zillion air conditioners palpitating. On second thought, perhaps he should call off this date with Portia. In hot, humid weather she was more irascible than a teething chihuahua.

The Falcon blasted out of the Lincoln Tunnel into Hoboken, New Jersey, home sweet home. Within minutes Floyd sprawled across his sofa, clenching a green bottle of beer. Now he was getting a little jittery: The actual wording of a proposal of marriage eluded him. Why hadn't his father told him how this went or at least left him a book? It was disgusting that once again he had to rely on Hollywood to see how these fundamental mysteries of life were supposed to go.

"Portia, my darling, I love you! Say you'll marry me!" Sheer 1930s drivel. She wouldn't faint, either.

"Hey Porsh, I was thinkin', maybe we oughta' try tyin' the knot someday." More contemporary but zilch dignity. Sitcom material.

"Okay Portia, I've had it. It's either me or the dogs. Make up your mind. I'll give you ten seconds." Now that had flair, guts . . . she'd make up her mind, all right.

Sighing, Floyd showered and shaved, surrendering to a fleet bout of diarrhea as the razor of reality drew nearer and nearer the soft throat of his dreams. The only equitable place to propose marriage to Portia was in bed, when reason was down, emotion was up, and her beeper was in the bathroom. Floyd paced between his closet and drawers, dressing sporadically. Maybe he could talk her into some moo-shi pork, naked, in his boudoir. No, no, only a coward would take such blatant advantage of the twentieth century; this was, after all, a business decision. Fully clothed, standing or kneeling, men had been asking, women feigning surprise, for centuries.

But forget the restaurant. Couples went there to have fights. How about a romantic stroll along the Palisades? They'd lean against a cool stone wall and listen to the rustling ivy as moonbeams enchanted Manhattan. At some point she would have to stop talking about poodles and Pomeranians. He'd let ten minutes elapse as the suspense mounted. A faroff gong would strike twelve.

"Portia," Floyd uttered to the hairbrush in his hand, "you must marry me."

He slowly put the brush down as a new thought staggered him: What if she said yes? Would she immediately throw out his corduroy slippers and force him to eat yogurt? What if she started bringing the dogs home? Worse, what if she relocated the Female Awareness sessions to his living room? It was goodbye to the Rod & Gun magazines, the rowing machine in the living room . . . for someone who worked twenty hours a day with animals, Portia had surprisingly little respect for *Homo sapiens* nesting instincts. Floyd had found that out when on her first visit Portia had removed the rainbow trout over his fireplace. To him it was a family heirloom; to her it was a dead fish encased in shellac. They had compromised by hanging it in the broomcloset.

It was time to go. His mind frothing like an overheated bouillabaisse, Floyd headed for Disraeli's, a posh cafe which had been first to capitalize on the exodus of the crippled affluent from Manhattan. The streetlights flicked on, pearling the tepid Hoboken cobblestones. Floyd walked swiftly down Hudson Street, deserted but for a few beer-addled engineers from Stevens Tech swatting at fireflies with old slide rules. They stared at Floyd as he hurried past; only a nerd would wear a coat and tie on a night like this.

Disraeli's had recently added a glass partition to the dining room so that its patrons could observe traffic in and out of the PATH tubes as they sipped peach daiquiris and discussed sublime reproductions of Victorian toilet bowls. Folder in hand, Portia sat inside reading. She was wearing his favorite white linen blouse. That was a good sign; she might sleep at his place tonight after all. Floyd stopped to catch his breath. Really, she was quite exquisite. Any man alive would want Portia to be his wife. She might be a daily tribulation, but she would never slide into booze, whining, or cellulite: Physically, mentally, Dr. Clemens was always going for the flyweight title. Kept a man on his toes. Floyd rather enjoyed that constant threat of a knockout; it kept his mind off the huge minuses in their relationship. He stared intensely at her through the glass. After a moment she turned the page, absently crunching a carrot between her front teeth.

A wall of cold air dashed him in the face as Floyd walked inside the restaurant. His pores shrank like frightened crustaceans. He walked to Portia's table, bending over her left shoulder. "Woof."

Portia jumped. "Ah, you startled me." Floyd kissed her ear as she closed a folder, *Hydrophobia and the U.S. Dog Food Industry,* and put it under her seat.

Floyd suddenly realized that he had forgotten the ring. He slid into his chair and drained a glass of water. How could he propose without a ring? The entire script depended on that prop! "What a day," he laughed shakily.

"Terrible. I lost two pugs."

Floyd squeezed her hand. "Nice to see you, beautiful."

A waiter approached the table with a wine bucket and raised a bottle of champagne from the slush as if it were a newborn seal. Portia inspected the label, sipping. "Fine." They watched as the waiter solemnly filled two flutes. "Cheers."

So she had remembered after all; the stars were with him. "Happy anniversary."

Portia put down her glass. "What do you mean?"

Screw the stars. They were just dying suns. "Three years ago today," said Floyd, "Batista introduced us." Batista was a pathetic cross between a dachshund and a retriever. Portia had been helping the animal recover from a slipped disc. "It was a perfect summer morning, no humidity, no smog . . . Batista was on a red leash . . . you had a white ribbon in your hair." Portia had worn it long then. "Remember?"

"Poor Batista." The dog had died of cardiac arrest while chasing a duck.

"What about my poor pants? That vicious beast tore them up. I was innocently opening my mailbox, if you would recall."

"Is that all you remember? Your pants?"

"I remember your pants, too. They were so tight I could ski on them." Those were the pre-Female Awareness days.

Sighing, Portia opened the menu. She was also wearing the lapis earrings he had given her for Christmas. Matched her eyes. If she'd just let her hair grow another eight inches, down to her shoulders again, she'd look sensational. But she'd have to quit wearing the serapes. Floyd pictured himself tearing the menu from her hands and hauling Portia off to the justice of the peace. No rings, no gowns, consummation across the hood of the Falcon: Portia would obey him forever. Ah, skip it. Now he was too hungry.

The waiter returned to the table. "Ready to order? Kitchen closes in five minutes."

"I'll have the Montrachet omelet. No salt, half the butter, and don't overcook it, please."

The waiter wished he were gay. Then he could come back with a snide retort and get away with it. Instead he looked scornfully at Floyd. "Yes?"

"Onion rings and a sirloin medium rare."

"Floyd, wouldn't you rather have fish?"

"Sure I'll have fish!" Floyd turned to the waiter. "And a bucket of steamers to start."

"Great choice." The waiter left.

Glaring after him, Portia drained her glass. Remembering his primary mission of the evening, Floyd poured them both some more champagne.

Now he regretted not having ordered an omelet himself. But not with goat cheese. That gunk tasted worse than joint compound. "There's nothing like a good steak," he said, "once every six months." Portia's lips flattened skeptically. "I'm starved," he continued, cheerfully sundering a prim loaf-for-two. Already the champagne was barreling through his system like a runaway train. He wondered why she had ordered it; Portia only drank on weekends.

Her mouth enclosed another carrot stick. Floyd knew she was analyzing the situation, wondering how she would treat a neurotic terrier under similar circumstances. Her teeth bisected the carrot again and again. "So," she chirped finally, "how were the airplanes?"

"Fine. But the rabble was unbelievable. They were coming in from Istanbul, Rome . . ."

"Why must you have this abnormal fear of Turks and Italians?" Portia interrupted. "Is it the color of their skin? The language?"

"What do you mean, honey? I was talking about the Americans."

Portia's indignation vanished like a purse in Times Square. "I see." She poured Floyd more champagne.

He lifted his glass. "Three years . . . can you believe it?"

Portia smiled ruefully as a pregnant nun. "All too well."

This was going to be one hell of a long night. He may as well get it over with. "Portia," Floyd began, leaning forward. He could feel his heart thumping uglily. "Let me ask you something."

Out of nowhere the waiter appeared with a tremendous bowl of steamers. Floyd recoiled as if he had been punched. He swept the champagne to his mouth so fast that a lipper splashed up his nose.

"Are these fresh?" Portia asked, ignoring Floyd's coughs.

"Chef shot them this morning." The waiter left.

"That fellow is not getting a tip," Portia said. "I don't like him."

"Cookie, just let the man do his job." Floyd swallowed a steamer, retrenching. He pushed the bowl toward Portia. "Try these."

"Shellfish contain high amounts of cholesterol and iodine."

"Mercury tastes great, too." Floyd swallowed a few more. "You know, I'm beginning to like that haircut."

"Hmmmm. So what were you going to ask me?"

"I forget."

Ominously mum, Portia consumed one clam. So far she had said less than ten words about dogs. "Come across anything interesting today?"

"Dope." Floyd chewed with deceptive vigor. "Watches and salami."

"How disgusting."

"Actually, it was a great salami. Just like one of my father's," Floyd said defensively, then realized he must quickly shunt this topic off tonight's agenda. Portia prickled whenever he talked about opening his own butcher shop. "Actually, we were all looking for someone known as Prong. He's probably the guy who torpedoed the Circle Line cruiser last month."

"Prong? What a strange name."

"He's supposed to have a pointed head."

"An acrocephalic? They're usually retarded. Did you catch him?"

"No, but we may have gotten a bum tip. Lots of people were wearing hats, too."

"I bet your friend George Hash was running this," said Portia.

"Hash got the tip, yes."

"Some tip."

"Come now, Portia, don't make judgments over one little episode. Hash is a great detective. He didn't mean to shoot that mastiff and you know it."

"Who said anything about a dog? His wife Pearl came to our Awareness discussion this week."

"Don't believe a word the woman says. They're divorced."

"He systematically robbed her of every ounce of self-respect."

"Is that a fact! Hash says she did the same thing to him!" Floyd finished the champagne. He had had three glasses, Portia one. This was no accident. "Let's not talk about them," said Floyd, pushing the clams away. "It's too hot."

The corner of his eye detected motion out on the sidewalk. Floyd turned his head and watched, stupefied, as a young Hispanic woman walked by. She wore a huge floral skirt. Her red bodice laced up the front, or tried to. The woman's black hair rippled over her shoulders like a velvet fog and she was definitely not walking to work.

Portia munched the last clam. "Poor thing," she said.

Floyd tore some more bread in half. Saying nothing, he swished it in the broth until both it and his stale lust had capsized. He had forgotten how powerfully gorgeous, tawny breasts could affect him. "How did Barbetta behave today?" he asked. That should buy him about thirty minutes to reconcentrate his thoughts upon Portia.

"Badly." The waiter cleared the clams away. "I got an invitation to speak at the international veterinary conference in July," Portia said. "It's in Switzerland this year."

They had made tentative plans to go camping. "Congratulations. Are you going?"

"We'll see." Portia beckoned the waiter. "Please bring another bottle of champagne."

What was this? If she intended to get him drunk, she could at least do it with something he preferred to swallow. "If you don't mind," said Floyd, holding up his hand, "I think I'll have a beer."

The waiter hesitated. Champagne was the primary weapon of couples like this. "Yes? No?"

"This is an anniversary," said Portia through clenched teeth. "Bring a half bottle."

Silence plopped over the table like a dull mother hen. "Barbetta," cued Floyd finally. He wanted to go to bed, alone, and dream about overstuffed black corsets.

"I don't want to talk about Barbetta," Portia snapped. "I want to talk about us."

Cripes, not again! Floyd ran a hand over his eyes. Each time she went to another Female Awareness session, Portia insisted upon applying her new knowledge to their relationship. Last night had been an epic, secret powwow. Floyd knew only that forty women had spent three hours behind closed doors then had all gone swimming naked in the YMCA pool. "Okay, darling," he said, "what did I do this time?" He looked at his watch. "You have three minutes, or ten thousand words, whichever comes first. Unless dinner comes first. Then we eat instead."

"Don't be childish," Portia said. "You avoid reality."

"Two minutes, fifty seconds."

"You're trying to provoke me, aren't you. William said to expect this." William was the woman who ran the sessions.

"William is a tactical genius. We could have used her in Vietnam."

Portia forfeited another ten seconds tapping her miniature, perfect fingers upon the tablecloth. Looking at them, Floyd doubted that his mother's ring would ever fit Portia; the entire setting was too ornate, too cathedral . . . too monogamous. It saddened him because his mother had loved the ring and adored the man who had given it to her. Ah, how times, how legacies, had changed. The only people who could openly adore anything now were the homosexuals. Everyone else had to split the rent.

Portia cleared her throat. "The subject last night was sexual independence." She leaned forward. "Does that mean anything to you?"

Obviously a trick question. He'd have to watch it. "Masturbation?"

"Damn! Can't you behave like an adult for once?"

"I am, baby, I am! Don't let it irritate you." Floyd looked at his watch. "Two minutes." Sparring like this always gave him a slight headache and a slight erection. If Portia kept up this pace, they'd have to carry him out of here. "Please continue. I won't interrupt any more, promise."

Portia patiently scrolled to the top of her lecture. It was professional habit: That smooth, merciless voice had broken the will of more opponents than had Stalin's best interrogators. No wonder she was the heaviest therapist in New York. Even as he sank, Floyd had to admire her. In all the earth nothing was more devastating than a woman with absolute control of her emotions. A man had about as much defense against her as he had against an axe in his toupee.

". . . this economic dependence has been used for centuries to keep the women tied . . ." When Floyd's father walked into the kitchen after a long day selling bratwurst, his mother would always throw down her wooden spoon and run to him. He'd twirl her around like a scarecrow and call her a lambkin or a pumpkin and sing along with the opera floating in from the living room. ". . . always taking advantage of their larger size . . ." Perhaps Floyd wanted Portia because she was easy to lift off the floor. Maybe her cooing to Batista that morning long ago had uncapped some forgotten homesickness in him. His mother had spoken to her husband in those exact soft tones which Portia used with her patients. Was he really only pursuing the shadow of his mother, hoping someone would spoil him again? Portia had insinuated this hundreds of times. He found it highly insulting but had said nothing since he had been taught to always treat women with courtesy. ". . . keeping them in skirts . . ." Portia had great legs. When she wore those narrow skirts with the slit up the side, he almost foamed at the mouth. But she only wore them to dog seminars, as the lower half of a business suit. The rest of the time it was unisex pants and those brutish brown shoes which were supposed to align the vertebrae.

"Three minutes," Floyd said, cutting his hand through the air. "That was a fantastic summary of two hundred thousand years of mankind."

"Personkind. You didn't listen to a word, did you."

"Would you like me to repeat it for you?" Floyd could recite this speech during a vasectomy. He looked out the window as the waiter exhibited and poured a split of champagne; now he was becoming melancholy. A couple had just walked by on the sidewalk. The man's hairline was beginning to emigrate and he carried a baby on his chest in a canvas sling. The woman, residually hefty, was berating her companion, puncturing the air with her fingers. Stroking the infant's head, the man said nothing.

"Anyway," continued Portia, "we got on to the subject of lovers and sexual independence. It was quite a revelation. Do you realize that not one woman in the class had been sexually satisfied in months?"

Now Portia had Floyd's full attention. "Including you?"

"Take Pearl, for instance. Hash's poor wife. Do you know that every night, when he thought she was asleep, he wrapped her hands around his penis and sang 'Blue Moon'?"

Floyd was horrified. "That bitch told that to a room of complete strangers?"

"Oh stop it! Women don't have these stupid macho hangups. Not only that, by the way. When Hash thought Pearl couldn't see him he—"

"Enough! I don't want to hear about it!" Several people at nearby tables turned their heads. "Female Awareness, my ass." Floyd emptied his champagne glass. "Change the subject, I command you."

The waiter returned, this time slinging a dish before Portia. "Your omelet," he explained unnecessarily. "Salad."

Floyd sniffed the air. "Smells like burning rubber."

"It's the cheese," said the waiter, arranging a steak before Floyd. "Onion rings. Catsup? Just a minute."

Four tines of Portia's fork pierced a yellow triangle. "Waitperson, this omelet is oversalted."

"It's the cheese, I told you." He had had it with yuppie gourmets tonight. They never ordered food which might spot their blouses or ties. "Enjoy your meal."

Inhaling deeply, Floyd leaned over his steak, a sizzling monument of muscle, steam, and black char. No meal in creation, since Creation, surpassed this. At certain times, neither could a woman. Salivating, he picked up his knife and began slicing off a black corner. Aromatic ruby juice dribbled onto his plate.

Portia picked at her salad. "I castrated Champ today."

"Christ Almighty, Portia," cried Floyd exasperatedly, flinging his knife down, "did you have to say that now?"

"Please control yourself. You're not auditioning for an Anacin commercial."

"My love," said Floyd, wiping his mouth with a napkin, "you are an absolute monster tonight. I am going home." Beget children upon this gremlin? Tomorrow he was going to call a psychiatrist. Male.

"Sit down!" snarled Portia, yanking his sleeve. "I'm sorry, really I am." Her cool fingers tantalized his flesh, full of promise. "I had no idea you identified so strongly with Champ."

Taking a deep breath, Floyd reached for his knife and began dolefully cutting the steak. Portia dissected her salad as if it were still alive. Neither of them spoke. From time to time Floyd simply looked at her and shook his head, chewing quietly. Portia alternately revolted, confused, and fascinated him. But this liberation nonsense was bordering on the obsessive now. Perhaps he had been mistaken not to stomp it out like some sinister beetle after her very first Female Awareness session. Portia had obviously misread his indulgence as tacit guilt; the balance of power between them had tilted perversely ever since. Perhaps a timely spanking . . . had that been her ulterior motive? To goad him into a spasm of weeping? Renunciation of America? Sex on her operating table? What was it about the strong, silent type which had suddenly driven women over the edge? This had all gotten out of hand after Vietnam, when one hundred million women were suddenly deprived of a Vesuvian emotional outlet. How could they return to humdrum boyfriends after pelting the National Guard with chicken gizzards? It had taken years to reacquaint these zealots with the Sisyphean challenge inherent in a ring around the collar. At last most of them were trying their luck as mothers. But not Portia. Oh no, she hung on to The Revolution like a bulldog with lockjaw. What a waste! If she approached marriage with half the energy she expended housebreaking beagles, they'd raise a passel of Mozarts. The woman would eventually come around . . . wouldn't she? He had already invested three years of his existence in her; it was too late to admit he may have been better off with anyone else. "Portia," said Floyd, "life is too short. Let's get married."

She speared a radish. "What's the matter, you pregnant?" The radish disappeared between her kewpie lips, never to roll again.

His blood turned to dust: Hash had tried to warn him. He wanted to kill her.

The waiter slid into port. "How's everything, folks?"

"Wrap this omelet, will you? I'm taking it to my dog."

Whistling, the waiter removed her plate. "Enjoy your steak?"

"Fine," croaked Floyd. He gazed out the window at the PATH tubes. Only executives and bums were emerging now. Their faces looked about the same.

"Waitperson! Two coffees, please!" Portia poured the last of the champagne into Floyd's glass. "What's so interesting out there?"

"Nothing."

"What's the matter all of a sudden? You look sunburnt."

Out from the shadows two taxis glided over the cobblestones, engorging the men in business suits. "Damn you anyhow, Portia, did you hear what I said a minute ago?"

She thought a moment. "You called me an absolute monster."

"No, I asked you to marry me."

Her light laughter tinkled over the table. All was lost. "You were serious?" The waiter set down two cups and very slowly poured coffee, absorbing every word. "Marry you? What do you think I've been trying to tell you all night?"

Hope whiplashed through Floyd like a scorpion's tail. "Are *you* pregnant?"

The waiter stopped pouring and stared aghast at Portia. She was the type who nonchalantly erased inconvenience with abortion.

"Bring us the check, please," said Portia coolly. "Don't stand there with your mouth open." The waiter hurried away. For a moment she studied Floyd's face, then sipped some coffee. "Let's backtrack a bit, shall we? Sexual independence."

"Your show-and-tell session last night."

"The last until October, you'll be glad to know. William is going to India."

"To overthrow the swamis or assassinate Mother Teresa?"

"Crap," said Portia tightly. Were Floyd a dog, she would have had him put to sleep by now. "I'm going to make this clinically brief. It's the only way to communicate with you." She leaned back, looking him in the eye. He knew exactly what was coming. "I don't want to see you any more. This relationship is finished." She snapped a toothpick in half. "It's nothing but dead wood."

Relationship was a neuter word. He detested it. Friendship, affair, marriage . . . these words described the tenuous bridge spanning two mortals with hearts and brains and an enormous leaden faith in the future. Relationship? That was something a circumference had with a radius. "Dead wood," echoed Floyd, caressing the words. "How poetic. And now I just float away after three years and five thousand ambulance rides?"

"Please understand," said Portia, "when I first met you I was a different woman. Insecure, one-dimensional . . ."

"Stingy, frigid, workaholic, so what? I like you the way you are."

Portia sat very still. Floyd thought he could hear her brain clicking like a Chinese abacus. After a few moments she blinked back to life. "That's the whole point, see. You don't challenge me."

Now it was Floyd's turn to play dead. He took a bit longer coming to. "I accept you, Portia, I don't challenge you." She did not move. Floyd doubted she had even heard him. "William has brainwashed you, my little chickadee. You can no longer distinguish between a lover and a lapdog."

"Leave William out of this," she warned, a little nitro seeping into her voice. "And don't drag my patients into it, either. You always were jealous of both of them." Floyd laughed, or perhaps hiccuped. Every time he stuck an oar in the water, he rowed himself a little closer to the cataclysm. "And don't just sit there grinning like a moron! That drives me out of my mind!"

Again the waiter appeared, carrying the check and a paper bag. "Clemens," said Floyd, "what went on at that meeting last night?"

Portia held a credit card in the air without looking at the waiter. "Add in eight percent for yourself," she said. "You have an attitude problem."

The waiter snapped his heels. "Anything you say, Sarge!" He left.

"Forty women turned up," Portia continued. "Nine of them were single. The rest in some way associated with men."

"No."

"One by one, we analyzed each relationship, trying to pinpoint what held it together. Don't forget, these women are all intelligent professionals."

"William knows better than to waste her time on godfearing immigrants. So? Come on, the suspense is killing me! What did you, William, and forty intelligent professionals figure out? What mysterious glue binds you to me? My shy smile? My CD collection? My undying patience with your fairy tales?"

"The Falcon."

This was below the dogs. "I don't believe it."

"Of course you don't believe it. You thought it was your penis, didn't you."

"My penis? You mean that thing I use to dust my boxer shorts?"

The waiter placed Portia's credit slip in front of her. She completely crossed out the figures in the box for the tip, signed it, and handed it back. "Thank you so very much," the waiter said sweetly.

"You're so very welcome," Portia mimicked. She returned to the carcass sitting across from her. "Don't pout, Floyd. You did very well in comparison to the other men."

"Yeah? What held their relationships together? Skateboards?"

"Cats. Boats. Season tickets to the Giants."

"Gee, did any of you girls mention children?"

"No. William disqualified children and religion."

"Of course." Floyd had a sudden urge to tear after that petticoated strumpet in the street, fling her over his shoulder, and run far, far away. Their children would all be swaggering infidels. Portia would be incapable of issuing anything but myopic runts.

"It's time for the second wave." Portia began neatly tearing the carbon paper from her credit slip into little squares. "Women can do anything— all by themselves."

"Isn't this a little rash, Portia? Do you really think you can get along without that Falcon?"

Her eyes could have been Zwingli's observing a voodoo festival. "We can get along without anything." She reached under her seat and retrieved the folder she had been reading. "You know I am very fond of you."

"Just go away."

"Someday you will understand that marriage only perpetuates the slavery."

"Good night, Portia."

"I will always consider you my best friend."

"Please get out of my sight before I kill you."

He watched her khaki pants march past a few tables towards the door. Never again would he balance that diminutive, delicious rear end in the palms of his hands. Portia turned left on the sidewalk, towards the clinic: This week she was running experiments on a pair of insomniac schnauzers.

"On the house, pardner," said the waiter, placing a brandy in front of Floyd. "You earned it."

Floyd could only nod his head, eyes shut: She'd be dropping in on Champ also. He wondered if the Dalmatian's testicles had stopped bleeding.

2

His key slid smoothly as a Latin lover into the lock. Stepping inside, Floyd clicked the door shut and stared into the hallway, waiting for his senses to infiltrate the night. First his ears located the refrigerator serenading the stove. Then he discerned the patient plop, plop of water falling from the kitchen faucet to a brimming cup below. Every fifth second another drop hurtled from birth to death, dissolved the moment it had formed a perfect tear. By and by the darkness distilled into familiar black clots within a diffuse gray sea: his sofa, the chairs, lamps, all exactly where he had left them a few hours ago. They seemed to be expecting him now.

He had been wandering along the Hoboken waterfront, half hoping a punk might jump him. Floyd's fists had not ached like this in years. His footsteps had startled the rats but no punks, who lounged elsewhere, lazily killing ice cubes: no point combing the streets if all the wallets reposed indoors, next to the air conditioners. Simmering dangerously, Floyd had found himself way down at the Lincoln Tunnel. The clock above the toll booths had read two-fifteen. He had looked across the river at Manhattan, wanting to uproot the island and fling it off the edge of the earth. No, fling it at Portia. Before going home he walked by the clinic. Her light was still on.

Floyd swung open his refrigerator and took a beer. It splashed down his throat like the first spring flood, recklessly waking life. Then he stripped to his shorts and skimmed to Australia and back on his rowing machine: nice try but rage still grizzled his stomach. He stepped into the shower, running the water as hot as possible. It rippled down his legs and slid easily away, perhaps into the Hudson, broth for the rats. Then Floyd jerked the faucet to cold. His epidermis shrieked and he wondered if heart attacks ran in his family: No one had really lived long enough to establish a precedent. Floyd gradually veered the water warm again. Only as he was soaping himself did he suddenly identify the pale blue column in the

34

corner of the shower as a bottle of Portia's expensive shampoo. He would rather have seen a copperhead. For some time Floyd stared at the plastic container through the steam. Then he twisted the top off and held it upside down over the drain, squeezing until it could only retch noisily. He threw it away.

Floyd poured himself a stiff drink and slid into bed. He was a little drowsy now. Fucking slut . . . several narcotic minutes passed. Then a lone bacillus of anger stirred in his brain, flicking on circuit after circuit as it made the convoluted rounds of memory. Soon he was totally alert, seething. She had first phoned him on a sweltering night like this, about the same time as now. "It's Dr. Clemens," she had said. "You met me two weeks ago on your front steps. I was walking a large black dog." She did not ask if the fang marks had faded from Floyd's shin yet.

He recalled the pleasant warmth which had rolled from head to foot at the sound of her voice. What a stupid, horny ass he had been. "Oh yes! Hi!"

"I know it's late. You weren't sleeping, were you?"

"No no no no no."

"Listen, I'm in a bit of a jam."

At this hour? Bail, flat tire, no gas. "You're out of gin."

Portia had said nothing. That should have been Clue One: Women without humor were like silk flowers, never fragrant, best eyed from a distance. Dolt! "Columbine's whelping and I can't reach her."

"Where is she, Roosevelt Island?"

"Please, this is no time for games. These pups are worth a fortune. Can you come to my clinic right away? Two-ten Washington Street? It's right around the block." Suddenly Portia had screamed. "Columbine! Stay!"

"What's going on," cried Floyd, leaping out of bed. "Are they mauling you?"

"My God! Just get over here!" She slammed down the phone.

So what had he done? Shot over to the clinic! Floyd cringed in shame: Men incapable of distinguishing between damsels in distress and Patton crossing the Rhine deserved to die. "What are you doing here this time of night?" he had asked as they tore upstairs.

"What does it look like?" she had snapped, running into the lab. "I'm running a few experiments. Columbine! We're back!"

"Hai! Hai!"

Atop a tall cabinet huddled a strange beast overrun with hair. A dog this impractical had to be gruesomely expensive. Floyd jumped on a stool. "Has she whelped?" cried Portia, grabbing his calf.

"You mean puppies?"

"Of course I mean puppies!" she screeched.

Floyd remembered something he had read in a Boy Scout manual. "Maybe she ate them already."

The hand around Floyd's calf constricted sharply. "Get that dog down here," Portia hissed, "before you terrify her into labor."

"Just let go of the leg, honey." With a grip like that, he had thought, she could give one hell of a hand job. A few moments later Floyd and Columbine were back aground. "Tell me," he had said, handing the dog over, "how did she get up there in the first place?"

Portia was busy inspecting her patient's genitalia. "Columbine thinks she's a bird." She put her down. "We have an hour yet before she delivers."

"How about breakfast? Ernie's Diner opens at five."

"No thank you. I have a lot of work to do here."

"Dinner then?"

"No thank you. I have a symposium to attend."

"Dinner tomorrow?"

"I make house calls on Thursday evenings."

"I have a house and I'll get a dog."

Portia had looked him coldly in the eye. Three years later, Floyd realized that she had not been playing hard to get after all. "Thank you very much for helping me, Mr. Beck. Let me show you out."

At the door he had paused. "How'd you know my name? And my phone number?"

"I sent the security guard to check you out two weeks ago, after you kicked Batista." Vengeful little twerp! How could he have mistaken paranoia for vigilance? Portia had opened the clinic door. Outside, night was languidly deferring to dawn, trailing a soiled blanket of humidity: Today would be another stinker.

His fingers had itched to run through her glistening hair; natural blonds were rarer than a Comanche in Budapest. "I have a station wagon," he had said, "in case you ever need an ambulance." Oh Jesus! Was a stupider man ever born? "By the way, what's your name?"

"Dr. Portia Clemens. I'm unlisted." She had shut the door.

The woman had had severe problems from the start, like a covair. Clown, fascinated by her disinterest in him, he had pursued her anyway. She was such an invigorating change from the women who tried to pick him up all the time in the convenience store. Floyd dragged to the bathroom and piddled away the last of Portia's French champagne: so much for special occasions. She was going to do it without him, eh? She wouldn't last two days without—the Falcon. "Damn." Floyd flushed the toilet. This time he left the seat up.

He wandered downstairs and poured another drink. Beyond the windows a bronze sky burnished a magenta horizon, pining for dawn. Floyd went to his music shelf. He had inherited quite a collection of recordings from his parents and Aunt Margaret, all of whom had shut themselves away with their phonographs when the going got rough. Floyd had continued the habit, but with compact discs. He slid one from the rack. Bartok string quartets? Forget it. He didn't need a musical depiction of slashed wrists. He tried another. The *Eroica?* Nix. Too many people playing nicely at once. Aha! *L'Histoire du Soldat!* He lifted the CD from its jewel box.

A trumpet bobbed in hideous, mechanical torment: Stravinsky grinned from his grave. Floyd looked slowly around the dim living room. First he spotted Portia's sweatshirt on his favorite chair. Marching tipsily, about in time with the music, Floyd balled it up and pitched it into the hall. There, half under the couch, lay Portia's running shoes. Floyd chucked them on top of the sweatshirt. Next came Portia's spare serape, two panties, forgotten bathrobes, shower caps . . . in three years she could never quite bring herself to move in with him. She preferred to keep his place stocked like some permanently reserved suite at the Holiday Inn.

By the time Floyd got to her books it was light enough to read their spines. *Canine Psyche,* Portia's beloved reference work, flapped into the hall like a surprised gander, as did *Happy Housebreaking* and *An Illustrated History of the Dachshund.* Over the years these squat, ugly volumes had overrun his shelves like pickerel in a pond, muscling out the daintier species. Floyd hadn't noticed them because they were all brown.

The trumpet blared foully, mocking something, as Floyd yanked a decrepit book from the shelf. A little spark flicked between his ears. He paused, then very slowly opened the cover: *The Recipes of Caspar Beck, Sausagemaker,* he read. Softly as a bed of coals, his past glowed inside of him, imparting heat, still alive. Suddenly Floyd missed his father terribly. He had not seen him in years and years; Caspar Beck had died when his son was seven, when Caspar was—Floyd counted on his fingers—thirty-five. Shocked, Floyd went to the window and studied the blinding horizon, realizing for the first time that he was now older than his father had ever been. What had he done to deserve more sunrises than Caspar? He took no more pleasure in a cold glass of beer, felt no more awe at Beethoven's Ninth Symphony than had his father. He had no wife, no little son, no butcher store, nothing anywhere near what Caspar had when life was yanked away from him: Wouldn't it have been cleaner for Floyd to have gone instead? Of course. But that would have been about as much sport for God, or Satan, or whomever tautened these brief lines, as reeling in a clam. Caspar had definitely fought all the way. He hadn't emigrated

from Switzerland and become the loftiest butcher in New Jersey only to
die in a stupid car crash.

Floyd stepped away from the window, not angry, not questioning
. . . not anything. Certain natural phenomena, like thunderstorms and
death, one simply accepted. He carefully turned the first yellow page of
Caspar's book. *Knockwurst,* he read in German: Forty pounds of boneless
veal, twenty of pork, eight different spices . . . he could still smell them
fresh from his father's smoker. The aroma made people stampede the
butcher shop. Floyd turned another page: kielbasa. His mouth flooded.
When was the last time he had chomped into one of those beauties?
What made that divine stench anyhow? He drew a finger along the
ingredients: fifty pounds of pork, twenty of beef, aha! juniper berries, a
mile of casings, three acres of garlic, whew, this read like the libretto of
Parsifal. Floyd continued: bratwurst. People came all the way from
Philadelphia for Caspar Beck's specialty. The man was a sorcerer. *Land-
jäger;* salami; mettwurst; easy to eat, treacherous to produce. He had
always wanted to get his hands into his father's sausage tubs. "Some day,
some day," Caspar told him. "We'll start with scrapple." So where was
the scrapple? Floyd pried apart two stuck pages and stopped, stricken,
staring at Caspar's compact, even block letters. *Floydwurst,* he read, and
beneath that, *For my son on his eighth birthday.*

Floyd's eyes filled with tears: Nice try, dad. Instead of shoveling Floydwurst down his throat, he had spent his eighth birthday in a funeral parlor
staring at two mahogany coffins and at Aunt Margaret, who had inherited
him. That was the day he aged sixty years. Aunt Margaret had not brought
a mute little boy home with her; she took in an old man who watched
the sun rise and the sun set but did not comprehend that thus what other
men called a day had elapsed. Since then Floyd thought in much longer,
amorphous units of time: the first had ended on his eighth birthday. The
second ended when he was seventeen. Right now, age thirty-five, he was
in his third day.

Those who toiled and planned according to astronomical days, Portia
for instance, found Floyd eerily static. She could not comprehend why a
man of Floyd's intellect and background would remain a customs inspector and investigator instead of trying to become head of the entire Treasury Department. It did Floyd little good to explain that once one let go
of days, one also lost touch with ambition: Portia kept making appointments for him at the psychiatrist, urging Floyd to talk out his childhood
trauma and become a normal individual. He had responded by listening
to his father's old recordings, assuring her that one Furtwängler *Lohengrin*
was worth ten sessions on a rented couch.

Stravinsky's trumpeter stridulated over a cliff, into oblivion. Never abandon hope, Aunt Margaret had told him from the day he moved in with her. Floyd dried his eyes. Hope for what? A wife? Children? Maybe he should hope to make the *Guinness Book of Records* as the world's oldest living stillborn.

Floyd turned the page. Instead of a recipe he read *Urs Eggli, Emwald, Switzerland,* and a telephone number. This must be the fellow who opened the butcher store in Bern with Caspar before he left the country. Caspar often said Eggli made the most sublime sausages in the world and that Floyd should meet him someday. Floyd closed Caspar's recipe book and placed it on an endtable; tonight he could not stand to delve further into these memories. Floydwurst . . . that had a nice sound. Too bad he would never know what it tasted like.

A cloud moved, the sun glinted upon the door of his linen closet, and Floyd stood up, reminded of his housekeeping. Portia's neat little smocks were about to take flying lessons.

Unaware that Floyd had entered the office, Albert McPhee leaned over his telephone. "Okay, we'll be there tomorrow as usual." He was probably making a reservation for himself and Frisk at the Great Neck Sheraton. They normally trysted there on Thursday afternoons.

Floyd cleared his throat and McPhee spun around. "So how was dinner, Romeo," he roared, slapping Floyd on the back. "Hot time on the old town? You're late."

"Overslept."

Not once in nine years had Floyd been late for work. McPhee squinted at him. "You sick? Your face looks yellow."

"Champagne." Floyd looked into the terminal. "What's up today?"

So last night had been a disaster. The poor kid had probably tried the missionary position. "The usual. But forget Prong. The informer made a mistake. He meant pointed chin, not pointed head."

"Yeah? I saw about ten thousand of them yesterday."

"So did everyone else. Hash should either make these people draw pictures or find himself a few English-speaking informers."

Molly Fiske floated into the office. Around her neck was the fuschia-and-green scarf McPhee had given her. Floyd saw at once that McPhee's mouth had recently made contact with every pore of her body. Women didn't glow like that from a simple application of talcum powder. "Floyd-Poo, you look awful." Her finger brushed his cheek. "Naughty boy didn't sleep all night, did he."

"Did you?" snapped Floyd. He left the office.

Frisk pulled the scarf away from her neck. "Is this hickey showing or something?"

"Naw, baby, he's just psychic." McPhee patted her behind. "You know that."

"So did he have a bad dream?"

"I think his little dinner last night blew up." A pat became a slap. "Scram. Take that scarf off and get to the station next to him. Tell the guy a joke or something."

McPhee watched her walk into the terminal and wondered how long this affair could go on. The highs were becoming higher, the lows lower, and longer. He should never have hired her; the girl would have been much happier in a post office. Through the glass McPhee saw Frisk say a few words to Floyd, who looked down at her a moment before turning moodily away. The little fool had probably told him the joke about the newlyweds.

McPhee had not seen Floyd look this whipped since his Aunt Margaret died. Poor Beck. He just didn't know how to navigate dames. He had never seen his father drunk and a little sour on domesticity; his mother died while the boy still worshipped her; then he had spent the next critical years with his Aunt Margaret, an admirable woman, but probably a virgin. This was no role model for a teenage boy. A couple rounds in Vietnam, Margaret with cancer, then smack into that unbearable little troll. No wonder the guy was a mobile hernia. He needed a woman like Frisk . . . McPhee suddenly peered through the window. Each time she laughed, her breasts wanted to bust through her blouse like newborn ostriches. Beck was the only guy in the terminal who never stared. It was a little unnatural.

Suitcases from Caracas began sliding intermittently onto the baggage wheels. Half of them probably contained dope, half of them religious figurines. The other half was clean. "Okay Beck, this flight's going to clinch it for you," said Frisk as they waited. "One decent watch and you're champ."

Floyd said nothing as the image of a castrated dog, whining in pain, came to mind. Did she just throw the testicles into the garbage?

"Hey, you hear what happened to Hash last night?" Frisk asked.

"What."

"He got nailed in the arm with a dart."

Floyd couldn't believe it. "From a Liberian barge?"

"Nah, they sank the barge. This was afterwards, cruising through the Village."

"Is he all right?"

"Sure, sure, just a little embarrassed. He tried to pick up a lesbian and her girlfriend blasted him."

Floyd frowned. "We talking business or pleasure here?"

"How should I know, lamb chop? Everyone's a faggot now." Frisk held her hand out to her first passenger, an obvious homosexual about fifty years old. "Passport."

Floyd inspected a group of women just back from a worldwide conference on birth control. They looked like ragpickers, perhaps on purpose. Then he cleared several Latinos in white hats and black moustaches. Two of them had sizzling women in tow; the others would acquire their own sizzlers before their second gin-and-tonic at the Palm Court. How the hell did these pomaded reptiles pull it off? An American would roll the same cigarettes, flare the same nostrils, make the same insinuations, and get himself slapped in the face. He was supposed to know better.

A raven-haired woman stood in front of Floyd. She wore a miniscule halter with no bra, like the women from the birth control conference, but the effect was radically different. It had to do with ulterior motive. Red leather pants restrained her sumptuous hips with excruciating difficulty. Her belt was just a tad too thick. Floyd toyed briefly with her suitcase. "Do you have anything else to declare?"

The ruby crucifixes in her ears shook. "Ehno."

"Do you see that inspector over there?"

"*Sí.*"

"She would like to see you."

The woman's eyes glittered at him. Without a word she picked up her suitcase. Floyd could hear her spike heels tapping against the linoleum and forced himself not to look. Why were fallen women always so beautiful? His headache yawned, stretching a fist through each ear, and awoke.

Seven hours later Hash found Floyd in the locker room playing stupidly with a sock. "What's up?"

"Not much." Floyd put the sock in a gym bag. "How's your arm?"

"Fine, fine." Hash slipped onto the bench next to Floyd. "And how are you doing, buddy?" he inquired, upbeat as a telephone salesman.

So McPhee had spilled the beans. "Fine, fine."

They sat a few moments. "Beer?"

"I should go home."

"And do what? Plot your revenge?"

No, plot his suicide. "Have another steak."

Hash clipped him on the back. "Welcome to the club, Becko."

A few years ago, as chastisement rather than a birthday gift, Hash had enrolled his wife Pearl in a real estate course. He was tired of her mousing around the house watching soap operas and leaving pink plastic curlers in her hair for days on end. If she felt too insecure to have children, the least she could do was sell backyards to those who did not. Within six weeks, Hash realized that his little plot had horribly backfired. Pearl fell under the influence of her instructor, Drusilla Cox, founder of Mighty Women, a consortium which was trying to buy up the cheaper half of Newark and rezone it into a new town called Femnia, New Jersey. Worse, Pearl started selling dozens of houses. Something about her droopy expression caused buyers to think she was giving them a good deal. Pearl's behavior changed soon after her commissions broke the hundred-thousand mark. She brought Hash's supper home in little white cartons; it tasted superior to anything she ever cooked herself, but that wasn't the point. Then her evening bookings prevented her from spectating at his softball games. Pearl turned her sewing room into a spare office. Hash finally blew up when, without his approval, she bought three tenements in the worst section of Newark; he had thought they were going to invest the money in krugerrands. They had a terrible fight and Pearl moved in with Drusilla Cox. Since his divorce, which fortunately occurred at the height of the sexual revolution, Hash had been voraciously frequenting singles bars, taking advantage of the flip side of women's liberation. Once he discovered that it was not only ridiculously easy but socially blasé to sleep with seven different women on seven consecutive nights, Hash modified his views upon sexual equality. He rather enjoyed ladies with the funds and the good taste to take him out for drinks, dinner, and weekends in the country in exchange for a few words of sympathy; such strains of feminist beatified a man's existence. The original heavies like Portia and Drusilla, of course, Hash would forever regard as upstream sewage plants, befouling the fauna below. Upon the advent of herpes, AIDS, and his own baldness, Hash's lechery had tempered considerably. He stayed with the same woman for an average of six weeks now.

Floyd and Hash drove to Hoboken. "Hey, the place looks great," Hash said as they walked up the front steps. Floyd had bought the house with some of the money he had inherited from Aunt Margaret. Lately he had been gardening more and more as Portia's schedule became crammed with summer patients. "Wish I had gotten one of these myself." Instead Hash had bought a split level in Teaneck. Now it belonged to Pearl. "No I don't."

Floyd checked his mailbox: no telegram from Portia. Tonight she'd call instead, begging for mercy. They went inside.

Hash immediately noticed the mound in the front hall. Floyd had probably made it sometime between midnight and dawn and then had become incapable of tossing it out. That was a bad sign. "Get rid of this stuff," Hash said. "Right away." He had dumped Pearl's things into garbage bags, put them on the curb the night before collection, then called her at three in the morning.

"What if she comes back?"

"All the more reason." Hash walked to the kitchen, remembering how sick he had felt watching Pearl heave garbage bags onto Drusilla's pickup truck in the dead of the night. He unpacked a few salads he and Floyd had just bought in Jennifer's Stove, the new gourmet shop which had replaced Rico's Shoe Repair on Washington Street.

Floyd took several bottles of beer. "Come on out back."

Heat lightning jagged overhead as they fell onto rattan recliners. Tonight there would be a storm; when the humidity got this thick, it never dissipated without a terrific fight. For a while Hash looked east, saying nothing. Very few back porches in the universe commanded the view of Manhattan as did Floyd's: Here one sat amid mountain laurel and dogwood and predominantly silence while not one mile away, smack across the Hudson, the Empire State Building brazenly poked the gods in the belly. No matter what the weather, what the hour, the view slapped the imagination. Pearl would have no problem getting a half million for Floyd's place, Hash thought. Then he emptied a bottle of beer. "So," he said at last, "she kissed you goodbye."

"No one kissed anyone." Merging saliva offended Portia's sense of clinical propriety.

They lapsed into a silence thick as blood pudding. "Did she say why?"

"I do not challenge her." Floyd got up and fiddled with the grill. He poured salt on the steaks; Portia had never been able to break him of the salt habit. "She said the only thing keeping us together was the Falcon."

"Now what kind of bitch would say something like that?"

"It was those goddamn Female Awareness sessions," said Floyd, slapping the steaks on the grill. "They brainwashed her."

Hash looked drearily up. "Beck," he said, "Portia ran those sessions."

Lightning teased the Empire State Building as Floyd and Hash discussed local drug and arms traffic. The Colombians kept raining cocaine on New York and the president kept denying the Coast Guard permission to mine the Hudson River, so the narcotics branch of every service was strapped to the max. Hash had just paid an informant fifty thousand dollars for implementing a seizure; customs rewarded its informants with a percentage of the total haul. Such generosity led Hash to some interesting conversations with all sorts of pimps, rats, and jilted girlfriends, the deadliest turncoats of all. Just this morning he had gotten an unusual tidbit from his Harlem informant about the Chinese using mutts as drug couriers. Maybe next week, when the subject of dogs was less fraught with personal indignity, he'd tell Floyd about it.

The steaks were ready. Hash opened a few containers. "Carrot and artichoke vinaigrette, corn with peppers and vidalia onions, orzo and marinated eggplant."

"Got any potato or macaroni salad?"

"Sorry, they don't make that kind of stuff any more."

A thick breeze rushed by the patio; soon it would rain. "She said I was jealous, childish, and predictable," Floyd said as they ate. He belched. "Am I a bore?"

"Give me a break."

"In three years I only went to one demonstration," said Floyd. "Remember when they tried to take away El Bandito's liquor license? Two hundred people marched on City Hall."

"Did you ever try tearing her clothes off and raping her?"

"Come on, you can't tear off smocks or those prissy little doctor blouses!" Floyd muttered. "Portia was less and less interested in sex anyhow."

"And you're sitting here crying that you finally got rid of her? What are you, a droid? A guy like you could walk into a bar and ten minutes later come out with the hottest tamale in the joint."

"Forget Hispanic women. They don't use birth control."

"Tamale is a generic term."

Floyd opened another beer. "I hate bars. The women there are pathetic."

"Where would you prefer to pick up a woman? The Salvation Army?"

"I don't like to pick up women."

"You prefer women to pick you up? I know just the spot."

Floyd thought a moment. "There's got to be a little fate involved here, George."

"You mean that shit called kismet?" Hash burped loudly. "Someday you're going to have to outgrow that puritanical upbringing. It's ruining your life."

"Wrong. Life is ruining my puritanical upbringing." Floyd swatted at a moth. "I am an old-fashioned man. Head of the house. Dad. Knit slippers."

"Forget it. No woman is ever going to knit you slippers. It's too demeaning."

"My mother knit. Aunt Margaret knit."

"That was twenty years ago, before they invented day care."

Thunder rolled heavily across the sky and its echo rolled back, slowly fading into the seams of the universe. Floyd was becoming sad. Portia had always been afraid of thunder. It reminded her how small she really was. "I miss her."

"How could you? She was never around! Look Floyd, you didn't have a chance. That hyena was born looking for a punching bag and a soapbox."

"Then she met William."

Hash choked on a beer. "Jesus! She had another boyfriend all this time?"

"William is a girlfriend. She runs the Female Awareness center in North Bergen. One day she brought her mutt Eleanor to the clinic for fungus treatment. It was downhill from then on."

A few stray raindrops hit the grill, hissing lustily. Then the lining of an enormous black cloud split with a roar. Floyd and Hash jolted to life, a little too late. By the time they brought everything inside, they were soaked. "I'll throw your stuff into the dryer," Floyd said.

"No, no, no problem."

"Cut it out, George. I've seen bandages before."

Hash reluctantly removed his shirt, revealing a large white patch on his upper arm. Two inches below glowed a perfect lilac set of toothmarks. Floyd winced. "Got you good, didn't she."

Hash unstrapped the holster from his ankle and lay it on the coffee table. As he peeled off his pants Floyd noticed a hefty welt on his back. "Bar stool," Hash said.

"What the hell did you do down there?" cried Floyd. Hash had a black belt in karate. From a barreling roller coaster he could shoot a candy apple off its stick. In eight years at a dangerous job, Floyd had never seen him with more than a scraped shin. Hash's adversaries he had seen with much worse. "Come on, tell me."

Hash got himself another beer as Floyd tuned in a jazz station on the radio. "There was this blond," he began, easing onto the couch. "Super tits. She was sitting alone at the end of a bar drinking a glass of milk. I sat down next to her."

"Were you waiting for an informant?"

"This was after work. She pretended to ignore me but I knew she was interested."

"How?"

"Because I ordered another round of milk."

Floyd scratched his head. He would have asked the woman if she had ulcers. "Then what happened," he encouraged.

"She said 'What are you doing here?' I said 'Same thing you're doing here.' Then all of a sudden there was this dart in my arm. Another beautiful blond about six feet tall came out of nowhere and sank her teeth into me like a mad wolf. It was unbelievable."

"Didn't it hurt?"

"Of course it hurt!" Hash exploded. He pressed the bandage gently with his fingers, seeing if the bleeding had started again. "While I was pulling the dart out, the first blond smashed me in the back with her bar stool."

"Didn't you fight back? They could have killed you."

Hash blinked slowly as an antique doll. "Floyd. These were gorgeous, gorgeous women. I just couldn't hit them."

"I don't get it. Why were they hitting you? Were they Swedish agents?"

"No, you moron! They were American lesbians!"

A classic arrangement of "Begin the Beguine" wound provocatively through the room. Floyd and Hash listened in silence, each dancing with an imaginary siren. The tune ended and the disc jockey, without speaking, broadcast another torrid ballad; it was one of those endless, steamy summer nights. "What a waste," murmured Floyd at last. "How could they."

Over the radio, a woman from another era sang the blues. She had lost her man. "They gave up on us," said Hash.

They dozed off like two cows under a July sun. When Floyd woke the rain outside had calmed to a filmy downpour. It was almost midnight and Portia had still not called. "She was so callous about it," he said. "Wore my favorite blouse, ordered champagne, all the while plotting the perfect moment to drop the bomb . . . I'll never speak to her again."

"You've said that before."

Floyd stopped breathing: Another woman had moved, miles under the mantle, the unseen, molten core of his existence. He could go for months unaware of her, then suddenly, with a sentence, feel the plates slip, feel her erupt to the surface, intensely, overwhelmingly alive, devouring years like so many brittle, dead sticks . . . ah, damn her. She had soured a lot of sweet things forever.

Hash rolled over. "Can I tell you something honestly?"

"Sure, what the hell."

"You can do better than Portia. She's nothing but a mannequin with a doctorate." Hash rubbed his bandage, looking almost proud of it. "I don't think you ever really liked her anyhow. She was a C-minus human being with a B-plus body."

Wrong about the body, but Hash had always been a breast man. "You're saying I deliberately deceived myself for three years?"

"Your subconscious was not deceived. You asked Portia to marry you with the specific intention of being ditched."

"That's ludicrous." Floyd poured himself a scotch; they had run out of beer. Tonight was just a bad dream stippled with phantoms. Tomorrow he'd wake up and find Portia doing fifty situps at the foot of the bed, grunting lightly. His heart told him she must be going through hell tonight, and his brain, wiser of the two, told him that she was off with William, studying maps of India. No, she didn't miss him at all. The patient had died and Dr. Clemens had moved on to the next case.

"So," said Hash, "what are you doing tomorrow night?"

"Memorizing the *Encyclopedia Britannica.*"

"It's Friday."

"So what?"

"Weekend, buddy! Party time!"

Floyd guffawed. "What are you, refried sophomore? Look at you, you're all chewed up! Now you're going back for more?"

"I know a great singles bar in Leonia. Dynamite women."

"Yeah? Blond with sharp teeth? Great at darts?"

"Be my guest. Sit here feeling sorry for yourself." Hash stretched his legs. "Tonight I'm going to find myself a proper lady. Just for a change. Skirts, shaved legs, perfume . . . there's got to be at least one left."

"There are about forty million of them," said Floyd. "All on Social Security."

The phone rang. Portia! Hash's eyes narrowed. "Don't be stupid," he whispered.

Half of Floyd tore for the phone; the other half ran away from it. As a result, he did not move. "I don't want to talk to her," he said. "Ever."

Hash picked up the phone. "Beck's Monastery." He listened a moment. "Who? Hi, Albert. No, he's okay. When? How much? Oiih, I'll be right down." He hung up.

Floyd handed him his dry clothes. "Where're you going?"

"Holland Tunnel. Lindley stopped a truckful of computers." Hash strapped on his ankle holster.

"Mind if I come?" Rain could drown one in memories.

Hash smiled. Floyd had been off Special Detail for a year; Portia had disapproved of grown men running around in the dark with loaded revolvers. Without him midnight raids had never been quite as sharp. "Sure." Hash pushed a fist into his sleeve, careful not to aggravate the bandage. "Thank you, Portia," he muttered.

"What's that?"

"Nothing. Let's go. You got gas in the Falcon?"

*   *   *

Six Tiffany chandeliers (plastic) drooped languidly over the bar, eaves-dropping on palaver below. The women caressed by their soft glow appeared supple and wise, the men, eternally strong. Here and there, tiny flames bloomed and vanished like fireflies above a Tennessee meadow. Each body at the bar leaned toward another body: Carnal gravity exerted maximum force on a weekend.

Floyd coughed. "There a nonsmoking section in here?"

Frowning behind a smooth smile, Hash led him over to the red marble bar (plastic) for which The Outpost was famous. All the seats had been taken three drinks ago by patrons who were just beginning to realize that only schoolteachers and disemboweled divorcés made an appearance before ten-thirty on a Friday night. "What'll you have," asked Hash.

"Beer."

Hash glanced swiftly right and left. "Two Pina Coladas, please."

"Beer, I said," Floyd corrected, cupping his hands around his mouth like a megaphone. "I hate coconut." A blast from the sound system cut him off.

"Quiet," Hash said, leaning an elbow on the countertop. "I know what I'm doing." Until the drinks arrived he bobbed his head in time with the oceanic music as if he had composed it himself. Floyd meanwhile looked uncomfortably around. Every woman within eyeshot sat openly appraising them, rapidly translating belts and biceps into a definitive tax bracket. For the first time in his life Floyd noticed that he was the only fellow around with his hair combed straight back. He wondered if perhaps a moustache, tennis shirt, tan, and two gold necklaces might make him a bit less conspicuous.

Their drinks arrived. "Follow me," said Hash, weaving through a field of athletic, laughing couples. He paused at a table snuggled by two nymphets drinking Pina Coladas. "Hi there," he said, sliding into the next booth.

"Hi," one of them replied, smiling with that side of her mouth which did not contain a straw. She was about twenty-one, Floyd saw, cute but a clone: Hair, clothing, posture, had all been copied from various caco-thespians who employed exorbitant publicists. Her friend seemed the type who would cry four minutes if her mother died and four weeks if her nail broke. It was beyond belief that he was expected to sleep with one of them tonight.

For several minutes, aware that the two ladies overheard them, Hash talked loudly about vacations. "Where are you going this year?" he asked. "The Riviera again?"

"Aghpf." Floyd pushed his Pina Colada away. "I thought maybe Perth Amboy."

"Idiot," whispered Hash, "I'm trying to help you."

One of the girls leaned over, tossing her hair, which already stood ten inches from her head, like a Visigoth's helmet. She looked at Floyd. "Got a match, lover?"

"We don't smoke," shouted Floyd as Hash drew a lighter from his pocket. Floyd twisted in the bartender's direction. "Would someone please turn that racket down?"

"Your friend's quite a number," said the girl, leaning over the lighter. Floyd did not like the way she guided Hash's hand toward her cigarette.

Hash displayed perfect teeth. "He's somewhat eccentric."

The other girl contemplated Floyd's haircut. "I adore eccentrics."

"I'm afraid I can't hear you," said Hash. "Why don't you two come sit here?" He smirked triumphantly across at Floyd. "That's much better. I'm George. This is Floyd."

"Roberta and Daphne," said the smoker. "I've never seen you two here before."

"You hang out in this place?" Floyd cried, looking darkly at Hash.

His friend merely raised his glass. "Pina Colada lovers of the world, unite!"

"Only a special man drinks Pina Coladas," said Daphne, clinking Hash's glass. "Macho but ultrasensitive."

Again Floyd twisted towards the bartender, who was busy making strawberry daiquiris. "Excuse me," he said, getting up.

"I'll have another," called Roberta. "Thanks, Floyd."

He did not like Roberta rolling her tongue around his name as if it were some red lollipop. "It's Inspector Beck," he said.

"What did he say?"

"You got me," Hash replied. "So! Are you two beautiful creatures roommates? Sisters? On leave from the caliph of Baghdad?"

Floyd guffawed loudly and headed for the bar. By now bodies choked the counter more thickly than algae did Lake Superior. "Hey Jack," he called. The bartender stood frowning into a mixology book.

"Excuse me," said a silken elbow to his right. Floyd ignored it; the voice contained not a speck of contrition.

"Hey Jack," he called again.

The bartender looked up from his shaker: No one but policemen and alcoholics ever called him Jack. Instinctually he knew he was dealing with the law. "What can I do for you?" He handed two White Cadillacs to a man wearing a bolla tie.

"First of all, you can turn that music down."

The bartender wiped his hands thoughtfully on a towel. The booze commission had just been in here last week trying to bust them for serving liquor to minors. They had no idea what a little lipstick could do to a twelve-year-old nowadays. "Sure thing." He rotated a black knob. "Anything else?"

"Two Pina Coladas and a draft beer."

"You don't fool around, do you, honey."

Floyd finally looked to his right. There sat a saucy brunette with terrific nostrils. He didn't know when she was born, where she aimed her life, what she thought of Palestine, but he'd only have to say "Try me" and he'd be screwing himself blind before midnight, no strings attached. If she couldn't keep up with him, tough: Lust was no charity bazaar. He felt his blood splashing downstream, towards its favorite dam. It had no conscience. "No, I do not fool around."

She toyed with her swizzle stick. "Too bad. We could have had some fun."

Floyd looked for the bartender. "Hey Jack, step on it."

"Out of coconut milk," the bartender replied nervously, rummaging on his knees through the mini refrigerator. "Just a sec."

Floyd cleared his throat. The smoke from her thin brown cigar bothered him. "Do you always speak so crudely to strangers?"

She blinked: deviation from the script. "You working for the Mormons?"

"Here you go," interrupted the bartender, placing three glasses on the counter. "On the house."

"Thank you." Floyd left a bill on the red marble bar. "Bring the lady a Bible." The bartender thought it was a drink.

By the time Floyd returned to the table, Hash had his arm around Roberta. That shocked Floyd; he was accustomed to Hash's arm around Pearl. "Where's Daphne?" he asked a little angrily, sliding into the seat. "Off powdering her nose?"

"Something like that," her friend giggled. "Whose drinks?"

A waitress in roller skates halted at Floyd's elbow. "Hi there," she cuddled, placing four more Pina Coladas on the table. "May I get you something else?"

Floyd looked across at Hash. "What would you like, George? An ice cream sundae?"

Smiling coldly at Floyd, Hash turned to the waitress. "A large guacamole, please. You do that so well here." The waitress spun away.

Roberta took one of the six Pina Coladas. "So let's party!"

Floyd peevishly fanned the air. "Would you mind blowing that in the other direction, sweetheart?"

"Hi gang, I'm back." Daphne slithered next to Floyd. "Where were you, Fred?"

"Floyd," he said, pushing her hand away from his hair. She had been smoking marijuana in the ladies room. "I should arrest you."

"Where did you find this guy, Georgie," asked Roberta. "He's weird."

Daphne lay a hand across Floyd's forearm. "No he's not. He's just a little kinky." She leaned over his ear. "I like that," she whispered.

"Excuse me," said Floyd, getting up.

"Now where are you going?"

"I am not feeling well. I should go home."

Hash stood up, passing a hand in benediction over the crop of Pina Coladas. "Ladies, amuse yourselves until we get back." His fingers crunched Floyd's elbow. "Two little minutes."

Antiphonal laughter, here coy, there hilarious, swelled at them from every table. Floyd led Hash behind the cigarette machine and whirled on him. "You fucking idiot," he snapped in a low voice. A nearby woman eyed them as she would prizewinning melons. "Cradle robber."

"Exactly what is the problem? Within one minute I hand you the best tail in this place and what do I get? Ayatollah Beck! Do you realize how lucky you are?"

"She smokes," said Floyd lamely.

"Oh crap, so what? You only have to put up with it til tomorrow morning!"

"That's really disgusting, George."

"Snap out of it, will you? What makes you think she wants anything to do with you after tonight?"

Such heinous thoughts had not indwelt Floyd's brain. "You're kidding."

"Welcome to the Space Age, Prince Valiant."

A dollar bill dangled between them. "Pardon me," smiled a woman with a flat face. "Anyone here have change?"

"Here you go, love," said Hash, digging into his pocket. Too late: She had already targeted Floyd. The man had no idea what an attractive sore thumb he made. It was beginning to irritate Hash. "Excuse us," he said, pulling Floyd away. "My friend was just going home."

"What a shame." Her eyes swooped down Floyd's thighs. "The night is so young."

"Bye, pal. Sorry you don't feel well."

"I make a great cup of lemon tea," she purred. "Cures everything."

Christ! Who told her she should act like this? Did she say the same things to the mailman? Did she get a volume discount on Wassermann tests? "Go home and drink it," snarled Floyd. He walked past the bar. The lady who had spoken with him before now sat toying with a neighbor's lower lip.

The street was shockingly quiet, the air Eden-pure. There were no women here. Floyd drove home but did not go inside; the walls had lately become echo chambers for his bleak thoughts. Instead he sat on his front stoop watching traffic pass randomly by. Witnessing the movement of others implied that he, too, was part of that dynamic continuum other people called life. Floyd knew that as he sat his heart sloshed blood from auricle to ventricle, his lungs bartered oxygen for carbon dioxide, and that by some alchemic miracle the enchiladas he had for dinner were transmuting into toenails. Yet he felt no wonder, no gratitude, at all. Those sensations tingled people who had something to live for.

He walked to Portia's clinic. Her office was dark: William had probably given her a ride to that veterinary conference in the Poconos. They were doing splendidly without the Falcon. Hash was right. He had ditched Portia because she didn't need him any more. Floyd chuckled sadly to himself, like a widower scenting his deceased wife's perfume on a passing stranger. Did Portia have any idea how her sisters behaved in places like The Outpost? Three years, numberless Female Awareness sessions later, did she once consider how many dozens of women in one tiny bar in one tiny town were blatantly available for the taking, like squished eggplant at a farm stand? Of course not! She had trained so much armament on the Floyds that she had overlooked the one billion Daphnes on her flank.

The hell with them all, Floyd thought, then ground his teeth: He could kill for a woman tonight. He didn't care what she smoked as long as she had two legs, two arms, two lips, and the software in between. No brain? No runes? Not to worry! He'd settle for skin! All she had to have was skin, room temperature: citrus to his scurvy. Why hadn't he just yanked the first fox who approached him tonight? What the hell was so antisocial about drilling a total stranger? Men had been doing it for centuries! They just didn't have to shell out for it now.

Floyd drove back to The Outpost. This time he had to wait half an hour to get in; after midnight even the wallflowers turned auctioneer. He looked around. Hash and his rareripe peach pies had gone. So had the woman at the bar and the woman at the cigarette machine. Only the bartender remained.

"Anthony?"

He looked down. Skidding past thirty, a little chubby: fifteen percent more epidermis than the average roast. Wearing her best jumpsuit and a bogus strand of pearls, good, good, trying hard. Before leaving home she had taken a bath, curled her hair, brushed her teeth, and slipped on a diaphragm. Floyd checked her lips for cold sores: zero. She'd invite him to her place because she had just blown two months' salary on a water bed. By five tomorrow morning, before the sun changed her from Scheherazade back to a squat little chamberpot, he'd be out on the street, free, already forgetting her name. "Close enough, honey," Floyd replied.

3

As she reached for a folder, the button popped off her waistband, disappearing into a box of silk swatches. A contorted bellybutton immediately peeped through the opening in her clothes, gasping for air: Since breakfast the dress had been trying to kill it. Viola Flury looked down, cursed, and continued sketching, resisting the temptation to undo a button in either direction of the ruptured waistband. The dress had not been tight last summer. Coquettishly snug, maybe, but never shrieking at the seams like this. No fair; she swam a mile a day, ate more vegetables than a giraffe, kept doing pushups, and in the end heredity would thicken her into a pudgy replica of her mother, who blamed everything on premature menopause but never stopped consuming layer cake. Criminy! When was the last time layer cake had passed her lips? Birthday last November! *Face it, Flury,* Viola thought, *the end is nigh.* After thirty-five years, tired of rolling ovaries into a womb which did not entertain them, her hormones were staging wildcat strikes. Two gray hairs insistently returned to haunt her left temple. As for energy, that struck out around three in the afternoon; Viola preferred hot tea and a good book to any night on the town now. Work? Routine as doing the dishes. Employees, accounts, came and went; the money remained constant. So did the pressure, of course, but therein lay the incentive to get out of bed in the morning. She had spent too much of her life in beds anyhow.

Viola slid the sketch into her briefcase and began digging around the box of silk swatches. Then she felt another pop and realized the front of her dress had sustained a second stress fracture. "Ah hell! Trixie," she called irritatedly, getting up, "do you have any safety pins over there? I blew a couple fuses."

"Sure." Trixie looked up from her computer. "Take four. I'm not sure two will do it."

"Thanks a lot, pal." Viola started pulling her dress together. "For six hundred bucks you'd think they could spare a little carpet thread."

"Obviously not a Pyrana product," Trixie said. "Long as you're here, want to see some numbers?" Her computer stopped whirring and sang a tinny B-flat. That meant it had finished swallowing data and was about to purge itself, like some electronic bulemic, into the printer. Indeed, seconds after the computer's little red lights ceased bleeping each other, the printer began gunning numbers at the green-and-white paper caught in its tractor feed. In about the time necessary for a secretary to utilize a strip of Correct-O-Type, the page was already sprayed with neat little columns, perfectly aligned, perfectly totaled. No wonder the accountants had lobbied so hard for this alchemic new tax reform, Viola thought as the paper inched toward the bin. They were being replaced by floppy discs.

She studied the printout a few moments before a line of zeros caught her eye. "What is this, Trixie, no more size-four pajamas? Only three more black peignoirs?" Viola peered at the lengthening figures. "No more size-four bikinis? What happened? Did UPS lose the last couple boxes again?"

"Nah, two Arabs came in yesterday and cleaned the showroom out. Said they liked petite women."

"Petite? They meant ten-year-olds. Anyone else buy size four yesterday?"

"I don't think so." Trixie watched as the totals leapt onto the page. "We sold nine thousand bucks worth of size four yesterday."

"Allah be praised." Viola pushed the fifth safety pin through her waistband. "I'll be out front. Run through an inventory of fours, would you? Just in case our friends come back for birthday presents."

Viola walked through a thick door into the showroom and saw that all of her salesgirls were busy: This week the National Rifleman's Association was convening at the Park Plaza Hotel a dozen blocks away. Ever since one of its members had bought some pajamas embroidered with a purple Colt .45 two days ago, the store had been mobbed.

Near the door stood a man wistfully holding a negligee in each hand, unable to choose between them. Viola walked over. "May I help you, sir?"

"This has to be just right," he said. "It's for my wife."

Sure, sure, and you're both Lutheran missionaries. "Is she fair?" Viola asked.

"Ah—she's black."

"Then take the green. She'll look ravishing."

"Right." The man paid with two hundred-dollar bills: no sense tipping off the fair one who received a cardigan sweater every anniversary. "Thank you."

"My pleasure." Viola checked around the shop and saw a regular customer. He dropped in once a week and never left without a morsel which, ounce for ounce, outpriced Beluga caviar. Maybe he was settling down: For three months now everything had been a 36C. "Hello, Dr. Bechstein."

"Good afternoon, Viola, you look splendid. How's your husband?"

"Fine, thanks." She glanced at the pink panties he was holding. "I just got them in from Switzerland."

"Exquisite. One does not see embroidery like this any more." Bechstein brought the panties close to his nose. "It's the Manhattan skyline."

Seen from Hoboken. "I've also got the reverse, pink on black, if you prefer."

"I'll have one of each. And what does a lady slip over this, might I ask?"

"Big Apples."

"Now that's clever. Give me two sets, one small, one medium." He winked at her. "Life goes on."

So it did; inconstancy was big business. Viola wrapped the packages and walked Dr. Bechstein to his limousine on Madison Avenue. "Remember, the blue box is the medium, red box the small. Don't mix them up or I'll be autographing your cast."

"Yes, yes, dear. Give my best to Eugene."

Waving, Viola went back inside. Now a man in a cowboy hat stood inspecting the Manhattan skyline. "Honeh," he said to her, "do y'ave somethin like this with downtown Houston on et?"

"No, but I could design a set for you."

"Ah'll take a dozen." He lay two bills on the glass counter. "But Ah want em red as a chili peppah with gold stitches. Nonna this pink and black business on mah secritarehs."

"No problem. May I show you anything else?"

The man glanced around. "Pehhaps somethin fo' ma wife. This me-chindise ain't quat heh style, howeveh."

Not her style with him, he meant. Viola brought out a bathrobe smothered with tiny cherries. The ruffles alone would obscure a Volks-wagen. "How does this grab you?"

"Divine, honeh! Pehfect!"

"I made that for a Bulgarian soprano. She wore it for interviews with *Paris Match*."

A salesgirl came to Viola. "Mr. Buffez on the phone, ma'am. I'll take care of the gentleman."

Viola excused herself to the back room. "Yes, Nestor."

"I just fired Wilma," said her partner. "She nipped a pint of gin for breakfast, then tried to snip appliqués out of silk again."

Viola sighed. They had six hundred tricot petticoats to get out the door by Monday. "I hope you have a replacement coming in."

"Not to worry, I found someone. Doesn't drink, smoke, yak, great with a pair of scissors. She wants to work sixty hours a week, she'll do weekends, and she's got two brothers who want jobs in the shipping department."

"Where'd you find her? In a time capsule?"

"No, the agency sent her. Look, Viola, can you come to the mill? The new samples are ready."

"How do they look?"

"Indecent. Every dirty old man in the country will buy one."

"For six hundred a pop?"

"Trust me. I know these things."

Viola had met Nestor twelve years ago at a masquerade ball. He was Mussolini, she La Sonnambula, wandering about the ballroom in several acres of lace and organza which had never quite made it into a wedding gown. Nestor had wanted to buy her costume for his date, a figurante who spent lots of time in dressing rooms. Viola disliked the woman on sight: all lacquer and elbows. Nestor? The only man on the floor with the balls to show up as a dictator. "Three hundred bucks," Viola had said, "and I don't dance." Two weeks later Nestor called, asking for another night-gown and a date. He got another nightgown. Within three months, he had bought eight. Then he asked if Viola would make him up a little teddy for the dancer, who suspected he was seeing other women. Nestor bought eight more teddies before Viola finally agreed to go out for a cup of coffee with him.

"I'm bankrupt," he had said.

"You're a shithead."

"Let's go into business together. You design, I'll sell." Viola had been doing nothing for two years but going to museums and ballets. She laughed at him anyway. "You'd be doing a tremendous service to humanity," he said.

"Male or female?"

"Both."

Their timing was perfect. Banks fell over themselves to loan money to an enterprise run by a Cuban and a woman. Within six months Pyrana, Inc. had four employees, then ten, then twenty, and still could barely meet the demand. Now that wives had joined the work force, husbands had a lot more cash to blow on their mistresses. Conversely, ladies were screaming for racy black slips to wear under their business suits, just in case they got run over by a CEO at the Telex machine. Another incorrigible segment of the population had never stopped giving, or receiving, lavish underwear throughout the last twenty years of social upheaval.

The Pyrana boutique on Madison Avenue became an overnight institution. Nobody custom-made garter belts any more. A lovesick advertising executive had no place to buy a few pairs of panties with his name embroidered across the fanny. Money meant nothing to seductresses of a certain age. In general, the more hopeless their infatuation, the more jagged with guilt and risk, the more Viola's and Nestor's clientele spent. Soon Pyrana had shops in Chicago, Los Angeles, Miami, and San Francisco, a city containing more transvestites per capita than a Halloween party. Thousands more customers across the country who still felt queasy buying lingerie in public ordered through the Pyrana catalog.

"See you later, Trixie," Viola said, swiping the inventory sheets from her desk. "I'm off to the mill." At the door she stopped. "If you have the time, could you please find those buttons for me? They're in that box of samples."

Trixie looked at the row of safety pins down the front of Viola's dress. "How many did you lose? Six?"

Years ago, before unemployment compensation, Trixie would not have dared say more than one. "Ten." Viola shut the door.

Thirty minutes later her black Porsche slipped into a parking slot at the plant in Paterson, New Jersey. Viola and Nestor had bought the place for peanuts a decade ago when everyone else was stoking wood stoves and Chapter Eleven forms. The company sold a mountain of his-and-her woollies that year; people could not bear to get out of their warm beds and face the gasoline lines. Pyrana, Inc. was soon able to transform the defunct mill into a glittery headquarters; the company needed the investment credits and its owners figured if they were going to spend sixteen hours a day in Paterson, they may as well enjoy it. Since his second divorce, Nestor had lived in the apartment over the executive offices.

"Hello, Mzzzz. Flury," the receptionist said, englutting her bubble gum. The front desk reeked of nail polish remover.

"Hi, Sylvia. Where's Nestor?"

"In back with Gina and Billy."

Viola walked down a long corridor and rapped twice on a door. "I said no more dictation, Henriette!" a voice shouted. "Make up the rest of the letters yourself!"

Viola entered the room. Nestor sat at a desk in his striped pajamas drinking a diet soda, watching two women in black peignoirs parade back and forth, arms up, arms down, turning, stretching, gowns drifting behind them like smoky shadows. Nestor studied their movements with the absorption of an astrophysicist rolling moon rocks. "I think you cut the ass too high," he said finally to Viola.

"I did not. Billy's got the belt too tight. Loosen it two notches, would you, Bill?"

Nestor let the road test run another minute. "Nope, it's still too high. Look how it pinches the crotch. Billy's getting sawed in half."

Viola sighed; Nestor was right. "I'll give it another inch."

His soda can clanked into the garbage. "But the gown's great. Floats like a dream. That really looks like lightning running down the back. Okay girls, thanks. See if they've got any bras finished for you yet." Gina and Billy left. Nestor stood up, adjusting his pajamas. He had stopped wearing suits when he moved into the mill six years ago. "What do you call that?" he said, noticing the pins on Viola's dress. "Designer punk?"

"Try designer flab."

"Sure." They headed toward the offices. "How's the shop?" Nestor hadn't gone to Madison Avenue in three years. Every time he walked in the store, he fired someone.

"Doing well on guns and Old Glory." July Fourth was two weeks off.

Henriette leaned out of a door. "Dingleball on line one," she called. "Whose turn is it this time?"

"Viola's," said Nestor, veering into his office. He did not get along with the Swiss embroiderer. The man kept trying to interest him in dirndl aprons. "I'm spray-painting garters."

"Give me a break." Viola took the phone. Four o'clock Friday and it had been a decent week; this call could torpedo everything. "Hello, Herr Dingle," she said heartily. "Don't tell me you've shipped the robes already!" Four-color changework, concatenating mistletoe and candy canes, their Christmas special. Two thousand of them should have been in the stores two months ago; this was one of those fine projects jinxed before the ink had dried on the drawing board. Viola listened a moment, bowed her head, and slowly massaged the bridge of her nose with two fingers. "We sent the pattern April tenth," she said. "You're only putting it up now? What textile strike in Italy? When? Why didn't you tell me this before? Of course I wouldn't have switched the order to Taiwan!"

Nestor tiptoed back into the office and leaned against the door, delicately plucking dustballs from his pajama bottoms. Dingleball never called unless a job got screwed up; he couldn't see wasting money on good news. "I need them in ten days, Herr Dingle," Viola said. "That means off the airplane, through customs, on my model's back. Is that possible or isn't it?" Nestor pretended to turn a huge, invisible screw through the air. Viola glared at him. "I don't understand. They just came back from a strike. Now you tell me they're all going on vacation?" Viola opened her desk drawer and twisted open a bottle of aspirin. "July first," she said.

"That is my deadline. There can be no exceptions. This is very disappointing. Yes, yes, of course it's not your fault. It never is. Thank you. Goodbye."

The phone crash-landed into its cradle. "Dingdong," Viola snapped. "From now on we're going to Taiwan." She pushed her intercom button. "No more calls on Friday afternoons, Henriette. Do you understand?"

"This is Thursday afternoon," the intercom replied.

Viola thoughtfully chewed another three aspirin. This was by far the worst news she had had all week. "How the hell did that happen?"

"We worked Sunday," Nestor said.

Viola went to the window and watched the gardener pat a little peat moss around the azaleas. Sundays still meant something to him; she envied that. Did he envy her barrowful of Ginnie Maes? "So tell me the good news."

"The white flannel pj's are a month ahead of schedule." Nestor scrounged his brains. "Shipping hasn't lost a package in three days."

Several aspirin detonated deep in Viola's throat. She picked up the top letter on her blotter, an invitation to appear on a television show about successful businesswomen. Success? Business? Woman? Bah, she just treaded water a little more spastically than everyone else. A sheaf of telephone messages, thick as flies on manure, clotted the desktop. "Leave," she told Nestor. "Go check out the bras."

One hour, many futile calls later, Viola decided to take a long weekend like the rest of the world. "Henriette," she called out the door, "can you break all my appointments for tomorrow?"

No answer. Viola stepped into the hall, peering right and left: deserted as a mosque on Christmas. Another surprise birthday party? Another fire in the kitchen? They couldn't all be in the john again. Curious, Viola walked down a long hall to the cutting room, where she saw twelve people huddled around a far table. It wasn't work-related: Everyone looked too animated. She headed over.

"Is it a boy or a girl?" she heard Henriette ask. "My God! Everything's so small!"

"It's a boy. You can tell from the ears."

"Can't be more than a few days old. The eyes are hardly open."

"Where'd you find him, Breeze?" Nestor said. "On the front steps?"

"In the dumpster. Wrapped in that scarf."

"He's really adorable, Nestor."

"Aw look, his poor little tummy's all scratched up."

"Stand back! He's going to pee!"

"Get him off the brocade, Luiza," Nestor shouted. "Now!"

Viola edged through the crowd. "What is going on here?" On a cutting table next to a fuschia-and-green scarf lay a tiny black dog. It seemed to be trying to swim. Viola looked at Nestor a few seconds. "Great," was all she said. "I'll call the pound."

Groans chorused from her employees' throats. "You can't, Viola! They'll gas him! Jesus wants us to keep him! We'll teach him to catch mice! It looks like an Afghanistan bloodhound!"

"That smudge is a mutt," Viola said. "People don't put pedigrees in dumpsters."

"Smudge!" The pup yipped from the table. "See! He likes that name!"

"Are we back in kindergarten, folks?"

"I'll take care of him," Richie volunteered.

"You stick to shipping," Nestor said. "When you get the hang of the Fed Ex forms, we'll think about trusting you with a living organism."

"Get back here, Richie," Viola said. "Nestor didn't mean it."

"So we can keep him?"

"No!" The phone on the cutting table rang, jolting Smudge's yipper into action. Ten maternal hands pulled the animal in ten directions. "Cut it out, gang! He's not made of rubber!" Viola lifted the receiver. "Pyrana, hello."

"Viola? This is Dr. Timm." Viola pressed a hand against her ear. Everyone was shouting at each other. Smudge was generating enough noise to keep King Kong at bay. "We have good news for you."

"I passed the Pap test?"

"Ouch!" shouted Nestor. "That runt bit me!"

"You're pregnant."

"What are you talking about?" Viola shrieked. "That's impossible!"

"The hell it is," Nestor snapped. "I'm bleeding."

"I'm in shock."

"Did you say you were bleeding?" Dr. Timm sounded alarmed.

"No, no, no! My partner is." Smudge skidded into Viola's elbow, howling piteously. Soon he would cry himself to death. "Give the poor thing something to drink, will you?" Viola said. "Not diet soda, Nestor, for Christ's sake! Dr. Timm, what do you feed a newborn pup? Milk?"

"Pup?" Timm didn't want to give the wrong advice and get slapped with a malpractice suit. "Make an appointment with me in the morning, all right? You're due—February tenth."

"I'll be thirty-six years old," Viola moaned. "The elastic's already shot."

"Get Smudge off that brocade," Nestor roared. "He's got two blow holes!"

"Bye-bye, Viola. Congratulations."

She collapsed across the table. "Who was that," cried Nestor. "Dingleball again?"

"Worse."

"The IRS?"

Viola opened an eye. Smudge was nosing in her hair, searching for a teat. She felt a delicate tug on her earlobe, heard a tiny sniff: mesmerizing. "It was my dear husband Eugene," she said. "He just postponed our safari twenty years." She slowly disengaged Smudge from her ear. The pup didn't like that. "Here, Nestor. Personnel is your department." She sat up; the crowd drew back. In twelve years Viola had still not been able to determine whether this indicated respect or aversion. She hopped off the table.

Nestor tucked Smudge into his pajama top. "End of intermission, guys. Kill the coffee breaks and manicures. Everyone busts until five o'clock." Nestor was a masterful proponent of free speech. Plus he knew that one didn't dare snap back at a Hispanic. That would seem racist. "I want you to meet the new cutter," he told Viola.

Cutter? What planet was this? "Who?"

They walked to a far table where a young Taiwanese woman was working intently. "Viola, this is Mai Ping. Mai, this is Miss Flury, your other boss."

Mai looked up. "Hi." Her scissors never stopped moving. Already a pile of appliqué oak leaves, twice the height of anyone else's, lay to her left.

"Terrific work," Nestor said, inspecting them. "You can go home now."

"Not five o'clock," she said, scissors limning another leaf.

Nestor shook his head; talk like that could get Mai Ping lynched. He lifted the top leaf from her pile. "Viola, come here. See how these look against the cape."

She had designed it last October, when Eugene had taken her to Vermont to see the dying foliage. Due February tenth? March, April, May tenth. Conceived May tenth. May? Impossible. Eugene had been fishing in Scotland. Wasn't she in Lucerne buying silk with Dingleball? No, that was April. The time zones must have bamboozled her ovaries.

"Well, what do you think?"

"Nice." Had May tenth been a Sunday? They aroused the beast in Eugene.

"Nice? Is that all you can say?"

"Colorful. Warm. Profuse. Nestor, I have to go home."

"First you've got to see the little gold acorns we're tacking between the leaves."

"Is this necessary? I'm in the middle of a mathematical problem."

"Viola, we've been over this a million times. There are twenty-three leaves and fourteen acorns on each cape. There's nothing to worry about. They all fit."

It had been a Sunday morning, all right. Eugene had returned from Scotland on Saturday afternoon, bursting with fish stories. He had fallen asleep at eight that night and awakened at four the next morning, ready for some heavy fly-casting. She remembered it quite distinctly now. *Viola*, he had whispered, rolling her over, *I can't sleep.* She had told him to get up and balance the checkbook. "Oiiiih."

Nestor looked at her oddly. "What's the matter? Now you don't like it?"

"No! It's gorgeous."

The lump under Nestor's pajamas began to whimper in frustration. For many minutes Smudge had been trying to coax some milk out of Nestor's bellybutton. "This afternoon is rapidly turning to shit." Nestor glanced at his watch. "Let's check out, everyone!" he shouted.

"Not five o'clock," said Mai Ping again as the other stitchers streamed by, gaping at her as if she were a derelict egesting in the gutter.

"Okay, honey. Shut off the lights when you leave." Nestor turned toward the shipping department.

"What are you going to do with that dog, Nestor?"

"Get him some milk." Nestor removed Smudge from his pajamas. "You know, I've always wanted a dog."

Viola did not go directly home; at rush hour, she could walk over the George Washington Bridge in less time than she could drive over it. Through the years she had learned to make the run about seven, seven-fifteen, after the commuters had buzzed each other's fenders, but before the suburbanites began streaming in for an evening's diversion; then she could get from Paterson to Riverside Drive in thirty minutes. Every morning, as the Porsche sailed by the hordes inching fretfully east on Route 4, Viola was grateful to be commuting west from Manhattan to New Jersey, and not the opposite. Her clutch wouldn't last six months.

At the door of her apartment she paused: burnt garlic and airplane glue. Her husband was experimenting again. Viola looked around the living room. "Eugene! Where are you, honey?" Metal clattered to the kitchen floor. Viola threw her briefcase on the sofa and rushed inside.

Eugene stood pouring gin over the incinerated remains of either a dishtowel or a fish. "Stand back, sweetheart!" he shouted through the smoke. "He's almost done!"

"I'd turn that flame down if I were you," Viola coughed, going for the exhaust fan.

Eugene lit a match. "Cajun sea bass!" he announced, flinging the match into the pan. The ensuing deflagration whooshed to the ceiling. After it had consumed the gin, it collapsed, leaving black stains on the copper hood above the stove.

"So where's the genie?" Viola said, trying to appear encouraging. "In that carton of ice cream?"

With a large spatula, Eugene was trying to disunite the contents of the pan from the bottom of the pan. "Ice cream? Didn't I put that away hours ago?"

Viola opened the freezer and removed a round container of pantyhose. Eugene hated to wear his glasses in the kitchen. "Sure."

Carefully balancing the pan, some bread, a salad bowl, and a red dish against his apron, Eugene kissed his wife's cheek. "No time for cocktails tonight, I'm afraid. The concert begins in an hour."

Ah cripes, Mostly Mozart! Tonight she needed something atonal, polyrhythmic, with tons of percussion. Shostakovich: Antheil: Mozart would drive her nuts. Viola took two bottles and followed Eugene to the table he had set on the terrace.

"This is going to be a super concert," he said. "All Schubert."

Ten times worse than Mozart: Schubert never knew when to shut up. Viola poured two glasses of wine and watched a tugboat patiently buck the Hudson. Above her head a breeze lifted the awning, softly ruffling its skirts. Otherwise all was quiet eighteen floors above the sidewalk: no birds, no humanity . . . here one waited as the sun, and time, slithered noiselessly below the horizon. But the sun came back in the morning.

Eugene ladled some fish flakes onto Viola's plate. "Did you have a bad day, love?"

"A typical one." Viola drank some mineral water.

"Did you swim this afternoon?"

"Ya, about a mile. Maybe that was too much." She looked at her plate. The salad she recognized. "Looks great, Gene. You're really getting the hang of that food processor now."

"One of the great inventions of the twentieth century. If something doesn't quite turn out according to blueprints, you just purée it." Eugene tasted the fulvous purée on his dish and took a long swish of wine. "Could have been worse."

"What was this originally, sweetheart?"

"Ravioli."

"Aha." Viola forced another forkful into her mouth. "So what did you do today?"

Eugene was an inventor. Before turning twenty, he held six patents. One of them, a miniscule valve which made centrifuges behave, earned him a fortune. Then Eugene became curious about fuel-injected engines. Within six years, he could have bought Chrysler; instead he invested in a row of castellated apartment buildings along Riverside Drive in New York. He and Viola lived in the top two floors of one of them. On his thirtieth birthday, Eugene decided to retire and take up fishing; his doctor had told him he needed more exercise. Since then, he had trolled on every continent but Antarctica and had invented dozens of items of fishing paraphernalia. Eugene was an authority on salmon.

"I'm getting set for Canada."

"Now? I thought that trip was off."

"Eh—MacArdle called me this morning. They're running late this year, it seems." Eugene took her hand. "I hope you don't mind, Viola. Spawning fish are so unpredictable."

Anything alive was unpredictable. Who would have believed five years ago that she'd be sitting on this terrace with a spouse named Eugene? Or that next year there would be three of them? Whoever wrote this script had not consulted her at all. Viola put down her fork; it was just as good a time as any. "So are spawning husbands, I'm afraid." She leaned back in her chair and sighed. "Nice work, Eugene."

For quite some time Eugene peered at his wife over his glasses. Then his countenance rose gracefully as a hot-air balloon. "We're pregnant!" he shouted. "Aren't we! By God, I love surprises, Viola!" He pulled her off the chair and twirled her around the terrace. "You fabulous thing, I've been waiting years for this!" He put her down in a chair and danced a jig. "I'm going to be a father. God, God, I don't believe it! This is better than three walleye salmon. It's better than the perpetual-motion machine. This is the invention of my life!"

"Sit down before you fly off the balcony."

Eugene was beside himself. He fell to the carpet and did two somersaults. Then he crawled to Viola's knees. "I'll cancel all my fishing trips. I'll invent self-changing diapers. I'll build a nursery."

"We're ancient, you big nut," Viola said.

"We're young, darling! Oh my God! I can buy model trains again!" Eugene bolted upright and tried to pour some wine. His hands were shaking so badly that he finally had to drink straight from the bottle. "We can go to Disneyland!"

Kids started smoking dope in kindergarten now. They lost their virginity before they lost their milk teeth. They couldn't even read Stop signs and they all hated their mothers. Ah, why even worry. A couple nuclear bombs would settle everything. "February tenth," she said. "Blastoff. Sorry about the safari."

"Forget the safari, I'm staying here! Wait, don't move." Eugene rushed inside. A few minutes later he returned with two cameras, a tape measure, and the bathroom scale. "Smile, Viola. That's nice. Stand up, would you? Turn towards the bridge. I need a profile shot."

"This is ridiculous."

Eugene snapped away. "Our scrapbook is going to start from the very beginning." He finished one roll of film and switched cameras. "Could you please undo those safety pins? Come on, be a sport. That's better. I do think you're beginning to bulge already, darling."

"The hell I am."

Eugene placed the scale on the floor and ushered Viola on top of it. "February tenth? How much did you weigh on May tenth?"

"I am not a fish. Put that thing away."

"But we need accurate records of this!"

"What for, the patent office?"

"Thanks, you can sit down now." There was no more film. "I've got to call my mother. She's always wanted grandchildren."

"Grandchild. Singular. One. If she wanted more, she should have hatched a few more herself."

Eugene led his wife to the swinging couch. "Tomorrow I've got to start seriously contributing to the MIT Alumni Fund. Would you just lie down here a minute? I have to check something." He knelt beside the couch and put his ear on her stomach. "Not much action yet, is there." He cupped his hands over Viola's navel. "Hi there, dynamite, how's the weather? Getting enough to eat? What? You want Mom to drink more milk?"

"I hate milk."

Eugene replaced his ear on Viola's stomach. "You don't want to be a wimpy little runt, eh. I understand. My mother did the same thing to me and I'm still annoyed with her. Pop'll take care of it, don't worry. Hang in there, kid. Over and out." He kissed Viola's belly and carefully placed a napkin over it, already tucking someone into bed. "Ah, this is agony."

"You ate too much Cajun sea bass."

"I can't wait until February. The excitement will kill me." On two knees Eugene slid up to her face. "Thank you, Viola." He kissed her hands and suddenly lay still. By the way he struggled to swallow she knew he was crying. She waited, stroking his back. "Do you know what the best part of all this is?" he whispered finally.

"No."

"You really are stuck with me now."

Were there kinder fates? Viola ran a few fingers through her husband's fragile hair. "Crazy man." She felt like sleeping for centuries. "Hey. Concert starts in half an hour."

The woman suddenly turned vengeful and suicidal. She had recently been thrown out of the house and her fiancé had been murdered, all because of a band of jewel thieves. Her only worldly possession was a horse which would inevitably bankrupt her. Distraught, she decided to burn down her father's mansion and roast herself as well; that would teach the old bastard to disinherit his favorite daughter. At her fiancé's pyre she heaved a brand into a mountain of sticks, howling in glee as the flames ate hungrily upwards.

Unable to move, Floyd watched the dancing yellow field engulf her. Even as her face disappeared, he could hear her singing ecstatically. For several terrible moments Floyd wanted to join her in the pyre. The woman was heroic, hypnotic, doomed . . . just his type. The father leaned from an upstairs window and realized immediately that the bucket brigade would never arrive in time; strangely enough, he did not seem surprised as the flames savaged him. Floyd saw several other people jump into the conflagration, yet he could do nothing. The fire ruled all.

Eonian minutes later, all was smoldering ashes. The woman had destroyed everything, including her horse. Floyd rolled over on the floor, spent; he wouldn't be able to speak coherently for days. That fiancé must have been one incredible motherfucker.

Someone pounded on his front door. "Beck, you in there? Beck!"

Hash may just as well have been pounding on his bedroom door thirty seconds after an orgy with the entire cast of "Dynasty." Torn between real, unreal, and superreal, Floyd remained procumbent, reluctant to become a mere human again, so soon.

"Beck!" At any moment Hash would break a window. He had done so before. Cursing, Floyd very slowly shuffled to the front door. Daylight, time, poked him in the eye.

"Where the hell have you been? Are you all right? I've been calling you all weekend! Jesus, you look a mess! What have you been doing to yourself?"

Floyd's dormant throat resisted speech. "Listening to opera." Now the spell was broken. He was furious with Hash. "You mind?"

"At six in the morning? Can't you sleep? Why didn't you answer the phone?"

"Unplugged it."

The white-and-black stubble on Floyd's chin glistened in the sun. Hair, shirt, eyes, a dissipated wreck: Floyd had been on another bender, all right.

Since Portia dumped him three weeks ago, he had rudely deteriorated. After one apathetic stab at a singles bar, Floyd had shut himself at home like a traumatized widow. The first weekend he listened nonstop to Bach. Last weekend he did a Proust marathon. This weekend, opera. What next, the Talmud? "Let me make you some coffee."

"What for? I'm awake."

"I'm not." Hash walked into the living room. Strewn about the floor lay pizza boxes, German/English dictionaries, beer bottles, apple cores, and at least fifty records in white dust covers. "What is this, the Reader's Digest Anthology of Beautiful Music?"

"The *Ring* cycle. Four operas by Richard Wagner."

"About what, a washing machine?"

Hash barely had the patience to finish a one-paragraph customs report. For twenty-five years, note upon note, Richard Wagner had tenaciously harvested his brains, constructing a world which he alone heard, and wanted. How strong was his will thirteen years into the mountain, two operas down, two to go? Certainly Hash would never know. "Very funny."

Hash picked up a record. *"Die Göttradamlingren?* Sounds perverted."

"Put that down!" Floyd snapped, snatching it away. "It's a collector's item."

"Easy, boy." Hash very carefully stepped between the records toward the kitchen, stopping to open the drapes and a front window. "You listened to all these? Straight? How long did it take?"

"Thirty hours and change. I have two versions."

A pox of bottle caps scabbed the kitchen counters. Hash opened a cabinet, looking for coffee. "I've been calling since Friday night. You missed quite a party. The women all had tattoos."

"Shucks."

"You on drugs or something?"

"No, are you?"

"So where were you Friday night?"

"Swimming."

Hash shook his head; he could just see Floyd in his little red trunks stroking doggedly up and down, up and down the pool, oblivious of the leers of more normal individuals. Floyd was always trying to improve his breast stroke. "I guess you're out of coffee," Hash said finally, closing the last cabinet. On the way out, he noticed an old book on the kitchen table. "What's this?" He read the open page. "Liverwurst? Is that the name of a guy in the opera or something?"

"That's a recipe for liverwurst."

After a moment, Hash laughed strangely. "I see. Of course. See you at work." At the door he paused. "By the way, today is Monday."

So? Did two suns rise on Monday? "Thanks for checking in. Really."

Hash slipped his Firebird through the Lincoln Tunnel amid a daybreak sea of inert, taxidermic heads: Weekends sucked the blood out of folk. It would take slathers of coffee, martinis, and coke to get Manhattan functioning again. What had these people done with themselves the past two days? Hash looked to his right. That guy in the blue Ford had watched baseball, swilled beer, and dreamt about blond bombshells who found hairy potbellies much more sensual than did his wife. Lolita there in the Datsun removing rollers from her hair? She had gotten herself sunburnt, drunk, then laid two days running. She had just moved to the city from the Midwest and was trying to become sophisticated as rapidly as possible. How about Joe Bowtie there in Volvo, chatting on car phone? He had run the local yuppie marathon (ten kilometers) on Saturday, gone skydiving Sunday. He'd walk on a cracked shin until Thursday, when the excruciating pain would finally force him to a doctor.

None of this stupidity topped Floyd's, though. Now there was a guy who not only knew how to destroy a weekend, but how to take out the week on either side. Thirty hours in seclusion with the Beatles, Hash could comprehend. But Wagner? Wasn't he the guy they played whenever politicians kicked the bucket? Beck would be a corpse for days, pallid, rigor-mortised with overtures and subplots. How could women find that dark stare attractive? Hash had seen the same look on mug shots of pornographers.

He cut off the man in the Volvo. Perhaps it was better that Floyd had not gone to the party after all; Hash might never have cornered that sensational redhead on the patio otherwise. Late twenties, she was at that awkward age when the body was still ablaze but the enthusiasm was cooling steadily as a pie on a windowsill. In another year she'd stop going to parties altogether and start videotaping interviews for dating services. It had taken Hash three hours of sophistic twaddling to convince her that casual sex disturbed him. Even after he had talked himself hoarse, she had remained skeptical, constantly glancing at her watch amid allusions to a sick cat. The episode had jaundiced his weekend. Was he losing his touch? Hash ran a hand through his hair. Balding? He spun the Firebird into the JFK lot. She must have been having her period.

He locked his car and walked toward the terminal. A 747 zoomed overhead, vibrating his toes. The redhead had left alone around midnight, without revealing her tattoo although he had asked specifically three times to see it. Bitch! Hash shoved open the gray steel door to the customs office.

"Hey, gorilla, use the doorknob," said McPhee, looking over his glasses. "What's eating you?"

"I hate screwed-up people."

"And you work in New York?" McPhee watched Hash pour himself a cup of coffee, misjudge its temperature, and choke violently. "What's gotten into you? Some little lady shoot you down?"

Hash had not become the Don Juan of the terminal by advertising his shutouts. "It's Beck," he snapped. "The guy's gone belly-up since Portia dumped him."

"Like what? He's been bagging people right and left. I'd say if anything his nose has gotten sharper."

"It's a sign of insanity," Hash said. "You know, like rabid dogs and water? Listen, McPhee, he's been acting like a psycho lately. That first weekend he shut himself in his room and played nothing but this spooky organ music for two days straight. Last weekend he read *Remembrance of Things Past* in one fell swoop. That's like a zillion pages."

"What's so strange about that? You should see my wife with her historical romances."

"You know how I found him this morning? In his living room with about seventy records. He had been listening to operas for thirty hours straight! The place was a wreck. You would not have believed his face when I came to the door. I thought he'd kill me. Then I go to his kitchen and you know what he's been reading between acts?" Hash threw the Styrofoam cup away. "Books about liverwurst!"

McPhee went to the coffee machine and thoughtfully pulled the spigot. Then he sat back at his desk. "That's pretty perverted," he said finally.

"I'm worried," Hash said. "Beck is too quiet. You never know what's going on in his brain. Always sits there looking at you with these eyes. This thing with Portia really put him round the bend. I'm not sure why."

"He's quiet because he's an orphan," McPhee reminded him. "His parents got killed by a drunk driver." Then McPhee remembered something. "Hey, his father was a butcher. Maybe that has something to do with the liverwurst."

"Oh, great! So Beck's regressing to his childhood? Next thing you know he'll get a fancy new car and drive it off the Palisades. I know how these things work. I took psychology in college."

"Can't you do something for him? Get him laid, maybe?"

"Shit, no!" Hash snapped angrily, startling McPhee. "I've tried. He's impossible."

McPhee considered the liverwurst, and Portia, again. "Is he gay?"

Hash scowled. "He may as well be. Women seem to turn him off."

"Does he turn women off, too?"

Hash thought about the ladies at The Outpost and the ladies everywhere he had ever been with Floyd. Then he thought about the redhead at the tattoo party this past weekend. Floyd would have sat in the far corner of the patio and sipped a beer, frowning at the celestial vault while everyone else tried to do a little socializing. Within ten minutes that redhead would have been sitting on Floyd's lap, begging to show him a weensy little tattoo five inches southwest of her navel. "Women go crazy over him," he said. "That's what I don't understand."

Hash's telephone rang. "Hello. Hi. Shoot." He listened a long moment. "Cossacks? Cassettes? Corsets? *Corsets?* You're sure. I'll look into it." He hung up.

"What was that," McPhee asked.

"My Harlem correspondent. Tells me I should start looking for drugs in corsets. I think that's what he said. His English is not superb."

"Is this the same guy who told us pointed head last month when he meant pointed chin?"

"Yeah. It's also the same guy who told me the Chinese were running drugs in dogs."

"Dogs? Sure he didn't mean docks? Or ducks? Like Peking ducks?"

"Maybe. I've been to Agriculture checking out the kennels every day and nothing's turned up."

"Great informant you've got there." Sighing, McPhee started reading a report.

Hash irritatedly flipped through the messages on his desk. "What's this now?"

McPhee finished the paragraph. It was too early in the week to fall behind. "Mama Juana. Lindley thinks he's getting restless."

Aldo Minsky, alias Mama Juana, imported and exported photographs of adulterated children without registering his product with the U.S. Treasury Department. For two years he had brilliantly eluded capture by turning into a Hasidic Jew, a bag man, or a stockbroker moments before Hash & Co. raided his various hideouts. Minsky's favorite getaway costume was that of a pregnant Puerto Rican; once he stepped onto upper Broadway in that rig, no cop alive could tell who was who. Hash had missed Mama Juana by inches several times and was becoming aggravated; the kids posing for the pictures all bore a faint resemblance to his nieces and nephews in Minneapolis.

Again the phone on Hash's desk rang. It was Lindley calling from Le Bagel on Forty-second Street, where he had been sitting all night pretending to be reading *Screw* magazine. He had just seen a suspicious priest enter the massage parlor beneath Minsky's photography studio. "Minsky couldn't be that blatant," Hash said. "Neither could a priest, I hope."

Lindley insisted the priest was the only guy in the area not glancing anxiously over his shoulder every two steps. "Okay, let's check it out," said Hash. "Pedrosian covering the back door? I'll meet him right away." He hung up.

McPhee looked up from his desk. "Try not to shoot the guy in the back, hey? The ACLU will string us up."

Hash made good time getting into Manhattan: Commuters were on vacation, tourists used the bus, and half the cabs were on strike. At the Queens Midtown Tunnel, Lindley radioed to report two young boys walking into the massage parlor with Betamax machines. Then a strange-looking van just pulled up outside the building. "What do you mean strange?" said Hash.

"Bunch of broads with bullhorns. Looks like a diversion."

Hash ran a few red lights; this whole cesspool was beginning to stink now. Juana had a genius for manipulating traffic jams and other inane, random occurrences to his advantage. He knew damn well that Lindley had been sitting in Le Bagel for three weeks watching him, waiting to blow his ass off. Reckless priests, boys with videos, ladies with bullhorns, all at eight o'clock Monday morning? Come on.

Attempting a short cut, Hash got trapped for ten minutes behind a garbage truck on Forty-first Street. During this time Lindley lost radio contact. By the time Hash got to the alley behind Mama Juana's, Pedrosian was ready to launch a few grenades. He had seen nine more boys with Betamaxes climb in through the fire escape. "They're shooting an orgy," he said.

Suddenly one of the boys upstairs screamed. "You're burning me! Stop!"

"Holy God, the bastard's doing a snuff movie," whispered Pedrosian. "Let's go."

Hash leapt for the fire escape. His injured arm gave way and he fell back to the ground, cursing. Several boys were crying fearfully up there now. "Give me a lift, will you," he said. Pedrosian stirruped his hands and Hash put a foot in. Soon he had crawled onto the lowest grate.

An explosion rocked the room. Hash ripped up the fire escape and burst through the window. Milky smoke clogged the air. Spotlights and Beta-max machines lay smashed on the floor amid a snarl of thick black wires, fake leopard skins, pizza, and pubescent buttocks. "Where's the priest?" he shouted. No one answered him. "Who was taking these pictures?"

"Uncle Larry," sniffled one of the boys. "He ran away."

"Which door?" There were three.

Each door got several fingers pointed at it. Hash ran through the middle one just in time to see a skirt depart the landing. He scrambled downstairs and into the street. "Oooafff!"

One of the demonstrators had tripped him. Another jumped on his back like a ruttish chimpanzee. Women again: Hash braced himself for more darts, this time in the groin. "Swine! You should be castrated!" the one on top of him yelled, pulling his hair.

"Off!" Hash shouted, trying to tear free. "I'm the law!"

The she-bear clutching his ankle bit him. "Sure you are, Dickie."

With terrible force Hash loosened the woman on his back. He lurched several feet down the sidewalk, dragging the second body along. About a block away he saw a pregnant Puerto Rican scurry fleetly around the bend: Minsky. Ten more seconds and he would vanish. Just as Hash kicked the woman off his ankle, another stood in his way. "Halt! I arrest you for crimes against half the human race!" she shouted.

He shoved her roughly aside although she would probably take him to court for assault and battery now. Where the hell was Lindley? Hash hesitated one moment, looking quickly right and left. That was all the time the woman needed to clout him with a placard. As he careened into a wall, Hash looked at her in surprise: The evil little pipsqueak had to be taking steroids. He staggered to the corner but Juana had dissolved easily as sugar in hot tea.

Lindley caught up to Hash. "You all right?"

"What the fuck do you think?"

"Sorry, there was a holdup at the bagel joint. The doors automatically locked."

Was Saturn impacting Pluto? Were the Russians bombarding New York with alpha particles? Hash rubbed the side of his head. "This is going to be a long week."

"Did we lose him?"

A thousand bagels, three weeks overtime, down the tubes. Lately Hash's department had been less cost-effective than Amtrak. "He lost us." Hash looked at the demonstrators outside the massage parlor. "With a little help from the peanut gallery."

"Who are those twats anyway?" Lindley squinted to read the signs. "W.H.A.P? Women Hate All Pornography? Give me a break. Do you think Minsky planted them?"

"See that little runt wrestling with the black guy?" Hash said. "She's going to jail."

"Looks like she's killing him."

"Go see what Pedrosian's up to. I'll take care of this." Across Forty-second Street two patrol cars, blue lights fulgurating, nestled in front of

Le Bagel as their drivers attempted to sort paying from nonpaying customers. Over on this side, WHAP had closed ranks around the boxing match, shouting encouragement from ringside. A herd of Japanese tourists, laden with expensive cameras, crisscrossed the street, blocking traffic as they crouched for zoom shots and mob scenes.

Hash strode to the combatants. "Knock it off, Mighty Mouse."

"He's resisting arrest," the woman snapped. Hash yanked her away. The man straightened his suit, mumbled something in French, and hurried off. He looked like a diplomat from the UN. The woman turned to Hash. "Get your filthy hands off me."

Hash marched her to a billboard and flung her against it. They wanted equality, didn't they? "Hands on the wall."

"Shove it," she said, kicking him on his sore shin.

That did it. "You little shit," Hash said. "I'm busting your nose."

"What's going on here," said a policeman. "Hang up the fangs, lady."

Hash trashed her against the wall again. "Treasury Department," he said, pulling an I.D. "I want this woman arrested."

"Bullshit! This is police harassment." The woman turned to her friends. "Look what they're doing to me over here!" Two Japanese tourists spun around, Nikons chattering. "Get this on film!" Several demonstrators ran over, shouting.

The cop had seen it all a million times before. He looked at Hash as if to say, At least they didn't call the *Daily News.* "Go back to your rain dance, girls. Now!" He waited until they had left. "What happened."

"Code E, Section Eight. This woman obstructed pursuit of a suspected criminal," Hash said, squeezing the back of her neck.

"What criminal?" she laughed derisively. "Don't tell me you were chasing that defenseless woman! She was eight months pregnant."

"That was the suspect?" the cop said to Hash. The Feds would dynamite the Statue of Liberty if someone told them she was semaphoring Moscow.

"Yes, that was the suspect," Hash snapped, "in his favorite disguise. It apparently worked."

"Where was your backup?" the cop asked.

"Trapped in the bagel shop."

"You had just one backup?"

"Look, let's not get sidetracked. Get these women out of here. They've wrecked a three-month investigation." Hash looked down. "I want Peanut here in handcuffs. She's been assaulting anyone who comes out of that massage parlor."

"We've been making citizen's arrests," she said. "On behalf of the women you've all been screwing upstairs."

The cop sighed. "Let me see your permit."

She pulled a green paper from her pocket. "This is unconstitutional," she said loudly to the Japanese photographers. "I hope you show all your friends back home what America is really like."

The policeman quickly read the permit. "Women Hate All Pornography? And you're Dr. Portia Clemens?"

"Yes, officer. We have permission to be here from eight til twelve. This afternoon we'll be at Radio City."

"What's pornographic about Radio City?" the policeman said.

"The Rockettes. They're an outrage."

"God Almighty," he muttered, handing the permit back. "You sure you want to get involved with all this, major?" he asked Hash.

Hash was studying her mouth. If Floyd had just spent a little time analyzing the seam between Portia's lips, he would have spared himself three years of humiliation. That tight little line cut from cheek to cheek, warping smiles, hospitable as a cactus. Enough women with such lips could annihilate civilization.

"Drop it," he said disgustedly.

"And what's your name?" Portia asked. "I'm lodging a complaint. Harassment and brutality."

"Lady, be a sport," the cop said. "He's just doing his job."

"Ha!" Portia hoisted her placard. "And the name is Dr. Clemens. Not Lady."

"My mistake, believe me."

Portia rejoined the circle of women picketing the massage parlor. As she bent over to get a bullhorn, Hash and the cop held their breath: Rear ends, unlike brains, were apolitical. For that moment, they forgave her. "Sicko," said the cop several moments after Portia had stood up again. "Doctor? Can you see her coming at you with a knife?"

"She psychoanalyzes dogs," Hash said. "Used to date my buddy."

"A guy?" The cop guffawed.

Hash tore his eyes away from Portia's skin-tight jeans, core three thousand centigrade: hardly the outfit to wear to an antiporno demonstration. She did it on purpose, of course. It supported her argument that men were beasts. "Thanks. Gotta run," Hash said. Circumventing the demonstration, he went into the alley behind Mama Juana's studio. A lot of wailing continued upstairs. Hash raised his arms and quickly lowered them: No way he was going to make the fire escape without Pedrosian's help. He pulled his walkie-talkie. "Lindley, you up there?"

"Under control. We're still pasting on Band-Aids."

"See you at the office."

Hash drove slowly as a grandma back to JFK. The first and last time he had seen Portia, she had beautiful blond hair rolling to her shoulders. He remembered quite distinctly the pink sundress she had worn when Floyd introduced them; the spaghetti straps kept falling down and finally she had just left them there. All night long she had drunk Cynar and talked about a cocker spaniel named Pushkin. She had been about ten pounds heavier then; voice, cheeks, everything about her had been fluffier, more feminine. No wonder he didn't recognize her now.

But she had not recognized him either. This disturbed Hash tremendously, as neither his height, his weight, nor his bonny demeanor had changed one iota. Were his eyes that forgettable? Had that much wavy hair just blown away? Blinded by that schmo Beck, had she really not noticed him at all? After one meeting, they had never met again. Why was that? Floyd had always mumbled some halfass excuse about Portia not liking men with guns, which made little sense since Floyd himself always wore one on his ankle.

Swerving in front of a limousine, Hash cut onto the airport ramp. He knew he was an extremely handsome man; mirrors and women told him this constantly. He knew he was a superb lover also; nearly all of his conquests cried afterwards. Two strikeouts in three days had to be an aberration . . . Hash just hadn't realized how vicious women became as they grew older. It didn't make sense. Theoretically, as their looks waned, they should be treating men more and more graciously.

Who needed this aggravation? From now on, he'd stick with eighteen-year-olds from The Outpost. They adored sophisticated gentlemen. Hash slammed the car door and winced: His shoulder felt like chop suey in a Mongolian hot pot. Mama Juana had outdone him again. Portia Clemens hadn't recognized him. By now they both should have been in jail.

Switzerland

"Pass the coffee, please. What a gorgeous morning! That view is just like the postcards, isn't it, girls. How did you sleep, Rhoda?"

"Fine until the goddamn rooster woke up. The coop must be right beneath my window."

"Don't complain, honey, the sheep are right beneath mine. Efff! This coffee's awful."

"They use different beans here, dear. Cut it with some milk."

"Nope, too fattening. Has your chef got any orange juice, Froy? Croissants? Egg MacMuffins?"

"Zis pension is not ze Ritzy Hotel. For breakfast ve have coffee and bread."

"I adore European bread. It's so robust. Nothing like that chemical fluff we have in America."

"This crust is some challenge. Do you ever serve white bread, Fräulein Moser?"

"No. Excuse me, I must go."

"Have a nice day, Froy."

"I can't eat this stuff, it's hard as a rock."

"What do you expect, Rhoda? It's been on the table since five o'clock."

"I'm not ready to climb that hill. Gad, I'd love to go back to bed."

"I don't know about your bed, but mine was like sleeping on a cauliflower. And the pillow must be stuffed with sawdust. Now I see why they don't need guns over here. They just hit people with their pillows."

"Girls, stop kvetching! It's just a little jet lag!"

"I can get by without anything but a decent cup of coffee in the morning. This swill reminds me of the stuff Louis my husband used to make. It took me two years to figure out that he always put a few drops of dish detergent into my cup. That was my punishment for not making the coffee myself like a good housewife."

"So why didn't you do the same to him?"

"I did. He moved out a week later."

"What's with these bastards? If they made decent money in the first place, we wouldn't have to go to work."

"I beg your pardon, Breeze. My husband Leonard has a fabulous job. That never prevented me from going to work the minute we returned from our honeymoon."

"I find that very understandable. It all depends on what the wife looks like."

"And what does that mean?"

"Well, it's just my theory. Suppose you were a blond bombshell, Harriet. Do you think Leonard would want you eating alone at strange restaurants, talking at strange conventions, knocking off a few brandies at two in the morning at the Chicago Hilton? Of course not."

"It may come as quite a shock to you to know that Leonard not only finds me attractive but trusts me implicitly. His idea of femininity is exceptionally mature. He detests bleached hair, for instance."

"And what does that mean?"

"Nothing, dear. Marriage is an eternal discovery."

"Yeah? The more I discovered, the less I wanted to be married."

"You must have married the wrong man."

"Make that men. Three of them."

"You've been married three times already?"

"Wipe that jealous frown off your face, Rhoda. It's tough going through life as a sex object."

"My, my, you flatter yourself."

"Let's see you in a bikini, Swallow."

"Never. Women who wear such clothes beg to be treated as sex objects."

"Is that the real reason you've never bought one? Give me a break. That's your fourth piece of bread."

"So what happened to your husbands, Breeze?"

"The first one, Jack, I had to marry. We had twins by mistake. In those days fathers were pretty good with a shotgun."

"My God! You're a mother?!"

"Technically, yes. I gave them away for adoption. I was too young to ruin my life with diapers and pediatricians. Besides, Jack was a moron. He looked like Clark Gable but he was content with a beer at six, hamburgers at seven, sex at eight . . . hey, what's going on in the kitchen? Sounds like a shelf fell down."

"That means the chef's home. Let's ask for a fresh pot of coffee. Yoo-hoo, chef! Hello? More coffee, please!"

"Sounds like he's bolting that little door in your face. Leave him alone, Rhoda. Men are such pains in the ass when they try to have temper tantrums. The only thing to do is laugh at them. That's what I did all the time with my second husband."

"Pardon my asking, but why did you get married again? It's just not necessary any more."

"Try that line again next time you run across a millionaire, Rhoda."

"My God, how cynical!"

"Oh come on! Don't tell me you married the godlike Leonard for love."

"I certainly did. There was never anyone else in my life."

"You have my sincere sympathy."

"So what happened to Number Two?"

"Stanley. The second time around I was more practical and married money. When Stanley ran out of it, all his charm disappeared. We did have fun while it lasted, though. The man was a perfect host."

"Sounds like prostitution, dear."

"Stuff it, Harriet, this was a business deal. Of all people you should appreciate that. Stanley got a great-looking dame and I got two years in a golden time warp. He took me out for dinner and disco six nights a week. We're not talking the local taco joint either, you understand. I still have the furs and dancing gear. In fact I brought a lot of those clothes over with me, just in case. The jewelry was repossessed. Stanley loved nothing more than showing me off. Unfortunately, he never told me he worked at the racetrack. One day at breakfast he announced that we owed forty thousand bucks to the credit card companies and from now on I was supposed to start cooking, cleaning, scrubbing floors . . . it was emotional rape. From the beginning the man had deceived me. I immediately got the marriage annulled. You can do that by mail, you know, with a credit card. Stanley had to go to jail for fraud."

"Sounds rather romantic, actually . . . a man bankrupting himself over you."

"Hardly, Rhoda. I got pretty sick and tired of staring at shrimp cocktails night after night. Anyhow, there was a bright side to this marriage. I became quite a connoisseur of fine food and restaurants."

"It takes more than two years of shrimp cocktails to develop a discriminating palate, dear."

"For a year Stanley wrote me letters from prison. He didn't comprehend that I had divorced him. He thought I had gotten a job somewhere and was paying off all his gambling debts."

"Just like a man, always expecting the good little woman to bail him out."

"Well, forget it. That kind of garbage belongs on 'Wagon Train.' Anyhow, I didn't get married again for another six years."

"However did you feed yourself in the meantime, dear?"

"I worked my butt off at a caterer's. Played the field. Had a fabulous time . . . did you notice, though, that all the men turned to shit around 1983?"

"Like what?"

"That was when I first began to notice how cheap they were all getting. They'd invite me to a great restaurant then expect me to foot half the bill. Or they'd spring for a weekend in Vail if I did both air fares. I started really getting aggravated when they couldn't even shell out for two movie tickets any more. Then everyone got herpes and they all began acting like a cross between a D.A. and Jesus Christ, asking you in ten thousand crude ways if you were contaminated. The only ones who didn't ask had herpes themselves, of course. Then all of them got their hair cut and became lawyers. They put all their spare cash into the stock market and condos. Then I noticed that they were all getting engaged, not to women in their prime, but to twenty-three-year-old bulldogs straight out of business school. At that point I panicked and married Marvin."

"I thought you said you loved your freedom, dear."

"I did, until I had to buy my own thirtieth birthday cake. Then I got hit with a real case of nostalgia for the good old days with Jack. Meat loaf started looking better and better."

"Did Marvin like meat loaf?"

"One better, Marvin cooked his own meat loaf, with truffles. He lived in a mansion in Westport and had a great job in advertising. He was decent enough in bed. I should have known there was a catch after he took me to Eleuthera for a week, all expenses paid."

"What was that?"

"His two kids. Brats looked exactly like his first wife. All day long I was schlepping them to dermatologists, karate school, bulimia therapists . . . on top of that, Marvin expected me to continue working since he was paying his first wife so much alimony. Once we were married, how many times do you think the bastard made meat loaf with truffles? Did the shopping? Picked up his shirts from the dry cleaners? Hah! His greatest contribution was to tell me when we were running low on scotch! I left after three months."

"Marry in haste, repent in leisure."

"There's nothing to repent, Swallow, and there's no leisure to repent it in. The hell with husbands. I suppose I'm destined to remain a free spirit, like my Indian ancestors."

"Look what happened to them, Tonto."

"Well! I suggest we all get going. Class starts in half an hour."

"Hold the fort, I've got to get some lipstick on."

"I thought you said you'd had it with husbands! What about this free-spirit business?"

"Rhoda, there's a big difference between a free spirit and a frump. And you never know what kind of Geronimo might turn up in these mountains."

4

The dollar hit a record high last week, leadening suitcases, subverting tongues. Floyd looked at the passengers hedging the Olympic baggage wheel and knew this would be a viperous afternoon: Nobody lied like the people who thought of Athens as one huge, open-air Bloomingdale's. They stepped off the plane wearing eight-hundred-dollar khakis and inlaid sunglasses, then expected him to believe they had purchased only two pairs of cheap sandals during a month on the Aegean. Did they have any idea he could smell penny-ante shoplifters before they even handed over their customs declarations? Of course not. They thought they were pretty clever stashing pearls in cold cream and medallions in elevator shoes like the countless stupid amateurs before them. Such people infuriated Floyd. Had they any panache, any respect at all for the opposition, they would shove diamonds up their nose and cuff links behind their sphincters, then swagger past him, pretending to sneeze. Rogues like that were as much fun to land as a champion barracuda. But this crowd had no appreciation of the fine art of piracy. They were just cheapskates skidding a bit beyond their credit limits; their ultimate goal was to beat the New York City sales tax. Exposure to enough of them year after year, like swamp gas, could drive a man mad.

The first six suitcases sliding onto the baggage carousel were tattooed relentlessly with the initials of their designer, who must have possessed the most miniscule penis in French history. There was no other excuse for such tasteless narcissism. Floyd frowned as a few more emerged from the bowels of the carousel: Even Richard Wagner only signed his scores once, for God's sake. He looked at Frisk waiting at the next station. "I don't think I'm ready for this," he said.

Frisk looked radiant. She and McPhee had probably gone to the Great Neck Sheraton for a ten-course lunch. They had returned through separate doors but the hair of both was still wet. For once Frisk had neglected to wear her Valentine's Day scarf. "Come on, Beckie, where's your sense of humor?"

That got smashed once and for all about three weeks ago. Saying nothing, Floyd looked again at the passengers heaving suitcases onto their trolleys. They reminded him of Wagner's Nibelungen horde stacking their ill-gotten riches ever higher, unaware that on the last page of the opera all creation would come tumbling down on them. Next time the Met mounted a new *Ring* cycle, they should use the JFK terminal as a backdrop. Everything they needed was already here: treasures, gnomes, thieves . . .

"Yoo hoo! Have a nice weekend?" Frisk asked. "Plenty of sun and surf?"

Sun? Daylight broiled his eyes. His neck was studded with buckshot. Surf? His brain typhooned with ten thousand leitmotifs. What weekend? Since last Friday he had been gone for years. How had Wagner thought up all those tunes? How did he keep that macaronic cast of characters straight? Floyd ached to go home and have another eighteen-hour go at the *Ring*. These tacky tourists were worse than the DTs.

Frisk hummed the "Lone Ranger" theme from the *William Tell* Overture. "Stand back, here they come."

An imperial woman avoided Frisk and swished her passport in front of Floyd. Four inches of brutal black eyeliner, earrings forged for a bull's nose, hips opulent as a yacht: Siegfried, phone home. Floyd looked over her visa and immediately felt very uneasy. Why hadn't she gone to Frisk's station? "Hello," he said pleasantly. "Are you traveling for business or pleasure?"

"Beezness."

Lie. That was no three-piece suit, honey. Floyd looked over the two valises on the conveyer belt. Both were infested with initials. "Would you open this bag, please."

She obeyed and before his eyes lay twenty pairs of panties, all shades of the rainbow and of deep midnight, brassieres ripe as summer fruit, made to be plucked, long black stockings destined for legs which were decidedly not in mourning . . . now that he had opened the suitcase, Floyd had to run his hands through it, so he very carefully lifted out a pink camisole. The Manhattan skyline, embroidered in black, rippled across the front. *Pyrana*, the label read. Gracefully as a cougar's tail his pulse dipped, and recovered itself. The camisole had never contained a body; it had no scent, no soul. Floyd dropped it back and picked up a set of lilac panties, size five. Piece by piece, slowly as a tortoise laying eggs, Floyd stacked the apparel on the counter, waiting for her to break. She merely watched him, tautly motionless. Finally he found the catch: false bottom. She was here on business, all right.

Cash traveled even better than polyester: The more one jammed in a suitcase, the less it wrinkled. There below the lining lay a meticulous mosaic, twenty by twelve by two inches, of hundred-dollar bills. It probably wasn't a donation to the Fresh Air Fund. Floyd looked ruefully at the woman; he hated to trash dreams. "That should cover your cab fare into Manhattan," he said. Behind the counter his knee pressed the alert button.

Without warning she pulled a tiny airline fork from her belt and lunged at his face. Beneath the Chanel No. 22 she smelled of fear: ta-ta, new life in the new world with new man. Floyd didn't want to see those black eyes two weeks hence, when she realized that no one would be rescuing her from the women's detention center. Damn, she was strong as Minotaur! Why kill him? She should kill her lover for packing the stash with eighty pieces of the wrong size underwear! That's what had blown her cover in the first place.

"Down, girl," said Frisk, chopping her in the kidney. With a shriek, the woman collapsed over the counter. By the time two security police arrived, Frisk had her handcuffed. "What'd you do, Beck, ask for her phone number?"

Floyd swabbed some blood off his neck. "Should have." He watched the police drag the woman away. She would make one hell of a rabid informer, all right. By the time she finished singing, her boyfriend would be lucky to find only three meat hooks in his back.

"You all right?" Frisk asked, turning. She saw the money. "Aha."

McPhee arrived with reinforcements. "Nice work, Beck. Get cleaned up. Hubble'll take over." He looked at the cash and at the black lace garter strewn lasciviously over the countertop. Then he remembered the three hundred chastened passengers standing in line behind them. Already quite a few were updating their customs declarations. "Button the blouse and get back to your station," he said to Frisk.

Floyd watched Hubble quickly repack the suitcase. The pink camisole with the black skyline somehow landed on top; that disturbed him much more than did the blood on his uniform. He broke away for the locker room. When he returned to the office with a clean shirt McPhee was sitting at his desk with a T-man counting the cash and feeding serial numbers to the computer. To their left was the pile of lingerie, again with the pink camisole on top, like a gypsy's queen of spades. This time Floyd walked over and studied it. Seventeen years since he had last touched her, she still exerted maximal magnetic force; his knees shook to even be near something she had made. He saw she had drawn the Manhattan skyline very precisely to scale, vantage the Jersey shore, perhaps from Hoboken, on the pier below his house. From his backyard he could have been looking at her without knowing it: Viola wore hats. Floyd slowly ran one finger down the pale pink silk. Only she could find such material. She knew it put a man in delicious agony: He wanted to peel it off and he wanted it to stay on. He wanted to touch it yet he knew the sooner he did, the sooner his proud lust would revert to putty. Had she perhaps held this camisole in her hands? The thought made his stomach fly. She was starkly, ferociously alive, buried with time but not with actual dirt. Only dirt worked.

"Eh! Quit handlin' state's evidence!" McPhee called. Beck looked as if he were about to eat it.

Floyd let the silk drift back to its sisters and went to the window overlooking the parking lot, half listening to McPhee drone hundred upon hundred as he peeled bills into a little pile. He felt sorry for the woman in jail. Had she only told him "Pleasure" instead of "Business," she would have been home free.

McPhee's phone rang. "Yo. What? That's impossible!" He cursed vitriolically. "Tell her to stick around and get the goddamn thing back," he snapped, slamming down the phone. "Fucking cretins."

Floyd looked over from the window. "What happened."

McPhee waved his hand through the air. "Botched a routine dropoff. You don't want to know about it." Which meant Floyd wasn't involved with the case so he didn't pursue the matter.

Frisk burst into the office just as McPhee was down to the last stack of cash. "So! Numbers!" She pulled out her little pad. "Quick! The next plane's landing in two minutes."

"Three-hundred-fifty thousand cash," said McPhee. "Get back to your station." He tried to sound annoyed.

"Way to go, Floyd! No one's going to come close to that this month unless they intercept a submarine." Frisk spied the pink camisole on McPhee's desk. "You're not going to chuck this into the incinerator, are you, boss?" She draped it over her blue blouse so that the Empire State Building and the World Trade Center each rippled languidly over a breast. As she took a breath the entire island undulated like a faroff mirage. Floyd and McPhee stood dumbstruck as a pair of milk cows. "Say, what size is this?"

"Not yours," McPhee suddenly snapped, tearing it away.

"Goodbye," said Floyd. He headed for the door.

"Hey, what's the matter with you two? Never seen underwear before?"

Again the phone rang. McPhee pounced on it. "Yo. No. Who? Ah, shit! I told him never, never to chase anyone on the Henry Hudson Parkway! Now he's stuck where?" McPhee's neck turned red. "Oh, great, that's just great! What am I supposed to do with an axle on Seventy-second Street?" He listened a moment, uttered a few maledictions, and hung up. "What did I do to deserve this? Beck, this is an emergency. Diorello just totalled the Chevy. Go inspect a few crates at Swissair for me, would you? Then get right over to the docks. Lindley and the dog are checking out a tanker with a phony manifest. Try not to get your ass shot off, half the department's already on vacation. Your Falcon's operational, isn't it?"

"What's so important at Swissair?"

"No idea. The expeditor's been hassling me all morning to run an express shipment through. Says he's got a raving Cuban in pajamas who refuses to leave his office without them."

"What's in the boxes? Cigars?"

"Just do it and find Lindley before he gets himself sliced into fish bait." McPhee looked at the scratches across Floyd's throat. "You do feel all right, don't you? Your neck looks like a strawberry sundae."

"It was just a fork."

Amazing what a little bloodshed did for a man's ego. "That's the spirit."

Floyd walked giddily to the parking lot and tried to unlock the Falcon door. His hands shook, but he hadn't slept in forty hours and she hadn't crept up on him like that in years. God, he hated ghosts! In a former life she must have been his twin, or a second head; in this life, the instant he saw her face, his blood recognized her and began clawing at his veins, wanting her back. So far his blood had gone almost eighteen years wanting. It was still functionally warm and red, but he knew it was only clocking in for work, like a clerk fifty desks back at an oppidan City Hall. Two or three times since she left his blood had perked up, drawn to an incomplete silhouette with Viola's eyes or smile, only to slow to its former pulse once the imposture had been discovered. For years now his blood had simply drifted, somnolent as the Mississippi, lulling Floyd into believing that it had finally dissolved this youthful shipwreck; then a woman from the office draped a pink camisole over her breasts and there was Viola, and there charged his blood, howling, jerking Floyd alive. He just wasn't used to it.

He lifted his forehead off the steering wheel. The blue sky singed his eyes and the Falcon suddenly reeked of dogs and hot plastic: reality: nauseating. He felt ill. Perhaps he should just die in this car, now. They'd find him in a day or two and tow the wreck away to a junkyard, no sanguineous bathtubs, no fouled sheets, kaput with a minimum of fuss in true Beck fashion . . . but then she would be free, wouldn't she. The idea galled him into remaining a mortal, no matter how unpleasant, a while longer. He started the car and a Chopin polonaise blurted from the radio. Floyd drove slowly over to Swissair, timing his arrival with the final cadence, and got out.

An eerie green light suffused the cargo terminal, creating the illusion of a dormant Atlantis. Floyd looked up at the green plastic roof and saw two giant fans twirling slowly as Sargasso seaweed; whatever currents they induced had dissipated long before reaching the floor many fathoms below. In the distance, industrious as a crab, a fellow was forklifting box after box of Japanese televisions into a tremendous pile, pausing to listen to the Mets game broadcasting throughout the cavern. To Floyd's left stood a flock of GE turbines. *This side up,* he read, upside down. The loading zone still smelled of fish although the uptown restaurants had retrieved their shipments hours ago. Floyd walked down a long aisle vallated by boxes from the Soo See Toy Company: Anatomically accurate horses and cows were supposed to be the hot Christmas item this year. He felt dizzy and paused to wipe his neck; it was still bleeding a little. When he resumed walking, his body seemed to drift above the floor like a lamprey.

In the office the lights blazed garish white. A secretary sat on her boss's desk, lazily swinging her leg as she watched him sign a few air waybills. The man didn't know it yet, but he was doomed: Four kids and one working wife could never prevail against an eight hour per day exposure to that callipygous white skirt. To Floyd the whole cycle was so stupidly predictable. Boss desperately needed good secretary; given the option, he always hired the most attractive candidate; several office crises, several costume changes later, boss invited worthy secretary to dinner; bang; indeterminate sordid trysts later, secretary left; boss once again desperately needed good secretary. No wonder the terminal was crammed with imports.

"Customs," he called. The woman jumped off the desk. She managed high heels about as well as a double amputee rowed a boat. "You needed something checked out?"

"Do I." The man compacted his cigarette into half a tuna on rye. "Right out here." Floyd followed him down a long lane of Swedish exercise bicycles. As the man crossed between the stacks from sunlight into shadow, his bald spot turned green to pink to green again. At last he stopped in front of a large carton. "Here's the paperwork. Looks like a load of nightgowns or something."

Something happened at the Mets game and the crowd in Flushing cheered like banshees. Floyd took the waybill. *From Dinglemann AG to Pyrana, Inc.*, he read, one gross of embroidered wool bathrobes, value twelve hundred Swiss francs apiece. "That's the second time today he's been hit with a pitch," the announcer croaked. "Watch out! Both dugouts are on the field!"

"Open the box," said Floyd.

"I hope there's no problem. That Cuban maniac will roast my ass."

Floyd watched the razor slice through the tape. "Where is he?"

"He's coming back at four. Said he had to buy a doghouse. The guy is nuts. Wears pajamas and these pointy alligator boots. Comes into the office at ten this morning with a little black puppy under his shirt and wants to have the nightgowns pronto for some television show. Blew his stack when my secretary asked if they were for 'The Colbys.' "

The forklift buzzed in the distance, overriding radio commentary, as Floyd turned a cardboard flap. The top robe lay folded in a plastic bag: innocent white this time. That was a joke.

"What are you looking for?" the man said, leaning over Floyd's elbow. "Dope? Microfilm?"

"Just checking." Floyd lifted the robe out. At the base of the V-neck she had begun a tiny green, red, and white helix. As the embroidery twined up the neckline the colors grew and separated; by the time it spilled over the shoulder, he could see that the green was mistletoe and the red and white were candy canes. Beautiful, very clever, but that was hardly enough: Viola was famous for what she did with her robes in the back, as if she knew that a woman was her most daunting as she turned away from a man. God knows that's what she had done to him for two insane years; maybe that's where she had picked up the idea. Dare he look? Again his hands started to tremble. The blood inside of them reeled in erratic eddies.

"Listen to that," the man said. "They're maulin' the pitcher." His face glowed like a Martian's in the pale green light.

Floyd shook the robe out of the plastic and turned it over. She did not disappoint him: Creeping over the shoulder, the two garlands met at the center of the back in a voluptuously embroidered white bow.

"What's up? You see something?"

Electrocuted, he couldn't drop it. This had to be some thoughtless joke she was still playing on him, wasn't it? Floyd folded the robe and put it back into the box, front side up. He never wanted to see the back again. "Nope." He gouged his signature on the customs declaration. "Get it out of here."

Floyd walked quickly out of the green cargo terminal into the glaring white parking lot. His head was on fire, but of course, hope never ran cold. Why a white bow? She knew what that was supposed to mean. Was she sending him a signal? Why presume he'd even see the back of one of her damn robes? She couldn't have the nerve to think he was still shadowing her career like some dull, adoring Rover. A white bow . . . Floyd rammed his key into the Falcon door. Viola was always the great surpriser. Maybe she drew that bow on the off chance that, halfway through a seduction, it would poke him in the eye, reminding him of a woman he had once left. That was too ridiculous, wasn't it. She had no reason to do that. Floyd and his cryptic signals were past history, dead as yesterday's dew. The bow meant nothing.

He slid into the front seat and gunned the ignition: down, blood. *Ride of the Valkyries* thundered from the dashboard and Floyd hooted. This day had to be a hallucination. It contained more bizarre coincidences than ten opera plots. Why? What next? He could sense destiny the way a horse sensed an earthquake: Orphans were thoroughbred psychics. Floyd suddenly whirled around, checking the back seat for a homicidal Cuban, for white ribbons, for Viola: nothing but a gnawed dog leash. Pain bolted like lightening through his eyes each time the cymbals crashed and still Floyd could not turn down the radio.

The Falcon smoked out of the parking space. Someday he'd have to accept the fact that she was gone. He had already rotted away half his life ringing the doorbell of an abandoned manor. And yet . . . wouldn't a signal be just like Viola, tucking clues into a labyrinth of silence and time and chance? What had she felt when she drew that white bow? Nostalgia? Hope? Hah, nothing? He didn't know. With her, maybe he would never know.

Ride of the Valkyries blared to a close. "Toscanini!" Floyd shouted, roaring onto the access ramp.

"Klemperer," corrected the radio.

Viola looked down the long conference table to a portrait of a salmon. In midafternoon, when the sun through the skylight struck it just so, the fish seemed alive as the day Eugene had painted it. Three walls of the conference room were decorated with a dozen trophies whose pulchritude had removed, temporarily, her husband's appetite. The fourth wall contained a huge, scarred rectangle of cork which Nestor had installed after Viola had flung an ashtray through Eugene's finest portrait of a mackerel during a particularly testy sales meeting several years ago. In less stressful times, the cork wall contained revenue charts and sketches of lingerie, as it did this afternoon.

Rising from her black leather chair, Viola walked to the smiling salmon and straightened the oak frame surrounding it. Where the hell was Nestor, damn him? He knew they had an appointment with the accountant at three. He should have been back from the airport at eleven. Actually, he should not have gone to the airport at all, but it was a halcyon June day and he wanted to take a drive in his new Buick. Muttering about important errands he had to run in the vicinity of the airport, Nestor had insisted upon picking up the shipment himself instead of sending Richie in the truck. The robes were delayed in customs and now she was marooned with Morton the accountant, who had been spewing numbers like a tickertape machine, sure that Viola had been following him with fascination and complete understanding this last hour.

"No, I don't get it at all," Viola said around four o'clock. The salmon had passed back into the shadows. "You lost me about ten deductions ago." Sighing, she leaned back in her chair. "Stupendous idea, this tax reform."

The accountant sort of chuckled. He hated his clients to think he was capitalizing on their misery, and at the same time he loved showing off his new Mercedes 560SEL. "Let's go over it again, just the main points, Viola. You should know what's going to be on the books next year."

"Great."

"First of all, Uncle Sam has done away with all the investment tax credits. You should seriously rethink buying those new sewing machines. I'd either hang on to the old ones another five years or lease new ones."

"The employees hate the old machines. Why can't I just buy new ones, Morton? I have the cash."

"You can't spend good money on plants and machinery any more. It's got to be invested in paper. Bank loans. Pension plans."

And accountants, of course. Viola frowned. "Leasing costs me twenty percent more than buying outright."

"And corporate income tax costs you twenty percent more than leasing, if you're lucky." The accountant shuffled some notes. "Oh, another thing you should know: Forget about building that new warehouse across the street. Instead we're going to rent the property, install steel shelves over a concrete slab, and put a tarpaulin bubble over the top. Then the whole thing can be regarded as steel shelving. That way we can deduct the rent. The shelves and the tarpaulin we'll expense out. We capitalize just the concrete slab." He thought a moment. "Could you get away with just a dirt floor?"

"What? You want me to store a million bucks of white panties over a dirt floor? Are you serious?"

The accountant frowned. "One million? Viola, that had better disappear by January first. State inventory tax has gone up five percent."

"Thanks for letting me know that when I was placing orders."

"Can't you sell everything for Christmas?"

"How am I going to move two thousand Statue of Liberty pajamas at Christmas?" Viola walked to the window and stared at the vacant lot across the street. Old Man Baldwin was walking his dog on it. "We took that pill out to dinner fifty times trying to sweet-talk him into selling his property. Now he finally agrees and you tell me to forget it."

"Yes, ma'am. I'm also telling you to watch your entertainment budget from now on. Business lunches and dinners will be only eighty percent deductible."

"I don't get it! I get stiffed for one hundred percent of the lunches and dinners! How come I can only deduct eighty percent?"

The accountant shrugged. "No one likes that one. It was a stupid little clause they slipped in just to pacify the middle class." He looked over his list. "Aha. Here's another one. You can keep the cars but you're going to have to account for every mile and every drop of motor oil you put into them."

"You mean log sheet?"

"Microscopic log sheet. Unless, of course, you prefer to trade in your Porsche for a delivery truck. That is obviously a business vehicle."

"Is that so? What do you deliver in your Mercedes?"

"Legal documents. Okay, let's move on. Currency transactions. We're going to have to report all overseas transfers over ten thousand dollars to the Treasury Department."

"For Christ's sake, are there enough trees on the planet to cover all this paperwork? How many extra bookkeepers am I going to have to hire to keep myself out of jail?"

"My firm can of course supply you with several part-time paraprofessionals."

"Why don't I just hire one full-time professional here?"

"Because payroll and unemployment taxes are going up again. So is the state income tax. They're also thinking of removing all the minority-worker credits."

Viola fell onto the sofa. Nestor had just hired another ten Asians. "Why do I even bother going to work, Morton? Why don't I just become a lifeguard, collect one W–2 form at the end of the year, and call it quits?" She threw a shoe at the cork wall. "We've busted our butts for twelve years! What did we do to deserve this?"

A pained look flitted across the accountant's face. "Your company makes too much money, Viola."

"I thought that was the point!" Viola threw her other shoe at the wall. "I'm going to sell this business and retire."

"I don't recommend that at this time unless you're prepared to set up a few nonprofit foundations and subchapter-S corporations."

"Forget it, I'm setting up a megilla trust fund."

"Hold off on that until I can check out the changes in the inheritance taxes, will you?"

The door burst open like a milkweed pod, emitting Nestor. In one arm he held a large cardboard box and in the other arm, Smudge the pup. "Hi Morton, sorry I'm late. I wasted this whole damn day at the airport. Henriette! Get in here with a milk bottle!" Nestor threw the box on the conference table and released Smudge on the floor. "Morton, be glad you never have to get involved with freight handlers or customs agents. They're much worse sons of bitches than the IRS. Bastards didn't clear the shipment until three this afternoon. Rush hour. Got a pencil? Thanks." He noticed Viola lying on the couch. "Hey, what's the matter with you? Too much chili for lunch?"

Viola sat up. "Nestor dear, how nice of you to drop by. Morton and I were just talking about lunches."

"Lunches? Did you eat in the cafeteria, Mort?" As he talked, Nestor tried to slice open the box with the accountant's mechanical pencil. "So how do you like my new cook? The Indian?"

"She's pretty terrible."

"I didn't ask you, honey." The box split open. "Ta-taaaaaa! The Christmas robes! Just in from Switzerland." He snapped one out full-length. "Joy to the world! Away in a manger!" Nestor remembered Morton, who was inspecting the tip of his gold pencil. "Happy Chanukah!"

From a distance, the colors, the proportions looked perfect. Viola smiled to herself: She was getting pretty good at this. "How'd he do on the embroidery?"

Nestor squinted at the collar. "Great. Terrific." He looked at Morton. "Every once in a while, for special projects, we splurge on Dingleball. The man's a Picasso. He just never heard of the word *deadline*."

"Let me see the back."

Nestor twirled the robe around. The smile on Viola's mouth momentarily let go at the seam, then reset itself. "Nice."

"How does it look in action?" Nestor asked, slipping the robe over his pajamas. He paraded around the conference table, swirling the wool right and left like an antebellum coquette. "Oh, thank you darling!" he said in a rapturous soprano voice. "I've been wanting a robe like this for years! Come here, you beast!" He switched to his normal voice. "What do you think, Morton? How would this look on your girlfriend? How do you like that great bow in the back?"

"Very attractive," said the accountant. "Is it warm?"

"Of course it's warm! These things are designed to be worn with nothing underneath!" Nestor cuddled his cheek into a sleeve. "Ah, exquisite. If I were a woman, I'd live in this robe. There's nothing like Swiss wool."

The accountant frowned. "That robe came from Switzerland?"

"Heinz Dinglemann and Sons," Viola said. "They have a plant outside of Geneva. Why?"

"Have you two been reading the newspapers lately?" Morton said. "Did you ever subscribe to the *Wall Street Journal* like I told you?"

Nestor turned the pockets inside out, inspecting the seamwork. "I only read the comics and the horoscope. Viola reads Ann Landers. The *Wall Street Journal* doesn't carry any of that important stuff."

"How do you two expect to keep current on business trends?"

"Who cares?" Nestor threw his hands in the air. "That's your job, Morton!" Smudge the pup yipped from beneath a swivel chair. "Henriette!" Nestor shouted out the door. "Where's that milk?" He picked the dog up. "I don't know why these scratches on his stomach don't heal faster. It's been almost two weeks now."

Ignoring her partner, Viola retrieved a shoe from the floor. "Is there something we should know about current business trends, Morton?"

"How about a textile war? Import quotas? Punitive tariffs of two hundred percent on all European goods? I hope you have your entire shipment of Swiss robes in the States. Uncle Sam's about to lower the boom."

"When did this happen?" Nestor said. "When we were in San Francisco?"

"How many robes did you pick up today, Nestor? Twenty-five hundred?"

"One gross."

"What?! Where are the rest of them?" Viola cried.

"That was it."

"No!" Viola flung her other shoe at the cork wall. Morton ducked just in time. "I don't believe this! He promised to send half the order! Now they're back on strike again!"

"Why do you do business with these people?" the accountant asked. "Can't you find a reliable source in Hong Kong? In Brooklyn? I've been telling you for five years to tighten this ship according to sound business principles."

"Yes, yes, Morton, thank you very much," Nestor said. He removed the white wool robe and straightened his pajamas. "We'll remember that next time *Forbes* magazine interviews us."

Henriette came into the office with a bottle of milk. "Smudgie! Where are you, pup? Woooo!" She crawled under the conference table towards the source of whining.

"How do you like our newest employee, Morton?" Nestor said. "Mr. Smudge, a vicious security guard."

"You put that dog on the payroll? I told you to freeze payroll!"

"He's only kidding, Morton," Viola said. "We're capitalizing Smudge instead. He's part of the alarm system."

The accountant hesitated; he never knew when these two maniacs were kidding him. It was that way with the whole operation. Twelve years running, he had yet to figure out how Pyrana, Inc. managed to keep making so much money. The people who ran it cared less about balance sheets than did an aborigine. One of them lived upstairs, had not worn a suit in years, and treated his employees like runaway slaves; the other one had a more volatile temper than a maimed cougar. Each time he left their office, the accountant changed his mind about Nestor's sexual orientation and his relationship to Viola. One week Nestor ranted like a neurotic queen, next week he never let Viola off his lap for an entire two-hour budget meeting. And Viola . . . now there was one stick of dynamite he would never allow anywhere near his lap. She'd blow his balls off. The two of those lunatics in one bed? Morton didn't want to be within fifty miles unless he had a comprehensive earthquake insurance policy. "Does the dog at least have rabies shots?" he asked in exasperation. "What if he bites an employee? Is that covered by your worker's comp policy? I never heard of a dog roaming around a legitimate business office. Never."

Nestor had put the white bathrobe on again and was giving the shoulders a stress test. "He's our mascot," he said. "Keeps company morale high. I'm writing off all the dog food under Advertising and Promotion. Hey Viola, Dingdong did a terrific job on the armpits. Ten rapists couldn't rip them out."

Something large thudded just outside the door. "It's Richie. I just finished the doghouse."

"Not now, Richie!" roared Nestor. "We're in the middle of a crucial strategy session!" He looked under the table. "Henriette, get the hell out of there and bring us a pot of coffee."

Morton cringed; he knew a dozen secretaries who had sued their employers for making such obscene demands. He leaned way over in his seat. "Thank you very much, Henriette," he tried to call under the table. Then he saw Viola crawling around the floor near his knees. "What are you doing down there? For heaven's sake!"

"Looking for my other shoe. You know, Morton, you've got a big hole in your pants right below the fly." Viola staggered out and reeled onto the couch. Her hair was gradually escaping from a nacre clasp. "Did you snag it on an adding machine or something?"

With the accountant's mechanical pencil, Nestor had meanwhile jagged open another box he had just brought into the office. He tossed the robe to the couch. "Try this on, V. I want to see how it looks with a pair of boobs inside."

Viola inspected the candy canes and the mistletoe sinuating over the white woolen neck and suddenly wished she were eighteen again. "This is a great design," she said, getting up. "One of my best." She slipped the robe on.

"Super," Nestor said. "Look at those candy canes now."

Viola swished to the side and her black hair fell completely out of the clasp. "Were you serious about that textile war, Morton?"

The accountant tetchily threw his mechanical pencil into his attaché case and slammed the lid. "In one month, you two are going to be selling those robes for a thousand bucks apiece just to break even."

"A thousand bucks? That kind of money I'd only spend on my mother," said Nestor. "Viola, call Dingdong right now."

"It's ten o'clock at night."

"So what? The guy's probably just getting back from yodeling club."

Sighing, Viola walked to the phone and punched in a dozen numbers. It was that type of thing which confused the accountant most: How could she remember twelve digits off the top of her head and still bobble which day of the week it was? "Yoo hoo, hello Herr Dinglemann. It's Viola Flury calling from America. Yes, thank you! We received them today. They're beautiful." That voice, too, he would never understand. The angrier she was, the more melodious it became. When she suddenly tossed in a few obscenities after a deceptively pleasant conversation, the effect was devastating. Morton would never forget the first time Viola told him she was going to chew his ass out. "Yes. Mmmm. I know you had a hard time. Yes, strikes are terrible things. We sympathize completely. How sad. But there's a serious problem. We only received one gross of robes. You had promised to send twenty-five hundred, didn't you?" She laughed lightly and Morton shuddered:

Dingdong was about to get nuked. "Really?" Viola looked over at Nestor, who was trying to gouge open the third box with the edge of an ashtray. "Is that so? Ha ha! Let's hope not! Would you mind reading me the air waybill number? Oh. Of course. We'll call you tomorrow then, at the office. You'll have it ready. Goodnight."

Henriette bustled into the conference room with three mugs of coffee and several pastries. "What the hell is this?" Nestor cried suddenly, pulling a brown apron from the box.

"She said it was zucchini and spinach muffins," Henriette said. "That's why they're green. Not to worry."

"Thank you so much, Henriette," fussed Morton. "Really, you shouldn't."

Viola rested her chin upon two fingers, watching Nestor fish several more brown aprons from the carton. The accountant had not seen her look so charming, so flirtish, in months. Her black hair looked ravishing over the white gown. "Dingle said he packed the first two boxes himself and had his mother pack the rest because everyone else was on strike. She may have split the shipment by mistake." Viola took a demure bite out of a muffin. "Then he told me his mother was half blind." Suddenly Viola whipped the ashtray at Nestor. It narrowly missed his ear and ricocheted sharply off the wall. "You stupid ass! I told you eight months ago this would be a disaster! Did you listen to me? Of course not!"

Nestor ran around to Viola's side of the conference table, knocking down a chair with the hem of his white wool bathrobe. "Shh, shh, we'll get them on time," he said, straightening her hair, fluffing her robe. The two of them looked like acolytes prepping for a Mass. "The rest of the shipment will come tomorrow."

"The hell it will! Dingdong thinks his mother sent it to Greece!" Viola roughly pushed Nestor's hand away. "I could strangle you."

Nestor looked helplessly at the accountant. "Don't pay any attention to her, Morton, she's hysterical. We're expecting a baby in a few months."

"You? You two?" Morton paled. "What happened to Eugene?"

"Nothing happened to Eugene!" Viola screeched. "He's fishing in Alberta." She picked up a brown apron. "I don't believe it. This is the story of my life. Everything turns to shit." She flung it back in the box.

"Sit down, Viola," Nestor said. "Everything will be fine. I'll get those robes for you if I have to fly to Greece myself. Ding just made a mistake with one box. You'll see, we'll get the rest of the aprons tomorrow."

"You mean the rest of the robes tomorrow," the accountant said, "ha ha." When no one else laughed with him, he dug into a muffin. "Effuiii."

"What's the matter now, Morton," Nestor snapped. "Did you think of ten more withholding allowances?" He bit a muffin. "This tastes goddamn awful."

"Thank that new cook of yours," Viola said. "I wish you'd fire her."

The accountant stirred a third packet of sugar substitute into his coffee. "Remember what I told you two about dismissal procedures. First you've got to make a list of complaints. Have her sign it. Get a few witnesses. Has she been pilfering spoons or something?" he asked hopefully.

"No, she's just can't cook."

"Did she falsify her employment application? Use bogus references?"

"Why can't we just tell her she can't cook?" Viola said. "For two months she's been poisoning us all."

"Could you back that up in court?" Morton looked at the muffins. "They're pretty grim, Nestor. Why did you hire her?"

"You didn't see the other applicants. None of them could even read a recipe. Plus she's an Indian."

"Indian? With that raunchy blond hair? Give me a break."

"Does she have a work visa?" Morton asked. "That could solve everything."

"Cheyenne Indian, Morton. Said she had been trampled upon all her life," Nestor said, remembering her emotional job interview. He swallowed some more coffee. "I'm getting a little sick and tired of this minority bullshit. I don't go around whining that I'm a Cuban, do I?"

"Only when you need a bank loan," Morton said.

"Can't we send her a registered letter saying if she burns the coffee one more time, she's hanging up her apron?"

"She'll probably take you to court for racial discrimination," Morton said. "This is a litigious society."

"Why can't all my employees be like Mai Ping?" Nestor said. "My new cutter. She's never late. She works all day. She never complains. She knows when Smudge needs his next bottle. She never asks for half a day off to help her mother-in-law move."

"Sounds too good to be true," Viola said.

The accountant poured more milk in his coffee and sniffed the cup before drinking. "I have an idea about this chef of yours. You could send her to cooking school. We can always use another business expense. Maybe squeeze a few brownie points with the review board out of it, too."

"What am I running here, a community college?" Viola cried. "Why don't I send myself to Acapulco for a few weeks while we're at it? Management Therapy for Pregnant Burnouts. How does that sound?"

"Ridiculous," said Nestor. "Drink some milk."

Morton abandoned his zucchini muffin. "One of my most important clients sent his cook to a special school and said it was worth every penny. Results were guaranteed. I'll get the details."

"What the hell, if I can't fire her, I may as well make the most of it," Nestor sighed. "I should learn never to hire a woman who cries at her job interview."

Mai Ping knocked once on the door and walked in. From her hand, like a fine catch of trout, hung several iridescent brassieres. "Mr. Buffez, I think we've got a problem."

"Is this important?" Nestor snapped. "We're in the middle of a crisis here. Oh, by the way, this is Morton the accountant."

"I've heard so many nice things about you," Morton smiled.

"Thank you." Mai Ping dropped a bra on the conference table. "What size do you think this is, Mr. Buffez?"

"34A."

"The label says 38C."

Nestor and Viola looked at each other like two parents who had just been told their son had tried to burn down the school. Nestor stood up. "I'll take care of this," he said. "Great seeing you again, Morton." White wool robe swaying gracefully at his ankles, he walked out of the conference room with Mai Ping. A few seconds later Viola and Morton heard him raise his voice. "Richie! Where the hell did that moron disappear now? Richie! Get this doghouse out of here! Damn that son of a bitch! He has less brains than a pair of panties!"

The accountant looked at Viola. "Does your partner have a sudden-death clause in his policy?" he asked.

First Floyd emptied half a bottle of gin into a beer stein: He wanted to avoid getting up every fifteen minutes for a refill. He blew the dust off a bottle of tonic and sprinkled a few drops into the glass. Limes? Unlikely, unless Portia had bought some for her Perrier. He found one hiding behind a withered cabbage in the bottom bin of the refrigerator, trying to look like a kiwi: another week and it would have succeeded. Off with its head. He piled three ice cubes atop the floating lime, shook briefly, and took a heavy swig. It tasted like a barium enema.

For hours he had been swimming mechanically as a paddle boat in the Jersey City pool. They had thrown him out at ten o'clock and still he had not even begun to tire; that white robe would keep him fibrillating between black dreams and electric hope well into sunrise. Before going into the backyard, he painted himself with mosquito repellant. It reacted with the chlorine already on his skin to form a paludal shield capable of repelling insects tonight and, should he expire beneath that serene yellow moon, at least until July Fourth.

Next Floyd pulled one of his father's favorite recordings from the music rack: the Franck Piano Quintet, apotheosis of the romantic age, music more purple than all his blood mixed with all the sky. Gin, stars, sumptuous air might beckon Viola's shadow, but this music would drop her smack on top of him, where he wanted her again. He pushed Play and passed into his shadowy yard, sinking into a lounge chair, closing his eyes as the scent of roses, or was it Viola, drifted over him, gorgeous and untouchable. Ice cubes clicked against Floyd's mouth as he lifted the glass and thought back half a lifetime to the first night he saw her. The terrain felt familiar and comfortable. Memory was a capricious mistress, one visit a doting mother, next visit a cackling Jezebel, but tonight memory loved him: Floyd had not visited in months.

The quintet sighed its first long, slow phrase into the night and melted back into silence, waiting for an answer. When one did not come, nor would one ever come, the phrase repeated itself, more gently, always with more anguish, finally fading into nothing. Franck, a church organist, had dedicated the quintet to a beautiful student named Augusta. His wife's name was Félicité.

The piano began to murmur and Floyd was back in Carnegie Hall, seat 25E, waiting for the lights to dim. Aunt Margaret sat in 25F, as she had for two decades on the second Tuesday of every month, passing him cough drops and explaining yet again why Beethoven was a genius. She had been dragging him to the chamber music series since his tenth birthday, hoping he would display an interest in playing the violin. For years Floyd sat in the darkened auditorium sucking cough drops, studying the faces of the musicians, wondering why they never smiled if playing the violin were as gratifying as Aunt Margaret described. When he got tired of that, he counted the gilt cherubs in the proscenium arch.

Over the years, Floyd began to socialize with the neighbors who, like Aunt Margaret and himself, held the same seats from season to season. The dowager to his left always wore black and a monstrous rope of pearls. Her perfume smelled like the hold of the *Lusitania* and when she clapped, the diamond rings on her frail hands chattered. The subscribers in front of Floyd, two men in fur coats, whispered in each other's ears between pieces and shouted Bravo whenever anyone played Tchaikowsky. The couple to their right usually talked French to Aunt Margaret during intermission.

The year he was seventeen, the opening concert of the chamber music season coincided with the third game of the World Series. Floyd was ticked with Aunt Margaret for dragging him to Carnegie Hall under such punitive circumstances and pouted in the bus all the way down from Eighty-third Street even though she took him out to dinner beforehand. He detested his new suit. He had an algebra test the next day. The only redeeming feature of tonight's concert would be seeing all the old cronies again after the summer.

Two minutes before curtain the whole gang was back except for the men in fur coats. They were never this late; their two empty seats stood out in the orchestra like missing front teeth, exposing Floyd. As the lights went down, finally there was motion in the aisle. With a pleasant smile of welcome, Floyd glanced up from his program notes into a thicket of black hair and felt his body slam to a halt. Pheromones cascaded into his bloodstream. He felt his skin bake, his vision telescope: adios, Beethoven. The music had shifted from a violin to the female of the species. Aghast, Floyd watched her shuffle along the row to her seat, bending a little at the hip. The Frenchman nearly bit her rear end.

She sat directly in front of Floyd and with one hand tossed her hair. It plumed over her shoulders, glinting blue then purple beneath the dim chandelier. Floyd wanted to straggle his nose through it, upturning ears and nape like an Alsatian pig sniffing out choice morels. He wanted to run her hair between his lips and see if it squeaked. He wanted to rub his belly over it and get himself all tangled up in that wavy black quicksand. He wanted to pull it back toward him so that her mouth would be pointed up at the chandelier, half open. Out tramped a string quartet and Floyd's hands flew furiously together: He wanted her to hear him clapping. The man sitting in the next seat whispered something; she nodded and the blue lights danced. Floyd's throat wobbled like the surface of an alligator pond.

The musicians opened their program with a long Schubert quartet, figuring that by the time they played all the repeats in the first movement, they'd be warmed up and the audience would have forgiven them all the horrendous intonation errors which had occurred the first time around. As they played, Floyd sat in torment, wanting the music to continue all night so that he could breathe on that black hair, and wanting the intermission to come, so that he could see her face. He sat still as a stone watching four bows curve through the air. Didn't she feel any heat from the row behind her? Once, between movements, she glanced at her chaperone. Diamond earrings: Most girls her age wore seed pearls. Her dress had not come from Woolworth's. Who was that old stiff anyhow? Her uncle? Her grandfather? Maybe it was her music teacher. Floyd pictured her with a huge wooden cello between her legs and wanted to deck the guy.

Finally the lights went up for intermission. Floyd could see that the Frenchman down the row didn't want to go for his customary stroll until the girl had passed with her rear in his face again. Therefore, Floyd tapped him on the shoulder and asked whether he thought Haydn composed better rondos than Schubert, and if so, why, and which rondos specifically. The Frenchman looked momentarily stunned: Floyd had said nothing but hello to him for eight years. As he was stuttering an answer, Viola and her escort shuffled to the aisle and vanished. Then Aunt Margaret put in her two cents, asking how was Toulouse this year, didn't everyone's hair look chic, et cetera ad merdium. The Frenchwoman wondered what had happened to the two men in fur coats. Then the lady with pearls, Madame Levitski, sashayed over to say hi, sandwiching Floyd between herself and Aunt Margaret. He knew that he was trapped there for the rest of intermission: No matter who played how, Madame was always reminded of a similar performance in the Old World forty years ago, and who sat where in the first tier, and who was sleeping with the queen. Aunt Margaret and the Frenchwoman could not absorb enough of these tales which Levitski was obviously fabricating as she went.

As the lights flicked for the last time up and down, just as Floyd saw Viola wedge back into the row, Levitski dropped her purse. By the time Floyd had retrieved both it and Madame's silver opera glasses, Carnegie Hall was pitch black and everyone had resumed a seat, including the string quartet. Now they were going to play a world premiere commissioned by the Ford Foundation. After two disharmonious phrases, the audience wished the Fords had just given the composer a new car and called it quits.

Again Floyd was left staring at the back of Viola's head. She had brushed her hair during intermission; the waves rippled twenty degrees starboard now. In twenty manic-depressive minutes the world premiere died violently and everyone more or less applauded except the man next to Viola. Aha! He was the composer! That explained the ingrown frown, the splenetic eyes . . . Floyd wondered what she could possibly find so attractive about him.

Throughout the second half, Floyd plotted his next fate-addled steps. He had to get her to look at him. Would they exit to the right or left aisle this time? Guessing wrong in this octogenarian crowd would be fatal. He'd have to head them off in the lobby, maybe shove the geezer into a revolving door and ask her directions to the World Trade Center. "Aunt Margaret," Floyd said the moment applause had dissipated, "I have to go to the men's room. Meet you outside in ten minutes." He tore off.

Posting himself behind a pillar, Floyd watched the audience seep, then flood through the lobby. His heart drummed his ribs, pumping an SOS to the legs: Run. Burning all reserves, his brain jammed that message. Floyd smelled perfume, mothballs, and car exhaust as drafts from the street swirled over the crowds, sucking them out to the sidewalk. Taxis squawked at limousines. Already his hands were beginning to shake; if she didn't come through those doors in another minute, his whole system would collapse. Too many forces were in opposition.

There she was at the far door, holding the old man's arm, her pale face bobbing amid the black coats and black hats like a loose pearl. Did he lock her inside, hidden from the sun, to keep her skin that bluish white? Was she human or vampire? Her stark melanochroid coloring lashed through the optic nerve directly to Floyd's gut: Perhaps he had skunk or zebra chromosomes. Black and white detonated his nervous system way back to the Cenozoic era, when things weren't quite sorted out yet. She turned her face in his direction and for the first time he saw her sparkling eyes. Overhead the dice clicked, God swore, and Floyd knew that he would spend the rest of his life thrashing stupidly against tides and men to be near them.

They passed in front of Floyd, who was doing a superb imitation of the pillar. "Not tonight," he heard her say, aloft between a scold and a laugh. No what tonight? No homework? No banana splits? Or was she referring to the string quartet? No encores tonight? What did that old fart say to make her eyes twinkle like that? "Are you going to practice arpeggios when you get home?" Floyd hated him. He had a thin, evil mouth which curdled at the ends like overcooked oysters. He combed his hair too much. He wore a silk scarf and cuff links, half investment banker, half Liberace. And he was not her uncle.

Floyd reached the sidewalk just as Viola and the man got into a cab heading east on Fifty-seventh Street. The last he saw of her was a hand, pale as her face, withdrawing into the back seat. Lost already; even then, as the cab merged into a galaxy of taillights, Floyd had a premonition that this would always be the pattern with her. He did not know for how long he would be slogging alone upstream, fate sealed, like a salmon; he did not know how they would finally connect, nor when he would learn her name. But he knew there would be an ending.

That was almost eighteen years ago. Floyd took a long swig of the gin in his glass and looked at the placid sky. The moon still shone; the roses still bloomed; the skyscrapers of Manhattan still clustered like concrete dreadlocks on Earth's poor scalp; he was still alone. Nothing had changed. The second movement of the quintet darkened from major back to minor, ending motionless as a lake at midnight. Was Franck still waiting when he composed that melancholy cadence? Or had his waiting ended and a knowledge much worse replaced it?

Saints waited; they thought the kingdom of heaven was at hand. Cowards and hypocrites waited for exactly the same reason. Which was he? Floyd knew only that he was no saint, and the gin was gone. He creaked off his chair and went inside.

On the end table near the liquor cabinet lay the book of sausage recipes Floyd had not yet reshelved from the other night. Caspar Beck's son froze in his tracks and slowly tiddled the pages to the recipe for Floydwurst. He read it over several times, trying to imagine all the ingredients in their final conglomeration: impossible. It had been too many years since he had tasted the genuine article. All the great butchers were dead and their shops had been converted to video-rental stores. Was Caspar's last creation destined for extinction, unrealized as his son's colorful dreams? Floyd imagined his father's soul roaming eternity, unable to rest until his son had closed the loop which a head-on collision had abruptly left open so many years ago.

Stealthy as a falcon, the last movement of the quintet whooshed into a half-step modulation. Floyd's hair stood on end; he had felt something huge, something beyond him, brush by. Gathering speed, the piece spilled toward its conclusion. How would it end, optimistic major or inconsolable minor? Had Franck finally touched the sun? Floyd did not remember so he waited, as always. The final phrase bolted like fire from a chimera's mouth: torrential open octaves, eternally, passionately empty, neither major nor minor, simply empty. No one would ever know how that circle ended but Franck, and God, and perhaps Augusta. Maybe that was the point.

Floyd put the recording away, scribbled a few words on a notepad, and turned out the lights. However, he did not go to bed. He got into the Falcon and zoomed toward the nearest all-night supermarket. Tonight he was going to satisfy filial duty and filial curiosity in one neat shot. For the second time in his weary life, he would break out of that silent, despairing bog which had stagnated him since he was a boy. He had last made the effort for Viola, who had pushed him right back into the marsh. His father would do no such thing.

The supermarket parking lot seemed unusually crowded for this time of night. Maybe it was an overflow from the bingo games across the street, Floyd thought as he nudged the Falcon into a remote slot. He took the only shopping cart available and wheeled it inside, frowning at the loud thunk it made each time the rear left wheel completed a revolution.

Instead of the saccharine Muzak he was accustomed to, "Get Off My Cloud" blared over the P.A. system. The supermarket had probably been held up again and now the managers were trying to discourage late-night shoppers from hanging around. They'd do that much better, of course, by killing the music completely.

Just as Floyd got past the bulletin board, a woman wearing spike heels and a pink jumpsuit passed in the opposite direction. "Hi," she gusted, stepping onto an exit mat. The automatic door blew open. "Try the frozen pizzas first." She winked and disappeared into the parking lot.

Floyd checked behind him; he thought she had maybe been talking to someone at the bulletin boards. Not so. Frozen pizzas? Why should he go there? Were they giving them away? Whatever it was, he'd be sure to avoid the area: Tonight he was on a cosmic mission. Floyd pulled his shopping list from a pocket and tried to read what he had recently scrawled under the influence of eight ounces of gin and two days without sleep. Quite a challenge: The words kept sliding up and down the page, multiplying into double, quadruple images like chromosomes undergoing mitosis. Mi-ma-num-margarine? That couldn't be right. Ah! Marjoram! The spice!

A man in a fake butcher's apron headed him off at the bottle return. "Here's your number," he said. "Good luck."

"What's this for?" Floyd asked. "The deli line?"

"Our raffle. Dinner for two at Disraeli's, the most romantic restaurant in Hoboken," the man said. Floyd noticed he was wearing a Store Manager tag. "Drawing's in fifteen minutes. Good luck!" The man hopped over to a woman pricing the gourmet croutons.

"Eleanor Rigby" hit the airwaves as Floyd wheeled his thudding cart past the cash registers. The entire checkout area was packed as Bedlam during a full moon. But something else was even more strange: Instead of drilling the cashiers with an evil eye or leafing sullenly through the magazines above the chewing gum, all of the shoppers seemed to be chatting and giggling as if the last thing they wanted was to get back home tonight. Floyd looked at his watch: eleven-fifteen. Where were the obese women with curlers in their hair? The engineering students from Stevens Tech in for their midnight fix of soda and pretzels? The morose bachelors and their single quarts of milk? Nowhere in sight. Frowning, Floyd steered his cart down an aisle. It would take damn forever to check out of here. His neck was beginning to feel as if a very poor intern had been practicing acupuncture upon it.

He stopped in front of the spices and started combing the shelf for marjoram. Floyd had no idea what it looked or smelled like. Finally he found a teeny cannister of the stuff. Was that enough? How much did he need for the recipe? Floyd pulled out his list again, finally got it to stand still, and saw that he had neglected to denote quantities. Thus he dropped five cans into the cart and started searching for mustard seed.

A woman braked her cart next to Floyd's. She wore a tennis outfit and one of those fluffy sports headbands that were supposed to look like designer squaw. "Hi. I'm looking for the basil," she said.

So what? She was tall enough to reach it herself. Then Floyd remembered his manners. "Here you go," he said. For that he lost his place and had to start top left on the spice rack again.

"Thanks a lot. My name's Susan."

And this was the supermarket, for Christ's sake! They'd be propositioning priests in the urinals next! Floyd hastily threw three bottles of mustard seed on top of the marjoram. "Is that a fact," he smiled, wheeling quickly away. His cart sounded like a huge metallic kangaroo.

Floyd made four passes of the meat case and still did not find one ingredient on his list. His progress was not assisted by the dozens of men and women conversing idly in his path, in no rush to restore the ice cream and microwave dinners in their carts to a gelid milieu. By now every muscle shrieked and his eyes were bloody lesions but Floyd was still aware enough to notice that something was going on here. All these people seemed to know each other. Was it the Hoboken Condo Association preparing for its July Fourth block party? That was two weeks off. Maybe they were shooting a commercial. Normal individuals just did not shop at this hour of the night in floral skirts and pastel cotton slacks. They wore housecoats with big chocolate stains and two buttons missing. Or bedroom slippers. Or ripped tee shirts and jeans, like him.

The sooner he got out of this charade of an anthill, the better: Nothing perturbed Floyd's concentration more than human propinquity. He joined a line at a special window marked The Midnight Butcher and reviewed the rest of his shopping list, planning his next moves. Floyd vaguely heard the first woman in line ask for ten pounds of veal birds. The second wanted a standing rib roast for twenty. A man needed forty quail. Was that ancient food grinder still in his basement? Where would he mix all this meat, in the kitchen sink or the bathtub? Where would he find juniper berries? Were they even in season?

The woman standing in front of him stopped humming along with "Light My Fire" and turned around. "Aren't the swordfish steaks gorgeous tonight?"

Floyd's train of thought snapped like a dry wishbone. Why bother a stranger with such a jejune observation? Didn't people have the dignity to just shut up and think for ten minutes any more? "Definitely," he replied. "And the smelts look ravishing."

That did not stop her. "You must be a terrific cook. I wish I had the time to do more. Between running my own law firm and renovating my brownstone, there just aren't enough minutes in the day."

"So quit the law firm and sell the brownstone," Floyd said.

"Ha ha! How tempting! Oh, it's my turn! Twelve pounds of your best lamb chops. Could you please remove every ounce of fat?" She smiled. "I'm having a little dinner party tomorrow night."

"How wonderful."

"I'm going to serve wild rice and mushroom timbales with the chops. And marinated pepper kebobs. I thought for dessert a lime mousse and Neuhaus truffles would do. What would you serve for an appetizer? A crudité dip? Or maybe a light fruit soup with fresh mint."

Floyd thought a moment. "Have you ever tried squid balls?"

"No! How do you make them?"

He cursed to himself. She was thicker than a phone pole. "It's a very complicated recipe. I'm not sure you'd want to hear the gory details."

"Of course I would! Please tell me."

The midnight butcher stuck his head out the window. "Twelve pounds of lamb chops," he said, handing the woman a large parcel. "Yes, sir?"

"I need fifteen pounds of pig snouts," Floyd said.

He could feel all activity within earshot immediately cease. The woman with the lamb chops didn't even try to close her mouth. "I beg your pardon?" the butcher said.

What kind of two-bit white-meat-only butcher was this? Wasn't he supposed to have the widest selection of the finest quality at the lowest prices in the universe? "Pig snouts," Floyd repeated, pinching his nose. "You know, oink, oink?"

"I'm sorry, we don't carry them. There is not a large demand."

"No? Is there a large demand for all that goat and rabbit you've got stuck all over the place?"

The butcher straightened his little white hat. "Maybe we could find a substitute. How about chicken feet? We have plenty of them."

"Forget it," Floyd snapped. "I don't do substitutes." He looked at his list for a long moment. The words on the white paper seemed to be skiing. "I need ten pounds of pork hearts."

The woman with the lamb chops looked as if she had been forced to swallow a live frog. "What in heaven are you making?" she said, staring openly at the scratches on his throat.

"None of your business!" Floyd looked at the midnight butcher.

"Well? Any pork hearts floating around back there? You have none out here, that's for sure." His eyes started to water; these fluorescent lights were murder.

"Eh—I might have one. Maybe not. Couldn't you use a beef heart instead? I think we've got a few of them in the back. The Italians use them for ethnic recipes."

"I said pork and I meant pork," Floyd barked.

"Go ahead, cry it out," the lamb-chop woman said. "That's what my therapist tells me, too."

"Screw your therapist!" The woman already had, so she looked offended. Floyd yanked his cart out of the butcher line. This whole expedition had hit quicksand. "I'm not even going to ask for hog bungs," he shouted over his shoulder. "I'm sure you don't have them either."

"Try the freezer case," the butcher called. "All kinds of things end up in there."

His cart shuddered violently as Floyd pushed it away. Somehow he landed in the frozen food section, an area even more jammed than the checkout counters. "Do the Twist" cawed from two gigantic loudspeakers. Every few yards stood a card table laden with cheese and toothpicks, or juice in Dixie cups, or tea sandwiches distributed by a man or woman in a striped apron like the store manager's. Abandoned carts strewed the aisle as their owners passed from table to table, sampling the scenery. Several people were actually trying to dance. No one at all was investigating the frozen pizzas. Over the gargantuan cooler hung a yellow banner with glitzy red lettering: It's Singles Night at Barrymore's!!!

A tremendous ball of steam erupted from a nearby electric frying pan. Floyd jumped, almost reaching for the gun strapped to his ankle. "Seafood twirls," sang the man with the lid in his hand. "They're great! Try one!"

"Thank you," Floyd said. The guy was trying pretty hard to look sincere. "Does this kind of thing happen often? Dancing and that music?" He took another seafood twirl.

"Singles night? Every other Monday. It's a big hit. The people love it. The store manager loves it. He moves more Brie and jumbo shrimp on these two nights than he does the whole rest of the month."

"Why is that?" Floyd chomped. "Are they on sale or something?"

"Hell no!" The fellow checked out the tins of spice in the bottom of Floyd's cart. "Let me give you a tip," he said in a low voice. "You won't have any luck with these women if you load up with stuff like Wonder Bread and hotdogs." He handed a seafood twirl to a mid-thirties jock who bore a disturbing resemblance to George Hash. "And next time, no offense, but put on a clean shirt and try to comb your hair a little better.

The competition is very rough." He stood up straight. "And don't wolf down all the food in sight. It turns the ladies off."

"Say, thanks. I'll remember that." Floyd thudded his cart into the thick of the crowd. He prowled along the freezer case, passing orange juice, then french fries, yards of pizzas and frozen dinners, and ice cream. Finally, at the far end, he came to a mound of giant frostbitten ovoids. Most of them appeared to be turkeys. Wait! There was a liver! And tripe! Floyd began furiously digging, piling the rejects on his left.

"Looking for something?"

Floyd agitatedly heaved a tongue onto the pile. There were only three balls left. All of them were turkeys. For a moment he drooped dejectedly over the freezer. As he straightened up his back popped like a live wire. "Not any more," he said. "Goodnight."

"You can't leave now! You'll miss the raffle!"

Floyd gave the woman his ticket. "I hate Disraeli's," he said, thunking his cart slowly away. He replaced the eight spice tins on their shelf, junked the cart, and walked toward the exit. The checkout area had not calmed down one iota; some woman had jumped into a man's shopping cart and put a little Fresh Produce sticker on her forehead. Everyone thought that was pretty entertaining. To the simian wails of "House of the Rising Sun," Floyd departed Barrymore's. He looked over the acres of cars in the lot and for a moment forgot how he had arrived.

He floated somehow home and flipped to the last page of Caspar Beck's book of recipes: Before falling ignominiously asleep, he had to make one last stand. Now was probably not the ideal time to introduce himself to a total stranger, but Floyd did not know how desperate he'd feel when he woke up. Meanwhile that loop describing Caspar mouldered, gaping, in purgatory. Floyd dialled a dozen numbers and heard a faroff honking, once, twice . . . this was insane. The number in Caspar's book was thirty years old.

"Hello?" he said in the Swiss-German dialect. He hadn't spoken it since Aunt Margaret died. It flowed best when he was a bit drunk, like now. "Is this Urs Eggli?"

There was a brief pause. "Who is this? Do you realize what time it is?"

"My name is Floyd Beck. I am the son of Caspar Beck, the butcher. You and he worked together in Bern many years ago. My father spoke about you many times. I'm very sorry to disturb you at this hour, but it's an emergency."

Urs tried to wake up. "Caspar Beck . . . went to America."

"That's right! He opened a butcher shop in New Jersey! That's where I'm calling from!"

For a long time Floyd heard nothing but static. "How is your mother Anna," Urs said finally.

The worms had finished with that shy, beautiful creature twenty years ago. The little mites with the pincers probably had dismantled her skeleton around 1975. Anna's son was just beginning to inhale the dust. "My parents died in a car accident in 1957."

"No!" Urs shouted. "Not both of them! Thirty years ago? And no one ever told me?" He swore at Floyd for a long time before calming down. "What is your name again? Why are you calling me with such terrible news?"

"It's Floyd. Floyd Beck." His voice started to break. Eggli sounded about to hang up. "Please listen to me. My father had a little book of sausage recipes. It is very important that I make one of them as soon as possible. But I don't know how. I can't find the ingredients. I need you to help me."

"You would fly to Switzerland? To make a sausage?"

"Yes! Yes! I'll get on the next plane!"

Eggli blew his nose. "I do not see that this is possible. I will be away in Egypt for two weeks' vacation. Then I go to my little cooking school in Emwald. I am a chef now, no longer a butcher."

"I'll go to your cooking school!" Floyd nearly screamed. "Please!"

"I am sorry, but there is no more room."

Floyd could feel Caspar disgustedly spitting into the clouds. "Can't we work out some arrangement? Can I wash dishes? Milk the cows? See you one hour a week? This is a life-and-death sausage I'm talking about."

"Let me think a moment," Eggli said. There was another protracted spell of static. "You are really Anna's son?"

"Yes! Her only one!"

"Listen. I have a cousin. She runs a pension. I believe she will soon be needing a chef. The present one is going to get married and move to Winterthur. Can you cook?"

"Of course! I've been doing it all my life!" Floyd lied.

Eggli remembered reading an article in the newspaper about the men in America and how they were all learning to cook, shop, and clean the house. In California the men were actually trying to bear children. "Let me speak with her. Perhaps we can arrange something. I would be interested to see you."

"That's the best news I've heard in years! Thank you! Thank you!"

"We shall see. I can promise nothing about these sausages. You will call me back maybe tomorrow? Not so early?"

"Of course! I'll call you at ten o'clock in the morning! Thank you!"

Floyd hung up the phone and let out a shriek. He kissed his father's decrepit book of recipes, wondering why it had fallen off the shelf into his hands now and not ten years ago. He had learned the hard way never to question The Great Choreographer too much; one simply danced, and tried to look thankful. "Emwald, here I come," he whispered to himself, or perhaps to Caspar. Then he plummeted onto the couch and fell asleep.

5

The U.S. Department of Agriculture forbade the entry of fruits, vegetables, plants, plant products, soil, meats, meat products, birds, snails, and other live animals or animal products into the country. This seemed to be a redundant, nonsensical rule to many incoming passengers, so they held on to their oranges and tucked those cute little ferrets into their hand baggage, disbelieving that one orange had the capacity to wipe out the entire Florida citrus crop or that one tiny ferret bite could turn their lower intestines into a fulminating Vesuvius for months running. Once caught in the act, the would-be smugglers emoted senility, ignorance, or shock to an unswayable customs agent, aware that the severity of their fines lay in inverse proportion to their thespian talent. The oranges and the ferrets, alas, ended up in bins or cages at an Agriculture lab, there to be analyzed and most probably destroyed, a fate their owners had not originally considered when bringing them in to the country.

Hash and McPhee walked along a row of neat white bins at the USDA New York facility, bypassing a half dozen chemists peering into microscopes. Customs agents often dropped by to doublecheck the contraband. "Have fun bowling last night?" Hash asked.

McPhee had been rolling balls along a narrow lane, but not in a bowling alley. "A blast," he replied, frowning to himself. He had been telling everyone Frisk and he had been at the target range: better change the subject before Hash asked how the team made out. "So! What are we looking for here?"

"Just nosing around." Hash stopped in front of a rack containing the lab's most recent acquisitions. He pulled a drawer and lifted out a bag of cocaine, poked it, sniffed it, and put it back. "Ho hum." He skipped to the next bin. "Smells dead, whatever it is." With two fingers Hash lifted a small gray spiral to the light, looking for irregularities. "Periwinkle. A fine specimen."

"What do you do with that thing?" McPhee said. "Load it in a sling-shot?"

"You eat it with butter and Pernod. Out of this world." Hash placed the periwinkle on the counter and slipped off his shoe.

McPhee bent a little closer. "Who in his right mind would swallow that."

Without warning Hash smashed the snail under the heel of his shoe. "God Almighty!" cried McPhee. "It's all over my shirt! What the hell did you do that for?"

Now the periwinkle looked like some fancy cookie. "An informant told me to check out the grocery store today," Hash said, looking closely at the remains. "Nothing here."

McPhee angrily wiped his shirt off. "Couldn't you have done that with an X-ray machine or something?"

"Why? That's no fun." Hash held a few more specimens to the light.

"Those are dead snails, period," McPhee snapped. He backed up never-theless.

Hash rolled them into the little bag. "I guess you're right." He pulled open the third drawer. "And what have we here?" He read the tag. "A Jewish watermelon!"

"Someone actually put that monster in a suitcase and schlepped it all the way from Israel? It must weigh fifteen pounds!"

Hash inspected the rind for suspicious indentations. "Come on, McPhee, this is nothing. Remember that Australian who tried to bring in an ostrich egg, then dropped his suitcase?" Hash replaced the water-melon in the bin and passed on to the next. Out came a mammoth salami. "Who confiscated this?"

"Beck. Must have smelled it right through the guy's luggage."

"He had one hell of a day yesterday, didn't he," Hash said, tapping the salami on the counter. "Up all night listening to those operas, then he finds this, then that dame tries to put a fork through his windpipe."

"He was a mess. I sent him to Swissair, then the piers. Lindley swears he took laughing gas before boarding ship. The whole afternoon he kept chuckling to himself and talking to the dog in that godawful Swiss-German. I wonder if insanity runs in his family. He reads poetry, you know."

"He needs to get laid," Hash said. "Severely. Maybe we could all chip in and rent him a hooker from that place on East Sixtieth Street." He looked slyly at McPhee. "Or just send Frisk over with a picnic basket."

"Frisk?! No way!" McPhee exploded. He cleared his throat. "I under-stand she already has a boyfriend."

"Oh. Too bad." Poor, guilt-crippled McPhee: His generation would always think of adultery as cardinal sin rather than the expansion of personal horizons. Hash returned to the contraband. "Salami is my one vice, you know. Full of fat. Chemicals. Salt. A good one wrecks your breath for days." He rolled this specimen over a few times. "Homemade. Look how bumpy the skin is. Smell that, Albert."

"I can. It stinks."

Hash withdrew a pocket knife. "Any pumperknickel in these bins? I haven't eaten since six this morning."

"You can't eat that! It's government property!"

Hash sliced the butt off the salami and put his nose to the flesh. "Great stuff." He made another cut about an inch away. "Beck says his father used to make these. People came all the way from Montauk for them. I can understand why seeing one drives him nuts." Then his knife hit an obstacle. "Whoa." Hash split the salami and removed a green stone embedded in its middle. "That ain't no peppercorn," he said. Within the next five inches, Hash retrieved six more. "I'd say they were emeralds."

"What colossal jackass would bring them in like that? The card says No Meat. No Meat Products." McPhee read the tag on the drawer. "Who's Alphonse Leduc?"

"Just a mule, McPhee, gone forever." Hash held the largest emerald up to the light. Oval cut, about two carats: Down payment on that Ferrari glittered mere inches from his pocket. What had he just whisked away from someone else? A year's supply of heroin? Arms for the glorious rebels? A Park Avenue penthouse? Somewhere a woman, always a woman. He slipped the gems into a plastic bag. "These should spice up the old customs auction."

Hash and McPhee completed the paperwork necessary for depositing the emeralds in the safe. Customs gemologists would be analyzing them tomorrow, determining which of earth's antediluvian veins had formed them, and which of earth's ephemeral lice had snatched them. The process wouldn't take but a few days; jewels, and their thieves, all had computer signatures now. "Hold on," Hash told McPhee as they were leaving the vault. "I have one more thing to check out."

They went to the kennels. It was past lunchtime and the place sounded as if all two hundred dogs were auditioning for the title role in *Salomé*. Each baying inmate, having been freighted from abroad to the States, would remain in quarantine for two weeks, trying not to exhibit symptoms of distemper or pestilence to USDA agents. If successful, the dog would then be free to soil the fire hydrants and front lawns of America, reunited with its doting master or mistress.

Hash walked thoughtfully by the cages, whistling softly. "What are you looking for?" McPhee asked. "An armadillo in drag?"

"No. But remember that tip I got about dogs running drugs?"

"Yeah," McPhee said. "You haven't found shit in the kennels here to back it up."

"I got two calls in the middle of the night," Hash said. "The first was from Berlin. Customs found a pug with a microchip sewn in its tail."

"Its tail? What's on the microchip?"

"They didn't say. Probably circuitry. The kind that runs submarines and the air conditioning at the Pentagon." Hash peered into a cage. The poodle inside of it tried to bite him. "They think someone over here plants a chip on Fido and ships him out with Mrs. Smith, who leaves him in quarantine a week or two, then delivers him to destination. Presto."

"If it's so foolproof, how'd they find the chip?"

"The pug was always scratching its rear end. The tail was a stupid place to plant it anyway." Hash stopped in front of a Chinese Shar-Pei. "Will you look at the wrinkles on that number. They could stitch the entire Tomahawk missile system to that mutt's face."

"So why did Berlin alert you?" McPhee asked.

"The dog left the U.S. from New York. They just thought we'd like to know." Hash played a moment with a beagle. "Then around three I got another call from my Korean in Harlem. He heard that five black mutts had just had operations, he didn't know what for, but it was supposed to look like they'd been scratched in a fight. Four of them were on their way to the Philippines."

"What happened to the fifth?"

"It got away."

"Where? In Harlem?"

"No, Paterson, New Jersey."

McPhee scowled at Hash. "Your informant couldn't be just making that up, could he? Sending you on a wild goose chase? I mean, that is one idiotic story. There are no supporting details. Who's the Dr. Franken-stein? Who supplies the microchips? Why ship mutts to the Philippines? And what kind of pup would run away in Paterson, New Jersey?"

"McPhee, the dog doesn't know it's Paterson." They arrived at the end of the cages. "No black puppies here, I guess."

"Of course not! That would be too easy! So what are you going to do?"

"Check it out. That's my job. I'll just take a little spin through Paterson this afternoon. It's a nice day. Haven't been there in years."

"You're going to find one dog in a city of one hundred thousand people?"

Hash shrugged. "Say one day the cutest little black mutt in the whole world sat whimpering on your doorstep. Would you keep it inside or would you show it off to your friends a little?"

"I'd take it to the dogcatcher. It might have germs. And it probably belonged to some little kid who was crying. I'd have to give it back."

"Aha." Hash wondered how a man so hopelessly shackled with probity could ever get it up with a woman not his church-sanctioned, state-recognized possession. Then he remembered that Frisk, if so motivated, could probably break Jerry Falwell into a Caligula in ten minutes flat.

"I thought your informant told you that dogs were running drugs," McPhee said. "Now he tells you they're running microchips? Are you sure he's not doublecrossing you?"

"Maybe," Hash said. "Maybe not."

Hash dropped McPhee off at JFK and continued to New Jersey. That salami with the emeralds bothered him. It was guaranteed to be confiscated; no smuggler alive would even dream of bringing it into the country that way . . . unless it was intended to be confiscated. Could there be a rat in Agriculture? Someone cunning enough to remove the emeralds before chucking the salami into the incinerator? How about a switch? A few years ago, Hash would never have believed it. Nowadays, when schmucks routinely sold their country out for a bit of extra pin money, he was not so sure. And what fiend could have hatched this dog business? Was life in a democracy so obscene? Did so much evil lurk in every shopkeeper, every CEO in the land, that destroying them could be construed a public service? Jesus Christ! If the son of a bitch sincerely wished to save the country, he should start by outlawing its Senate and House of Representatives. Americans would instantly make him a national hero.

Hash merged onto Route 80 and turned his radio sky-high. It was too lovely a day to contemplate the death of his society. Sunshine incandesced the Airstreams waddling along the right-hand lane. A horde of six-cylinder mules, laden with canoes and pup tents, sped west with him towards the mountains, streams, and mosquitos. Unaccustomed to distances greater than ten city blocks, dozens of vehicles had already collapsed, radiators panicking. Many prospective campers were also busy changing tires as others in their party wandered towards the roadside trees.

The first of the Paterson exits appeared and Hash decided to swing through downtown, refreshing his memory. He and Pearl used to come here dancing on weekends, before discos became drug bazaars. The city was supposed to be on the mend. For years, Paterson had languished in urban thrall, its decrepit mills and factories awaiting resurrection as luxury condominiums awash in tulips and custom baby carriages. The developers had had to wait, however, until Hackensack and Teaneck became unaffordable, impelling desperate commuters ever westward from Manhattan. That had finally happened and the visionaries who had bought up all the abandoned lots along the Passaic River were at last talking turkey with the architects and zoning boards. Paterson was the last pocket of reclaimable wasteland before Ridgewood and Franklin Lakes, whence the upper class had fled in the first place eighty years ago, when white was white, black was black, and Puerto Ricans lived in Puerto Rico.

Hash sailed off the exit smack into a slum. These shoulder-to-shoulder tenements had been built at the turn of the century with compact Italian and Polish laborers in mind; the present inhabitants slam-dunked basketballs through hoops attached to the telephone poles, still pursuing the American dream. Hash killed the radio and drove slowly along the wide street, subtly scanning the sidewalks and porches for a small black dog, trying not to look like a cop. Everyone he passed stared suspiciously at him: Aside from diapers and cocaine, his face was the only white object in sight.

Eventually he wound up in the retail district of Paterson. Here and there shopkeepers were furling steel jalousies which they hoped would preserve their storefronts until they returned from lunch. One was yanking a rack of men's suits off the sidewalk as an assistant followed with a large orange sign. Hash passed a three-block void inlaid with chicken wire and concrete icebergs. Then the stores resumed: plants, wigs, checks cashed, and that shoplifter's paradise, Woolworth's. Graffiti swirled over every immobile surface. Most of the parking meters had been decapitated and their spindles now anchored lamed bicycles and agitated dogs, some of them black but none of them small. Pushing huge strollers, mothers in platform shoes ambled along the sidewalk. Maybe half of them would return to high school in the fall, leaving Junior with grandma as they went to study American history and reproductive biology, two semesters too late.

Hash was becoming depressed. He should have spent the afternoon at Coney Island, scanning the sea for enemy submarines amid the bikinis; his chances of finding one were about as even as his chances of finding a black mutt in Paterson. Maybe the informant was jerking him off; he had not exactly come to Hash's attention with a list of stellar recommendations. Drugs, Hash thought, drugs in corsets. Chinese drugs in corsets? Chinese dogs in corsets? What the hell was a corset anyhow? And who would sew a microchip in a pug? He stomped on the brakes as a juvenile stepped in his path: the kid's radio was almost the size of Hash's Firebird. On the kid's heels walked a pair of very fat ladies, regal and awesome as blimps. Hash wondered what it would be like to lie next to such an immensity, much less mount it: One breast alone could crush his skull. Then a band of Girl Scouts, at least a couple of them pregnant, crossed the street. That must look terrific when they tried to sell cookies. The moment the road cleared, Hash zoomed ahead. He'd had it with downtown. There was something very aggravating about people whose culture was so deliberately different than his own.

Driving into a less congested area, Hash bought a carton of orange juice from a Vietnamese superette. He felt much more comfortable in this neighborhood, perhaps because the Patersonians here were six inches shorter than those downtown. Hash leaned against a mailbox, wondering where he would run were he a dog. Into a sewer? An alley? Damn, couldn't that informant have been more specific? What kind of mutt? Long legs or stubby legs? How old? How'd it get away? Did it just fall out of a car?

An Asian teenager with a headset over his ears walked by. At least this kid had some respect for the public airwaves. "Excuse me," Hash shouted, jumping in his path.

The fellow exposed his ears. "Yes?"

"I wonder if you could help me. I lost my little black dog a few days ago. Have you seen one around?"

"What's the reward?"

The kid was assimilating fast. "Police," Hash muttered, showing his badge the way the cops did on television. The boy's eyes doubled. "You see a dog?"

"Nope, sorry. Try around the old factories. There are lots of dogs there."

"Doing what?"

"Roamin' around, eating garbage."

"Which way?"

"Follow the old railroad tracks. Can I come along?"

"I'm sorry, son, this is not a television show." Hash thanked the boy and sped off.

The railroad tracks had not been used much after all the factories went under. Hash wondered what could have killed Paterson. Bayonne? The minimum wage? In some places the tracks disappeared completely under a pane of macadam, surfacing a block later in a field of goldenrod. The sparse houses finally ended and high wire fences began poking out of the crabgrass, promising to electrocute anyone who touched them although one glance beyond the peeling exclamation points indicated that no one had paid an electricity bill here in fifteen years. Though filthy now, the old stone factories had lost none of their original grace, as if the architects had sensed that someday, upscale couples would be steaming broccoli therein.

The tracks suddenly terminated into an invisible station. Hash got out of his car and surveyed the desolate area. In the distance a demolition crew was eviscerating an old mill; clouds of plaster rose from a dumpster parked at its side as wall after wall slid down a two-story chute. Then he stopped short. In front of him stood a rickety building with a sign over the door: Feinstein Corset Company. Three ancient Cadillacs sat in the lot. Hash knocked and walked in.

Three old men, none of them Chinese, sat playing poker and smoking cigars in the seedy office. "I'm looking for Feinstein," Hash said.

"Dead," one of them replied. "Are you going to make us an offer or waste our time?"

"An offer? For what?"

"The building. Don't even think of anything less than two million. A developer from Poughkeepsie is coming over this afternoon. He's serious."

Why should these three risk anything on dogs and drugs if they were going to clean up on real estate? "Sorry," Hash said. "I think I'm in the wrong building." He walked down the street, still looking for dogs. The terrain did not look promising. It contained no garbage cans, no wood-chuck holes.

He stopped in front of a fanciful mass of pink granite: Now there was a classy renovation. Nothing Pearl had done in Newark came close to this. Business or condo? Hard to tell. The windows all had curtains but the parking lot was full. The yard was exquisitely manicured. No sign of any kind stood outside: Whoever lived there cherished privacy. Then Hash saw a man in pajamas run out the front door, race to his car, grab a newspaper, and rush back inside. The fellow's elaborately embroidered bathrobe ruffled in the wind as he disappeared through the ponderous oak doors.

A window to the right swung open and Hash saw the fellow angrily defenestrate three or four brown aprons onto the bushes below. Then a shoe came flying out. A woman holding a telephone to her ear leaned over the granite sill and called someone's name. Around the side of the building scurried an old man in overalls, who handed the shoe back. Then the window slammed shut. A few moments later the doors trembled and out staggered a fellow with a large wooden box. It appeared to be a doghouse. As he struggled down the stone steps, the man in pajamas burst out of the building, bellowing unmercifully at the fellow's neck. Both disappeared around the back.

Intrigued, Hash moseyed up the walk. He was almost to the front steps when the man in pajamas reappeared. Hash could almost see the man's blood boiling and decided to be ultradiscreet: Urbanites nowadays were as apt to wear Uzis as bifocals. "Excuse me," he said. "Do you live here?"

"Yes, I live here! And I don't need encyclopedias!" The man was holding a lump under his pajamas. Hash hoped it was a loaf of bread. "What do you want?"

"I wonder if you've seen a stray dog in the neighborhood. It ran away a week or two ago."

"Why'd it run away? What does it look like? The man tied a big bow in the front of his bathrobe. The lump became lost in the folds.

"It's a black mutt."

"How big?" Hash's hands described an amorphous mass. "That's not much help. Why don't you just get another one? Your kids won't care."

"I don't have kids," Hash said irritably. He was supposed to be the guy asking questions. "I just want to take it back where it came from."

"Look, I'm a busy man. What's the dog's name?"

Hash hesitated a moment too long. "Blackie." He saw the man didn't believe him.

The doors behind him swung open and a gorgeous woman stepped out. Hash nearly fell to his knees. "Nestor, darling," she said. "Get inside this instant. I'm about to kill the cook." She looked imperiously at Hash and he felt like crying. Where had this lunatic found such a woman?

"Excuse me, I have work to do," Nestor said, swishing by. "I suggest you ask around the Chinese restaurants downtown. They're always out here with nets and baseball bats." He joined the woman at the top of the steps. They were wearing the same white bathrobe but she had a ruffly summer dress under hers; the effect was strangely erotic. Normal people did not wear wool bathrobes in June.

Hash watched the oak door slam after them. One second later it swung open and a woman with two baby bottles bustled out, calling "Smudgie, Smudgie" as she disappeared around the side of the building. He could not be sure, but Hash thought he saw a small black object scurry across the foyer inside just as the door slammed shut. He had to have been mistaken. It was a black Manx, or a baby panther. Or his imagination. That woman would never have tolerated a mutt in her mansion.

For another half hour Hash crawled around Paterson. Then he went after the submarines off Coney Island.

Viola slammed the door. "Who was that talking to you?"

"Some bogus dogcatcher," Nestor said, striding toward the cafeteria. "I saw through him right away. Tried to tell me he was looking for a mutt named Blackie. He wanted to take Smudge away and sell him to a laboratory. I know how these things work." Nestor removed the pup from his pajamas and inspected its stomach. "They were already torturing the poor guy," he said. "Look at those scratches. I should call the police and have that pervert arrested."

"What's his name? Where's he from?"

Nestor frowned. "He didn't tell me." Smudge's tiny pink tongue lapped his finger. "Henriette! Where's the milk?" Nestor cuddled the pup to his nose. "No one's ever going to slice you up again, tiger," he whispered. "I'll kill the bastard if I ever see him again."

"Will you forget that dog? We've got a problem in the kitchen."

"What now? I forbade her to make anything that didn't come in a can."

Viola stopped. "Smell that delicious aroma, Nestor."

"What is it?"

"Beef stew from a can and foam from the fire extinguisher. It's all over the kitchen. Oh God, she's a disaster. We've got to get rid of her."

"We can't, honey," Nestor said. "Morton's been through that already."

Henriette caught up to them. "Gloria Budd from *OmniFem* is here for the interview, Viola. I put her in the greenhouse."

"Remember to water her in two weeks," Viola said, walking away. "I've got a business to run."

"Hey! You can't do that to national television!" Nestor cried. "This is free advertising to two hundred million people! I promised Gloria we'd show her the Christmas robes and give her a little scoop."

Viola studied Nestor as if she were about to sculpt him in purest gold. "Think about that a moment, Nestor. What if one percent of one percent of the population orders one? I'm only twenty thousand short."

"Wrong. Nineteen thousand eight hundred short. We can still make it. Dingleball's sure the strike's almost over. And he found the missing robes."

"Sure he did. In Crete." Viola looked at Henriette. "Tell this woman that I feel disgusting. I look disgusting. The last thing I want is to be seen on television. Why can't Nestor do this interview? He's the idiot who schedules them all."

"Because I'm not a successful businesswoman, dear," Nestor said. "I have not shattered the bonds of male tyranny and made stockbrokers weep into their martinis as I walked by." He slapped open the cafeteria doors. "Breeze! What have you done to me, you halfbreed? I thought you people knew how to cook over an open fire! Damn you anyhow!"

"Where is she," Viola said, turning. "Let's get this over with."

"In the greenhouse. Don't you think you should take that bathrobe off first," Henriette suggested.

"Here, hide it. What time are the Lungs getting in? One? This is going to be one hell of a quick interview." Viola strode into the greenhouse.

A meticulously assembled woman stood peering into the hollyhocks. Viola didn't like her white business suit at all. It couldn't decide whether it was a bridal gown or a straitjacket. "Gloria Budd," the woman said. "I'm so pleased to meet you, Ms. Flury."

"Likewise," Viola replied, sitting on the rattan rocker. "I have about fifteen minutes to talk to you. No personal questions about my partner or my husband, please. And go easy on the women's lib angle, if you don't mind."

Gloria thought Viola was kidding. She motioned to a cameraman, checked her file cards, and sailed right in. "Good afternoon. This is Gloria Budd for *OmniFem.* Here we are in the fabulous greenhouse of Pyrana, Incorporated, Paterson, New Jersey and with me is Viola Flury, the force behind a tremendous empire of women's lingerie. Ms. Flury, how do you do it?"

"How do I do what?"

"Everything! Let's back up. How did you get started in this business? The fashion world is so very, very tough. Where did you go to school?"

"I didn't go to school. I spent my childhood studying to be a figure skater."

"How fascinating! What happened?"

"I couldn't cut it."

"I see! How bold of you to admit that . . . how very honest . . . touching." Gloria did her best to look pained. "Then what happened?"

"No personal questions, I said."

"Let's skip a few years then. You met Nestor how? Apprenticing on Seventh Ave?"

"At a masquerade ball."

"Now that is romantic. That is destiny." Gloria turned to the camera. "Nestor Buffez, a Hispano-American, is Viola's business partner. They were in this together from the very beginning." She leaned confidentially over her subject. "Did he ask you to dance?"

"He wanted my dress. For his girlfriend."

"Your dress? You must have made it yourself. How did you get into design, Viola? It's such a brutal field."

"I had always sewn my own skating costumes. It wasn't a long leap from there to lingerie."

"I see! You were obviously right on the mark because your company became an immediate success. You knew what American women wanted. Tell me something . . . do you think that, because of your sex, it was more difficult for you to achieve recognition?"

"Of course not."

Gloria tried another tack. She wasn't getting enough social-message material here. "Don't you agree that women's lingerie should be designed by a woman, for a woman?"

That sounded like a tampon advertisement. Viola cleared her throat and followed the loops of a bumblebee amid the ivy. "A woman buys lingerie to seduce a man. A man buys lingerie to seduce a woman. Who designs it is immaterial. No more liberation questions, please."

Gloria scanned her clipboard. "Tell us about this fantastic mill, Viola. How did you find it?"

"Nestor and I were driving around one afternoon in 1973 looking for the Feinstein Corset Company. Our car ran out of gas right in front of this building. It was for sale."

"You took a tremendous chance, buying in Paterson . . . Pyrana was one of the first companies to locate its worldwide headquarters in what can only be described as a slum. That took vision and remarkable courage."

"If you insist. Nestor felt at home here."

Gloria nodded uncertainly. "Well! Can you describe what happens in this building?"

"One hundred people make underpants."

"Oh ha ha! Give us a little more than that, Viola! Take us from A to Z with"—Gloria held up the pink camisole embroidered with the Manhattan skyline. "This little nothing."

Viola looked at her watch: five more minutes of propagandist baloney and she could return to work. Not one interviewer in ten years had asked her why she really put in eighteen-hour days. "I designed that for a UN diplomat who was being transferred to Brussels. He wanted something which would bring back fond memories of New York."

"You do a lot of commissioned work?"

"Yes."

"For celebrities?" Gloria's eyebrows levitated into her bangs. "Could you name a few?"

"No. Lingerie is a private affair."

The greenhouse doors burst open and in swished Nestor. He had changed to a fresh pair of pajamas and brushed his hair. "Gloria, how are you, darling? It's been years, hasn't it!" He was laying on a heavy Spanish accent which Viola had not heard since they had applied for the last bank loan.

The newswoman perked up. "Nestor Buffez," she said, kissing him as if they had spent many, many happy hours together in some important location, "what a delightful surprise." She motioned him to sit next to Viola on the rattan rocker.

"I hope my partner hasn't been giving you a hard time," Nestor said, sliding casually into place beside Viola. "She's expecting her first baby, you know."

"I was just leading up to that," Gloria lied. Nowhere on her cue cards was pregnancy mentioned. "Viola, that's fabulous. You must be thrilled. Like so many women across America, you've postponed motherhood until your career was established. What sort of changes will this bring about in your life?"

She'd probably never take the extra lard off and that would drastically reduce the likelihood of an extramarital affair. From now until she died, she'd have to act responsibly and with dignity. Her sketches would eventually lose that hungry, lustful edge and start looking like mom's hobby. Her entire existence would be sucked up by a few pounds of alternately gurgling and colicky flesh and she'd never forgive Eugene for accidentally domesticating her. "I suppose my husband will have to start using seat belts."

"We already have a day care center here at the mill," Nestor interrupted. His pajamas looked somehow incomplete now without a sombrero. "And we're finishing a wonderful playground out back." He burned his dark eyes into Gloria. "We want our employees to be happy here. They are our most important asset."

Gloria's thoughts roamed outer space. "It is always obvious when a woman runs a company. The priorities are very different."

"Oh *sí, sí,*" Nestor agreed. "You know, Gloria, as the years go by, I understand more and more how lucky I am to be working with Viola. She is a very liberated lady: committed, compassionate, sophisticated . . ." Nestor was about to say "sexy" but caught himself just in time. "I hope you will forgive me for barging in on your interview. I know this is a program for women."

"Thank you, Nestor. If only more men had your attitude. Tell me . . . do you think, because of your Hispanic origins, it was more difficult for you to achieve recognition?"

Nestor did his finest imitation of Louis Leakey contemplating a fibula. "I harbor no grudges. Today I am a success." Suddenly he leapt from his seat. "Gloria! I must show you our latest arrival!"

Viola stood up. "If you'll excuse me, I have some important calls to take."

Nestor blocked her path with the Christmas bathrobe he had just happened to bring in with him. "Viola is such an artist," he almost shouted as one hand shoved her back into the rocker. "Look at this gorgeous design."

Gloria motioned for a camera to zoom in. "Lovely. Stunning."

"This is for the holiday season," Nestor said, his accent verging on gibberish. "Try it on, Gloria." He swathed her in white wool. "Doesn't that feel like heaven?" He turned her back to the camera. "See this exquisite embroidery. This robe will soon be available in all our shops across the country. Any woman who is becoming tired of diamonds and pearls should ask for one of these. We have only made a few because these are so special."

"How much does this robe cost, Nestor?"

"More than a bottle of perfume and less than a fur coat. That is all a lady needs to know." Nestor removed it from Gloria's shoulders. "If you would excuse me. I must speak with some architects. We want this playground to be just right." He kissed Gloria's cheek. "*Adiós.*" He departed like a triumphant matador.

For some moments Viola and Gloria sat in silence. "What tremendous vitality," Gloria finally remarked. She straightened the microphone on her white lapel: human-interest time. "Just a few quick questions, Viola, before we let you go. What do you do for relaxation?"

Shout at morons in Switzerland. Exchange ulcers with accountants. Go blind over inventory printouts. Look forward to textile wars. "I swim." That was the closest she'd ever get to figure skating.

"And is your husband supportive of your work?"

"I wouldn't have married a man who was not."

Gloria waited but nothing else came. "You're quite recently married, aren't you?"

"Two years."

This was tougher than skinning a porcupine. Gloria wished Nestor had stuck around; he could have fielded a few questions about homosexuals in the marketplace and lingerie as an instrument of feminine power. Viola Flury was a mental case. Didn't she watch television? Didn't she realize how many people would just die to be on *OmniFem?* There was something unholy about a person in this day and age who did not wish to be interviewed. "May I ask how you met your husband?"

"He was a regular customer at the Madison Avenue store."

"Oh? What was he buying?"

"Lingerie for his first wife." Viola rose from the sofa. "I think you have enough material here. It was a pleasure to meet you, Gloria. I'm sorry I don't have any more time today." At the door of the greenhouse she turned around. "The robe is six hundred and fifty bucks, by the way."

She went to her office and tried to catch up on phone calls. Half the people who had called her when she was out were now out themselves; they'd be sure to call back the moment she left. Around one Nestor walked in and flopped onto a chair. He had been haggling with a manufacturer of bra hooks for most of the morning. "Why must females have breasts," he said, pouring himself a drink. "They make life impossible for us all."

Viola skimmed through a pamphlet about Brazilian cotton and spun it into the waste basket. "Nice schmoozing with *OmniFem*, Nestor. Bring your tortilla press along next time." She inspected a yellow baseball cap with *Pyrana, Inc.* across the brim. "I ordered a load of these for the company picnic."

Nestor opened one eye. "Nice." He swallowed the last ice cube. "I had to show her the robe, you know. It was a great opportunity."

"Of course."

"Come here a minute."

Columnists, counsellors, preachers, executives, everyone with a functional frontal lobe in fact, advised against sleeping with the same people with whom one shared the copier. They thought it decreased productivity. They never calculated, however, the millions of brain-hours squandered daily as the American workforce attempted to smother lust under a soaking blanket of good sense: Nothing shorted out concentration like pent-up sexual curiosity. It was much better to sleep with the person in question, shatter all those pleasant daydreams in one rude shot, and return to the copier as if nothing had happened.

Viola climbed upon Nestor's lap and picked a blue thread off his pajamas. "What now."

"You're annoyed, aren't you."

"Yes! I'm tired of this lady tycoon bullshit! No more interviews. If you want publicity, play up the Cuban-makes-good angle for a couple months."

"They prefer you, Viola. You're such a perfect subject."

"I have nothing to say and I'm not a role model."

"It's just a game," Nestor said, curling her black hair behind one ear. "If it doesn't amuse you, we'll stop."

"They don't even realize when I'm laughing at them anymore," Viola said. "What the hell kind of fun is that?"

Henriette more or less knocked before walking in. "Hi, guys. Your friends are here."

"Put them in the conference room," Viola said, sliding off her partner's lap. "And for God's sake, don't bring in any coffee unless you make it yourself." She turned to Nestor. "What did you do about lunch?"

"I sent Breeze into Wyckoff. She's picking up some quiche at a caterer's. Said she had made something much better but I told her to freeze it." Nestor stood up and straightened his pajamas. "How charming do you feel, lady tycoon?"

"Charming enough to nail this deal."

The Lung brothers, three Chinese silk merchants, were standing in front of Eugene's portrait of a salmon, smoking cigarettes, when Viola and Nestor walked into the conference room. "Good afternoon, gentlemen," Nestor bowed. His voice contained not a speck of a Hispanic accent. In fact it sounded almost Etonian. "We are honored that you could visit the headquarters of Pyrana, Incorporated." Introductions were made, hands clasped. Viola presented each of the Lungs with a baseball cap. "How about a little tour of our plant?"

Viola zeroed in on the eldest Lung brother, Kew. He was the one who signed the checks. For half an hour, as they shuffled through the mill, she talked to him about silk. She showed him what they were using at the moment, where it came from, how much it cost, and why she had used it. The mill was immaculate as an operating room: All week long Nestor had nitpicked the custodian staff to the brink of rioting. And somehow he had gotten all the ladies to wear skirts today. Smudge was temporarily out in the yard with his babysitter Mai Ping. The Lungs were fascinated with purple brassieres and received an assortment to take back to China with them.

Nestor leisurely rounded his party back to the conference room, mixed the Lungs a martini, and delivered a profuse toast to international commerce. He had used this speech to great effect on any number of occasions and was almost beginning to believe it himself. No signal for lunch came, so Nestor poured another round. He was planning to take the Lungs to the golf course this afternoon and wanted to insure they all played the game American-style.

Finally Henriette, wearing a Pyrana baseball cap, wheeled a cart into the conference room. On top of it stood several bottles of wine, a salad bowl, and a foul-smelling tart bearing resemblance to a quiche only in that it was round. Viola broke away from Kew Lung, who had been at the window admiring Smudge's doghouse, and started tossing the salad. The bright orange dressing unnerved her stomach.

Nestor joined Kew Lung at the window. For a moment they watched Mai Ping run Smudge through the treadmill. "How do you like my doghouse," Nestor said.

"Very nice," Kew said. "Your dog is new?"

"Yes. So is the girl exercising him. She is my best employee," Nestor said. "Chinese, by the way." Kew Lung beamed. "I wish I had fifty more of her." He returned to the conference table. "Our chef has prepared a special American lunch which we hope you will enjoy."

Saying nothing, Viola started slicing the tart. It resisted division: There seemed to be large, tough objects suspended under its ripply epidermis. "Nestor, pour our guests some wine," she said. "I'll have this ready in just a moment."

The Lungs sat down and watched Viola saw away: In their culture, the presentation of food was as important as the deglutition of it. She finally freed a piece.

"What this is," Kew inquired. "I have never seen such a dish before."

"You haven't?" Nestor exclaimed in surprise, leaning over the table for a closer look. "That is hotdogs and sauerkraut, an American favorite, in the form of a pudding we call a quiche." He smiled proudly.

"Hot dog?" one Lung asked. "You eat dog in America too?"

"No, not dog. See that long reddish sausage sticking out the side? That is a hotdog. It is made of beef and pork and fine spices." Nestor beamed at Viola. "Keep slicing, my dear, before everything gets cold."

Soon all five of them had a robust wedge on their plates. It looked as if Breeze had piled some hotdogs onto a pie crust, buried them in old sauerkraut, poured milk then eggs over the top, and plastered the mess with a pound of American cheese. "*Bon appétit,*" Nestor toasted, raising his wine glass. "Long live the Pyrana-Lung silk connection." He shoveled a heaping forkful into his mouth and chewed for many moments. "You will be surprised to learn that the layer of cheese is hot and the hotdogs are cold," he said finally. "It's quite a complicated cooking technique but our chef is a master."

The Lungs ate with martini-induced gusto, sure that whatever the heads of Pyrana, Inc. served them must be rare and exquisite indeed. Nestor managed to engorge the contents of his plate by flushing it downstream with several glasses of wine.

"You're not eating," he said to Viola. "Aren't you hungry?"

She stood up. "Excuse me a moment. I'll be right back." She went to the bathroom and was sick. It was the first time her body had reminded her that she was going to be a mother in seven months whether she liked it or not.

"Viola," Nestor called softly, knocking on the door. "Are you all right?"

She came out. "What the hell happened to the quiche? Don't tell me she picked that cow pie up from a caterer."

"I have no idea. But Morton's shipping her to cooking school if it's the last thing he does." Nestor stopped at the door of the conference room. "You're white as a snowball. Maybe you should go home."

"I don't want to go home. Eugene has the place crawling with carpenters." Viola opened the door of the conference room. The odor of sauerkraut nearly emptied her stomach on the spot. "Whoa," she said to Nestor, and took one deep breath. Viola quickly shook hands with the Lung brothers. "I'm very sorry, but an emergency has come up. I must leave. Have a wonderful time at the golf course. I'll see you soon."

"Maybe at the silk convention in July?"

"That's right, it's in Montreux this year," Nestor said. "We'll definitely be seeing you there."

"That would be lovely," Viola chimed in.

Nestor accompanied her out. "Why don't you lie down upstairs?"

"I'll go swimming, thanks."

Before leaving, Viola called Morton the accountant. "Where's that cooking school," she said. "That cretin is going there tomorrow. She almost poisoned the co-signers of a six-million-dollar contract."

"Oy, that's bad. I don't know if your liability would cover poisoning. Hold on." Morton shuffled some papers. "Here. It's in Emwald, Switzerland. The chef guarantees results in three weeks. He teaches everything from soup to nuts. Class is limited to ten students."

"How much," Viola interrupted.

"Four thousand bucks, including air fare."

"You kidding me? I'd rather pay that in unemployment comp!"

"Would you? She'd probably sue you for discrimination. You'd end up paying forty thousand in damages. Have you been reading any of that material I've been sending you about hiring and firing women?"

"I give up," Viola said. "Enroll her in the next course. Maybe she'll bag herself a rich Italian and decide to stay over there."

"How are those robes coming along? The trade talks have broken down again."

"They're in transit," Viola said, hanging up before Morton could predict more catastrophe. She drove to a health club on Route 4, slipped into the pool and for a long while just floated, not thinking, allowing the clear, open water to slowly blanch her brains. She swam a few laps, concentrating on form, watching the turquoise tiles slide placidly by: After she quit figure skating, Viola had become a swimmer. She kept it up now because she hated jogging and refused to participate in an aerobics class with twenty toothy, grunting women. Water was sensuous, quiet, and it could swallow her easily and forever. On still summer nights, when she alone tantalized a black lake, Viola thought about that.

Late in the afternoon the black Porsche slithered back into Manhattan. Viola swung open the apartment door. "Eugene! I'm home!"

Most of the foyer floor was gone. Viola stopped short and peered down the crevasse, half expecting to see a smoking meteorite eighteen floors below.

Eugene removed a few nails from his mouth and looked one flight up. From his carpenter's belt hung a hammer, a square, and a bag of drywall screws. Plaster dust floured his eyebrows. "Hi, honey, you're early! How do you like it?"

"What have you done to our house, Eugene?"

"This is the two-man slide to the nursery, remember? For when we have to get down here fast? When the baby's crying?"

He had shown her the blueprints about a week ago, when Dingleball's aprons had first defoliated her groves of reason. Viola vaguely remembered throwing her hands in the air and telling her husband to do whatever he wanted. "I thought we were going to think about this a little more."

"There's no time, Viola! I only have seven months and three days! The slide has to go in first because it's attached to the pneumatic cradle rocker. And that's attached to the lullaby system." Eugene handed a tape measure to a passing carpenter. "See how thick that wall is, would you? As long as we're here we may as well tear it down."

"Hold on a minute! Which wall? I don't remember any of this, Eugene."

"I'm getting a few more ideas as I stand here. We should probably put a little wading pool in the corner. You can float the baby around in it while I read Cicero. Hey! Guess what came in today! The *Goldberg* Variations! Remember that stereo belt I made with the pillows? Now we can hook it up to your stomach at night."

Instead of Bach, wouldn't it be much better for the child to listen to sewage sloshing around its mother's intestines? That way it wouldn't exit the womb with unrealistic expectations of the world outside. "What are you going to do about this hole in the floor? Wait until someone falls into it and breaks a neck?"

"No, no. Before the crew leaves they're going to put up a temporary rail."

"And when is that?"

"Right away. We weren't expecting you home so soon, darling."

This was her punishment for trying to take the afternoon off. Viola went to the library and searched for the mystery she had been intending to read since Christmas. She looked twice along the bottom shelves, which Eugene reserved for new acquisitions, and saw nothing but a slew of baby books. Viola opened one about breast feeding: Her husband had underlined pithy passages and written notes to himself all over the margins. Without doubt he had done the same to every manual on the shelf. Was it really necessary to read five conflicting theories of toilet training? Did parents really have to know precisely why their Jojo liked rattles but didn't like teddy bears? Who gave a damn about the influence of mobiles upon an infant's eye-to-hand coordination? Americans slurped this scholiastic drivel by the ton and their children still turned out to be ten times more aimless than a drunken harlequin. Where was the book titled *The Joys of Judicious Horsewhipping?* How about *Ten Thousand Ways to Make Junior Earn His Allowance?* They had been out of print for thirty years.

Viola finally found her mystery squeezed between several carpentry manuals in the bathroom. She went outside and tried a few pages. The first paragraph read like morphine and the terrace was too hot. She wasn't tired enough to take a nap but she was too tired to drive back to Paterson and close up the office. It was too late now to take a spin to the Madison Avenue shop. She should have called Dingleball today, not that he could have given her any good news about the textile strike, but he should be needled daily until she received her shipment of white robes. Viola walked to the edge of the terrace and let the wind ruffle her hair. She watched a traffic helicopter drone above the Hudson, counting the vehicles pasturing upon the rush-hour freeways.

Disaster was nigh; she didn't know where, or when, but it was palpable as the humidity soddening the breeze. She had first felt it the moment she sketched the white bow on the white bathrobe and now Dingleball had proven her intuition right. Viola did not understand. Orders had been late before, shipments lost, designs misplaced, and in the end, she and Nestor had been able not only to jig past catastrophe, but to laugh about it afterwards. That would not happen this time. Who was sticking pins into a voodoo doll?

Bah, she imagined things: a sign of maternity intersecting desperation. Viola turned away from the wind. Luck could return, ambition rekindle: Once the hormones called it a day, the blood was never quite as red again.

No cars riled Hudson Street. The birds were still bundled to their branches, waiting for light to crack the east. Floyd sat on his couch staring at the clock above the mantel. The hands only moved when he dozed off:

Time did not enjoy being observed at its nefarious task. Reluctantly the minute hand faded north. There: four o'clock. Floyd picked up the telephone and dialled Urs Eggli.

"Good morning," he said in the Swiss-German dialect. "This is Floyd Beck again. Remember me?"

"Of course, Anna."

Floyd hesitated: Was Eggli senile? His father had never mentioned the man's age when he told stories about him. "Were you able to talk with your cousin in the pension?"

"Yes. She indeed does need a cook."

"She does?!" Floyd jumped off the couch, knocking over his beer. "That's great news! When? How soon?" Carefully lifting the phone, he walked into the kitchen and got a sponge.

"In two weeks. July sixth. That is Monday, no? You will cook breakfast and dinner in her pension. In return I will help you make this sausage."

"That is perfect," Floyd almost shouted.

"You sleep in the pension," Eggli said. "In a little room by the kitchen. It is very clean and has a shower. You stay there for three weeks, during my cooking school."

"What sort of things am I supposed to cook? Ten-course banquets? How many people? Does your cousin have a microwave oven?" Floyd finished mopping the beer and took the sponge back to the kitchen.

"I cannot answer all of these questions. This is a very small place high in the mountains. I will tell you in advance that this is a pension for women only. My cousin does not like to have men under her roof. She is a very proper and modest woman. I assured her that you would keep to yourself."

"I intend to, believe me."

"May I ask what sort of things you cook? My cousin would like to know."

Floyd happened to be standing in front of his freezer. He whipped it open and read off a few boxes. "Fettucine Alfredo I make all the time. Flounder Florentine. French Bread Pizzas. Creamed Chipped Beef. Macaroni and Cheese Casserole Deluxe."

"This sounds very impressive but much too fancy."

"Never mind! We can have peanut butter sandwiches."

"I need, please, some documentation. Could you send me full references and a photograph for my cousin?"

"Of course, at once."

"I will send you a map and a brochure of my cooking course. You must also bring formal clothing for special occasions."

"Yes! Thank you, Mr. Eggli. This is a dream come true."

"For me also. I must go."

What did he mean, for him also? Eggli must be dying to get his hands on Caspar's secret recipes. Formal clothing? Floyd laughed out loud: Why not. He was up for anything. Switzerland! Mountains, fresh air, pure snow, a luxury hotel, Floydwurst . . . and a secluded pension for proper and modest women. No thieving magpies, no Portias, no aggressive bow-wows for three weeks. He felt like Adam getting another shot at the Garden of Eden. Nothing prevented him from staying there and opening a butcher store in a picturesque Alpine village. He just might find himself a sturdy Swiss wife and leave this Babylon America. Begin all over again on the other side of the ocean, just as Caspar had, but in the reverse direction. The idea had a certain perverse symmetry.

At eight o'clock, shaved and ironed, Floyd was at JFK. He found McPhee standing morosely at the coffee machine, chewing a fake chocolate eclair. "Hi Albert," he said. "Could I talk to you a moment?"

McPhee glanced sideways. His pasty face looked as if he had attached it to an air compressor and pumped thirty pounds of mustard gas beneath the skin. "Sure."

Floyd hesitated. "Are you feeling all right?"

Last night Frisk had told McPhee she was quitting her job and she never wanted to see him again. She couldn't handle the commuting. "Sure, what's on your mind?"

"I need to take three weeks off. Starting July Fourth."

"Forget it," McPhee chomped. "No way."

"Then I quit," Floyd said, walking off.

McPhee expected he'd be punished for his sins, but not this soon. "Hey! What's gotten into you? Everybody just can't jump ship like this!" He caught up with Floyd. "Run that by me again. Everything but the quitting part."

"I need to take three weeks off. For private reasons." That didn't seem drastic enough. "Private medical reasons."

"You sick?" McPhee scanned Floyd's face. Today, for the first time in weeks, Beck didn't look like a reject from the waxworks.

"I will be if I don't get this problem taken care of."

It was that lesbian dog doctor again. "Where are you going?"

Floyd's brain skipped a groove. "Florida."

"In July? Do you realize how hot it is down there now? How fast microorganisms multiply in all that sweat?"

"McPhee, no more questions. I have to know today."

The supervisor sighed. "I'll see what I can do. This really catches me off balance, Beck. I hope it's necessary."

"It's life or death, believe me."

McPhee's mouth suddenly fell open. The eclair had stained his tongue completely brown. Frisk had just walked through the office, en route to her station. She had gotten a haircut and was wearing, for the first time, red lipstick. She was not wearing her habitual Valentine's Day scarf: This was serious. She looked older and a little tough, like trussed fowl. McPhee couldn't believe she was here, not after last night. What new form of torture was this? The Look-But-Don't-Touch-Inspector-Fiske Routine?

"Hello, Floyd," she called. "Plane's about to land."

"Guess I'd better get out there," Floyd said. He went to his station. Next door Frisk was skidding a ballpoint pen through a customs form. Within a few lines it bolted from her hands and spun to the floor. Floyd picked it up. He didn't need much imagination to figure out what had happened; Frisk was emitting more gamma rays than a fractured reactor. "I like your haircut," he said, handing her pen back.

"Thank you." Frisk's fingers poked the computer at her waist.

Floyd saw the corner of her mouth tremble and wondered what miniscule event had turned the tide. One dried-out turkey club too many from room service? Another Sunday sunrise on an empty pillow?

Then the passengers hit. Once again a dozen permutations of the Casual American paraded past Floyd's station. In no way was he going to look like one of these when he went to Chef Eggli's hotel. Tourists really got out of hand in the summer, for no mitigating reason. The weather was hot; clothing was cheap; everyone wore less of it. Why, therefore, couldn't a guy with enough cash to fly to Timbuktu and back spare a few extra bucks for a decent pair of socks? Aunt Margaret would never have let him out of the house looking like some of these people. She had taught him that it was always better to be overdressed than underdressed for the occasion: a European attitude with its roots in kings and crowns and order. No wonder Americans didn't relate to it.

Every so often, like a lily blooming in the swamp, a delectable woman would filter past Floyd. He would smell her perfume, observe her clothing, then try to imagine what he would cook for her were she up in the mountains in a pension. Simple things: chicken, vegetables, little soups . . . hmmm. This could be a problem. Next station, Frisk was dissecting the suitcase of any man who bore the slightest resemblance in age, height, or hairline to McPhee. Everyone else she just flushed through. Floyd tried to keep an eye on her as he sifted through his own lines, but quickly realized this was unnecessary: Nothing concentrated the antennae like rage.

A fresh crowd began hauling luggage off the carousel. He didn't have much time. "May I ask you something," Floyd said to Frisk.

"What the hell."

"Are you a good cook?"

Her red lips compressed. "What kind of stupidassin' question is that?"

"Would you give me a few cooking lessons this week? Show me how to make things like chicken rice soup? Pot roast?"

"Don't tell me your dog doctor never taught you to cook like a good boy."

"No, she never did."

"So why do you want to learn now?"

"Now's a good time."

Frisk slammed her conveyer belt on. "Let me think about it."

After the next planeload, they took a break. Floyd hovered over Frisk, telling all the stupid jokes he could remember. She had done him the same favor about a month ago, probably with the same jokes; no matter. The point was not to laugh at them, but to advertise that she was too miserable to laugh, period.

Hash strolled by for a slug at the water fountain. "Good afternoon, all." He whistled. "That is some haircut, lady. Did you get the supervisor's approval before making yourself into a fire hazard?"

"Go fuck yourself," Frisk said, walking away.

Hash looked askance at her receding backside. When he paid women compliments, they usually responded more positively. "What was that all about?"

"You stupid idiot," Floyd said. "Are you blind?"

Now Hash peered at Floyd. "What's going on with you two?"

"Nothing."

That recent fog no longer opacified Floyd's eyes. His whole demeanor had risen about six thousand fathoms. Hash decided to let the matter drop for the moment. He'd get to the bottom of this after a few beers on Floyd's back porch. "What are you doing the next couple nights? I need an extra pair of eyes."

"I'm busy."

"Doing what? You just said it wasn't a woman! I thought you wanted to get back into Special Detail."

"I have a lot of shopping to do."

"For what? The complete works of Dostoevsky?"

"Clothes."

"Why, are you going somewhere?"

"No. I mean yes, I might be going away. Maybe on vacation."

"Where to? You didn't tell me about this."

That's because Hash would never trash his present life and fly three thousand miles in pursuit of a sausage: That was about as moronic as listening to opera for two days straight, or reciting Tennyson to the moon. Floyd waved his hand through the air. "I was just toying with the idea, that's all."

Hash remembered reading in his college psychology course something about the sudden fantasies and mood swings of people who had recently received emotional shocks. He forgot what the exact treatment was but seemed to recall something about playing along. "Well, great," he said finally. "Let me know if it's a fishing trip." He took a long drink of water. "By the way, remember that salami you nipped a few days ago?"

Floyd watched Frisk come out of the ladies' room and return to her station. With each step her breasts teetered like buoys in a placid bay. "What about it."

"There were six emeralds inside."

This seemed to amuse Floyd. "Someone's got a sense of humor."

"Well, I don't," Hash snapped. "You would not believe the bullshit that's been coming down the last few days. People are insane." They watched Blustein from Agriculture haul a huge cactus to the incinerator. "You up for a few beers tonight? Maybe at The Outpost?"

"I've got to get to bed early. I have a lot of studying to do. Maps."

It had to be a woman. "Are you free this weekend for a little investigative work?"

Floyd sighed. "Like what."

"I'm trying to locate a courier in Paterson." Hash omitted mentioning that the courier was a dog. He did not know how completely Floyd had recovered his sense of humor since Portia had exited. "I was out there this morning looking around and came across a very odd place. I don't know, I just have this feeling that something's strange there."

"What is it? A house? A storefront?"

Hash had already done a bit of research. "Called Pyrana, Inc. It's like a factory but people live inside of it. They make fancy underwear by day. God knows what goes on at night. Wacko operation, almost reminded me of a commune. When I was there the other day, two of them came to the door wearing fancy white bathrobes. They started arguing about their cook."

A little vein on Floyd's temple commenced a quavery march. "Odd."

"You should have seen this one maniac. Wore green pajamas. Latino, good-looking guy, about our age, combination Napoleon and the Tooth Fairy. He's definitely not on the level."

"Who else."

"God, I wish I knew, Beck. I think it was his wife. Black hair. Her face was pure white. I can't describe the effect. It was like a queen of the vampires looking at me. I thought I'd melt."

"What makes you think it was his wife?"

"She called the guy darling in that special bored way." Hash glanced over. "Well, are you interested? Want to watch the place with me?"

"No!" Floyd stalked off.

Rattled as if Floyd had exploded a paper bag right next to his ear, Hash went to the office and sifted through the papers on his desk. He called his Korean informant in Harlem but received no clearer information regarding the black pups and corsets. He called Agriculture to see if they had analyzed the salami yet: of course not, this was summertime. Half the staff was studying mammalian behavior at Coney Island. And what the hell was going on with Beck? He didn't really think Hash believed all those inept lies about clothes and maps, did he? The guy had been avoiding Hash for weeks, ever since he had brought him to The Outpost. Ever since Portia, actually. Hash was getting tired of it.

"McPhee," he said finally, "I think I need a vacation."

"You shithead, don't even contemplate it!" McPhee snapped. "No way until August!"

"What's going on here?" Hash shouted back. "Is this whole fucking station going berserk?"

Frisk sailed into the office, done for the afternoon. McPhee stared at her new haircut, praying it was a wig so that he could tear it off and make like it was yesterday again. "Don't look for me at the target range tonight, Albert," she said pleasantly, grabbing her jacket. "I'm teaching Beck how to make pot roast."

Hash looked up after she had gone. "That weasly schmuck told me he was studying maps tonight."

McPhee did not answer; he was busy rearranging the customs inspectors' schedules. Beck was going on a three-week leave of absence immediately, even if it meant McPhee had to work the short shifts himself. Florida, eh? McPhee would have preferred Floyd to take a six-month sabbatical to Pluto.

6

No drum majorette, no fire chief across the land could hope for a balmier July Fourth. For the first time in years, the holiday occurred on a Saturday. A placid breeze blossomed at seven in the morning, swished the humidity into the Bay of Fundy, and nestled over New York, talking to itself. The sun arose in a benevolent, satiated mood, having spent the previous twelve hours singeing Australia. Flocculent clouds bobbed along the airstreams, admiring the shadows they trailed upon the verdure below. Indeed, this was a day when even the most fanatical Communist would be grateful to be in America.

The inhabitants of Cliffside Park, New Jersey, lined Anderson Avenue for the parade which would begin at ten and end by noon, dovetailing nicely with their picnic plans. Besides the fire department, the high school marching band, and the Elks, this year's expanded cavalcade included several floats which had been constructed by local merchants and organizations at the behest of the mayor, who was upset that his patriotic speech had endured ten minutes longer than last year's entire parade.

Flag in hand, George Hash stood at curbside with Roberta and Daphne, the two women he had met at The Outpost, watching a marching band blare by. Once these ceremonies were over, they planned to shoot out to Sussex County for some hamburgers and skinny dipping. On the way back to work, Hash would drop the girls off at the Statue of Liberty for tonight's fireworks. Hash had invited Floyd several times to join them; however, scheduled to fly out of JFK that evening and obligated to pack his clothes, bolt his house, and otherwise prepare himself for a monthlong absence, Floyd had demurred.

Roberta took a swig of her diet cola. "That's some mother fire engine."

"You can get a free ride in the hook and ladder truck after the parade," Hash said. "Want to?"

"Yeah, that would be fun."

Daphne hiked her sagging tube top back to her armpits. "I think I'm getting a sunburn," she said. "Where's that baby oil, Ro?"

As the pair oiled each other's shoulders, Hash ogled the thighs of the bypassing color guard: Few sights in all creation quickened him like a woman's stockinged leg rammed in a boot going hup-two-three-four. And he adored those teeny skirts, swishing in march time, which barely covered the ass. Chubby women, flesh rich and dense as triple cream, looked particularly succulent in these outfits.

"I'm hungry," Roberta said.

"There's a fruit stand around the corner," Hash replied, eyes loath to leave the baton twirlers.

"I hate fruit. Anything like a pizza joint around here?"

Hash directed them to a point four blocks off and gave Daphne five bucks: Today the girls would buy beer, Hash would buy food. "Don't stay too long," he said. "The parade's almost over." He slid his wallet back into his pocket. "I'll meet you at the hook and ladder truck in fifteen minutes."

The girls backed into the crowd and Hash reverted to the parade, too late to catch the tail end of the baton twirlers. Instead he faced a float in the shape of a whale, property of the local environmental group. The people surrounding the whale were not in uniform, nor were they marching briskly in consonance: They were distributing pamphlets to the bystanders. Hash scowled at the fellow attempting to hand him an envelope for donations to Worldwide Whale Day. "This is July Fourth," he snapped. "Give me a break." Where the hell were the color guard? The Women's Flute Brigade of Weehauken?

The whale bobbled off, a squadron of Shriners in its wake. Then the mayor passed, waving to his constituents from the rear seat of a Duesenberg as a drum and bugle corps, predominantly male, aimed a popular opus of John Philip Sousa at His Honor's shoulderblades.

Hash's mouth dropped when he saw the following attraction: WHAP, headed by none other than Dr. Portia Clemens striding purposefully as Joan of Arc down the center of Anderson Avenue. Hoisting a red-and-white banner, she wore the same skin-tight pants as when she had tackled him in New York a while back. The other ladies in her crew preferred the Charlie Chaplin look, or a combination of overalls, undershirts, and hiking boots. They were chanting "Por-no No No, Por-no No No" in a rhythm which clashed with the Sousa march preceding them. Perhaps attracted by Hash's malevolent stare, Portia glanced at the spectators: A little smile crimped her lips as she recognized him and marched by.

That scorn tainted the rest of the parade, if not the day, for Hash: Mere sight of the woman affected his digestive tract like a pailful of carbolic acid. Hash waited for Roberta and Daphne at the hook-and-ladder truck for twenty minutes, fuming at the crowds swirling around the booths which many of the marchers had set up at the terminus of the parade route. Where had those two bimbos gone now? Too late Hash recalled that there was a record store next to the pizza parlor.

"Hello, officer," said a voice behind him. "Still looking for pregnant women?"

Within the last few weeks she had acquired a tan and a splash of freckles. He wondered what sort of bathing suit, if any, a feminist wore. "If it isn't Dr. Clemens," he replied. "Still raining on the parade."

"I'm touched that you remember my name," she said. "Our little demonstration in New York must have made quite an impression on you."

"Not really. My name is George Hash."

Dismay marbleized Portia's face. This stranger had just revealed that he knew much more about her than she would ever willingly divulge to him. She did not know how intimately men talked with best friends about their women; but she knew that Floyd and Hash had spent many midnights together over many bottles of beer. By sheer osmosis, he must know her very well.

Portia studied Hash's eyes. "Now I remember you," she said. "We met once. Your wife's name is Pearl. A lovely woman."

She knew damn well they were divorced. "You ladies spent the whole afternoon chatting about fleas and rabies," Hash said. "Delightful."

Roberta and Daphne suddenly returned from deep space. "Georgie," Roberta said, blowing a huge pink bubble with her gum, "come up in the hook and ladder with us."

Portia looked at the pair, then graced Hash with another of those derisive smiles which enraged him. "Your nieces?" she inquired innocently.

"No, much better than that. Roberta and Daphne, this is Miss Clemens. We're going to pick Floyd up and go out to the country this afternoon."

"We are?" Daphne squealed. "I just adore that kinky guy! I can hardly wait to get him skinny dipping."

Were he a god, Hash would have rewarded Daphne with immortality. "Ladies, why don't you stand on line for the hook and ladder ride? I'll be there in a moment. Then we're off to the lake."

Portia watched them run off. "I see you two boys have been amusing yourselves."

"Floyd's never looked better," Hash lied. "There's nothing like sex with a teenage nymphomaniac to get the rust out of your system." He glanced down at Portia and pretended to act startled. "Oh, pardon me! I'd forgotten that such talk offends you."

"You stupid ass," Portia said.

Hash smiled: He had scored twice now. The lady was not made of solid wood, as he had thought. "Well, I should be running. We've got to get Floyd back from this picnic in good time. He's flying out of town tonight for a month." He winked at Portia. "With another woman. Don't tell Daphne, it'll break the kid's heart." He turned to go. "Hey, how are your dogs? You still performing lobotomies over at that clinic?"

"Much more interesting stuff than that, Mr. Hash."

A little latch clicked in his brain and he took another look at Portia, this time not as a professional neuterer, but as a criminal of major stature. Idiot! Why hadn't he thought of this before? Of course she would be the perfect person to implant a microchip in a dog: She had the technique and she had the warped brain. She hated men so violently that overthrowing the country George Washington had created would barely begin to appease her. Hash could easily picture Portia bent over a slashed, anesthetised pug in the deep of the night, holding a microchip to the light with a pair of surgical tweezers, then placing it perfectly in the open wound, sewing it up . . .

Portia walked away. Hash caught her by the arm. "Wait a minute."

"Oh, now we're a cop again?" she said. "Shove it, cowboy."

He released her; Roberta and Daphne were calling to him from the front of the hook and ladder line. As he watched Portia stalk off, Hash wondered if she blurted secrets in the throes of sexual pleasure, and if so, what they were.

When her eyes opened she was lying on her back, hands folded serenely across her stomach, in the pose of a newly-entombed Juliet, or Sleeping Beauty awaiting the kiss of Prince Magic. Viola never slept on her back; it was a precarious attitude in which to leave the body unaware. With a minimum of effort, an attacker might slit her throat, bury a dagger in her belly, or, were he a randy male, edge in half a rape before she came to her senses. Why was she in this position now? Because of the Goldberg belt, Eugene's first paternal invention. He had amputated the ear cuffs from six pairs of headphones and sewn them into a wide, fluffy cummerbund which Viola was to wear over her stomach when she went to bed. A little wire ran from the side seam into a CD player which Eugene had bolted to the nightstand: He wanted his heir to absorb the *Goldberg Variations* along with the more mundane nutrients in its mother's placenta. The child would emerge a genius.

Without disturbing the Goldberg belt, Viola moved her head sideways to read the clock: almost seven. Eugene was snoring lightly alongside her, four fingers draped over her arm. He could not sleep unless some portion of his flesh touched hers: She was his connection to slumberland, he said. Viola slowly turned her head to the other side and studied her husband's face in the rich yellow light. Even after two years, waking up with Eugene in the same bed still surprised her. Not that it was an unpleasant surprise. It was like getting home from the store and finding that she had unintentionally bought unsalted, instead of salted, cashews: not exactly the taste she had in mind, but in the long run, probably healthier. Viola blew a shock of hair off Eugene's eyebrow. He looked so young. Misled by his pink cheeks and cherubic demeanor, people habitually underestimated his age by fifteen years. They were off by twenty when he wore a hat.

Eugene's lithe snoring suddenly ceased and he opened his eyes. "Euclid," he said.

"I what?"

"Euclid. That's what we're going to name the baby. If it's a boy."

"Euclid Phillips? You can't be serious."

"The father of geometry. Civilization owes a great debt to Euclid."

"Let's not be the first to pay it off, Eugene. What will his friends call him? Yuke? Clid? The boy will murder us in our bed before he hits eighth grade."

Eugene looked hurt. "Why can't they just call him Euclid? No one ever called my father Fin or Ass. They called him Phineas."

"That's what he thinks." Viola kissed her husband's cheek. "Go back to sleep, honey. Let's forget the Greeks and Romans for a while. Can you think of some English names maybe?"

"There are several from Arthurian legend," Eugene said, drifting away. "Mordred . . . Godfrey . . ." The snoring resumed.

Viola hoped the baby would inherit its father's ability to fall asleep and remain thus for many hours. Eugene did not know how unusual this gift was, but he had not slept with many men in the upper-tax bracket. Unwilling to let the day go, overleavened with tomorrow's agenda, they fretted in their beds; at four in the morning they were still making telepathic conference calls. When the alarm clock finally sounded, they lunged at it, bodies wound up like tin soldiers responding to a dawn artillery raid. A woman could keep them under the sheets only if she had set the alarm for a half hour earlier, and even then, their minds were already on the counterattack. Viola laughed to herself very softly so that Eugene would not feel the mattress quaver, and wake up. What made her think of him, she wondered; it had been years.

Eugene's hand slipped off his wife's arm. He turned over and backed up so that his rear end snuggled Viola's side. She patted his hip, dubious and amused that there lay her co-contributor to the gene pool: not quite the six-three, pearl-toothed, bemuscled, nimble model she had ordered from Divine Providence. His character contained no flecks of cruel, brute passion which she had previously found so indispensable in a man. Eugene was simple sunshine, no twisted ravines, no brumous moors. She had not expected that such a personality could have contented her so. The men she had previously known, and loved so hopelessly, prided themselves upon being more complex than that.

Eugene had been one of the first customers to walk into her Madison Avenue shop when it opened ten years ago. Viola remembered him distinctly: He bought a black peignoir embroidered with flamingos and a half slip, size eight, for a woman he would only describe as "my lovely perch." After three years Viola finally realized this meant a fish, and that Eugene could bestow no higher compliment upon a woman. Besides the usual holidays, he visited the shop at irregular intervals, needing a gift to commemorate Thomas Edison's birthday, or an anniversary of the first moon landing, or the invention of the steam engine. If Viola was busy, he waited for her; if she was not in the shop at all, he came back another day. Suddenly he did not return for two years. Viola noticed his absence after several weeks and assumed he was wintering in Florida or damming the Nile. After six months she began to worry: Eugene was a mugger's Golconda. Finally, when she sent him a Christmas card which did not come back by April, she knew that something had happened to either him, or to his perch: He was not the type to vanish without saying goodbye. She missed him. He was a customer of wealth, taste, and mischievous imagination.

He finally returned one miserable March morning. Viola was pulling underpants over half a mannequin and at first didn't recognize him; he had lost a lot of weight. That made him look older. "Eugene!" she called, ditching the panties, crossing to the other side of the shop.

He looked as if he had had a serious operation and was still a little suspicious of survival. "Hello," he said. "Thanks for the Christmas card."

"Is everything all right?"

"Yes." His eyes roamed her face and Viola knew that something had happened to the perch. "You're looking well."

"You too." Viola put a hand on his arm, perhaps in sympathy. "May I show you something?"

"I was wondering if you would be interested in doing a little project for me."

"I'd be delighted."

Eugene removed a silver case from his pocket and held a tiny fishing fly between two fingers. "I've always been very lucky with this," he said. "I wonder if you would be able to embroider it on some blue silk for me."

Viola looked at the brilliant yellow feathers specked with black. "What would you be making this into, Eugene?"

"A robe."

Several times over the following weeks he came back to review her sketches and choose the silk. Each visit he looked a bit ruddier. She noticed he had stopped wearing his wedding ring and wondered about the recipient of the new robe. Whoever it was, he'd spoil her. "Viola," he said in May when the robe was finished, "I'm going to have a little party this weekend. I'd be delighted if you could make it."

"What's the occasion?"

"The two-hundredth anniversary of the invention of the hydraulic pump."

From their wayside conversations, Viola knew Eugene was an inventor and that he spent a lot of time fishing with friends. "Sounds great," she said.

"Do you play bridge, by chance?" Eugene said.

Was he kidding? She hadn't remained in the same chair for over twenty minutes since her dentist had capped a molar in January. Even the hairdresser couldn't get her to stick around for a blow dry. "Not in this life."

"I see. Never mind. We'll also be showing movies of our last expedition on the St. Lawrence River."

Thus Viola showed up at Eugene's apartment dressed like a librarian going to a bookmark exhibition. The moment he answered the door in a morning coat and waders she knew she had drastically misjudged him.

"Viola," he said. A half-naked woman in a toga flew through the air behind him. "How sweet of you to come." In one hand Eugene held a glass of champagne. With the other he drew her inside.

Laughing, drinking, looking nothing like her idea of inventors and anglers, one hundred people milled about Eugene's tremendous apartment. Off in the corner a pianist was slushing through "Autumn in New York" as couples swayed gently against each other, osculating sporadically. Very few guests were actually sitting on Eugene's furniture; rather, they draped over the arms and backs, stood on the cushions, and blew bubbles through little plastic hoops as they conversed with vicinal heads. Overhead flew several miniature dirigibles, motors purring as they skirted the upper bookcases and occasionally bounced into a wall. The waiters serving champagne were all dressed as monks; about the room stood people in the garb of priests, game wardens, Balinese princesses, and French generals. It was difficult to say whether these were actually costumes or the typical attire of the people who wore them. Viola quickly saw that everyone in here had two traits in common: lunacy and great intelligence. The combination was extinct in her line of work.

Eugene removed a glass of champagne from a silver tray. "Long live the hydraulic pump," he toasted. "Would you like to see the game room?"

He showed her twenty people locked in an intense duplicate bridge tournament; the prize was a week for two in Paraguay, a country which Eugene felt had been unjustly neglected by American tourists. A large and enthusiastic crowd was watching fish movies in the music room as *La Bohème* boomed through the speakers. Before removing his waders for the evening, Eugene retrieved six huge lobsters from a tank in his downstairs laboratory and handed them over to the cook, who was preparing a midnight supper. He took her on a tour of his laboratory and told her all about his inventions. From the moment Viola walked in the door, in fact, he did not leave her; only much later, when everyone had gone, did Viola realize that Eugene's guests had taken one look at him with her and left them entirely alone.

The party gradually dissipated around eight in the morning when, in a breakfast ceremony, Eugene awarded the tickets to Paraguay to a fellow dressed in a kilt and bow tie. The two of them were sitting on the balcony eating lobster, watching sailboats slither up the Hudson, when the last dishwasher finally left. "That was a wonderful evening," Viola said. "Thank you for inviting me." She did not, however, get up to leave: That would hurt. Somehow over the past twelve hours, with mere words and soft dancing, Eugene had grafted himself onto her, filling all the holes of the decade since he had first wandered into the shop on Madison Avenue. She felt she had known him all her life.

Eugene lay his fork down; Viola thought he was going to offer to drive her home. "Would you marry me?" he said.

"Excuse me?"

"I know that you have no need of a husband and that you must hear requests like this every week, from men you would consider much more seriously than me. But ever since I saw you ten years ago arranging undershirts in your window, my life has not been the same."

She couldn't even swallow so Eugene continued. "Now that I've finally gotten you here, and am in a position to even ask you to stay . . ." He smiled sadly, like an old man who had outlived his entire family and realized there would be no one at his own funeral now. "I know this is sudden but please say yes, Viola. Life is so short."

When in this age, from whom, would she ever hear a confession like that again? "Yes."

"You mean that, don't you."

"I mean it."

He kissed her hand and looked at her for a moment. "Thank you. You've made me the happiest man alive."

Hardly; he was ninety-nine percent there already. They married at City Hall two weeks later. One of Viola's wedding presents was the bathrobe with the yellow flies. Another was a honeymoon in Oregon for the opening of trout season. Eugene was a model husband, perhaps because he had already had years of experience. He gave her room and he came in close with that delicate, perfect timing of men who realize that they need their wives much more than their wives will ever need them. Before seeing the justice of the peace, Eugene had changed his will, making his future wife sole beneficiary of his estate. His immediate, absolute trust humbled Viola: She had thought they were going to the lawyer to draw up a marriage contract. Once again, she had underestimated Eugene. The man preferred to live in another age, when Earth was a miraculous, ever-ameliorating planet and promises, once made, were kept.

Eugene sighed and woke up. "How's my baby?"

"The big one or the deaf one?"

He looked down. "You don't like that Goldberg belt, do you."

"I don't know. Maybe if we piped a little Stockhausen through it once in a while I'd feel a little better."

Eugene put an ear to the belt. "It's almost over. Then we can get up." His mouth played with her left nipple a moment. "I've always been fond of Mildred, you know."

"Mildred who?"

"The name Mildred. Old English. It means both mild and strong."

"Sounds like a manicurist."

Eugene's mouth crawled to the opposite nipple and stayed there a while. He wanted to get Viola in shape for heavy nursing. Then he suddenly leapt out of bed. "My God, the glue's set on the cradle!"

"Will you stop this, Eugene?" Viola cried. "You're driving me out of my mind!"

"Don't get up! You'll tear the wires!" Eugene rushed back to bedside. "I'm sorry, darling. That was thoughtless of me." Again he listened to the Goldberg belt. "Okay. The coast is clear."

Viola tore the contraption off and went straight to the bathroom. "There's a company picnic today," she said. "I hope you can interrupt work on your pneumatic cradle rocker long enough to eat a few hotdogs with my employees."

"That's right! What time are we leaving?"

"We should get out of here by eleven. It starts at noon."

"This is Saturday already? How did I lose a day?"

Viola dressed and went shopping for maternity clothes. The preponderance of outfits with starched white collars and big puffy sleeves put her in a foul mood: Already mothers were mentally rolling back the clocks, trying to look like overstuffed children. She finally found a voluminous sundress and one sailor outfit. When its charm waned, she'd wear pajamas like Nestor. Or she'd lop a foot off a few of her robes. Even in truncated form, at least they were her style.

Eugene was applying the final daubs of shellac to his new cradle when Viola returned. "Look at this, honey," he called when he heard the door slam upstairs. "It's almost done."

Viola looked into the hole in her foyer floor. There stood Eugene, paintbrush in hand, poised over a cradle about the size of a Honda. He had been working on it for three weeks. "Come on down," he said. "I can hardly wait to show you this. Take the slide."

"You do plan to put stairs in here, don't you," Viola said, brushing her pants off. "I can't see your mother taking a slide to the nursery."

"We're going to have a mini-elevator," Eugene said. "Over there, in the corner. It will be voice-activated. Goes up when someone recites 'Humpty Dumpty,' down when it hears 'Jack and Jill.' "

"Aha."

Eugene held up a sack of potatoes. "Now watch this," he said, placing it in the cradle. A few lights above the headboard came on and the cradle began very slowly rocking. Soft music trickled from the speakers recessed in the sides.

"*Adagio for Strings?*" Viola said. "Really, Eugene."

"Shhh! Watch this!"

Another red light blinked, a hatch opened, and a warm bottle of milk descended from overhead. Gently as a blind kitten, it located the sack of potatoes, probed it in various spots, and finally wormed the nipple through an air hole in the plastic. "It's programmed to find the mouth," Eugene said. "If it hits an ear by mistake, the drip mechanism will close."

"What if the kid's lying on its stomach? With no diapers?"

Eugene had not considered that. "Hmmmm," he said. "I'll have to rewrite the program a little. Thanks, sweetheart." He scribbled on a pad. "I'm still waiting for a few parts to come in. Then I can install a computerized rattle and a TV in the headboard. Thought I'd put together a little video program."

"Of what?"

"Oh, dancing triangles and parallelograms. Elementary geometry."

With a cradle like this, parents would bore the kid stiff thirteen years before he or she became a teenager. "It's super, Eugene," Viola said, kissing his cheek. "You should patent it."

"Never. This remains a Phillips family treasure. You never know. We might have to use it again."

She looked at her watch. "We've got to be out of here in fifteen minutes. Nestor will kill me if I'm not at that picnic by noon. That's when he's choosing the softball teams."

Eugene regretfully put his paintbrushes away. "How about Edwina," he said.

"No more names until the amniocentesis!" Viola pressed a few fingers into her forehead, probing for the shrapnel. "I'm sorry, Eugene. The humidity gives me a headache."

"Let's forget the picnic. We'll stay inside and read all those school catalogs I got in the mail."

She'd rather hang-glide naked off the World Trade Center. Viola left the nursery. "Don't forget your flippers."

Pyrana, Inc. held its annual July Fourth picnic at a park along the Palisades. Nestor had begun the celebration seven years ago, when personnel fornication reached its preherpes peak; he felt, aside from the obvious patriotic overtones of the day, that this would be a fine opportunity for those employees conducting intramural affairs to get to know the children and spouses of their lovers, and perhaps feel impelled to break off the exhausting liaisons which had commenced at the Christmas party six months ago. The idea worked for two years. Then the spouses of the employees began having affairs with each other. At that point, of course, the July Fourth picnic had become tradition and Nestor could only smile pleasantly and distribute hotdogs to the new rash of adulterers which he had created.

It was an exhilarating drive out of Manhattan until Viola got a speeding ticket for doing eighty on the George Washington Bridge; she had been trying to make up the half hour lost as Eugene sought his flippers amid the rubble of nursery construction. Then she missed the turn to the picnic and had to zip another exit up and back on the Palisades Parkway as her husband delivered a soporific lecture upon the perils of exceeding the speed limit and how these habits must change in the future. They arrived at the picnic well after Nestor had divvied the employees into teams.

He was standing on the pitching mound distributing baseball caps. "Well! Where have you two been? Interviewing nannies?"

"Very funny," Viola said, snatching a cap. "How's everything going?"

"Fine. Terrific." Nestor sniffed the air. "Smell that roast pig. You can guess who's not cooking today." He had hired a caterer to take care of the picnic.

"Where's your date, Nestor?" Viola asked. "Weren't you going to bring one?"

"Forgot. Where's that mutt? Smudge! Here pup!"

The dog came skidding around a picnic table, barely outrunning a marauding toddler. Smudge had just about gotten the hang of using four legs at once now and was putting on a little weight. He looked like a hairy balloon. Nestor caught the pup and tucked him under an arm. "I forgot the leash," he said. "This beast is going mad in the great outdoors." He looked around. "I don't suppose anyone here has a spare." The only animals in leashes were *homo sapiens*, age two.

"We could tie him to my fishing reel," Eugene suggested. "It's twenty-pound test line. Then he could roam in a hundred-yard range."

"Great. Thanks, Gene," Nestor said. Eugene hurried to the Porsche. Nestor turned to Viola. "You look a wreck today. Where did you find such a foul outfit?"

"Hey pal, you can go shopping for me next time. I thought it would be bad policy for both of us to show up in pajamas."

"Why? Everyone thinks we're married anyhow."

Viola scowled at the towering Palisades. That would have been one week of bliss followed by extortionate hell. "Which team am I on?"

"None. You're the scorekeeper. I don't want you getting hurt."

Viola waved to a few men she vaguely remembered from previous picnics. "I'm not Grandma Moses, for Christ's sake. And I'm about ready to bash the both of your heads together."

"Who? Me and Eugene? For taking care of you?"

Mai Ping, Nestor's favorite employee, came to the pitcher's mound. "Here you go, honey," he said, handing her a baseball cap. "You're on the red team."

Panting, Eugene returned with the fishing line and slipped a loop through Smudge's collar. "There we go." The dog scuttled away like a turtle on speed the moment its feet touched the grass. "I'll just tighten the tension, Nestor. That'll tire him out a bit."

Viola pouted. "I'm having a hotdog."

"No you're not. I've given orders not to serve anyone until the sixth inning." Nestor cupped his hands over his mouth. "Okay everyone, let's get this game rolling! Work up an appetite!"

"Which team's Eugene on?" Viola asked.

"He's the batboy. I don't want a repeat of last year." Eugene had gotten hit in the ear with a wild pitch. "Get over there, Gene. The bats are in the pickup truck."

Viola looked at her partner. "And what are you? Umpire?"

"Spectator." He accompanied Viola to the grandstand behind home plate, pausing once to reel Smudge in a few yards. The employees and their spouses, as they did every year, watched the Cuban in pajamas and the woman in the pink sailor outfit, the balding batboy, and now the dog on a fishing line, cross the field. Few people believed that the batboy had actually married, much less impregnated, the sailor; others thought the sailor and the Cuban in pajamas were siblings. No one could figure out the dog on the fishing line. All they knew for sure was that, between the three of them, they could probably buy the Metropolitan Museum of Art. Somehow it didn't make sense.

Nestor and Viola sat in the front-row void which their employees had created for them. The pitcher threw his first strike. "Hey, did you see yourself on *OmniFem* last night?" Nestor said.

Viola had completely forgotten. "No. How was it?"

"Gloria did mucho editing. Cut out all but your most flattering feminist remarks. She used mostly me, actually."

"Surprise."

Nestor gave Smudge a bit more line so that the dog could reach a distant sandbox. "The L.A. store ordered two thousand robes this morning. Said the phone rang off the hook after the show."

"Damn you, Nestor," she said between her teeth, "I told you that would happen." Someone hit a triple and the wooden bench vibrated beneath them. "So did you call Dingleball this morning and ask him for the two thousand robes?"

"No answer. It's Saturday."

Viola watched an employee step to the plate. That woman would collect a nice, neat paycheck every Thursday. She'd punch out at five, free, and step into a separate existence devoid of Pyrana, Inc. If the mill burned down, if no one bought red garters that season, if Dingleball sent four million robes to Mars by mistake, that was not her problem. She had not seen the company when it was just two innocents in a dingy fifth-floor walk-up. To her, Pyrana was inextinguishable and impersonal as Fort Knox; Viola was the duchess who went on TV between trips to the bank. That woman would go home tonight, sunburnt and barmy, and not once would textile wars or capital gains taxes have troubled her mind. A picnic was a picnic. "Call Dingleball when you get home," Viola said. "Tell him you and a bayonet are flying to Switzerland."

A caterer motioned to Nestor from the side of the grandstand. "Hold this for me, will you," Nestor said, handing Viola the fishing rod. Soon he returned. "They left two kegs of beer in Paterson. I'll go pick them up."

"Should I come along?"

"Nah, you hold the fort. And the dog." Nestor drove off in the pickup truck.

Viola tucked her black hair under the baseball cap, letting the breeze relieve her shoulders. Today she would have liked to drive way upstate and find a secluded lake, get naked, and float with the fish, away from Eugene, away from Pyrana, away from cribs and cradles, and slowly convince herself that it was all right to bring another life into the world. She looked around the bleachers and the playground: children everywhere. Each one of them had a mother who had weighed the odds and then damned the torpedos. Why were her hormones taking so long to persuade her brain that maternity was a woman's most sublime calling?

Eugene came to the stands and sat beside Viola. No one needed a batboy. "How do you feel?" he said. "That sun too hot?"

"No, no."

"Hello? Ms. Flury? We saw you on television last night," said a voice behind Viola. She turned around and saw the wife of a sales rep with a baby on her lap. "Didn't we, Lois?" The slumbrous Lois did not confirm. "I had no idea you met Mr. Buffez at a masquerade ball."

Those were the days when Nestor was still enamored of women. Now he preferred the company of dogs. "That's right." Viola felt a small tug on the fishing line and checked that Smudge had not gotten himself wrapped around a water fountain. The line disappeared behind a hemlock.

Eugene turned around and spotted Lois the baby. "What a lovely child," he said. "Exquisite as a Raphael. How old is she?"

"Five months."

Eugene played with a tiny toe. "Does she have a good appetite?"

"Never stops. I'm feeding her every two hours, day and night."

"Is that so? Bottle or breast?"

"Eugene," Viola said. "Restrain yourself."

"Good old mother's milk," the woman replied. "But I suppose I'm taking a chance. Last time I got severely cracked nipples."

Eugene shook his head in sympathy. "Were you nursing too long? Was it winter? What kind of salve did your doctor prescribe for that?"

"If you'll excuse me." Viola turned back to the softball game. Richie the shipping clerk stepped to the plate, swung, and missed. He changed bats.

Eugene patted the blond furze on Lois's scalp. "Does she sleep well?"

"Not this one. Screams all night long."

"We're expecting our first child in February," Eugene said.

"So I hear. That's fabulous." The woman shifted the snoozing Lois to her shoulder. "Are you going to childbirth classes yet?"

"They start next week," Eugene said. "Viola and I can hardly wait."

Richie took another vicious swing at a pitch and clouted himself in the shoulder instead. "Will you look at that klutz," Viola remarked. "He thinks he's still in the shipping room."

Eugene and the woman didn't even hear her. Now they were debating the merits of a diaper service versus throwaways. "How many do you go through a week?" Eugene asked.

"Depends on Lois's plumbing," the woman said. "You should have seen her brother when I switched him to mashed potatoes and peas."

Lunging at the sphere hurtling toward him, Richie finally got his bat to connect with the softball. It shot straight into the line of hemlocks behind first base. Then a loud squeal split the air.

"Shit," said Viola, reeling in the fishing line. It snagged on a lawn chair. She threw the pole down and tore into the trees. There lay Smudge, whimpering feebly upon a cushion of moss. "The ball's over here," Viola muttered to the first baseman. "It hit Nestor's dog."

The fellow came rushing over. "Oh Jesus, he's gonna kill me."

Richie burst into the bushes, saw the damage, and repeated verbatim the sentiments of the first baseman. He dropped to his knees and touched Smudge. "You all right, fella?" In reply the pup yipped sharply. "Looks like a nosebleed and a busted ribcage. Maybe a hemorrhage," he told Viola.

"Don't be asinine," she snapped. "Where's the nearest vet? I'll get him patched up before Nestor even gets back. You can tell him a kid sat on the dog."

"There's a clinic in Hoboken," Richie said. He gave Viola directions.

"Would it be open on July Fourth?"

"It's always open. I took my spaniel there on Christmas."

Eugene and Mai Ping tromped through the underbrush. "Viola? What's going on?"

"Smudge stopped a line drive. I'm taking him to the vet."

"Let me come along. I'll drive."

The dog would bleed to death by the time Eugene poked down to Hoboken. "You and Mai stay here and pacify Nestor. That's much more important." She bent over the dog. "Smudge, you're just a little bruised." The pup made no sound as she lifted him. "I think he just got the wind knocked out of him."

"So how come his stomach's bleeding?" quavered Richie, about to cry.

"He just scraped it," Viola said. "Get back to the game. Everything's under control. Nestor is not going to come after you with a baseball bat."

Unconvinced, Richie receded through the hemlocks. Viola wrapped Smudge in the first baseman's sweatshirt, lay him in the Porsche, and blew out of the parking lot. Traffic was sparse. In fifteen minutes, Viola arrived at the clinic. She rang the bell, banged the knocker: nothing. "Damn." She kicked the door and it suddenly swung open.

Dressed in a clean, white smock, Dr. Portia Clemens studied the intruder, then the intruder's foot, for an exaggerated moment. "Yes?"

Viola immediately disliked the woman. She had stared very inhospitably at her pink sailor outfit. "My pup's hurt," she said. "Are you the nurse?"

"I am Dr. Clemens."

Big deal. She didn't have to say it as if she had discovered penicillin. "Could you please check my dog? He was smacked with a softball."

"Where is he?" Viola led Portia to her car. Smudge lay whimperng on the front seat. "You picked a wounded animal up and carried it?"

"What was I supposed to do? Float him down the Hudson?"

Leaning into the car, Portia began expertly probing Smudge's potbelly. "This is totally irresponsible. Where was this dog's leash?"

"He was on a fishing line."

"He's bleeding."

"I know that."

Portia gently picked Smudge up and carried him inside. "Wait here, if you don't mind," she told Viola outside a door marked Laboratory. "This is a restricted area. Please fill out a registration card as you wait."

Viola agitatedly paced the cool, gray hall, wondering what Dr. Clemens was doing in a laboratory on July Fourth while the rest of America belched its way through parades and hortatory speeches. Antiseptic hung in the air like a dowager's perfume. Diplomas lined a long stretch of the immaculate walls: Dr. Clemens had more degrees than a thermometer. After the sheepskins Viola strolled past a gallery of dog photographs. Each was neatly labeled with the dog's name, malady, and date of discharge from the clinic.

Viola was standing in the farthest corner of the hall staring at a picture as Dr. Clemens emerged from the laboratory with Smudge. "Your dog is fine," Portia called.

Viola did not move. "Who is this," she said.

Portia walked over and peered at the picture. "That's Champ, a Dalmatian who has undergone one of medicine's first male-to-female sex changes."

"Who's the man," Viola said. The eyes, though made of paper, bored through her stomach. His mouth remained nocturnal as ever, still waiting for moonrise before smiling. He still combed his hair straight back; was that white frilling the temples, or a reflection of the glass?

"That's Floyd Beck." Portia looked at Viola. "Do you know him?"

"We went to concerts together when we were young. I haven't seen him in years."

Portia was no idiot. "Really? Floyd never mentioned concerts to me."

Viola had never mentioned concerts to Eugene either. "How is he?"

"Fine, I suppose. I'll be seeing him this afternoon."

It was indirect contact but Viola's pulse withered anyhow. She did not like the thought of Dr. Clemens and Floyd seeing each other for any reason. "Is that his dog?"

"Champ is my patient. Floyd has little interest in my work. He's a customs agent." Portia blew a speck off the picture. "Actually, I haven't seen him in weeks. Too busy."

Then she was more insensate than the walls of her clinic. Viola took Smudge. Across his stomach was a little bandage. "He's all right?"

"Puppies are very resilient. Could you tell me a little more about the cuts on his abdomen? The wound apparently reopened a little."

Viola remembered Nestor saying something about the dog having been abused. "I think he tangled with a tomcat." She reached for her wallet. "What do I owe you?"

"Fifty dollars."

Viola pulled out a hundred. "Sorry. Hope you have change."

Portia disappeared into the office. Again Viola stared at the picture of Floyd. His eyes hadn't changed a bit. She wondered if he had finally forgotten about her.

Portia met Viola at the front door of the clinic. "Here you are. You have filled out a registration card, I presume?"

"On the desk." Viola thanked her and drove away.

Floyd and Frisk had just about finished washing the dishes when the timer above his oven went off. He flung down the towel in his hand and slipped on a pair of potholder mitts which were supposed to look like beagles. They belonged to Portia but she never used them. "Well, what do you think," he said.

Frisk poked the meat loaf. "That's done." She stuck a fork in the potatoes. "So are these." For the last ten days, directly after work, Frisk had been teaching Floyd what little she knew about cooking. He had told her he was going to Florida to care for a sick uncle. Floyd had learned to boil noodles, potatoes, and cabbage, and had familiarized himself with such esoterica as peas and now meat loaf. Cooking procedures were much simpler than Floyd had thought, although he still had trouble with coffee. Last night they had tried to make an apple pie, failed abysmally, and decided to stick to stewed prunes for Uncle's dessert.

Floyd pulled out two plates. "It's kind of a hot day for meat loaf but someone's got to eat this stuff." He was flying to Europe that evening.

Frisk removed her apron and sat at the table. "Too bad your uncle doesn't have a grill," she said, handing Floyd a knife. "Half-inch slices."

He began carving. "Where'd you learn this recipe?"

"My mother. She said the way to a man's heart was through his stomach." Frisk guffawed. "What bullshit. Men don't have hearts. They don't have balls any more, either."

He did not know what to say. In two weeks, Frisk and he had not divagated from the subject of Food, purchase and preparation of. The name McPhee had not once come up. But a lowgrade tension had developed in the kitchen: A man and a woman did not spend ten consecutive evenings placing comestibles in their mouths without wondering a little about the other's grander appetites. "Men are just a bit confused lately," Floyd said. "I can swear to that."

"What's so confusing? You love someone, you get married."

Exactly what Floyd had thought many years ago. He had lost out to a third wheel also. Poor Frisk: The rage would seep into her bones and remain there forever, like carbon 14, unless she neutralized it with a better man. "McPhee's been married for thirty years," he said. "You weren't even born when he already had two kids. No amount of meat loaf is going to make him forget that."

Frisk's face went bright red. "You know about Albert and me?"

"The whole department's known about you two for years."

She slowly swallowed a cheekful of potatoes. "I guess you know why he approved your vacation leave so fast then." Frisk pushed her plate away and walked out to the deck. For one moment, watching her rippling, liquid rear end, Floyd wanted to drag her by the hair into his bedroom and rip her clothes off. Then he thought, no. Not when she was in this vitiated condition. She'd hate him afterward. And not today. He had to finish packing. This was not the time to raid McPhee's mistress. Sighing, he followed her to the deck. She was right: Men had no balls any more.

Frisk stood calm as an elm looking across the river at the Empire State Building. "I miss him," she said.

Oh God! Suicide! Floyd hugged her consolingly, glad that sunlight blinded him; were the moon in his eyes, he might be tempted to kiss her instead. "Poor baby."

He couldn't believe he was out here saying this, or hearing this. Two weeks ago she was just Frisk, Aphrodite of Customs & Immigration, McPhee's TNT, the lady who ran the monthly contraband contest among the agents. Now he didn't know what she was, but she was careering in his direction. Still, Floyd couldn't let her go; Frisk felt like steel and velvet and peaches in his arms.

"Ahem! Excuse me!"

Floyd and Frisk flew apart like an exploding grenade: Hash stood at the edge of the deck. "What in Jesus are you doing here," Floyd said.

Hash grinned and Floyd could have belted him: He thought he had interrupted some sort of indolent, booby sex game. "Happy July Fourth. I just wanted to say goodbye before you left tonight, Floyd. Figured you'd be out back. Hello, Friskie. You look staggering, as usual."

"Aren't you supposed to be working?" she said.

"Tonight."

Round the bend tumbled Roberta and Daphne. Forward momentum ceased the moment they saw Frisk: Few items shocked more than the unexpected presence of a woman. "Hi girls," Floyd said. "Long time no see."

"Hi Floyd." Roberta's face could barely cut a smile. "I guess we'll wait in the car. Forget the double date, Daph."

"One minute and I'll be out," Hash called. "Why don't you change into your bathing suits?"

"You told us not to bring any." The girls left.

"Would you believe nieces," Hash said. Frisk's frown was embarrassing him.

"No." She went into the kitchen.

"Listen, I'm really sorry," Hash said, hopping onto the deck. "I had no idea you guys were getting it on like this."

Floyd suddenly yanked Hash by the collar. "She's teaching me to make meat loaf, understand?" He flung him disgustedly away. "Sorry. I guess I need this vacation."

"I'll say." Hash straightened his shirt. Now was obviously not the time to bring up Portia; Beck would strangle him. Meat loaf? Who ate that but the inmates of prisons and insane asylums? "The girls and I thought you might like a little swim before you took off. Clear your head."

"Thanks, I've got to finish packing and mow the lawn." Now Floyd felt a bit sheepish. "Beer? Would you and the girls like some lemonade for the trip?"

"No thanks." Hash followed Floyd into the kitchen, where Frisk was finishing her meal. "You mean you two really were making meat loaf?"

"What does it look like," she said, "pea soup?"

"See you at the office, honey," Hash waved. He and Floyd walked into the living room. Folded neatly upon the couch lay sweaters, jackets, and aprons. "You're taking all this stuff to Florida?" Hash asked. "Won't you be a little hot?"

"Air conditioning," Floyd said. "It's wicked down there."

From the bannister hung a brand-new tuxedo and two expensive suits. Floyd did not spend the money he had inherited often, but when he did, chunks of it disappeared. "What's this for?" Hash said. "Your fishing trips?"

Floyd kicked himself for having brought Hash through the house instead of walking him around the side to his car. "Night life."

"I thought you said you rented a trailer in a mobile park."

"So what if I did?" Floyd snapped. "They organize games and stuff."

"Where exactly is this place in Florida," Hash said. "Someone should know where you are just in case an emergency comes up."

"Frisk knows," Floyd lied. "But she's not telling, so don't ask."

Hash believed that. At the door he stopped. "I hope you get better, Floyd, really. You haven't been yourself at all." He was depressed that, for all his thousands of hours and dollars trying, he could end up with nothing better than Roberta and Daphne while Floyd had the run of creatures like Frisk and that she-dragon Portia for practically nothing. "Meat loaf," he muttered to himself. "I never would have thought of that in a million years." He shook Floyd's hand. "Have a wonderful vacation. Don't sleep with any alligators."

Floyd watched Hash dispiritedly tread his front steps and for a moment was tempted to call him back and tell him everything. But Frisk was here and he detested maudlin farewell speeches. He went back to the kitchen.

She had just finished her meat loaf. "I should be going," she said. "My sister is having a barbecue and the whole family will be there. Whoopee."

The last time his whole family had been together was in a funeral home twenty-seven years ago. She had no idea how lucky she was. "Does your family know about McPhee?"

"My sister does. She told me from the beginning I was wasting my time." Frisk took her plate to the sink. "I didn't believe her."

Floyd realized that besides family, she had something else he had never had: consummation. Which was the slower death, forever wanting the lover one had never had, or wanting back the lover one had forever lost? It depended upon the quality of consummation, he supposed. God forbid that it should be all one hoped for. He took his plate to the sink. "I don't know what to tell you."

Frisk wrapped the meat loaf and potatoes in some foil and wiped the table. "You know what kills me?" She threw the sponge in the sink. "I'll never have his children."

"Have someone else's children," Floyd said. "The kids will never know the difference." He packed the contents of his refrigerator in a bag and gave it to Frisk. They walked to her car. "Thanks for everything," he said. "I appreciate this more than you know."

"Ditto," she said, patting his cheek, convinced he had dragged her through this little cooking class rigamarole strictly to take her mind off McPhee. "Write me a postcard from Florida. Let me know how your uncle's doing."

Again Floyd had a pang of conscience; this time he responded to it. "I'm not really going to Florida. And I don't have an uncle."

She was quiet for a moment. "I don't get it."

"I'm going to Switzerland to make sausages."

"Is this some sort of yuppie wine-tasting vacation?" No wonder he had kept it a secret. They would have laughed him out of the terminal.

"My father was a butcher," Floyd said. "He had a book of sausage recipes. One of his old Swiss friends is going to help me make them."

"What for?"

Well, dear, life is but a dream. I was sitting at home, innocently crying into my boots, listening to the Franck Quintet, when the Angel of Death made another pass over the couch. Knows me well. She's been flying lower and lower all the time and one of these days She's going to land on me. I have no heirs and no family. But I have a sausage which bears my name. Count Waldstein had a sonata, Mae West had a life preserver, I have a sausage. Once before that angel makes a final recon, I'd like to taste the creation which makes me immortal. "Just for the hell of it."

She didn't understand but he hadn't told her enough. "My lips are sealed."

"Thanks. Dinner and dancing when I get back?"

Frisk got in the car and contemplated the steering wheel a moment. "You're an unusual guy," she said. "The only one I know who hasn't tried to screw me after ten minutes of chitchat."

From this angle he could see acres of breast, yards of eyelash, miles of hair: No man alive wouldn't want to conquer this flesh. "Maybe I'm a coward," he said.

Frisk gunned the ignition. "Have a great vacation."

"You still going to be working when I get back?"

"I don't know."

Something inside him paled as she drove away: stupid, stupid timing, signature of F. Beck's life. Once again he seemed to be diving into a beautiful pool which someone else had just drained. Floyd watched Frisk's car zip around the bend at the foot of Hudson Street. Why was it that every woman he had ever wanted drove like a terrorist? He went inside and picked up Eggli's modest brochure describing his course. The pictures far outshone the copy:

> Chef Urs Eggli, reknown chef, teaches for three weeks every July ten fortunate students who gather at the Hotel Badhof in scenic Emwald, thirty minutes by train from Montreux, Switzerland. Students learn the basics of gourmet cooking in an intensive 21-day session in the hotel kitchen. Four nights per week they learn the basics of fine service when they serve the guests at the hotel. The famous esthete Count Zimstein attends all public classes and imparts his knowledge of impeccable mannerisms to the students, thereby rounding their education in a superb style.

One more time Floyd read the letter he had received from Chef Eggli's cousin:

> *Dear Mr. Beck,*
>
>   *Thank you for sending me your picture and fine résumé. I am sure that a man who works for the U.S. Treasury Department will be a serious and industrious chef at my pension. In exchange for making breakfast and sometimes dinner, I will give you a room of your own and meals. I hope you will not eat too much. My cousin is thrilled that you will be coming and promises me you shall behave like a gentleman. Your simple duties as chef should leave you much time to study sausages with him.*
>
>   *With best wishes,*
>   *Fräulein Erna Moser*

Floyd put the correspondence away and began packing for the pension: slacks, shirts, aprons, cookbook. Then he packed his two new suits and tuxedo for events at the Hotel Badhof: In no way would he be mistaken for the thousands of Americans who slouched past his station at JFK each week.

Done, Floyd stood the two suitcases by the door, changed into an ancient bathing suit, and mowed his lawn. The sun's amorous fingers tingled his shoulders and crickets sprang out of his path. In the street two students from Stevens Tech slid a Frisbee along the wind. Random cherry bombs and ladyfingers crepitated in the distance, reminding Floyd that this year he would miss the fireworks on the Hudson River. He put the mower away, got a beer from his refrigerator, then sat on his deck, not thinking, aware of nothing but his flesh absorbing the sun. Across the river the Empire State Building waited for night to rekindle its upper stories. Floyd stared at the tall island: man's version of God's Alps. This same evening he was leaving one for the other.

The doorbell rang. Floyd frowned, in no mood to stress his brain with the formation of speech. It rang again, longer this time. He walked to the front door, wondering who had any business with him on July Fourth. Maybe the students had lost their Frisbee on his roof again.

There stood Portia, queen of hornets. An arctic wind whizzed through Floyd's chest. His nervous system immediately jolted him one step backwards. It did not quite get him to slam the door in her face, however: Aunt Margaret's years of etiquette instruction jammed that SOS. He stared at Portia's brown cheeks, nattily freckled by the sun. In summer she spent a lot of time in the backyard of her clinic teaching the canine equivalent of basic training. She wore a V-neck undershirt beneath a pair of denim overalls lopped at midthigh. Even the hiking boots and thick socks couldn't make her legs look bad. On a leash panted a splendid Dalmatian.

"Hello, Floyd," she said. "Champ and I were passing by and thought we'd wish you a bon voyage."

As ever, a conflicting squall of emotions drummed over Floyd. He wanted to hug Champ, kick Portia, and, most importantly, find out how she knew he was leaving and if she knew where he was going. "Thank you," he said curtly, then dropped to his knees and ran a hand along the Dalmatian's spine. "Hey, Champ, howya doin', old boy."

"Champ is no longer an old boy," Portia said. "She is a bitch."

Floyd's hand paused midway between the dog's head and tail, then fell to the side. Champ licked his cheek but, it seemed, more diffidently than in the past. Floyd could not bring himself to look the dog in the eye. Slowly he got to his feet. "So castrating him wasn't enough," he said. "You're too much, Portia."

"Now that is a strange reaction. Everyone else has been congratulating me." Portia saw the two suitcases. "You're leaving tonight, I understand."

"Who told you that?"

"George Hash. I had quite a chat with him this morning. He and two—shall we say—companions were at the Cliffside Park parade."

Floyd wondered why Hash had not mentioned this to him. He also wondered what Hash and Portia could possibly have talked about—besides him. They had absolutely nothing else in common.

"May I come in? I've been meaning to speak to you about something for quite a while. I won't be long." Behind Portia's head a Frisbee glided gracefully through the air. Floyd wished he could change places with it: The fewer minutes Portia needed for a speech, the more arsenic she had distilled into every sentence.

"I don't have much time," Floyd said, opening the door nevertheless: Once he stepped onto that airplane, this segment of his life, Portia included, would break off like a floe from an iceberg, bob downstream, and melt into history. "Let's sit on the deck. Beer? Lemonade?"

Portia and Champ walked through the living room, noses in the air, alert for ducks or another woman. "What's that delicious smell in here? Have you been cooking?"

"Meat loaf."

That did not quite answer Portia's question but she did not pursue the matter. She tied Champ to a post on the deck as Floyd poured some lemonade. "So. You look well."

"I've been well, thank you." Champ sat down on her haunches and stared at him. Floyd wondered if she still lifted one leg to pee.

"How was your swim today?"

Swim, swim, water, fish, swim, Hash, aha! Portia thought he had gone with Hash and the Space Shots. Floyd grinned slowly. "Very refreshing."

That irritated her because she smiled pleasantly, with her lips shut. Floyd could afford to be a little hospitable now. "And how's your social life?" he asked.

"I have no time for dabbling in the opposite sex, if that's what you mean," Portia replied. "Between Champ, the clinic, and WHAP, it's been brutally busy."

"WHAP? What's that now?"

"Women Hate All Pornography. This summer the campaign goes into high gear. In fact I ran into your dear George at a demonstration a few weeks ago. Knocked him down by mistake and he claims to have lost a big bad criminal because of it. He's quite a pathetic liar."

Hash had not told him about this episode either. Floyd wondered what else Hash had kept to himself over the past few weeks. "Speaking of liars, how's William?"

"William is in India leading a week of protests in Bombay." Portia ran a hand through her short hair: Another inch and she would no longer look as if she were recovering from a severe infestation of scalp lice. "I might join her in Europe in a few weeks."

An ice cube nearly slid into Floyd's lung. "Where in Europe?" he coughed.

"I'm not sure. There's a symposium on German shepherds in Vienna. And there's a schnauzer conference in London in two weeks. I've been invited to speak at quite an important veterinary convention in Montreux. I believe I told you that last time we met. I'll go if I can bring Champ along. She's a critical part of my lecture upon the sexual psyche of dogs."

"You'd never get her past quarantine," Floyd said. "She'd never make the airplane ride. The time zones will kill her. Forget Montreux." It was less than an hour from Emwald.

"There's going to be an international women's conference in Geneva at the same time. William plans to attend that with a delegation she's bringing back from India." Portia sighed. "We're having trouble finding a room, though. There are supposed to be NATO or SALT talks happening. Everyone's getting put up farther and farther out of town."

"I said forget Montreux," Floyd repeated. "Go to Vienna."

"We'll see. I'll have to look into this quarantine business immediately. It's too bad you're leaving tonight. Perhaps you could have helped me."

"Sorry." It would be worth delaying his takeoff a day just to insure that Champ never got one paw off United States soil: Floyd would screw that bitch's papers up so badly that Agriculture might have to incinerate her. He'd call Hash from the airport tonight and ask him to intercept the paperwork . . . among other questions.

"So where are you going for your vacation?" Portia interrupted.

"Florida."

"At this time of year? What's down there? Disney World?"

"No interruptions." He swished the ice cubes in his glass. "So what brings you here, Portia?"

Champ yipped from the corner; maybe she had cramps now. Floyd watched Portia kneel and gently pull the dog's ears, whispering consolation. Once upon a time she had done the same to him. "I have a business matter to discuss with you."

She was going to sue him for throwing all her textbooks out. She wanted to rent a room downstairs for laboratory specimens. She wanted to buy the Falcon. "Shoot."

"I would like you to inseminate me. I will pay you a thousand dollars."

A rash of firecrackers spit into the air. His blood surged: It thought the woman had propositioned him. But she hadn't said "make love" or "sleep with" or even the honest "fuck." *Inseminate* was the word she used: That was something Champ used to be able to do. That was something which syringes did all the time. "Inseminate," he said softly. The word hissed like a cobra. She and William had probably spent many hours discussing that thousand-dollar honorarium. Anything less would seem amateur; anything more would sound illegal. One thousand dollars wasn't bad for a few minutes' labor; on the other hand, it wasn't even a penny per spermatozoon.

"No," he said.

"Why not? Think about it, Floyd. The child would be well cared for and, judging from our backgrounds, healthy, intelligent, and attractive."

"Who's the father? You or William?"

"You're the father, of course. What a silly question."

The kid would never learn to fish; that was murder. The kid would never play football; that was aggression. The kid would never wear high-heel shoes or lipstick; that was victimization. The kid would never play with dolls; that was brainwashing. The kid would never, ever be allowed to eat a sausage. By the age of ten, however, the kid would be convinced he or she grew up in a terrible land where men did nothing but rape women, seize their inheritances, and chain them to potato mashers while they meanwhile caballed on Wall Street. "How dare you even ask me this? You know how I feel about children of my own."

"I had hoped you might have moderated your views by now."

Was doing it all without men moderation? Not two hours ago, Frisk had stood on his deck mourning that she would never have McPhee's children. Now Portia wanted to borrow a teaspoon of semen. "If I loved you, I might consider it," Floyd said.

Portia glanced sharply at him. "You loved me enough last time we met."

"That was last time."

She scowled: typical male treachery. "What does love have to do with it anyhow? I'm paying you a thousand bucks! You don't even have to think. I'm not asking you to take the kid every other weekend. I'm not going to file a paternity suit." Portia exasperatedly flicked a ladybug off her knee. "Just close your eyes and pretend I'm someone else."

Floyd stood up. "I've got to leave."

"I know a dozen other men who would have jumped at the chance."

"So start asking them, sweetheart. You are not going to have my baby."

The blond hair on Portia's legs glistened in the sun as she unhitched

Champ from the post. "You're the most selfish, stubborn bastard I ever met."

Floyd patted Champ's head as Portia led her off the deck. The animal seemed to walk differently now; he couldn't tell whether it was from all the stitches or the pendulous weight recently shed under the tail. "You're not going to get both of us to donate our balls to science." They arrived at the sidewalk. "Someday I'll feel flattered about this, I'm sure."

"You've changed, Floyd," Portia said somewhat wistfully. She and Champ walked a few steps away then turned. "By the way," she said too nonchalantly, "Viola Flury asked about you today."

Down, blood. He kicked at a grasshopper. "Did you see her at the parade, too?"

"No, she brought a hurt pup to the clinic. Saw your picture with Champ in the hall."

"How is she?"

Portia did not have to answer that question. But perhaps she figured the airplane might crash tonight and Floyd should die, as always, an incurable romantic. "She's still a very beautiful woman, if that's what you wanted to know. Goodbye."

Floyd took a long shower, clamped his house shut, and drove the Falcon to the airport, where he'd stash it for three weeks behind the customs terminal. The crew would keep an eye on it. He checked in at Swissair and called Hash, who had just returned to the office from his afternoon natation.

"Shouldn't you be on a plane," Hash said. "What's up."

"Do me a favor. Portia's got a Dalmatian she's thinking of bringing to Switzerland with her in three weeks. Maybe."

"What for? Protection against all those guys in lederhosen?"

"Says she's got a veterinary convention. If you see the dog in quarantine, would you make sure it flunks? I don't want it to leave the country."

Floyd had never asked Hash anything like this before. He must be desperate for revenge. "Sure. But why?"

"It's a threat to mankind. Trust me."

"Anything you say, buddy." Hash waited a moment. "Portia's not going to like this."

"I'm sure you can handle her," Floyd said. "Gotta run. Thanks."

Hash mumbled a farewell, sure that Floyd knew all about his two encounters with Portia. "I'll keep an eye on your house."

"Thanks." Vastly relieved, Floyd hopped down the ramp onto the airplane. Too many emotions had galloped through him today and he could no longer distinguish Portia from Frisk from Hash from Viola from

Eggli. There would be time to cud that all over at the pension. He looked out the window as the plane lifted off. Beneath him, all over the black countryside, girandoles sprouted in the night like the sneezes of angels. As he swallowed a sleeping pill, Floyd prayed that he would awaken in Geneva, and not next to Caspar.

7

The train droned along the rails, swaying its passengers into a narcotic silence. Most of them had long ago shed their newspapers and knitting and now either dozed, heads lolling into the seat cushions, or gazed out the windows, blinking sporadically as ancient tortoises in the sun: They traversed the same scenery every day and were no longer mesmerized by horses, chalets, or the Lake of Geneva far below. The tracks bisected the vineyards which rose sharply from the edge of the water and terraced far up the mountainsides. Flowers surrounded each cottage and the women picking them all wore skirts and thick shoes. In the center of each village rose a church spire, advising parishioners of the correct time. Cows outnumbered cars.

The Lake of Geneva, Lac Léman to the poets, lay black as onyx under the morning fog. Gauging by the mountains delineating its shores, the water must be very deep, very cold, and thick with monsters. Floyd saw no swimmers and only a few sailboats moored close to each other, huddling as if to protect themselves. Across the lake, in France, the snowy peaks of the Dents du Midi dipped in and out of the fog, teasing the eye.

An hour out of Geneva, at the far end of Lac Léman, the train pulled briefly into Montreux before climbing into the Bernese Alps. Floyd got out at a tiny village and waited for a local train to tuck him even further between the mountains. Beside him on the platform waited an old man with an elaborately carved walking stick. He looked Floyd and his baggage up and down, nodded his head, but did not smile. In the street a little bell tinkled as a boy and his goat ambled past. There was no other movement, no other sound, anywhere. Floyd could hardly believe that the stupendous peaks in front of him were not a combination of plastic and optical illusion. He could almost hear their immensity. They threw all perspective awry. They were definitely alive: God frozen.

Another dark green train finally slid alongside the tiny station. Floyd

165

and the old man climbed aboard and rode across narrow bridges, through long tunnels, higher and higher into the Alps. The moment the train wound past one bluff, another stood in its way. Floyd could not pry his eyes from the window, unable to decide whether looking down or looking up caused him more vertigo. Hoboken grew on this same planet? How insane.

The conductor poked his head into the somnolent car. "Emwald," he announced, drawing the door shut. Floyd jumped up, yanking his suitcase from the overhead rack. He waited anxiously for the train to stop; the moment the station ceased moving, he pushed his suitcase against the doors and toppled onto the platform. A farm wife in heavy black skirts alit after him and rustled into the street. The conductor peered out of a window, saw that they had not fallen out by mistake, and drew the train away.

Floyd had memorized the directions to Fräulein Moser's place, an unnecessary precaution considering hers was the only pension in Emwald, and arrived minutes later, soaked and gasping: In her letter describing the unparalleled view from her veranda, Fräulein Moser had not mentioned to Floyd that Luthergasse lay on a sixty-degree incline, nor that her pension perched at its summit. A huge cowbell hung next to the front door. Mopping the sweat raining from his eyebrows, Floyd pulled the tough leather cord. He jumped at the thick noise which echoed through the valley. He pulled the cord again, less robustly this time. Still no one answered.

He walked around back. In a lounge chair reclined a woman with a book on her stomach and a box of chocolates at her side, absorbedly reading. Her black-and-white hair had been pulled into a bun the size of a loaf of pumpernickel and upon her nose drooped the lower halves of a pair of glasses. She had crossed her plump legs at the ankles and was consuming about three bonbons per page turn.

"Excuse me," called Floyd in Swiss-German. The woman flattened the book against her breasts and glanced over. "I'm looking for Fräulein Moser."

Either the novel had hit a seduction scene or Moser did not want to stop eating chocolates; very reluctantly she rousted herself from her chair. "If you are looking for rooms, I am sorry. This is a pension for women only."

"My name is Floyd Beck, your new cook."

"Ah! Yes! Mr. Beck!" She studied him very carefully, finally satisfied that he indeed resembled the picture she had received. "Urs told me you were only coming tomorrow. This is a fine surprise. Now you will cook dinner tonight."

Were she a man, Floyd would have told her to forget it, he had three thousand miles and a Lethean train journey to shake off. But she had called him Mr. Beck, something no woman had done in years, and considered his arrival a fine surprise. Only a cad would reply that he preferred to sleep. "Certainly."

"Let me show you to your room. You must wash up." Fräulein Moser nipped one last chocolate and went inside.

Floyd took a final glimpse of the mountains before following his new employer. His eyes needed a few moments to adjust to the dim interior of the pension. Everything was spotlessly clean and frugally decorated, perhaps as an example to the clientele Fräulein Moser wished to guest. Wooden plaques painted with flags of all the Swiss cantons decorated the white walls. At his left was a modest sitting room which contained a half dozen chairs, many pillows, a sewing machine, a fireplace, and a pay phone. In the window slept a calico cat. Fräulein Moser's quarters were behind the sitting room, on the side of the building with the best view. "And now we have the kitchen," she said, walking past a staircase. Suddenly she stopped. "You must never go up these stairs," she said. "The women sleep up there."

"I would never consider such a thing unless a life were at stake," Floyd said.

This reply pleased her. "So. Here is the kitchen." She led him into a dining room containing six tables. Upon each stood a little vase of flowers. More wooden plates hung on the walls.

Floyd cleared his throat. "I had not expected quite so many people," he said.

"Do not worry, we are very rarely full. Emwald is not a tourist village. This week I have only two guests. Soon they leave. Next week I have three more coming in. They go to my cousin's cooking school and stay for three weeks. So you do not have a difficult time."

Not if he remembered how to peel potatoes. "Thank you very much for hiring me, Fräulein Moser," Floyd said. "I am very grateful."

"Not at all. You phoned Urs at just the right time." She opened the door to the kitchen. "Here is where you will work."

Floyd's stomach curled around a kidney as he saw first a water pump, then pots and pans hanging from the ceiling, the knife rack, the ancient stove, and the thick wooden table awaiting him. His eyes cut across the room in search of a microwave oven: sorry. He was lucky to even have electricity. The thought of being responsible for the transmutation of potatoes into rösti, apples into tarts, almost made him cry: He was out of his mind to have come here. Without Frisk standing by with a spatula, he couldn't boil water. "Perfect," Floyd said.

"Now. For breakfast we have bread and coffee. This is very easy. The baker will bring the bread. You make the coffee and boil the milk. We begin at six o'clock and end at seven. I do not like the women sitting and gossiping in my pension."

"That suits me fine."

"For dinner we eat at six. I will put on the table what you should cook."

If she put esoterica like eggplant, leeks, and chicken liver on the table, he wouldn't last a day. "I'll be glad to do the shopping for you."

"No, no. I must control the costs. We cannot be eating such things as meat loaf here every night."

"Of course. That's very wise."

Fräulein Moser walked to a far counter. "When the dish is ready, you will open this little door and slide it out to the dining room. Then you will shut the little door again. I do not want the women to be seeing you. This only causes problems. I will tell you once more that I will not have you socializing with the guests."

Floyd didn't understand why Moser was belaboring the point. "My only interest is in making your breakfast and dinner, and studying sausages with your cousin. That leaves very little time for the women in this pension." The altitude must be giving him a headache. His stomach was empty and confused, and said so.

Fräulein Moser heard it. "There is still some bread in the cupboard. Now I take you to your room." She walked through a door at the rear of the kitchen into a tiny chamber with a tiny window. "Here is your bed." She meant cot. "And your little bath. Very modest, but it is private."

"It's perfect."

"You have your own entrance here," Fräulein said, swinging open a broom closet. A heavy rifle fell out.

"Watch out!" Floyd shouted, diving on it. "God Almighty! Is this thing loaded?"

"Possibly. I had to shoot a few stray dogs several months ago." Each citizen's house contained such a rifle which the men brought home after their military service. The Swiss were still convinced that other, less fortunate, countries harbored a desire to invade them.

Floyd unloaded the rifle as Fräulein Moser retrieved several scattered cabbages. "You should never leave a loaded weapon anywhere. That is very dangerous."

"Yes, yes, so are stray dogs! They eat my chickens!" She stood the rifle back in the broomcloset. "So. Through here is your private entrance."

Floyd peered into a small excavation which went almost straight down. It looked more like a well than a tunnel. "Interesting."

"Yes. During the war my father built this in case of attack. The other end comes up in the bushes behind the train station."

"No one else knows about it?"

"Only Urs and I'm sure he has forgotten."

"And I'm supposed to use this?"

"Yes please. I will not have you using the front or the rear door along with the other women. I let you unpack. Each time you take a shower, I charge you two francs for hot water. You must buy soap. Perhaps today you pay a small visit to Urs in his hotel. Then you come back at five o'clock and make our supper."

"Where is the hotel?" Floyd asked.

Fräulein Moser led him to the backyard and pointed across the valley. A medieval fortress nestled in pine trees on the opposite mountain. "The Badhof is a very famous and exclusive hotel, very close to the thermal springs. The food is excellent. It is a short walk from here."

A short walk for the Green Giant, maybe. "Thank you," Floyd said. "I will unpack and go."

"I will call Urs and tell him to meet you there at three."

He hung his suits and tuxedo into the small armoire in his room, took a shower, and put on a tie: Moser had said exclusive. He slipped Caspar's recipe book into his pocket and ducked into the tunnel. It smelled like dead bones and bay leaves but it worked. Floyd pushed open a door at the opposite end and found himself right behind the train station, in the bushes, as Fräulein had predicted. *Private Tunnel. Trespassing Forbidden,* read a tiny plaque. The citizens of Emwald had obeyed that for forty years; such a sign in Hoboken would guarantee instant invasion. Floyd brushed off his pants and looked around. He walked to a tiny inn and gulped four cheese pies with two beers. Then he bought a case of beer and stashed it in the tunnel. Enervated by the pristine air and that euphoria which accompanies lack of sleep, he took a walk through the village. It was hard to believe that people lived here for real, and not for display purposes only, as in Williamsburg, Virginia. He followed the signs pointing up to the Hotel Badhof. Suddenly Floyd's thighs began to boil so he paused to catch his breath. Emwald lay far below, in the valley.

A white Mercedes whizzed by, nearly knocking him down a ravine. The wild man at the wheel stomped on the brakes, looked back, and rammed the car into reverse, speeding toward Floyd as if he were a hit man wanting to complete the job. "God damn you!" Floyd shouted in dialect, leaping across the road, rolling into a tree. "Are you out of your mind?"

The man lowered a tinted window. Sixtyish, he looked like a cross between Santa Claus and Rasputin. "God strike me dead, you look just like your mother."

Floyd got up and brushed his clothes off. The recipe book had snapped in half along the spine and pebbles imbedded the precious pages. "You're Eggli?"

"You still speak the dialect. I congratulate you." Eggli swung open the passenger door. "Hop in! I'll drive you the rest of the way."

A rank, morbid odor permeated the car, reminding Floyd of the nights the Falcon had shuttled gangrenous dogs to the morgue. He looked into the back seat.

"You smell my Gorgonzola," Eggli said. "This morning I picked up a trunkful in Ascona. It's magnificent. So! Did you have a good trip?"

"Yes, thank you. I'm all set up at the pension. Your cousin wasn't expecting me until tomorrow."

The Mercedes skidded behind the hotel into a parking space, spraying gravel everywhere. "Don't pay any attention to that stupid woman. She's been in the mountains too long. She's beginning to look like one herself." Eggli jumped out of the car. "So! Help me now with this cheese! I have a thousand pastries to make for this evening."

Flipping open the trunk, he threw five wheels of Gorgonzola at Floyd. "Follow me." Eggli hopped into the enormous hotel kitchen and tore the cork off a bottle of brandy. "Put it there," he pointed to Floyd, "on that table." Then he guzzled the liquor straight from the bottle. "You have given me a great shock, Anna."

"I'm Floyd. My mother was Anna."

"Yes, yes. I know what her name was." Tying on an apron, Eggli wheeled around the kitchen, berating and patting a half dozen sous-chefs before finally returning to the center table. He stared at Floyd's eyes for an uncomfortable period of time. "Come back tomorrow," he finally said. "I can't stand to look at you any more today."

"What about my sausages?"

"The hell with your sausages!" Eggli roared. "Get out of my kitchen!"

Dazed, wondering if he wasn't still dreaming this all from his deck in Hoboken, Floyd stumbled back to his tunnel. He had difficulty lugging the case of beer through the narrow passageway to the pension.

On the table lay a dead chicken, five onions, and a basket of strange, coarse greens. This was not a combination which Frisk had gone over with him. It did not take Floyd long to decide that stew was his only hope. He filled the largest pot in the kitchen with water, got it to a fine angry boil, then heaved the chicken, the onions, and the greens inside, slamming the lid on. He set his alarm clock for one hour and collapsed upon his cot.

An unusual odor danced in his nostrils as the alarm went off. Floyd awoke totally disoriented: He never slept in the afternoon. Tidbits of the day swished through his mind and finally formed a sodden whole. He leapt out of bed and ran to the pot on the stove. The liquid had boiled off and everything was beginning to hiss, so he upended the pot into the sink. The chicken looked awful. Its feet and beak had fallen off and its feathers were all stuck in the greens. Dinner started in ten minutes. Floyd lifted the chicken out of the sink, plopped it on the wooden table, took a cleaver from the wall, and desperately hacked it in half, heartened to see some white meat poking from the ribcage. Working quickly, he tore the meat from the bones and tossed it into a serving dish. Then he ran back to the sink and retrieved the five onions. They reminded him of the softballs he used to find in Aunt Margaret's rainbarrel. Floyd chopped them up and threw them atop the chicken. Then he began plucking brown and white feathers from the quaggy mass of boiled greens. Just as the cuckoo clock struck six, Floyd slid open the little door above the counter. Fräulein Moser was waiting on the other side.

"Thank you very much," she said. Then the door slid shut.

Out in the dining room Floyd could hear forks clicking and the voice of Fräulein divulging tomorrow's weather forecast to her guests. They were not a loquacious bunch. His head dropped against the counter; an indeterminate time later, three empty dishes and one empty serving plate were returned to him. Floyd washed everything and toppled into his little bed. Within moments, his body was still as the mountains outside.

His brain, however, was too agitated to immobilize. Floyd dreamt briefly of Frisk throwing a Dalmatian into a pot of boiling water, explaining that whenever in doubt, Floyd should make stew. Then he dreamt of Portia sitting on his deck shaving her legs and armpits as Eggli threw firecrackers at the Hudson River. He dreamt he left his front door wide open and Hash was inside with Fräulein Moser, eating sausages in his bed.

He half woke up. Floyd's mottled thoughts circled to a remote volcano which had begun to smolder again: Viola. Portia had actually seen her. Oh God, that was getting very, very close. He wished he could borrow Portia's eyes, to see what Viola looked like after all these years; Portia's ears, to hear her voice; Portia's skin, so that he could touch her cool hand. Instead he had only a sea of dreams in which Viola swam, forever seventeen. She had been asea for so long that the thought of her floating so close to harbor, and again stepping into reality, terrified him. His sea would then be empty.

Floyd drifted back to sleep. He dreamt he was in Carnegie Hall, at the second concert of the season, waiting in the dark for either Viola, or the two men in fur coats. If the men in fur coats returned to their customary seats in front of him, that would mean that Viola and her chaperone had been given their tickets for an evening and he would never see her again. But if she returned . . . most likely she had a season subscription and he would be seeing her six Tuesdays between now and June. Floyd sucked tensely upon the cough drop Aunt Margaret handed him, every nerve concentrated on the empty seat in front of him, as Madame Levitski told tales of tonight's violin soloist. She had known him back when he had had more hair and a Hungarian accompanist.

There was movement in the aisle and Floyd glanced slowly over. A purple beret capped those black curls and she was wearing a light perfume. He nearly cried with relief. At the time he thought he could never thank the two men in fur coats enough for sacrificing their seats; that opinion, of course, would flapjack violently over the next seventeen years. She sat directly in front of him and glanced at the side loges. Floyd noticed for the first time a mole on her left cheek, stark as a raisin in vanilla ice cream.

Madame Levitski's anecdotes wound down as the lights dimmed. "Don't you wish you played the violin, Floyd?" she asked.

If he did, the girl would be staring at him in admiration instead of whispering into that old geezer's ear. "Now I do."

"It may be too late," Levitski said, raising her opera glasses. "Your hands are already formed."

At intermission, he got up and followed them, never taking his eyes off Viola's green miniskirt. When she outgrew it, someone else could use it as a potholder. She had athletic calves, knees compact as fennel: Floyd wondered if she took dancing lessons. They strolled arm in arm down the musty corridor, talking in low voices. Viola suddenly giggled. Floyd stopped dead: She couldn't be sleeping with that man, could she? When they got to that age their balls reeked worse than a horse's. They snored and when they woke up in the morning, their breath corroded brass bedposts. Their skin squished and squirmed like those oily dead ducks Aunt Margaret cooked for Thanksgiving. They got it up about as decisively as a water balloon. Their tongues got fat and their fingers got cruel. She wouldn't lie down naked beside something like that, would she? Floyd's eyes moved after her just as a ray from a hall light caught Viola's heavy gold earring. It was not the sort of jewelry a schoolgirl bought for herself, nor received from her parents.

On the mezzanine they passed another couple. "Hello, Richard," the man called, veering his wife over.

Richard, eh: aptly named after all those evil English kings. The girl and Richard stopped. Floyd came up very close behind them, pretending to be studying the historic photograph of Carnegie Hall on the wall. "This is Viola Flury," Richard said. He did not add "my niece" or "my student" or "my secretary." They chatted awhile about the concert and how they would all get home during this nonsensical cab strike. Then Viola excused herself to the ladies' room.

"I must say, Richard," the man remarked after a short silence, "you've outdone yourself this time."

"I'm afraid I have," he replied.

Floyd didn't want to hear any more. He went to the ladies' room and paced outside the gold and white door, weighing the consequences of introducing himself to the girl named Viola. Once he eked his name out, what was he supposed to say? "Would you like to take a spin in my aunt's Studebaker?" How about "I like your hair?" How pathetic. A familiar frost crept up Floyd's legs as he realized that any moment now, she would appear. He planted himself outside the door.

It swung open and there she stood, pale as a unicorn. She had painted her lips pink. Where, in which life, had the threads come unraveled? In which life would they reunite? Viola hesitated, looking around. Her eyes hit him in the chest, flashed up to his face a moment, then moved on. As she walked by he could smell her lily-of-the-valley perfume. Floyd felt sick. He returned to his seat and fused his nose to the program notes, ignoring Aunt Margaret, who stood yakking with the French, and Madame Levitski, who was fishing beneath her seat for a leather glove.

Viola . . . his fourth-grade teacher's name was Viola and she had been named after the instrument: taut, varnished, unplayed for centuries. The Viola in front of him was named after the flower. Paralyzed and mute, Floyd watched her slide back into her seat with Old Richard, finally disappointed that she did not turn around. Why should she, though? How many times in five years had he looked at the folks behind him? How did he know there wasn't a woman insane with lust shuddering an arm's length away?

Floyd spun around. Two Chinese women sat talking with a fat man in a bow tie. The man nodded and smiled pleasantly at him.

December slipped away, then winter. Five times, at each intermission, Floyd followed Viola to the ladies' room on the mezzanine, standing in exactly the same spot outside the door, eyes pouncing on her the moment she emerged. In February she finally started making the connection. By March he had her flustered. In April she reacted. Rather than rejoining Old Richard at the bar, Viola walked straight at Floyd. The strawberries on her silk dress nodded in time with her steps; few women wore any underwear at all in those days. Floyd knew she was going to break the silence and swallowed half his brain.

"I don't know who you are," she said. "But you're beginning to bother me."

So she had blue eyes; he had stared at many moons wondering about that. He wanted to lay two fingers on her lips and run them slowly down her white chin, to her throat. But it was way too soon. Suddenly the panic and the desire left him and he was only very sad: This was impossible. "Good," he said, breathing on her face.

She wound her arms around his neck and kissed him passionately. That revision of history jolted Floyd awake like a whack at a Balinese gong. Immediately he knew he was not in Hoboken because his feet hung over the edge of the bed. Where were the streetlights? The death rattle of distant mufflers? His brain told him his eyes were open, yet no signals relayed to the optic nerve. Adrenalin splashed into the blood: He had never been buried in such total night before. Then a clock struck four and Floyd remembered where he slept. He stared straight up at the ceiling, breathing shallowly, still weighted by Viola. He chuckled to himself. She had not kissed him at all. She had tossed her hair in his face and paraded back to Old Richard.

Floyd stumbled into the kitchen and pumped himself a glass of icy water. Then he put his head under the spigot and yanked down on the handle several times. Vivid dreams were crueler than death. They released the soul, allowed it to flutter in perfect happiness, then dashed it back into its bleak, carnal cage. Oh God, he came here to forget, not remember! He straggled back to bed, damning Portia. Had he agreed to inseminate her, she would not have flung that parting sally at him: She knew it would have made him impotent.

Until dawn, Floyd drifted between discomfiting visions of Urs Eggli and Fräulein Moser. He could not sleep in such oceanic silence; his body distrusted it. The baker finally roused him at five by knocking on the kitchen door with two loaves of bread. Floyd took a shower, then boiled coffee and milk. Again, Fräulein Moser did most of the talking at breakfast, this morning about the demise of a beloved canasta partner. Her voice carried distinctly through the partition into the kitchen.

She came back to visit after he had washed the dishes. Her enormous bun was freshly tacked to the rear of her head, stretching her forehead back. "Very unusual coffee," she said. "You are not using too many beans? Not more than eighty?"

"You want me to count the beans?"

"Of course. And you slice the bread a little too thick."

"Excuse me. I'll be more careful next time."

Fräulein Moser inspected the pot which Floyd had just washed. "Good. Very clean. I think you will be fine. I never had such a chicken stew as last night."

Floyd remembered a few lines Frisk had fed him for such emergencies. "Thank you. It was organic." He hung his apron on a hook. "I must be off to see Chef Eggli. We have some recipes to study."

"That is impossible. He has gone into the mountains to rest before the start of his cooking school."

"He's already in the mountains, for Christ's sake! When's he coming back?"

"Friday. He telephoned me last night when you were asleep. He said that you should take long walks and become accustomed to the climate. I think you have upset him."

"Well, now he's upset me, so we're even."

Fräulein Moser felt sorry for Floyd. Urs had not warned the boy that he was unstable. "I tell you what, Mr. Beck."

"Just call me Floyd. My father was called Mr. Beck."

"Do you like jigsaw puzzles? Do you play cards? Canasta, by chance?"

"I used to." Aunt Margaret had forced him to be a fourth on many a rainy afternoon.

"So. You take a long walk all around the mountains. You come back at one, after lunch. We will play canasta this afternoon for several hours. Then you make dinner."

"That sounds good."

"Do not forget you owe me two Swiss francs from your shower this morning."

"I'll bring it to the game."

Floyd walked into Emwald again. The few villagers he saw did not converse with him: The mountains had stolen their tongues. What would they talk about anyhow? Cut out crime, pollution, gridlock, the Mets, three million women, and there was nothing left but cows and chocolate. He would need a few more days to downshift from urban to alpine metabolism; maybe Eggli taking off was not such a bad idea after all. Floyd walked through a pine forest on the outskirts of Emwald and discovered a little lake. It was the most perfect picnic spot on earth. He'd come back the next day, with lunch.

Fräulein Moser and two friends were waiting for him at one o'clock in the garden. Floyd felt immediately at home with his three canasta partners, who dressed and spoke like outdated versions of Aunt Margaret. Spinsters had formed the bedrock of his childhood. There had been many in his family. Caspar's mother, Floyd's grandmother, was the only child of nine to have married; her eight sisters preferred to knit unimpinged by gruff demands for beer and conjugal awfulness. Aunt Margaret had been engaged once, but broke it off to sail to America and become a governess. She lived in New York for years, raising the children of a very wealthy family; Caspar, her nephew, conveniently furnished her with an orphan just as the last of her charges went off to boarding school. By that time Aunt Margaret had become quite an affluent woman thanks to some shrewd investments in the stock market which her employer had recommended. Floyd grew up in her East Side apartment amid a constant stream of dowagers and nannies, who gathered there for teas, cards, and all major holidays. They adored him. He was a lovely, quiet child, not at all like the brats they were paid to look after. Soon they had him playing canasta and backgammon three nights a week.

Fräulein Moser and her friends played cards with a virginal viciousness which Floyd remembered well. As the sun crept from peak to peak, nudging shadows along the grass, he slowly got his game back. "It is almost dinnertime," Moser announced, way too soon. "Perhaps we do this again tomorrow."

For five days, as the Alps slowly dissolved the demon Time from Floyd's veins, he walked in the morning, played cards all afternoon, boiled dinner, then slept all night. There was nothing to worry about here; the mountains kept evil, and memory, away. Sunsets lasted eons. Snowbells carpeted the fields. No one here knew who he was and no one back home knew where he was. Floyd was free.

"My boy," Moser said one afternoon after a particularly intoxicating backgammon match, "three new guests will be coming to the pension tomorrow morning."

"That's very nice." He couldn't care less.

"We will perhaps make a little lunch for them after their trip, no? I buy some knockwurst that you boil for me. They will be going to my cousin's cooking school."

"That means Urs is coming back tomorrow."

"Yes, yes," Fräulein Moser sighed as she dealt the cards. "I do not know when we will be able to play canasta again."

"We'll play tomorrow afternoon," Floyd said. "You'll see."

The next morning he awoke very early. The sun had already tinged his room flamingo. Until the baker arrived with the bread, Floyd lay in his cot listening to the birds and the occasional chime of the village clock. He watched the walls slowly incarnadine. He had not felt this cleansed and untroubled in years. After breakfast he took a long walk in the forest with a little book of poetry and sat by the side of his secret lake, reading. No one ever disturbed him there.

When he returned to the pension, Fräulein Moser had placed a small pile of knockwurst and potatoes on his kitchen table: just like home, thirty years ago. Floyd threw everything into the stewpot and finished the poems as they boiled.

A grumble of the floorboards indicated that several bodies had entered the dining room. Floyd slid open the little door, pushed out the knockwurst and potatoes, shut the door, and waited for Moser to commence her habitual mealtime monologue.

Instead he heard a woman say, in English, accent Brooklyn, "This looks fabulous, Fräulein Moser."

Floyd clutched his heart and pitched forward: an American. He felt violated. Then another voice said, "I could eat a horse." There were two of them out there. This was disaster.

A third voice said, "My Gawd! I haven't eaten a hotdog since the Bicentennial!"

Paradise down the tubes! The last people he wanted polluting his cloister were Americans, variety female! How dare they come here! What were women doing at a cooking school anyway? Wasn't that like a slave going back to the plantation for Remedial Cotton? Their voices sawed through the pine boards into the kitchen, blah-blahing about the incredible train ride, the unbelievable mountains, the fabulous valleys: Fräulein Moser was hit with more stupid questions than a toll collector on the New Jersey Turnpike. She had obviously not spoken English in quite some time and was having trouble comprehending many words.

Finally she made the mistake of asking if the ladies' husbands had sent them to cooking school. Floyd cringed at the response she received. Snorting, the first woman snapped that her husband, cheap bastard, had never offered to send her anywhere but Weight Watchers. The second said her husband cooked for himself. The third said she would consider such a suggestion grounds for divorce. At this point the conversation took a speedy turn downhill as the women explained to Moser how spoiled and impotent American men had become. Floyd could not believe what he was hearing. It sounded like Portia all over again, somewhat less strident, but much more frightening: The plague had spread to the general population.

When they started talking about the great new generation of women which they of course represented, Floyd couldn't stand to listen any more. He banged around a few pots, momentarily silencing the new arrivals. Then he put his head under the water pump, to convince himself this was really happening. He never wanted to see them. He did not want to cook for them. The thought of washing their dirty dishes insulted him.

After lunch they had the gall to knock on his sliding door and yoohoo impertinently into the kitchen. Floyd felt like flinging the mop at them. Instead he took their plates to the sink and washed them in the hottest bearable water. Fräulein came into the kitchen as he was finishing up.

"Urs called," she said. "You must go to the hotel at once."

Floyd sighed: goodbye, canasta. "I did not know these were American women coming."

"You are not going to be chasing them now," Moser said. "I had a terrible problem with my last three cooks and American women. They go to my cousin's school and come back at night all crazy."

"I will have nothing to do with them," Floyd snapped. "In fact, I don't even want to be sleeping under the same roof." He moodily returned to the dishes in the sink.

Moser could not believe her good fortune. "They will not bother you much," she said. "Just an hour at dinner and breakfast. The rest of the day they will be with Urs."

"What do they do at night? And when do I see Urs myself?"

"Four nights a week they will remain at school to serve the guests in the hotel. You will see Urs perhaps on the other nights."

"All this coming and going gets me nervous," Floyd said. "Emwald is a tiny village."

"That is why you have a tunnel," she said. "Now you go see Urs. Do not be late returning for dinner. We eat at six o'clock sharp."

Glancing often over his shoulder, Floyd walked up to the Hotel Badhof. The three times a car passed, his stomach rolled itself into a tight little ball, trying to hide.

Chef Eggli stood beside a wooden table bashing a mound of dough with a rolling pin. He looked as if he had been skydiving into the flour barrel. "Puff pastry," he shouted at an assistant. "After sixty years it still gives me trouble." Then he spotted Floyd and scowled. "It's you again, Anna."

"My name's Floyd. My mother's name was Anna." Floyd approached the wooden table. "How was your rest in the mountains?"

"Just one moment, can't you see I'm busy?" Eggli walloped the dough a few more times. "Bah! Put it back in the refrigerator!" he instructed the assistant. Then he proceeded to a table stacked with peeled carrots and starting rapidly mincing them. "I have a small problem," he said to Floyd. "You must help me."

"Then we can make the sausages?"

"Yes, yes, we'll make the sausages! Listen to me. Did you read the brochure I sent to you about my cooking school?"

"Many times."

"Then you know that four times a week the students cook for the public. They are critiqued by my old friend, Count Zimstein. He is an expert upon manners and proper service. He is indispensable to my course."

"What can I do?"

"I just received a telephone call from the count. He is very ill. He ate a poisonous mushroom. He will not be able to come to Emwald now and help me." Eggli scraped a mound of carrots into an aluminum bowl. "You must substitute for Zimstein."

"I don't think I can do that."

"What do you mean? You only have to eat and make stupid comments."

"They'll know in two minutes that I'm an imposter."

"No they won't. You speak the dialect, not English. You wear a nice suit and comb your hair. Believe me, no one will mistake you for an American."

"I don't know the rules of etiquette."

"What? Didn't Anna teach you anything?"

Floyd looked around the kitchen. An assistant in the corner stood grinding meat into a large plastic tub. "I thought I came here to learn about sausages."

"This is an emergency! Caspar's damn sausages can wait another few days!"

"Let me think about it," Floyd said.

A carrot ricocheted off Floyd's chest. "No thinking about it! You do it!" Eggli passed to another table and began cracking eggs into a crock. "Caspar would have assisted me without question in an instant. He would never resist such an opportunity to eat, drink, and tease the women."

"I do not tease women."

"Why not? Are you a homosexual?"

"Where I come from, men don't dare tease women. They'd get their nuts diced like the carrots in that bowl."

Eggli plunged a massive whisk into the eggs and started beating. "It is hard to believe that you are Caspar's son. Go away now. I have to make two hundred vegetable soufflés this evening."

Floyd walked down to the lake and plopped against a tree, watching the clouds float over the mountains. He wondered why Eggli, who had been so eager to bring him over here, now displayed no interest whatever in the Floydwurst. Since his arrival the chef had stared oddly at him, called him nothing but Anna, lammed into the mountains, and now had asked him to step in for some flimflam Count Zimstein for his cooking school. Floyd had not anticipated that the chef would not lunge upon Caspar's book of recipes with the same frenzy which he had: Wishful thinking, once again, had torpedoed sound judgement. The chef was obviously down a quart and everything, Floyd now saw, had happened too easily. Yet he could not shake the feeling that this trip was inevitable and significant, Eggli or no, Floydwurst or no. He skidded a stone into the water and watched the ripples disturb the lake, wondering who would be throwing what at him next.

Last night Eugene announced that he would be abstaining from sexual intercourse with his wife until their baby was born; he had read somewhere that odds were one in one hundred million that an orgasm would dislodge the embryo from Viola's uterus. In the meantime they should cut back to light petting and brushing each other's hair. Fellatio was entirely acceptable, of course. Viola had told Eugene to invent his own fellatio machine and had spent the night on the living room couch, without the Goldberg belt. Breakfast this morning had not been a cheerful occasion. Eugene was petrified that his wife's rage might result in a miscarriage and got up at five to make strawberry crêpes, attempting to appease her. After a few petulant bites, she threw up.

The rain had caused an accident on Route 4 and Viola was trapped in her Porsche, unable to urinate, for almost two hours. When she got to work the accountant Morton was already waiting for her in the conference room, peevishly wiping mud from his pants as he checked the payroll printouts. An employee had splashed him in the parking lot. "Good morning, Morton," Viola said, removing her raincoat. "Where's Nestor?"

"Here." Viola looked under the table. Nestor was lying on his side next to Smudge, trying to get the pup to play with a bone. "I think he's finally beginning to walk again. I don't like this bleeding, though. It's not healing properly."

"Give it another couple days, will you?"

"What happened now," Morton said.

"The dog got smacked with a softball at the July Fourth picnic," Viola told him.

Nestor crawled into view. "Viola's not telling me who hit the ball. She knows I'll fire the guy. Then I'll kill him. Maybe I should kill him first. That's what worker's comp is all about, isn't it?"

"That is totally absurd," Morton snapped. "You cannot fire an employee for playing softball, Nestor. The Division of Employment Security would string you up."

Nestor flopped into a chair and poured himself a cup of coffee. "I can't have any fun any more. Coffee?"

"No thank you."

Nestor bit into a slice of banana bread. "Go ahead, Mort, it's good this time. I have a new chef. We shipped that Indian cretin off to the cooking school you told us about."

Viola selected a corn muffin from the tray. "Did it really have to be Switzerland, Morton? I mean, aren't there any cooking schools in Buffalo or Trenton?"

"Look, you two were desperate. We needed a four-thousand-buck write-off. And I told you the results were guaranteed."

Nestor suddenly slapped Viola's hand. "Put that coffee down! No caffeine!"

"What the hell's the matter with you? This is for Morton!"

"Sorry, V. Looked like you were about to drink it."

"Okay, let's get down to business," Viola said, glaring at him. Of course she was about to drink it. Eugene didn't allow her to touch the stuff at home. "I have to get to the shop this afternoon."

Morton napkined the spilled coffee from his green accounting pad. "Did you get all your bathrobes in for Christmas? There's going to be a textile war in August. No doubt about it. The talks broke up for good."

"Dingleball finally found them in Crete," Viola said. "They were all water-damaged."

"He's making another shipment as fast as possible," Nestor said. "I told him I was flying over in two weeks to pick them up personally. I think that impressed him."

"You scared the guy out of his wits," Viola corrected. "Nestor told him he had strangled men in Cuba for rolling cigars wrong."

"My God!" Morton screeched. "Please don't say that to an American client! Once the ACLU hears about it, we're finished!"

"Calm down, Morton, I haven't strangled anyone in years. It hurts my hands."

The accountant snapped open his briefcase. "I thought the Swiss were more dependable than this. How did you two manage to find the only imbecile in the entire country?"

"We met him a couple years ago at a silk convention in Florence," Viola said. "Nestor's going to meet him again at this year's convention in Montreux. Dingdong's plant is only a half hour away."

"Well, Nestor, then you can drop in on your cook, too," Morton suggested. "Make sure you're getting your money's worth. I don't think the school's far from there. Take a few days in the mountains."

"I hate mountains. I like beaches. Sun. Water."

"How about hot springs? Mineral baths? The cooking school is part of a famous spa."

Viola scowled. "Now I'm paying for her to take mud baths, too? She'd damn well better be able to make lobster bisque and Beijing duck by the time she gets back, Morton, or I'll strangle her myself."

Morton plunged into a tendentious monolog concerning the perils of opening a shop in London as Nestor played with Smudge and Viola dusted the portraits of fish upon the walls. Then Viola lay down on the couch and appeared to go to sleep. Finally, when Nestor put Smudge down, crawled to the couch, and began giving Viola a back rub, the accountant threw his pencil at the cork wall. "Are you two even listening to me?" he shouted.

"Of course we are," Viola said without opening her eyes. "You just said rent would be forty-two hundred pounds a month. That means we'd have to sell one hundred six pairs of panties each week just to break even."

"Let's do it anyway," Nestor said, moving his fingertips to Viola's other shoulderblade. "What the hell, I like England."

"Did you hear what I just told you about taxes? Import duties? Registering every damn garter in the store with Scotland Yard?" Morton said. "And don't think for one minute you could wear those pajamas on Bond Street. They'd lock you up."

"These are my working clothes," Nestor said. "They are not pajamas. Next time you come here, Viola will be wearing them also."

"She will? And will you be wearing her dresses?"

Viola got off the couch. "I can't find any decent maternity clothes, Morton. It's easier to just wear pajamas." She looked at her watch. "I've got to get out of here."

"Just one moment now! We have to talk about that warehouse across the street. You have two dozen zoning appeals to sign. Then we're going over the midyear balance sheets. I don't want any surprises this December again." Morton had spent last New Year's Eve hastily jimmying funds between eight holding companies and overseas accounts.

Viola slouched into a seat at the conference table and began peremptorily reading the legal documents Morton handed to her for signature. After the first few she just began scrawling her name across the dotted line before shoving it over to Nestor.

"You call that a signature?" he said. "Smudge could have done better with his paw and a stamp pad."

"Just shut up, would you? All these papers give me a fucking headache."

"Well, pardon me," Morton drawled. "These papers just saved your company thousands of dollars. And if you want a real headache, try to run my office some time. I'm just waiting for the day they discover that carbonless copies are carcinogenic."

Viola stood up. "Look, we're all cranky today. Let's can this meeting and reschedule something next week. The midyear totals can wait another few days."

The phone on the conference table rang. "It's Eugene for you, Viola," said Henriette. "He said it was important."

Viola picked up the handset. "Yes, dear. Fine, thank you. Tonight? Oh come on, Eugene! Is this necessary? I see. Right." She shoved down the phone. "Crap."

"What's the matter?" Nestor said.

"Eugene's got a midwife coming to the house at six o'clock for an interview."

"A midwife?" Morton cried. "My God! What does he think this is, the Middle Ages?"

"She's supposed to be teaching us breathing exercises," Viola sighed. "I am somehow not looking forward to the three of us on a blanket in the living room." She took the last corn muffin. "I'll call you from the shop this afternoon, Nestor. Bye, Morton."

The door shut. Morton looked at Nestor. "Is Viola going to continue working after this baby?"

"You don't think she's going to stay at home helping that nut Eugene invent a perpetual motion machine, do you? She'd jump off the balcony in three weeks."

Morton uncomfortably cleared his throat: Eugene was an old friend. "She seems preoccupied and somewhat irritable lately."

"She's pregnant, for Christ's sake! This business with Dingleball has upset her. That's why I'm going over myself to straighten the guy out. Don't worry, in a month she'll be back to normal."

"You should maybe start thinking about buying her out, just in case she decides to retire. I can start drawing up some papers."

Nestor patted Smudge's torn stomach. "Let me tell you something, Morton," he said. "If Viola retires, I retire." He put the pup on one shoulder. "Believe me, it won't happen, not while she's married to Eugene. See you next week."

It had stopped raining and the sun was making up for lost time. Viola took a quick swim at the athletic club and continued to the shop on Madison Avenue. She hadn't been there in a while and wanted to check out the new window display. Midtown traffic was exceptionally docile: Even women in high heels dared to be jaywalkers today. Viola parked the car and walked up to her boutique.

In one Pyrana window posed a mannequin, its back to the sidewalk, Christmas bathrobe draped over its shoulders so that the heavy embroidery was displayed to fullest advantage. In the other window two faceless black mannequins lounged in yellow panties watching a yachting video. Evocatively crumpled at their feet lay a set of women's and men's underwear and a life preserver. Viola walked inside, tallying customers: two Arabs, three businessmen, one woman. Everyone seemed to be buying but the woman. In her hand was a credit card receipt for almost three hundred dollars and she wanted to know exactly what her husband had purchased here last month. Viola rolled her eyes at the salesgirl and cut through to the rear: Another dilettante playboy had neglected to check his pockets.

"Hello, Trixie," she said to the bookkeeper. "Is Stanley still around?" That was the window dresser.

"He left. Why? Don't you like the new display?"

"I want that white robe out of the window immediately. It makes me nervous."

"It should. We sold ten of them this morning. If it hadn't rained, we would have sold out. Now I think you still have three left."

"What the hell did he put that in the window for? I told him to wait until we had stock!" Viola grabbed the phone. "Doesn't anyone around here follow directions?" She dialed Stanley's home number and got his lover. "Hi Paul. Where's Stan?"

"At the doctor. He has a sore throat."

"Tell him I called, would you? Thanks." Viola hung up. "Why doesn't that fucker just use a rubber? Wouldn't that be easier than having a blood test every ten days? He's never home any more."

"You got me," said Trixie, typing an envelope.

"If anyone calls, I'm in the window. What should I replace the white robe with? What's in stock?"

"The pink flamingos on orange silk."

Viola returned to the showroom and got an orange robe from a drawer. As she stepped through a small door into the display window a van, crusted with rust, gurgled to a halt in front of the store. Viola pulled the shade, slipped the white robe off the mannequin, and reclothed it with the flamingos. This robe didn't drape the same as the white one so she took a few moments adjusting the mannequin's arms.

She pulled up the shade. On the sidewalk not ten steps from her front door marched a dozen women in a tight little circle. Each of them toted a placard: *Down with Sexist Lingerie,* she read, then *Outlaw Lace,* then *Garter Belts = Fascism.* A limousine halted behind the van and she saw Dr. Bechstein, one of her oldest customers, emerge. "Damn," Viola said, retreating speedily from the window. She rushed to the sidewalk and took Bechstein's arm.

"Hello, my dear," he said. "What's all this commotion?"

"A few people want me to start making hair shirts."

"You two!" shouted a voice behind them. "Don't go in there!" Viola continued walking Bechstein into the store. "You're financing slavery!"

"I'll be with you in a minute," Viola said to Bechstein, shutting the door behind him. She turned around.

In her path stood Dr. Portia Clemens, the veterinarian. For a long moment neither of them moved. "Well, well," said Viola finally. "So this is what you do for a hobby."

Portia let the bullhorn drop to her side. "I certainly hope you're not buying lingerie here."

"I would never do that. I own the place." Viola sailed inside, smiled to her customers, and telephoned Nestor from the back room. "Get over here immediately," she said, voice shaking. "We have a severe problem."

Nestor had not heard Viola sound this bad since she told him she was pregnant. "What is it, babe? Those two transvestites bothering you again? I'll tear them apart."

"A bunch of women are demonstrating out on the sidewalk. I can't handle them."

"Give me a clue, V. Is it the Salvation Army? The Moonies?"

"Feminists."

"Ah, shit." Customers were more repelled by them than by typhoid fever. "Hold on, I'll be right over. Go sit in the back and sketch me something nice. Ruffles with red-and-white polka dots. Don't even think about that garbage out front."

"Their leader is the vet who sewed Smudge up," Viola sniffed. "This short blond bitch. I just can't take her. I don't know what's the matter with me."

"Nothing, sweetie! I'll be right there."

He was, in twenty minutes: Nestor had floored both the accelerator and the horn all the way into Manhattan. He zoomed up Madison Avenue and, horn still blaring, crashed his Buick right onto the sidewalk in front of the boutique. The women scattered.

Portia charged the car. "Are you out of your mind, you swine? You could have killed us all!"

Nestor hopped out, his canary yellow pajamas ablaze in the afternoon sun. Portia stopped dead in her tracks: Nestor bore a powerful resemblance to Floyd. "You stupid shit," he said to Portia in an undertone. "You mutilated my dog."

"What are you talking about? Who are you? I've never seen you before in my life!"

Nestor drew Smudge out of his pajama top. "Look at my pup's stomach. You did the worst hack job on his stitches I ever saw." His voice never rose above a whisper. "He bleeds every night thanks to you, you incompetent bitch."

Portia leaned over. "Let me see those stitches."

Nestor swooped Smudge above his head, out of reach. "Not on your life! You'll split the guy in half!" He looked at the demonstration, which was losing steam without Portia infusing heat at the bullhorn. "And you have the gall to be parading around the sidewalks instead of studying surgery." Smudge yipped, fearful of heights. Nestor returned him to his bosom. "He's all infected, too."

"Show me that dog," Portia shrieked, stamping her foot.

"How much malpractice insurance have you got?" Nestor displayed Smudge's stomach to Portia. "Where'd you get your license, Haiti? Hey! Don't touch!"

She gasped. "This dog needs immediate attention." Portia put her bullhorn to her mouth. "Sisters of WHAP, I must go. Continue as planned." She looked at Nestor. "I assume you can drive that tank to my infirmary without killing us all."

"Get in," Nestor said. "You really belong in the trunk." The Buick tore off.

Not one minute later, a police car rolled onto the sidewalk. Without Portia, who had taken off with their permits, bullhorn, and animation, the members of WHAP were forced to either disband or spend the rest of this sunny afternoon indoors, under arrest. The van chugged off, wounded, and disappeared around the corner of Eighty-sixth Street.

Viola came onto the sidewalk and leaned into the police car. "Thank you, gentlemen."

"Bunch of nuts," the patrolman at the wheel said. "They're not even funny any more."

"Hope they didn't scare your customers away," the other said.

A smile tilted Viola's pale white face. "My customers live dangerously," she said. "And they know about the rear exit." She asked for the sizes of the officers' current inamoratas and told them to stop by on their way into work the next morning. Then she went into the back room and began sketching something in red-and-white polka dots for Nestor.

He, meanwhile, had raced to New Jersey as if the four tires of the Buick alone stood between him and a radioactive cloud. Portia had strapped herself into the seat, saying nothing as pigeons and pedestrians flurried out of their path. Every time he hit a red light, Nestor cooed to Smudge, who nestled in his habitual cocoon. Portia he ignored completely.

"Is Viola Flury your wife?" she finally asked.

Nestor skidded out of the Lincoln Tunnel. "Where's this place of yours now?"

He followed her into the infirmary. A few people sat in the waiting room, reading animal magazines. Portia held out her hands, regaining a tad of authority. "You may wait here as I examine your dog," she said.

"The hell I may," Nestor said. "I'm watching every move you make."

No man had dared address Portia so disrespectfully in years. Under normal circumstances she could counterattack savagely; however, she was unsure how to handle a Hispanic in pajamas. She did not want to squash the ego of a downtrodden nonwhite; on the other hand, this man spoke English flawlessly. The pajamas threw her. She couldn't tell if he was straight or gay. He was handsome enough to get away with both. Even in this day of open communication, the man's language stunned her. He had to be rich to get away with such outrageous bluntness. Where were the diamond rings, the limousine, the rest of the male toys? She couldn't figure out the dog at all. Men in power positions went for pointers and purebred hounds, not mutts. And he was in thick with Viola Flury. For some reason she could not thoroughly analyze, this irritated Portia more than anything. She found Nestor a ferociously attractive man. "Very well," she said, "come inside."

He followed her into the enormous laboratory, watching without comment as Portia washed her hands and donned a white smock. She switched on the light above a white table and looked expectantly at the bulge in Nestor's pajamas.

Whimpering slightly, Smudge curled around her hand as she lifted him onto the table and very gently probed his stomach. "There's something beneath his skin," Portia said. "It's working its way out."

"And you didn't see that last time?"

Portia ignored the accusation and ran her finger over one of Smudge's cuts. "It feels like a tick."

"Tick?! Where?"

Portia guided Nestor's finger over the little lump, hoping for some reaction at the contact of their flesh: null. "I'll be damned," he said. "Are you going to take it out?"

"Normally, I would not have time. But I happen to have a cancellation."

"Cancellation, my ass. You'd still be pussyfooting up and down the sidewalk if I hadn't dragged you back to work." Nestor looked at his watch. "May I use your phone?"

"Over there," Portia snapped.

He dialed a number. "V? You feeling better, baby? You did? Red-and-white polka dots? I like it. Good for them. Did they use their billy clubs, I hope? Too bad. Those birds had no business being out there in the first place. Ah well, maybe next time." He glanced over at Portia, who was swabbing Smudge's stomach with antiseptic. "I'm at the vet's. She thinks Smudge has a tick on his stomach. That's why he hasn't been healing right. No, no, go home. I'll see you later. Okay. Bye." Nestor returned to the table. "Thanks."

Portia prepared an injection of procaine. "He's going to squeal a little," she said. "There's nothing I can do about that."

"Mother of God! Don't you people believe in gas?"

"I'm not going to knock out a five-pound pup," Portia snapped. "Just hold him steady," Portia said. "This will hardly hurt." Smudge disagreed.

Finally the anesthetic began to take effect. Portia cleansed the wound on Smudge's stomach. Then she poked around with a pair of surgical tongs. "Here's the culprit," she said, extirpating a small black nodule.

"That is not a tick," Nestor said. He thought back to the stranger who had recently made insidious inquiries about Smudge.

"How did it get there?" Portia turned the microchip over. "What is it?"

"The former owner abused him," Nestor said. "I think that's some sort of electrode."

"Who would do such a thing? What's his name?"

"I don't know," Nestor said. "But I remember his face."

Portia carefully placed the microchip in a dish. "This is the most appalling perversion I have seen in years. I certainly hope your pet has not sustained any lasting psychological scars. He might be in for lifelong therapy."

"That is bullshit," Nestor said. "My dog is perfectly fine. Just sew him up, please." He watched Portia draw some thread through a needle.

"The symptoms of neuroses are not immediately apparent. Does he cry in his sleep? Does he urinate in his bed? Does he chase mice? Does he bark at crocodile shoes?" Portia cut the thread and rolled Smudge back onto his feet.

"Are you kidding? He sleeps all day. In my shirt. Except when Henriette feeds him his special formula, buttermilk and tuna fish. Then he goes to the doghouse with Mai Ping and runs in a treadmill."

"That's disaster," Portia said. "The dog will become irreparably confused."

"Nonsense," Nestor said, rolling Smudge back into his pajamas. "How much do I owe you?"

"One hundred ten dollars. In-house surgery." Smudge began to cry. "You see what I mean," Portia said. "He's an angry animal."

"He's hungry and his stomach's in ribbons," Nestor retorted, removing his wallet. "And the prices you charge are outrageous. You deserve every malpractice suit you get." He handed the cash to Portia and turned away.

"That fee includes removal of stitches and an introductory hour in therapy," she shouted after him. She did not want Nestor to leave the lab. "You forgot your evidence."

He was already halfway down the hall and she still did not know his name. Portia caught up with him at the door. "And you forgot to fill out a registration card."

"What for? I'm not voting here."

She walked him to the Buick. "Here is my business card. Please call if you have a problem with your pup. Remember what I said about that first therapy session."

Nestor tossed the card onto the dashboard and leaned out the window. Portia thought finally he was going to introduce himself and, of course, thank her. "You know, I detest pushy women," he said. "They're totally unnecessary." The Buick blasted away.

Portia knew that she had found her inseminator.

Since receiving the bulletin from Berlin customs, Special Agent Hash had been vigilantly patrolling the USDA kennels in New York for a dog implanted with microchips or microfilm. For one week he had found nothing but sullen hounds and vicious terriers awaiting emancipation from their cages and was beginning to shelve the whole investigation when, on the eighth day, he came across Champ, beloved pet of Dr. Portia Clemens, who wished her Dalmatian to enter Switzerland with her one week hence.

"Look at this, McPhee," Hash said, stopping in front of the cage. "I think we've got something here."

McPhee was recovering from another hangover, tenth in a row since July Fourth, when Hash told him he had interrupted Frisk in the arms of Floyd Beck. McPhee knew all too well what she was like before long goodbyes. "Such as," he said without enthusiasm.

Hash pulled Champ's papers. "Portia Clemens wants pooch to come with her to a veterinary convention in Montreux. That's Switzerland. I don't like that." Floyd hadn't liked it either. He had called Hash just before leaving for vacation asking him to ambush the dog's papers for the good of mankind. Hash got an Agriculture official to spring Champ from her cage. "Could we check this dog out?"

"Just came into quarantine this morning," the man said. "What would you like to see?"

"Her stomach, for starters."

Champ was induced to lie on her back and get petted. "I don't believe this," Hash said. "It's covered with stitches. She couldn't be that obvious. She couldn't think we're that thick, could she?" He grabbed the papers from McPhee. "What's the explanation."

"Sex change operation," McPhee read. "Can you beat that?"

"Beck escaped from that woman just in time. I think." Hash chuckled. "We'll ask Frisk."

McPhee wanted to bash him in the face but restrained himself: Hash wouldn't be making these terrible insinuations if he knew the truth. "She could have planted half a Univac in that mess," he said, staring at Champ's belly. "Are all those tits fake now?"

"I'm going over to her clinic and ask a few questions," Hash said. "Normal people just don't schlepp Dalmatians to Switzerland."

Hash drove to Hoboken, imagining how Portia had spent the rest of her July Fourth once all the parades were over. He drove past Floyd's house, checking that it was secure. Things were very quiet at the terminal with Beck gone, McPhee drunk, and Frisk working the piers: Hash felt like taking a week off himself, just to relieve the tedium.

A huge black Buick blocked the entrance to Portia's clinic. Hash put his Firebird into reverse and began to squeeze into a parking slot halfway down the street. He had just turned off the engine when who should emerge from the clinic but Portia, accompanied by that maniac in pajamas from Paterson. Hash nearly choked to see a small black dog in the man's arms. He watched Nestor get into the Buick and roar away. Portia stared after the car for a considerable length of time before returning inside.

Hash sat in his car for an even longer time before turning the ignition. Dog; drugs; corsets; so his informant hadn't been conning him after all. Portia and Nestor were in this together, weren't they. She was avenging forty male presidents and he was avenging the Bay of Pigs, three-piece suits, who the hell knew. Hash merged his Firebird into the Holland Tunnel, imagining the look on McPhee's face when he learned what Hash had pieced together from just a few disjunct clues. Such investigative brilliance could land an agent in Washington, at the head of the Customs Service. Smiling, Hash sped up the ramp into Manhattan. Southern women were famous for their hospitality.

8

"Eggli? I think he's cute."

"I think he's nuts. Did you see the look in his eye as he was carving up those radishes? Calling them Caspar?"

"Girls, the man is an artist and entitled to his eccentricities. I thought it was a splendid first day of class. Scrambled eggs will never be the same for me."

"I thought it was kind of anal to spend half a day on pots and pans."

"You obviously have much to learn, Breeze. It's a shame that you spent more time ogling that Danish student than you did taking notes."

"Oh, you noticed that?"

"Everyone in the class noticed it, dear. Really, did you have to ask him to tie your apron for you? It's the oldest trick in the book."

"He didn't seem to mind."

"He's gay, Breeze. No straight guy would have fluffed up the bow like that afterward. And did you see the way he was staring at Eggli? Mooooo."

"Crap! Why is it that the only decent men left are married or gay? I was hoping that things might be a little different in Europe."

"Men are alike all over the world, I'm afraid. Animals. I don't know why you even bother with them any more. Aren't you happy single?"

"Sure I am. But men are such fun to play with."

"Efffui! I suppose you consider herpes, VD, and AIDS fun also."

"Get off the pulpit, Swallow. When was the last time Leonard made you crazy? Don't look so outraged, I know how these things work. You've been married how long? Twenty years? If you sleep with the guy once between now and Christmas, consider yourself lucky."

"Or unlucky."

"You two find these crass comments amusing. Go ahead and laugh. Just remember I'm still the one who's married, and you're not."

"Big deal, I could get myself married in a week if I tried. Rhoda might have a problem. You look a little over the hill, lady, if you don't mind my

192

saying so. Why don't you color those gray hairs? Get that lard ass down to a size ten?"

"What the hell for? This is my natural state, something I couldn't say for you. And I already told you I'm not interested in the dear boys. All they do is drink your booze, fuck you badly, then disappear."

"What do you mean badly?"

"Badly. Epileptic chipmunk. I haven't had a decent lover in ten years."

"Why is that, you poor thing? Don't you explain beforehand exactly what suits you?"

"Do you?"

"Of course! Men are much too thick to figure out these things for themselves."

"My God, you actually said something bad about Leonard. Let me get this on tape."

"Breeze, cut the crap, this is a serious discussion. What did you do, Harriet?"

"Simple. One night I said to Leonard, 'My dear, you are a good provider and an excellent bridge partner. However, you are one dismal flop of a lover.' "

"How'd he take it?"

"He called his mother."

"Jesus Christ! What did she tell him?"

"She said she should have told his father the same thing forty years ago. From then on it was total, blissful obedience. So you see, you must lay down the law at the very outset. Men are insecure, stupid, and generally as incompetent at sex as they are at everything else in life."

"For years I thought it was me."

"Of course not, dear! Haven't you ever heard of pearls before swine?"

"Sure. But I thought I was the swine."

"You are really fucked up, Rhoda."

"Louis my husband did this to me. But I finally began to dig myself out. I joined a group called Gynamite. It saved my life. I never knew how to get along without the bastards until I joined that group."

"I myself belong to a group called Feminine Destiny. It meets once a month at the most popular singles bar we can find. We must be on the same wave length, Rhoda."

"You two call that a wave length? I call that a beeline to hell."

"You have no idea what you're talking about, Breeze."

"We all know what we're talking about. M.E.N. Look, I agree they're ridiculous. I just don't compare horror stories with twenty other sad sacks to feel a little better."

"Emotional support and growth is hardly a horror story."

"Give me a break, misery loves company. I'd rather be venting my rage on another man. That's what I call emotional growth."

"Excuse me, ladies. Ze dining room is now closed for ze evening."

"What? It's only seven o'clock, Fräulein Moser! What are we supposed to do until bedtime? Read? You got a television here?"

"You take a valk. You write postcards. You sew in ze drawing room. Breakfast is at six tomorrow morning."

"I'm going to do some aerobics in the back yard. Your chef laid it on a bit thick with the carbos tonight, Froy."

"You do not like ze spaghetti? Zen vhy did you eat it all?"

"We were very hungry from our day at class."

"How vas ze class? You learn about eggs and pots today, no?"

"That's right. It was incredibly fascinating."

"Eggs and pots? *Mein Gott.* Please bring your plates to ze little door. Ze cook vashes zem for us."

Floyd ducked out of the way of the sliding door just in time to avoid being seen. He washed the dishes, crawled through Moser's little tunnel into Emwald, and walked to the Hotel Badhof, where Eggli was in the throes of dinner. The chef stood before the gas stove, tossing trout and almonds in a frying pan as he shouted over his shoulder to various assistants ranging the kitchen. Each time the oven door opened next to Floyd, luscious roasts and soufflés emerged. "What is it, Anna, I'm busy now," Eggli shouted, poking the trout. A glob of hot butter singed his finger. "Damn, he got me!"

"I'll step in for Count Zimstein," Floyd said. "He starts tomorrow night?"

"Yes, fine! So what shall we call you? Son of Zimstein? Hans! Get me that tureen!"

Floyd thought a moment. "Count Carnegie."

"Ah! Like the famous delicatessen in New York? I have eaten there many times."

"That's right." Floyd hopped out of the path of a standing rib roast. "I'm still not quite sure what Zimstein was supposed to be doing."

"Simply eating and making editorial comments. It adds a bit of elegance to my class. You make things up as you go. That's what Zimstein did."

"I'll try my best."

"Just come here at eight o'clock with your tuxedo. And make sure you comb your hair and wear a bit of perfume. Look at this trout! Wouldn't you be proud to smell so delicious after you were fried?"

"Certainly."

"What's the matter with you, Anna? You look upset."

"I'm not upset. And will you please stop calling me Anna? My name is Floyd. Anna was my mother. Me Floyd. Floyd. Get it?"

"I cannot help it. You look exactly like your mother. It still startles me. Don't ever wear a dress in my presence. I would die of shock." Eggli threw sliced leeks and two sausages into a pan. "What an aroma! Goodbye, I have no more time tonight."

"Remember why I came here," Floyd said, looking at the sausages.

"Of course I remember! Caspar whispers it to me at night. Now will you get out of here, Count Carnegie? Hah! Why not Count Corned Beef?"

Floyd left the kitchen, wondering about the long-range effects of searing stoves upon the brainpan. Why must Eggli keep calling him Anna? Caspar never mentioned that Eggli knew his mother. He just said that he and Eggli were buddies before Caspar married and left the country. Perhaps Fräulein Moser could furnish some clues; he'd ask her next time they played canasta.

Floyd walked into the forest to his lake and sat against a pine tree, watching the sun set. He did not want to return to the pension before those three bitches had retired for the evening; their voices cawing downstairs would bore straight through the walls into his bedroom. Christ! Couldn't they talk about anything but men? In the two days since their arrival Floyd had overheard nothing but the sins of Louis, Leonard, and those three hapless clods who had attempted to marry the Indian. By tomorrow they'd probably start dismantling the penises of these gentlemen, comparing tales of inadequacy. What happened to the days when women like Aunt Margaret could sit in a parlor and chat for hours about lace and applesauce? Or children? Floyd snorted: God forbid that any of these hellions actually propagate.

An image of Portia breast-feeding an infant as she shouted imprecations into her bullhorn sprang into Floyd's mind. He sighed: There was no escape. Such women were everywhere, and reproducing, like mosquitos and goldenrod. Mankind would survive, but at an effort. At least mosquitos and pollen had the courtesy to be seasonal. Why this obsession with proving half the human race useless as an appendix? Let them stock up on frozen sperm, ship all the males to Australia, and see how paradisical the world became. Without a target for their henpecking and their lascivious wiles, women would have to rebound their frustrations and ambitions not upon the docile sex, but upon other women. Within a few months they'd make male aggression look like Aunt Margaret's games of musical chairs.

Floyd looked across the lake to the pine forest on the other side. Already it lay in deep shadow; once the sun set behind the mountains, day capitulated almost immediately to night. He wondered who owned the forest. There were no houses on the shore, no châteaux halfway up the mountainside . . . one morning he would like to hike over there. Or he'd swim. It didn't seem like a long way. The lake was surely as cold as the snow which melted into it from the mountaintops. Floyd walked to the shore and put a hand in: The water was startlingly warm. Then he remembered the hot springs beneath the valley. He wondered why no one ever swam here instead of the little pools behind the hotel. No stern lifeguard; no attendant with a little white towel; no ceramic tiles; just fathoms and fathoms of black, sultry warmth. Floyd rolled up his sleeve and swished his arm through the water. It enveloped his flesh like a lonely widow. He hadn't been swimming in a long time and his body wanted to be floating again, half earth and half sky, more fish than man. Floyd stripped and slipped into the water: Pleasure swallowed him. He floated on his back, paddling occasionally and nowhere, watching the mountains slowly fuse with the black sky until there was nothing but night buoyed by a tremendous, monolithic silence.

Ah, Viola. Last time he had seen her they had been in a lake at dusk floating just like this, watching a tiny white gash of moon peep above the horizon, not touching, then fingers touching . . . thinking about it still made his guts turn. He remembered pulling her to the shallows and finally after two years wrapping his arms around her, whispering her name as her skin touched his chest: Home sweet home. His fingers snagged in her heavy black hair. He remembered holding her like some huge white water lily, not understanding why such beauty should exist, nor pause with him now. Where her skin met the air, he smelled roses and warm cream. It was not soap; that would have dissipated into the lake. This came from inside of her, and he had smelled it before, across aisles, across intermissions, across dreams. Finally he couldn't stand the not knowing and moved his lips along her cool shoulder, breathing her rather than kissing her. She sat so very still that he almost stopped. Joy, pain deep as the lake dissolved him: He was going to drown. That's what he had always wanted.

Floyd quietly paddled back to shore and dried himself with his shirt. He did not care to recall the rest of that evening. The valley had quickly become cold: The mountains, alive by night, breathed on it. Floyd pulled on his clothes and returned to Luthergasse. Emwald, cows excepted, already slept. Only one light remained on upstairs at the pension. Floyd wondered if it was the Indian, the fat crab, or Leonard's Prize, snug in her narrow, lumpy bed. Getting along fine without men, eh? He'd soon see about that.

In four days of class, Chef Eggli had coasted through rolls, eggs, raw vegetables, and cheese pies. Now his students were going to work on their serving skills. All ten of them clustered the oversize wooden table in the center of the hotel kitchen, scuffing dust from their white gloves and black jackets. "Attention, class," announced Chef Eggli, rapping a wooden spoon upon the table. "We are about to meet the public. Let me go over a few points. First, I assume you all have some experience presenting food to others. Although this is an informal buffet tonight, please remember the correct procedures we have gone over in class. The guests of the Badhof are used to being pampered. They pay well for the privilege." He looked pointedly at Breeze. "I want no stupidities. This is not a social occasion. You stand behind your assigned entrée and you serve it to the guest. That is all you do." He straightened his high white toque in the reflection of a frying pan.

Harriet Swallow, attired in an ill-fitting tuxedo, raised her hand. "How many guests will we be serving, Chef Eggli?"

"Thirty or so. And do not forget what I said about Count Carnegie."

Rhoda raised her eyebrows. "I thought your brochure said Count Zimstein. What happened to him?"

"He died," Eggli retorted. "I hope you don't mind. Have no fear, Carnegie is equally as capable of observing you and correcting fine points of etiquette. Tonight, because it is our first outing, he will not criticize your blunders. But just tonight."

"What does he look like?" Rhoda asked.

"You will find out soon enough. For the moment he will remain incognito." That way, if Floyd messed up, Eggli could still scramble for another substitute. "Any guest could be Count Carnegie, remember that. Five marks against you, and you are finished with my course. I send you home. I do not care how much money you have paid to come here. I have no sympathy with imperfection, nor with slow learners."

"Do we get a refund," Breeze asked.

"No! You pay the penalty of wasting my time!"

"Chef Eggli," Rhoda said, "this was not mentioned in our pamphlet. I do not know whether you have the right to do that."

"No? Let me tell you something. If you want rights, you stay in America and send telegrams to the president. My class is a privilege, not a circus." He looked at the other students. "Are there any more questions? Then go to your dishes and check that they are perfect and the silverware is spotless."

Chef Eggli looked anxiously into the empty dining room of the Hotel Badhof. He had told Floyd to show up at eight, go through the buffet line, and sit at the reserved table in the west corner. He was to eat very slowly and speak only the Swiss dialect, or English with a heavy accent, to anyone attempting to converse with him. Simple. Still, Eggli was worried. Caspar Beck had been a merciless practical joker. "All right," he called. "Out into the dining room." He inspected each dish as it was carried by.

Harriet Swallow passed with a platter of deviled eggs. "Where's your parsley," he roared. "Where did you learn to cook, the New York prison system?"

"Parsley is so old-fashioned, Chef Eggli," Harriet announced. "In America, the vogue is to present dishes without garnish. We call it minimalist cuisine."

"I call that naked cuisine. If Count Carnegie were keeping score tonight, you'd have one point against you already. Get back to the kitchen and make me a decent-looking platter. Pfuiiii! Americans!" Chef Eggli passed five male students. Then Breeze came by with a basket of rolls. "Where are the tongs? You serve rolls with your fingers at home?"

"Sure. And I don't wear white gloves at home, either. I find it a little pompous."

Chef Eggli bopped Breeze on the head with his wooden spoon. "I give you a choice. Either get the tongs or get the next plane out of here."

Rhoda was standing behind Breeze. "I protest all this violence. You're harassing the women in this class."

"Eh? Women happen to be the stupidest members of this class. Get over here." Chef Eggli pushed Breeze out of the way and sniffed Rhoda's stuffed tomatoes. "Too much garlic," he said icily. "Serve it with a smile, if possible."

"That is demeaning," Rhoda answered. "You have no right to ask me to do that."

Chef Eggli turned to the student standing behind Rhoda with a bowl of strawberry salad. "Do you believe what you hear, Hein?"

"Uncredible."

"You men are trying to intimidate me," Rhoda said. "It's not going to work."

"Get into the dining room," Chef Eggli snapped. He was about to smack Rhoda on the head with a wooden spoon but suddenly thought better of it.

Finally the ten students had arrayed themselves behind the buffet table.

Eggli nodded to the maître d', who swung open the dining room doors as the harpist in the corner began daubing at a bit of Debussy. Gradually the room filled with impeccably dressed guests who did not look in the least in need of hot mineral baths. They filed past the buffet choosing bits of this and that before returning to their tables and visiting with the wine steward.

Precisely at eight o'clock Chef Eggli saw Floyd walk through the door. His appearance was beyond perfect. The boy was born to wear evening clothes. In his lapel he wore a snowdrop and he had combed his hair straight back so that the grey streaks rippled just above his ears. Graceful as Valentino, he moved towards the buffet table. Floyd could tell the boy was up to something; he had seen the same cunning in Caspar's face when he was playing his terrible jokes on people. The entire dining room noticed the stranger. He had definitely not been soaking himself in the baths this afternoon with everyone else.

Floyd took the plate which a gloved student handed him and edged slowly along the buffet table, accepting tidbits from the servers on the opposite side. He met the Indian first. Originally she must have been an attractive brunette, but the lifelong strain of emulating a Las Vegas chorine was taking its toll. Now her hair looked too blond, her nails too red, her rear end too tight; by the lines on her face Floyd suspected she either smoked or drank to kill the hunger pangs. She reminded him of a fading lioness, still sinewy and sharp, but aware that the cubs were outpacing her.

As Floyd passed she stared so openly at him that Eggli pinched her rear end. "Rolls," he hissed, padding behind the line of students. Floyd timed it perfectly, moving on so that he was just out of range as she lifted her tongs.

Floyd needed a moment to decide whether the next woman behind the buffet was Leonard's Prize or the fat crab. They were both pudgy. However, the one behind the deviled eggs looked a little softer around the edges: Leonard's mitigating influence. Floyd guessed she had not been contradicted in the last forty years. It showed in the arch of the eyebrow. He smiled at her, said nothing, and held out his plate. Harriet ladled a deviled egg smack on top of Floyd's duchess potatoes. "Oh I'm so sorry," she said. "Excuse me."

Eggli stalked behind her. "Idiot," he whispered. "Imbecile."

"She is not," Rhoda cut in, then noticed Floyd. Even after years of behavior modification, sight of a handsome stranger in a dinner jacket still killed the current . . . momentarily. "Stuffed tomatoes," she said, not smiling. Floyd knew she would have smiled had she dressed a little more becomingly, say, in a tailored blouse and maybe a pair of earrings, like Harriet. But Rhoda had chosen to wear no makeup and a jacket cut for six dead pillows. The double chin and the crewcut did not complement each other.

"Tank you," said Floyd, proffering his plate. Even Rhoda was not bad-looking. None of these women were bad-looking. They just sounded ugly through the kitchen wall.

Floyd meandered to the end of the buffet and continued to his table in the corner. He was the only person in the room dining alone, a fact not unnoticed by those ladies seated with less invigorating commensals. Aunt Margaret's two decades of etiquette training finally paid off: With an aplomb which nobody would have mistaken for an American's, Floyd lifted the correct fork, the correct knife, and commenced eating his dinner, occasionally smiling at the harpist. Finally Eggli had to swing by and pretend to ask how dinner tasted. "Stop this, you fox," he muttered, elaborately pouring some wine. "You're disrupting my class."

"I have no idea what you're talking about."

"Of course you do. Finish your dinner and get out of here immediately. I should have known a son of Caspar Beck would do this to me. I see history repeats itself."

A fine redhead loomed behind Chef Eggli. "Hello Urs," she said in the dialect, allowing the chef to kiss her hand. "Your students did quite well. Who is your friend?"

"This is Count Carnegie," the chef replied disapprovingly. "He just happened to be driving through Emwald on his way to Gstaad."

Floyd stood up. "Good evening," he bowed. Had Aunt Margaret been around she would have rewarded him with a chocolate. "A pleasure to meet you."

"You are Swiss?" the woman said, hearing the dialect. "I am surprised that I do not know you."

"Yes, yes," Eggli interrupted, "Carnegie has been abroad for years. Please return to your table, Angela, I cannot see what my students are up to if you stand in my dining room like this. Thank you." The moment she left, he turned on Floyd. "What in the name of God are you doing to these women?"

"Nothing. I'm just sitting here counting the peas on my plate."

"I give you three minutes to finish the peas and go home."

Another woman said hello to Chef Eggli and introduced herself to Floyd. Suddenly he felt as if he were back in The Outpost, but all dressed up this time. Floyd put his napkin down, shook the woman's hand, and excused himself: On this side of the Atlantic, he would do the pursuing.

He walked back to the pension, opened a beer, and stared out his little window at the moon. Hours later, far from sleep, he heard Harriet, Rhoda, and Breeze come crashing in, complaining about the lack of streetlamps. That made him smile.

Floyd awoke with the sun and boiled the coffee. He sliced up the bread, slid it out to the kitchen counter, and waited. Fräulein Moser ate and left. Around half past six the three classmates stumbled down to the dining room.

"So how'd you sleep, Harriet?"

"Not well. I believe the goat has moved beneath my window."

"You made quite a spectacle of yourself in class last night, if I say so myself."

"In what regard? Please pass the bread. The coffee's undrinkable this morning."

"I saw you dump the deviled egg right on that guy's mashed potatoes. Eggli was choking. You never got your wits together after that."

"The man startled me."

"He startled me too, honey, but I didn't go flinging rolls into his fruit salad like a sixteen-year-old."

"Whatever are you suggesting, Breeze?"

"One damn gorgeous man . . . when was the last time you conned Leonard into wearing a tuxedo? I think he winked at you, Rhoda."

"I would have slapped him in the face."

"Sure, sure. You two are so full of shit I don't know whether to laugh or cry. He was sitting by himself in the corner, but I'm sure you two noticed that."

"What is the point of this, Breeze?"

"Look, we're in the mountains. Leonard's probably sweating bullets on the A train. Rhoda's little feminist group is in a pup tent talking about orgasms. I won't tell anyone if things get a little retrograde up here. Did you see those two phony sexbombs trying to pick him up?"

"That was disgraceful."

"Ah! So you noticed!"

"What has gotten into you, Squawfoot?"

"I'm just trying to see where you two stand. I suppose you've told me. So let's get this straight: If the guy shows up again, he's mine."

Conversation vanished. Behind the sliding door, Floyd began to wonder if the three women had perhaps flown out the window. Finally he heard a knife clink china.

"That's a rather juvenile statement, don't you think, Rhoda?"

"Very aggressive. Very hostile. How you could get so worked up over a total stranger disturbs me, Squawfoot. You have a lot of hangups to work out of your system. Think about it. A man like that has probably used and discarded hundreds of women. Don't you think it a little odd that he should be alone in the middle of nowhere? Did it cross your mind that he was probably cruising for another victim? Look how he was making eyes at Harriet."

"He was doing no such thing, I assure you."

"Come on, don't cover for the bastard. Then you saw how quickly he left. He probably arranged to meet that redhead upstairs. Such men are never satisfied with just one woman. They have to screw everything that moves. It's a game to them, like skeet."

"Thank God I think of men the same way."

"Efffuuiii! What an unbelievable statement!"

"You two really have no idea what the word liberation means. Instead of trying to make men think like women, why don't women just think like men? Then we're all equal."

"It's too early in the morning to get into this. I've already got a splitting headache from this coffee. Either of you have any aspirin?"

"Sure. In my room. What are we studying today?"

"Eggli's reviewing the buffet. Then I think we're doing tea sandwiches."

"When the hell's the chapter on coffee?"

"Rhoda dear, you're not feeling well."

"It's PMS. Yet another delight of being female."

"That's the spirit. Let's get moving, gang. Eggli said he was going to start handing out demerits for being late. He wasn't serious about shipping people home after five, was he? My boss would kill me."

"The idea is tempting, dear."

George Hash awoke at six in the morning and ran twice around the local reservoir. He took a long shower, shaved, and dressed very carefully. Then he drove to Portia's clinic, arriving shortly before seven. She was already out walking a few patients so he picked up coffee and croissants from the local donut joint and camped out on her front steps. On the way in he had again passed by Floyd's empty house. Hash wondered how his friend was doing in Florida; Floyd had been gone almost two weeks and no one had heard a word from him. He had given McPhee a phone number with a bogus exchange. At first Hash thought Floyd had taken off with Frisk. Wrong: She and her supervisor were playing zombie in New York. Then McPhee had shocked Hash by mentioning that Floyd may have gone for tropical-disease treatment in the Everglades. Why hadn't Floyd confided in him, Hash wondered. Was he that sick? He hoped it wasn't one of those desperate spiritual journeys which men of sudden middle age felt compelled to take: Floyd's soul would have had a much clearer understanding of Flesh vs. Immortality had he borrowed Roberta and Daphne for three weeks. Maybe he had gotten an invitation from a high school sweetheart to visit Disney World. Hell, maybe he just wanted to fish. Whatever the reason, wherever Floyd was now, Hash missed him. He flung the tail of a croissant into the garbage. The donut joint should have stuck to donuts.

Towed by two Great Danes, Dr. Portia Clemens tripped around the corner. She looked luscious: white shorts, black linen blouse . . . sandals would have rendered her legs a bit more user-friendly than those leaden hiking boots. "Donner! Blitzen!" she called. "To the left. Left!" Then she saw Hash. "Get off those steps! There's no room for you and two dogs!"

Donner slipped by Hash's left while Blitzen, blocked, immediately started to whine and chase her tail. Hash had never seen such behavior in a Great Dane. "That dog has a problem," he said, scuttling off the steps.

"That's why she's here," Portia snapped. "I hope you realize it will take an hour for me to unwind her now. Perhaps I should send the bill to you."

"If you can't see over a Great Dane, you shouldn't be walking one," Hash said. "And I'm here on business."

"I didn't think you'd be asking me out to breakfast. Hold this a moment for me, please." Hash was handed Donner's leash. Portia collared Blitzen and started talking into her ear as the two of them walked in circles at the foot of the steps.

After a few minutes, Donner yelped. He was becoming jealous of all the attention sucked up by his sister. "Take that dog inside, will you," Portia commanded. "Give him to the assistant in the office. I'll be there in five minutes."

There was no way to refuse without seeming piggish. Hash was beginning to see why Floyd had become so taciturn over the last few years. "I don't have all day, madame."

"Don't call me madame," Portia replied. "I don't run a whorehouse and I don't live in France."

"You might be better off if you did both," Hash snapped, stomping inside. He waited exactly ten minutes, then returned to the front door. By this time Portia had gotten Blitzen to lie on the sidewalk. "May I ask you a few questions, Dr. Clemens?"

"Just keep your voice down," Portia sighed, rubbing the dog's ribs.

"It has come to my attention that you have a Dalmatian in quarantine."

"That's right. Champ. She's going to Switzerland with me next week. I'm bringing her to an international veterinary conference in Montreux."

"Tell me a little more about Champ," Hash said. "How did she get all those incisions on her belly?" He watched Portia's face very carefully.

"She has undergone a series of operations over the past months. Her health is now perfect." Blitzen seemed to be dozing off.

"Describe the operations, please, in detail."

Portia looked up. "What is the problem? It's none of your business what happens in my surgery ward."

"Would you object if we X-rayed Champ before she left for Switzerland?"

"I certainly would! She's had enough X-rays to last three hundred dog-years! If you want X-rays, come to my office. I have dozens. Otherwise, forget it."

Hash watched an emergent stockbroker walk by, en route to the PATH station. That man had an easy life: He, his wife, and the people he worked for all shared the same concept of society. "What are you going to do with the dog in Switzerland?"

"Exhibit her as part of my lecture. She's unique."

Hundred of conventioneers, plenty of opportunity to make one more incision, hand that microchip over . . . Portia had thought it all out, clever girl. But it took more than chutzpah to become foolproof. Hash pulled a picture of Nestor Buffez from a pocket. He had snapped it in Paterson as Nestor was getting out of his Buick. "You wouldn't happen to know this man, would you?" he asked, dangling the picture in front of Portia's freckled nose.

Beneath the tan her blood froze, tingeing Portia's cheeks a disagreeable ochre. Her tiny mouth fell a tiny bit open, reminding Hash of a sunfish gasping for air. "I've never seen the man before," she said finally. "What is his name?"

After all those hours in Female Awareness, Hash had thought Portia would be a more accomplished liar than this. "Fidel Castro," he said. "You don't remember seeing a man who looked like this carrying a small black dog into your clinic, would you? Last Wednesday, perhaps?"

Her eyes darkened from jade to pewter: Portia's brain was soldering one zillion stray connections. "You're harassing me," she said finally. "Floyd put you up to this."

"Floyd?" Hash was stunned: The name had clouted him out of nowhere, like a boomerang. "He's got nothing to do with this."

Portia's fingers ceased massaging the Great Dane's gigantic ribcage. "Up, Blitzen. You're all better. We're going inside."

"I have a few more questions," Hash called.

"Get a subpoena." The door of the clinic slammed an inch from his toes.

A new Telex lay on Hash's desk when he returned to the terminal that morning. Apparently a little black dog with recent wounds on its belly had turned up in Vienna. Its purported owner, Josephine Smith of Nashville, was scheduled to retrieve her pet from quarantine in one week and take him to the opera, or whatever one did with mutts in Austria. One hour later, Hash got a second Telex from Vienna informing him that there had been a fire in the kennel and that the dog, if not roasted like its fifty neighbors, had escaped into the streets. There was no hope of ever finding the mixed breed among the thousands already roaming the city.

This made him very angry and somewhat impetuous. Hash drove to the Pyrana plant, waited a few hours, and finally tailed Nestor to a pet store, then a travel agency. He thought it irregular that the president of a large company would not have his secretary make all reservations for him from the office. Therefore Hash entered the travel agency, exhibited his badge, and learned that Nestor had just booked himself on a flight to Geneva leaving the next week. Hash went directly to McPhee and told him he wanted to raid the Pyrana plant and seize the pup before Nestor and Portia decided to do something rash; McPhee, however, did not think there was enough evidence to warrant a raid. He suggested instead that Hash have a forceful chat with the Cuban during office hours. The whole case mystified McPhee. He did not understand why Hash was becoming so engrossed in a few dogs while the pornography and drug files on his desk multiplied like spirochaeta in a sewer.

Hash reluctantly took McPhee's advice. He picked up a phone. "This is George Hash from the Customs Service," he said. "I would like to speak with Mr. Buffez."

There was a short silence ended by the explosion of a wad of bubble gum. "I'm sorry, he's testing underwear and cannot be disturbed," Henriette replied. "Who's this again?"

Hash repeated himself. Henriette thought he represented a talent agency. "We do not need any more models at the moment," she said. "Call in a few months." Then she hung up.

Thus Hash decided to intercept Nestor on public property. Around closing time he drove out to Paterson, posted himself across the street, and watched the Pyrana lot empty except for a dozen, six, then three cars. After a half hour the woman with the raven hair emerged with Nestor, who walked her to a Porsche and spent another fifteen minutes dangling over the window like a moonstruck lover. Eventually the Porsche rolled away. Instead of getting into the Buick, however, Nestor returned to the mill. An hour later, an Asian woman got into her white Toyota and drove away. The sun took forever to set and Nestor remained inside: still testing underwear? Or was he working on little black dogs now? Hunger sucked Hash's stomach as he tried to analyze Nestor's connection to Portia. Where would a Cuban anarchist meet a radical veterinarian? Why would Portia deny knowing Nestor? Why were they both going to Switzerland next week? And what was with that canine abomination named Champ? Hash wished Floyd was around to bounce ideas off of. He was great at pulling pattern from coincidence; it agreed with his philosophy of life.

As the stars came out Hash noticed a light flick on way upstairs: the corporate penthouse, of course. He groaned. Nestor was home for the night. He wondered what had driven the Cuban to buy a ramshackle mill and sink several million dollars into it for the sole purpose of manufacturing underwear. Ten years ago no one would have invested in such a risky concern. How did Nestor Buffez know that women would start wearing lingerie again? Or that men would dare buy it again? Maybe he read different magazines, or didn't believe what he heard on television. Maybe he had hit different singles bars. Maybe it was all a front for something much bigger: Pyrana imported and exported all over the world. How very convenient.

Suddenly the Cuban popped out the front door of the mill and jumped into the Buick. Hash's heart started to chug as he followed Nestor to Dominick's Pizza on Market Street. Oblivious to the stares of the teenagers belaboring the pinball machines, Nestor swished inside, spoke to the kid behind the counter, sat at a front table, and waited, staring fitfully out the window. After many minutes he got up, yelled at the kid, and sat down again. He seemed to be very edgy. The kid finally brought a pizza to the table. Nestor glanced at it and began gesticulating angrily. The kid took it away and began flinging another island of dough into the air behind the counter. Nestor bought a can of soda. Then he pulled the pup out of his pajamas and began playing with it.

A white Toyota crawled in front of Hash's parked Firebird. He saw the Asian woman who had just left the mill honk and wave at Nestor, then turn the corner. Hash watched fascinatedly as a few girls drifted from the pinball machines to Nestor's table and hovered dotingly around the dog. The kid brought a second pizza which seemed more acceptable to its purchaser. Everyone had a slice and Nestor yelled at the kid, ordering a few more. Soon he had a fairsize audience around his table. Hash tried to imagine, without much success, what Nestor was up to: Amateurs were so problematic. They did nothing according to the rules of criminal behavior. Why was he displaying the dog in public? Was he going to hand it over to one of the girls, who would in turn deliver it to a phony Mrs. Jones? Who was that chick in the Toyota? Maybe Portia had telephoned and panicked him and he just wanted to get rid of the animal but couldn't bring himself to abandon the pup behind a garbage can. As Nestor's table became more crowded, Hash suspected that some type of switch was about to take place. He decided to drift inside and order a meatball sub.

No one noticed his entrance. Even the kid supposedly making pizza leaned, two elbows over the counter, mesmerized by Nestor's dog story. "It's too early to tell," Nestor was saying. "The vet told me the mutilation might cause permanent damage to his personality." His audience murmured angrily. Newborn babies could be left out to desiccate in the trash, impure heroin could turn a classmate's brain into blancmange, but when the CIA tried to rearrange a puppy's bellybutton, that got to be too much. Then Nestor saw Hash. "Holy Mother of God, it's him!" he shrieked. "The cannibal! He's come back to kill my dog!"

Hash had just raised his hand to wave hello to Nestor when a large pizza pie hit him in the face. Had he been attacked by a giant, boiling squid in the middle of Times Square, Hash could not have been caught more off guard. The pizza wrapped halfway around his head, covering his ears, blinding him, choking him, and of course, burning him. The pan bounced noisily to the floor and tripped him. Then, before he knew what was happening, every kid in the room was on top of him. The fellow behind the counter threw a couple more pizzas into the fray, aiming at Hash but without as clear a shot as he had had before. Nestor leapt in over the top as if he were going for a touchdown, squashing all below.

Had Hash been in sharper physical condition, he would have been better able to defend himself; however, his right arm and his back had still not mended from the barroom attack of weeks ago. And, no matter what his state of readiness, one man did not disengage himself from fifteen adversaries quite as easily as he passed through a receiving line. Each time Hash got a good grip on one of the enemy, there seemed to be a piece of pizza in the way, or a sneaker in his nose. Nestor was continually trying to strangle him. "Call the cops, you idiot!" he screamed at the kid behind the counter. Hash took the opportunity to bash Nestor on the jaw.

The scuffle was a bruising, sloppy stalemate until Nestor suddenly noticed that the girl to whom he had handed Smudge for safekeeping now crouched a few feet away biting Hash's shins. He scanned the room just in time to see Smudge scamper out the door into the street. Nestor emitted a terrifying shriek. "My dog!" He relinquished Hash's throat and tried to free himself from the pileup, stamping on whatever lay beneath his slippers. He had just about made it to the door when, at maximum velocity, he skidded on a piece of pizza. There was a sickening crack as Nestor slammed into a pinball machine. "My dog," he croaked from the floor, rocking with pain.

When the police arrived, all of the kids except the one behind the counter had vanished. Hash lay serenely recumbent, spattered with tomato sauce, maybe blood; Nestor was whimpering profanely under a table, clutching an elephantine ankle. "What happened here, Tommy," the police officer asked the boy behind the counter.

"Please get me a towel and some ice water," Hash said from the floor. He still did not open his eyes. "My face is burned."

"First call an ambulance," Nestor said. "My damn leg's busted." He looked at Hash. "You touch that dog and you're going to be one sorry motherfucker."

Picking a dainty path between the floes of pizza strewing the floor, the policeman brought a towel and ice to Hash, who looked more tractable than the Hispanic in pajamas. "What's your name," he said.

Hash draped the towel over his face and poured ice water over it. "George Hash, Special Agent, U.S. Customs Service. On assignment. I.D.'s in my pocket."

"He wants to kidnap my dog," Nestor said. "He's been performing experiments on him."

"Where's the dog."

"He bolted," Nestor snapped. "What would you do if you saw Dr. Frankenstein coming at you just when your skin got back to normal?"

"Is this true," the policeman asked Hash.

"No," said the towel.

"Mind if I take a look at your I.D.," the policeman said. If that revolting mess at his feet was a special agent, he'd hate to see what Customs was hiring as routine inspectors. "Thanks." He pulled the I.D. and looked at the man in pajamas. "Major Hash is a Customs agent," he called.

"Oh Christ, who cares? Where the fuck is that ambulance?"

"What's your name?"

"Nestor Buffez. I live down the street. I just stopped in here with my dog for some chow. Then this dick walks in and waves hello as if he's trying to pick me up or something. The place went nuts."

The policeman looked at Tommy. "What happened."

"There was a fight."

"I can see that. Who was in it and who started it?"

Tommy did not want to admit that he had been a bit trigger-happy with the pizzas. "The guys were in here playing with the machines. They got a little out of hand."

"Do you have any idea where you are, major?" the policeman asked Hash. "Paterson, New Jersey. This is not the same as Sun Valley, Idaho. I know the kids who come here. Six of them used to be prostitutes. One of them tried to kill his own mother. Another stabbed his teacher in the neck with a screwdriver when she asked him to multiply six times eight."

"I knew I should have gone to the Chinese takeout," Nestor said.

"You would have been in fifty pieces by now," the policeman said disgustedly. "Asian gangs fight with knives, not pizzas."

The ambulance arrived and carted Nestor away. "What about my dog?" he said. "Ouch! Damn you! Can't you see I'm not dead yet?"

"We'll find your dog," the policeman said.

"He's a little black mutt. Name is Smudge. One thousand dollars reward." The stretcher bearing Nestor exited. "I'm filing suit. Infringement of civil rights. My lawyer's an activist." The ambulance doors shut.

"Was that guy for real," the policeman asked. "What's with the pajamas?"

"He sells pajamas," Hash said, slowly rising to a sitting position. "Lots of them." He removed the towel from his face.

The policeman winced. "Would you like to file a report?"

"No, drop it. We'll be seeing more of each other later. And he's not going to file suit, believe me."

"What did he do?"

"I'm working on it," Hash said. "Finding that dog would help." He limped toward the door. "Nice arm, Tommy," he said. "You should be in the majors."

At the same time that Hash had been jogging around the reservoir in preparation for his sunrise conversation with Portia and the Great Danes, Viola was rustled from pastel dreams. She felt Eugene's hands just below her breasts, gently stroking her stomach, and half rolled over: He was going to make love to her after all. She hadn't thought he'd be able to abstain for seven more months, as he had so confidently predicted last week. Since then, in retaliation, she had gone to bed naked; her flesh, so blatantly available, had finally worn him down. She smiled: Eugene was lazy and sensual in the morning. Viola put her arms around him.

"The Goldberg belt," he whispered. "It's slipped."

Cancel the day: Viola lay very still as Eugene softly tugged the Goldberg belt from her ribcage south to her abdomen. "How did this happen," he wondered. "It was snug when we went to sleep. Your stomach is becoming more convex, I notice. I might have to make some modifications in design." He centered the ear cuffs in the Goldberg belt. "You aren't trying to sneak this off when you think I'm sleeping, are you? I might have to put in a bottom strap."

"Like a chastity belt? Go right ahead." Viola rolled over, thwarted.

"Darling, please lie on your back. This should be balanced stereo."

"Eugene," she muttered, "I would have loved to sleep for one more hour. Wouldn't that have been healthier than one more go at the *Goldberg* Variations? If the kid doesn't know them by now, we've hatched a moron."

Her husband had not considered this. He apologized and got out of bed to make breakfast.

Viola stared at the ceiling awhile then took a shower. She felt like a huge slug: Maybe it was the humidity. She dressed and went out to the terrace. On the table Eugene had already placed a huge glass of milk, Birchermuesli, fruit salad, and buckwheat pancakes. He folded the *Financial Times* and anchored it under a flower pot. "How's your appetite, sweetie?"

Gone. The heavy breeze rippled Viola's shirtsleeves: Manhattan would become a cauldron by noon. "Eugene, I must talk with you."

He kissed her hand. "What is it."

"You're driving me out of my mind with this baby. I don't want to see any more midwives. I don't want any more breathing exercises. I don't want you reading me any more books when I'm trying to eat. I don't want to hear about names. And I want those carpenters to get the hell out of my house." They would be arriving in ten minutes.

Eugene sipped some orange juice. "I suppose I've overdone it."

Viola had been expecting rebuttal, denial, and accusation. Now, instead of feeling morally triumphant, she felt guilty. Eugene wanted this baby fifty times more than she. He was already the much superior parent. What was she bitching about? Would she prefer a husband moping around the house, sullen at the prospect of demotion to second place in his wife's priorities for the next twenty years? The poor man had done nothing but ejaculate at a catchy time of the month. "That's all right," Viola said miserably. "Forget it, you're doing fine. It's me."

"You're going to love this baby," Eugene said. "You'll see."

"That's what the wife is supposed to be telling the husband."

"Times have changed." Eugene moved his chair next to hers. "This is still the greatest thing that's happened to me. Besides you."

Viola picked at a strawberry. "We should take a vacation. Maybe next week. Go somewhere quiet. I could straighten myself out."

"That would be great, but the electricians are tearing the place apart. If we go away now, they won't come back for months." Viola said nothing. "I know! Let's go to a concert tonight. I'll get us tickets to something good."

"No Schubert."

"No. We'll go out to dinner and have a nice evening." A carpenter pounded on the door. Eugene kissed Viola's cheek. "You look quite beautiful these days. I can't describe it. There's something about your face."

Try round. Viola got up. The breeze had not been able to dry her hair. "See you around six, pop."

She drove to Paterson and killed the morning on the phone with smarmy retailers, suppliers, and sundry irritants who forever promised what they could never deliver. July was a terrible month in which to conduct business: Those who were not physically at the seashore were mentally crabbing. Lunch hour widened anywhere from ten in the morning til four in the afternoon. No one from California to Miami was eager to discuss the upcoming spring collection of lingerie. And of course there was Dingleball in Switzerland, who had accomplished less than nothing: Now he had run out of red embroidery thread. Since hearing that Nestor was flying over to personally pick up the white robes, Dingleball had become irrational. Each time Viola spoke with him on the phone now, the man sounded as if he had been inhaling laughing gas. Orders for the robes, meanwhile, increased daily. The advertising staff felt that not having an item in stock was no reason not to run copy on it.

Late in the afternoon Viola found Nestor in the fitting room studying Gina and Billy, who were modeling prototypes of the polka-dot lingerie which Viola had just drawn. He didn't like it. She didn't like it. The models didn't like it. Finally he sent them away. "What a shit day," he sighed, flinging a can of diet soda into the wastebasket. He punched a button on the telephone. "Henriette! Call the vet for me."

"Henriette's on vacation," Viola said. "And don't ask the temp to do it, she has no idea how to use a Rolodex." She sank into a chair. "Why do you need a vet?"

"Smudge is crying all the time. I think he's having psychological problems. He might need therapy."

"Maybe he's teething. Why don't you just leave him out in the doghouse a few days? He's getting too big for your pajamas anyhow." Viola cleared her throat. "I've been meaning to talk to you about that dog."

"You want me to get rid of him, don't you."

"Look, I know you're attached to the animal. He's very cute. Everyone loves him. But he can't be wandering around the mill any more. Morton's getting paranoid that an employee is going to trip over him and sue us for a million bucks."

"Morton has no vision," Nestor fumed. "After ten years he still tells me to wear suits to work. He gets upset when you throw shoes at him during board meetings. Just because he doesn't see an Irish setter at E. F. Hutton, he thinks dogs should live on farms. And no matter what we say, he keeps making the mistake of thinking this is a textbook operation." Nestor shot a rubberband into the overhead lights. "He can't comprehend it's just something we do to amuse ourselves."

Viola walked behind Nestor's chair and put her arms around his neck. "Keep the dog if it makes you happy," she said. "But please don't bring him back to that bitch of a vet. I can't stand her."

"You're angry at her for that demonstration in front of the shop."

"I don't like her, period." Viola stood up. "She's going to wreck your dog. That's the job of a therapist. Otherwise she'd be putting herself out of work. You thought Smudge was perfectly fine until she planted these ridiculous ideas in your head."

"He cries too much. I think he has nightmares."

"Sure he does. He dreams you're going to bring him back to the clinic."

Someone knocked on the door. "What now," Nestor shouted.

In walked Mai Ping. "Mr. Buffez, I wanted you to check out this new appliqué before I started cutting them all out."

Nestor inspected a beautifully embroidered hotdog Viola had designed on July Fourth, after the company picnic. It was going to be one of their fun summer items next season. "Nice job," he said, handing it back. "As usual."

Mai looked at Smudge whimpering on his master's breast. "Is he hungry?"

"No, Mai." Nestor sighed. "Just unhappy." He handed the dog over. "Take him out to the doghouse, would you? You're the only one who can get him to use the treadmill."

Mai left. Nestor stared wearily into space. Viola picked up a polka-dot brassiere Billy had discarded as she was leaving. "What a flop. I'm losing it, Nestor. Haven't drawn anything worth keeping in months."

"No, you haven't." Nestor never lied. That was one reason they had been unable to remain lovers.

She smacked him in the back of the head. "That's not what I wanted to hear."

"Then draw me something decent."

"Try it yourself if you think it's so easy."

"I never said it was easy. I said it wasn't very good."

Viola went back to her office, locked the door, and fooled around with a few floral designs. They weren't very good. She looked out the window for inspiration. Forget the sky, an overworked subject. Ditto flora and fauna. How about the parking lot? Wouldn't that be romantic? A doghouse, maybe? The facade of the Feinstein Corset Company? Viola sat at the drawing board and tried to imagine what she would wear were she intending to seduce . . . whom, damn it? There was no one left. For seven years Nestor had inspired her most voluptuous and erotic designs. Then, one irresistible spring night, she had made the mistake of realizing the inspiration. That killed not only her imagination, but Nestor's marriage to the ballerina as well. After that she had foundered upon lust for a while, then Eugene started visiting the shop. He had fueled two years of very subtle, fantasical design. Viola had won awards for many of them. Then she had married him and that particular fount sputtered dry. These men were not deficient lovers. But imagination was a hound, charged more by pursuit than by the kill.

Finally Viola put her pen and ink away: useless. As the belly grew, the libido shrank; God only knew how long it would take for her to relate to extravagant lingerie once the baby arrived. Maybe Pyrana should go into seraphic nightgowns and Victorian petticoats for a few years, capitalizing upon the neofascism which was sweeping the country back into monogamy, virginity, and Sunday school. Bah. Nestor would quit and she hated flannel. Viola drove moodily home. Nothing depressed her more than a vacant imagination.

Eugene took her out to dinner and made a heroic effort to not once mention cribs, midwives, or nurseries. However, this forced him to discuss even more unsavory topics such as current events and the daily tribulation at Pyrana, Inc. with his wife. Viola was becoming despondent. When she iterated that Eugene had better bag the carpenters and make one last fishing trip while the going was good, conversation ceased altogether.

Hoping to uplift the evening, Eugene took his wife to Carnegie Hall. He had gotten excellent seats which were eerily close to those which Viola had occupied long ago with Richard. She could barely bring herself to sit in them. But Eugene knew nothing about Richard except that he had been her patron and that he had died; she had never told him about the chamber music subscription at Carnegie Hall nor the two years she had

lived with Richard. Had he known, Eugene would certainly not have
bought these tickets.

Tonight a string quartet was performing an all-Beethoven program.
Viola shut her eyes as they filed onstage: She was revisiting a concert
which had occurred eons ago, when she was fairer game. Nothing had
changed. The musicians dressed exactly the same. They bowed like four
old men and their faces were still dour, tense, weighted with unimaginable
burdens. Applause crepitated through Carnegie Hall like a familiar, dark
tide; the chandelier diffused that same soft, yellow light over the red seats.
Viola clutched Eugene's arm. He leaned over in the gloom. "What is it,
darling?"

"Nothing." The quartet began to play and Viola cleared her throat:
Instead of Eugene, there sat Richard. Her brain swam in a deep circle,
still unable to sort hatred from love, and thus was marooned in an everlasting sea of anger that swept beyond Richard to the outmost fringe of her
life. He owned a ski lodge in Lake Placid and was introduced to Viola by
her coach during the junior national championships. She was fifteen and
he awed her: so dark and powerful and wise. He came to the rink every
day for two weeks to watch her practice, left for a month, then returned
on weekends, sitting silently in the stands, following her legs across the
ice. One evening Viola's coach took her aside and said that Richard had
taken an interest in her career and that she should consider herself extremely fortunate. Richard had brought her to New York when she was
sixteen, straight from a knee injury at Lake Placid, to study ballet and take
a break from the rigors of competitive figure skating. Her parents in St.
Louis had no idea that Richard was more than a sponsor, and that she
had no intention of stepping into a pair of skates again. They began to
get the idea, though, when she didn't return to Lake Placid the next fall.
In three years they never quite made it to New York; going out to dinner
with their omniscient, infallible daughter and a man twenty years older
than they was not the Flurys' idea of a family outing.

It had all been so long ago. She hardly remembered any of it; the brain
had cauterized so much. Even now, surrounded by familiar lights and
sounds, she had to struggle to convince herself that one Tuesday a month
she used to come here with someone named Richard and sit in the dark,
barely touching his elbow, insanely happy. For the first year, anyway. After
that, it had just been insane. He had been away a lot and she was left alone
in his enormous brownstone staring at a collection of minor Watteaus and
Fragonards and a housekeeper named Hiram. Then there was Floyd.

The quartet began a slow movement and Viola sighed. She had probably ruined the poor boy. She could still see him standing outside the ladies'

room at every intermission, arms folded across his chest, waiting for her to come out. He had the most beautiful quiet eyes, and he never spoke. For one year, concert after concert, he just watched like a loyal dog, as if he knew that someday she would break. She began to think about him at odd moments, wondering who he was, and why he looked at her like that. Maybe he had seen her skating somewhere.

In October of the second year Richard went away for two weeks and they had missed a concert. The next month he was overnight in Chicago and Viola decided to go to Carnegie Hall by herself. She had to get out of the apartment. She missed the boy with the gentle eyes and she was angry at Richard.

At intermission she came out of the ladies' room and there he stood, right outside the door, not across the way as usual. He startled her. "Where's your friend," he said. She could not place his accent. It was not New York.

"He couldn't come tonight," Viola said. "How do you know about my friend?"

"I sit behind you."

She was as shocked as if he had been peeping into her shower. For one year he had been an arm's length away from Richard and her? Damn, she had intended to keep the two of them completely separate, like Africa and Australia. "Why didn't you introduce yourself," she snapped.

"Why didn't you turn around?" He smiled to himself, as if the answer was obvious. "Your name is Viola."

He was beginning to frighten her. Normal teenage boys did not speak this way; they hawed and blushed and stared at her breasts like drugged mules. This one was like an early edition of Richard. Perhaps that was why she didn't run away. "How do you know?"

"I overheard your friend."

"What's your name?"

"Floyd Beck."

"Where are you from?"

"New York."

"Where in New York?"

He lived less than ten blocks away from her. She could run into him on the sidewalk at any time. Viola realized that this would not be terrible. "I have to go."

"I'll take you to your seat."

"I'm not going to my seat." She had gone home like a good girl. But she never whispered in Richard's ear again, nor let him kiss her hand, at Carnegie Hall: Floyd was watching. Long, long ago. Now he was a customs agent and she was a mother-in-waiting. It needn't have turned out that way.

Viola did not talk much in the cab home. "You're tired," Eugene said.

"Beethoven." She pinched his nose. "Great concert, Eugene. Thanks."

The phone was ringing as they walked into the foyer. Viola scrambled around the hole in the floor which still irritated her each time she had to circumnavigate it. It was a constant reminder of how events had continued without her permission. "Hello?"

"Hi."

"What's the matter?" Viola said.

"I'm in the hospital with a broken ankle."

"What?! How did that happen? Are you all right?"

"No. It hurts like hell." Nestor sounded pathetic. "Smudge ran away."

"Where are you? I'm coming right over."

"St. Elizabeth's." This was down the road from the mill. "Don't bother, Viola. Visiting hours are over."

"Forget visiting hours! I'll see you in fifteen minutes." She hung up.

"What happened?" Eugene asked.

"Nestor managed to bust his ankle and lose his dog. He's in the hospital."

"That's terrible. We'll go right over."

They arrived at the hospital forty-five minutes later and found Nestor in a private suite. His right leg swung in a giant cast and he was angrily flipping through a *Watchtower* magazine. "What took you so long," he fumed.

"Eugene drove."

Eugene gave Nestor some Belgian chocolates and a box of cigars. "How long will you be here, sport?"

"Two days. I snapped the ankle in three places."

Viola sat on the bed and took Nestor's hand. Cotton hospital pajamas were not quite his style. "What happened?"

"I was eating a pizza at Dominick's, minding my own business, talking with the locals, when this goon walked in. Remember the guy who was after Smudge? It was him again. The kid behind the counter hit him in the face with a pizza and there was a fight."

"I don't understand," Eugene said. "Why did the kid hit him with the pizza? That could be dangerous. Was the man threatening him? Or you? Why do you call him a goon?"

"Nestor believes the man was performing experiments on Smudge," Viola explained.

"Really? Now that's intriguing. Experiments of what nature?"

"Calm down, Gene," Nestor said, waving his hand in the air. "Let's not get sidetracked." He unwrapped a cigar. "Turns out this dope was a customs agent."

Viola felt the blood ebb from her fingers. "What does that mean?"

"I don't know," Nestor said. "We'll find out soon enough, I'm sure. Half the agency will probably be swarming the plant any day now, asking all kinds of questions."

"Questions about what? Pizza?"

"The dog, honey. Smudge."

"But I thought you said he ran away. How did that happen anyhow? Can you pick up your story where the customs agent got hit with the pizza? Or a little before that?"

"Eugene, give Nestor a break. This isn't an inquisition."

"It's simple, really," Nestor said, lighting the cigar. "The kid behind the counter is jumpy. He gets held up a lot. Once he started heaving pizzas, everyone began to fight. Smudge ran out the door."

"Why did you bring the dog with you?" Eugene said. "I thought pets were not allowed in eating establishments."

"We're not talking La Caravelle here, Gene. Damn, where's my dog? How can I sleep knowing he's lost on the streets of Paterson?"

"He's black," Eugene said. "He'll blend in with the alleys."

"Someone might shoot him," Nestor said. "Think he's a rat or something."

"Will you two stop this," Viola interrupted. "We'll find him, Nestor. There's a more important problem we've got to think about."

"Don't tell me Morton didn't renew our health insurance."

"Switzerland, remember? Silk convention? Dingleball? Airplane?"

"Nestor can't possibly fly in this condition."

"We know that, Eugene," Viola enunciated through her teeth.

The white smoke from Nestor's cigar curled gracefully as a honeysuckle into space. "You go, V," he said. "You need a break anyhow. I'll take care of these customs agents."

"Viola cannot take such a trip," Eugene said. "Not in her condition."

"I'm perfectly fine," she almost shrieked. "You're just afraid I won't wear the Goldberg belt."

"What's that?"

"Nothing," Viola snapped. She looked at Eugene. "I'll be going to Switzerland for a few days. Would you care to join me?"

Eugene had been married long enough to know that both a yes answer and a no answer would be equally unacceptable. "Let me sleep on it," he said.

A nurse irrupted into the room. "Where did these cigars come from?" she demanded, snatching the mundungus cylinder from Nestor's lips. "You people? Visiting hours are long over. You must leave immediately."

"See you tomorrow, Nestor," Viola sighed, slipping off the bed. "Can I bring you anything?"

"My dog and that goon's ass."

9

Chef Eggli irritably rapped his wooden spoon against a large kettle. He had not slept well: Caspar and Anna had been galloping through his dreams. "Attention, class," he called. "We are going to review our buffet. Then we will finish the day studying knives."

"Just one quick question, chef," said Breeze, raising her hand. "Which of those guys last night was Count Carnegie? Was it that hunk with the black hair?"

"Never interrupt me!" he shouted, flinging the spoon into a cauldron of chicken broth. "How dare you show such disrespect?"

Rhoda frowned at Harriet. Although she had disapproved of the question as well as its response, the latter came from a male and therefore demanded the sharper reprimand. "Let's not overreact, Chef Eggli," she tut-tutted. "This is not the court of Louis Quatorze."

"No, it is not. Louis Quatorze is dead. I am not. My kitchen is my court. And you now have one demerit for your stupidity." Chef Eggli straightened his apron. "Let that be a lesson to all who cannot take orders." He looked pointedly at Breeze and Harriet. "Count Carnegie is indisposed. He ate a few poisonous mushrooms. Do not expect him to return to our classes."

"What?!" Harriet cried. "That's impossible!" She had intended to interview him for her exposé upon cooking schools.

"He's the other half of this course," Rhoda fumed. "I'm seeing the Better Business Bureau about this. False advertising can lead to criminal prosecution, you know."

The male members of Chef Eggli's class looked at one another and shook their heads: *Gottinhimmel*, couldn't a guy even eat a few poisonous mushrooms any more? They could not figure out why these women had paid thousands of dollars and flown thousands of miles just to harass a helpless cook; wouldn't it have been more challenging to make eunuchs of all those cowboys who smoked Marlboros? Maybe this was some sort of perverted feminist safari, quarry Eggli, who had the bad luck to teach a course in a scenic location. The man was obviously not a misogynist. He didn't care if he taught men, women, or robots as long as they shut up and followed his directions. But he was in a no-win situation. If he ignored their incessant nitpicking, he drove the ladies into a frenzy. If he fought back, they buried him in statistics. And most critically, he didn't have the sense of humor to laugh and start calling everyone waitperson.

Eggli and his men were stymied. Aggression from their own kind they could handle; nothing in the history of the human race had prepared them for the revolt and subsequent aggression of women. Who was going to stay home and look after the tots? Who was going to mend their socks, arrange the cocktail parties, and hem draperies? And who the hell was going to make them feel like a demigod for getting out of bed in the morning? Upon such details rested the survival of civilization. Maybe in a few years one of these men would be able to invite Rhoda into the parking lot after class and thrash out their differences; right now the concept contradicted everything their mothers had taught them. Given enough time, and enough Rhodas of course, black eyes would cease to present an ethical problem. Meanwhile the men would just have to tread water very carefully, trying not to distract the predators prowling below them. Thus the other students in Eggli's class restricted their disapproval of Breeze, Rhoda, and Harriet to inimical glares and silence. They had come here to cook, after all, and not to debate the morality of serving unborn calf to counts, a dialogue about as productive as a thermonuclear exchange.

"The buffet," Chef Eggli continued, ignoring Rhoda's hints of a lawsuit, "on the whole was a success. Our guests seemed to enjoy it."

"How about that guy in the corner," Breeze persisted. "The one sitting by himself. Did he like everything?"

"He liked ze harpiste," said a deep voice from the rear of the kitchen.

Chef Eggli and his students looked behind them. There stood Floyd in a fine black suit, a large bouquet in his hand. *"Go'verdammi,"* swore Eggli under his breath. The boy looked exactly like his mother Anna with a short haircut. The chef was not used to her back in the same room with him after all these years, still young, while he had gotten old and thick. It made him doubly crazy. "Are you trying to kill me, Anna?" he croaked in the dialect. "I thought I told you last night to leave the dining room."

"May I see you a minute, Chef Eggli," Floyd called affably in the dialect.

The chef tore over to the corner. "What the devil do you want?"

"I think you need help," Floyd said. "Those three women are ruining your class."

"Is that so? How would you know that?"

"I've been here watching you a while. I also hear what they say at the pension. If this keeps up, you won't even get to boiled eggs in three weeks. Rhoda will sue you. Harriet will boss you to death. God only knows what Breeze will do to you."

"This is none of your business."

"Yes it is. I don't want you in an insane asylum before you help me make those sausages." Floyd glanced at the students and was pleased to see the three women staring at him. "I have a plan. You must trust me."

"I trusted you once and never will again."

Floyd had no idea what that meant, but wasn't about to get detoured. "Let Count Carnegie replace Count Zimstein. I promise I'll be nothing but exquisitely polite and proper. I've had a lot of experience with such women in America. You won't recognize them after one week."

"Chef Eggli," called Rhoda from the wooden table, "how much longer will you be using class time talking to that man?"

"I vas chust leaving," Floyd smiled to Rhoda, picking up his bouquet. "Are you going to let that bitch sit on you for another three weeks?" he said to Eggli.

"I'd rather jump off the Matterhorn."

"Trust me. I won't let you down," Floyd said. "Not this time," he added, shooting in the dark.

"My, that's a gorgeous bouquet," Breeze called. "I adore flowers."

"Whoever sent that woman here should have their heads examined," Eggli said. "She's stupider than a cow."

Floyd walked over to Breeze. "Zen you may keep zem," he said, presenting her with the bouquet. He returned to Eggli. "Until tomorrow?"

"I'm not sure," Eggli said. "This seems somewhat risky."

"Chef Eggli," called Harriet, waving a pamphlet in the air. "I've been re-reading your brochure. There are some egregious inconsistencies here which we must discuss."

"You come tomorrow," Eggli muttered to Floyd. "Before I kill them all." Floyd left and Eggli returned to the wooden table in the center of the kitchen.

"Thanks for the flowers," Breeze called. "Who was that guy, chef?"

"That was Count Carnegie," he snapped. "He's feeling much better now."

"He's going to be at class tomorrow night then?"

"That's what the brochure says, doesn't it?" Chef said, snatching the pamphlet from Harriet's hand. "I wouldn't want to mislead you with false advertising."

As Chef Eggli reviewed the buffet with his students, some of whom were not listening as acutely as others, Floyd walked back to the pension for a canasta game with Fräulein Moser and her friends. It was another gorgeous summer day; the clouds had shredded themselves crossing the Alps. Floyd's three canasta partners were waiting for him in the backyard, drinking tea and eating chocolate balls. "You are all dressed up," observed Fräulein Moser, dealing the cards. "Was there some occasion at the hotel?"

He lay a box of fancy biscuits on the table. "I'm substituting for Count Zimstein. He's too ill to come to the cooking school."

"Then you see the ladies from my pension?" Moser frowned.

"They'll never know I'm your cook. We tell them my name is Count Carnegie."

Fräulein Moser contemplated the cards in her hand. "This does not sound very good."

"No, it is very good," Floyd said. "The ladies from your pension think they are better off without men. Urs and I must show them how stupid they are."

"Urs is terrible at playing tricks. His temperament is very fragile. He has had an unfortunate life."

After a few rounds of canasta, which he lost, Floyd said, "I did not know that Urs knew my mother as well as my father."

"My boy, Urs was going to marry your mother until Caspar took her away to America. My poor cousin spent ten years in a complete stupor. Then he started to cook again."

"He calls me Anna occasionally," Floyd said.

"Yes, yes," Moser sighed. "He believes she will return to him someday. It is very sad." She popped a chocolate into her mouth. "He was quite curious to see you."

The sun slowly rolled from peak to peak as they continued playing canasta. Floyd imagined twenty years hence, when he was old and alone, receiving a phone call in the middle of the night from a son of Viola's, begging to come study customs violations with him. He wouldn't ask any questions either, would he; Floyd would probably do Eggli one better and buy the kid's ticket for him. And what if the boy had a dark mole on his left cheek, just like his beautiful mother? What if the boy's face was pale white and his hair black and his eyes sky blue? Would Floyd, befuddled in time, forever wandering in the dark, perhaps call the boy Viola, still wanting her so much that he would not care how foolish and senile he sounded as long as he could say that name again, and remember what hope felt like? God! Would she have children without him? How would he feel seeing a boy half Viola, half another man, innocently poring over customs manuals, asking questions, having no idea of the lost dreams his existence represented? No wonder Urs had taken off into the mountains; Floyd wondered how he had brought himself back to Emwald at all.

He lost another game of canasta. "Did my father really steal her?" he asked Fräulein Moser. "Did Urs just wake up one morning and they both were gone?"

"Yes," she said. "He did not see it coming."

Of course he didn't. Passion had zero peripheral vision. Floyd got up from the table. "Well, ladies, I must get dinner started. Perhaps we can play again tomorrow."

"Yes, yes," said Moser. "Take a few cabbages from the closet. I have a bit of ham on the table. I suggest you could bake it for a change. We've had enough stews for a while."

"Certainly." Floyd excused himself and changed into cooking clothes. As he took several cabbages from the broomcloset, he noticed that Fräulein Moser's rifle was missing from its hook. Had she been out shooting stray goats again? The thought made him uneasy; this afternoon he noticed that Moser had trouble telling queens from kings from jacks. She could easily shoot a horse by mistake. Floyd hacked up the cabbages, arranged them around the ham, and slid the casserole into the oven. Then he discovered that the World War I appliance was not electric, but gas: Frisk had not covered this possibility with him. How did these things work now? Floyd vaguely remembered his mother bending over the stove with a match. He turned the switch on, heard a fine hiss, lit a match: There was supposed to be a hole in here somewhere, wasn't there. He swished the match around in the dark. Nothing happened. How could his mother have done that to Eggli, Floyd wondered. She was not a cruel person. She was very quiet and gentle, almost invisible. Maybe the chef had imagined everything. Maybe she had one day smiled at him and he mistook that for everlasting love.

Boom! went the stove in Floyd's face. He blew backwards, smacking his cheek on the wooden table. Several chairs bashed into the cupboard.

Fräulein Moser came in just as Floyd was regaining his feet. "You're bleeding! What happened?"

"The oven sneezed," he said. He got a few ice cubes from the freezer and held them against his cheek. "No problem. I'm all right."

"That stove is impossible. My mother hated it. Some day I will get a new one." She inspected Floyd's wounds. "You will need stitches. I will call the doctor in Emwald."

He put his face beneath the pump and flushed icy water over his eyebrow. "Fräulein Moser," he said, "I noticed your rifle is missing."

"Yes, yes. There was another disturbance in the chicken coop."

"Why didn't you tell me about it? I'm a good shot."

"You were out swimming in your little lake." She left the kitchen and returned shortly. "The doctor will come to the pension and sew your eye. He will charge you twenty francs."

The doctors he knew would charge two hundred francs to pick up their telephones. "Thank you."

Fräulein Moser looked at the casserole. "You do know how to bake a ham, don't you?"

"Of course," Floyd replied, laughing insincerely. "Why do you ask?"

Moser retucked a few hairs into her mammoth chignon. "Never mind. You are a fine canasta player."

At six o'clock, neatly staunched and stitched, Floyd poured himself a beer and leaned against the counter, waiting for Breeze, Rhoda, and Harriet to enter the dining room. Chairs scraped against the floor. "My God, baked ham," he heard Rhoda say. "That imbecile finally threw away his stew pot."

"We certainly eat simply here," Harriet said. "Fräulein Moser is a frugal hostess."

"Don't you two get enough cream sauces and chocolate pastries from Eggli all day long? You trying to run your cholesterol count off the charts?"

"I suppose you're right. These mountains do stimulate an appetite, though."

"Fight it, Harriet, it's all in your mind. I lost four pounds since getting here," Breeze said. "Now I'm going to fit into that black jumpsuit for tomorrow night."

"What's tomorrow night?"

"Count Carnegie goes to cooking school. I've got to thank him for that gorgeous bouquet and maybe get a phone number."

"Why do you bother, Breeze? Do you know what your chances are?"

"What the hell, one in a million. Still better than yours."

"That means nothing. I'm not in the least interested."

"You shouldn't be. He didn't even notice you. Calm down, calm down! It's your own fault. You dress like a bum who just rolled off the bottom of a B & O railroad car. What's the point? Do you want to make sure the guy loves you for yourself? That approach might work if you were twenty-one years old and living off a trust fund. But guess what. You're one out of two billion eligible women. I don't even know if you could pick up a gorilla in your present condition."

"Don't pay any attention to her, Rhoda. She's a desperate old nag."

"And you're not? Jesus Christ! At least I admit it!"

There was a long silence punctuated by the ding of teacups against saucers. "Let me tell you something, Breeze," Rhoda finally said. "For ten years I got dressed up just like you do. I plucked my eyebrows, shaved my legs, wore perfume . . . and in the end, it didn't make a damn bit of difference. Louis dear still preferred to screw his secretary. The woman was ugly as a mouse. A bimbo with boobs I could maybe forgive. Maybe. But not that sour little twat."

"There you are, Rhoda. His ego was desperate for adoration. Once you started making money he knew you didn't need him any more."

"Is that so? I told him fifty times a day I needed him to help with the housework, help with the laundry, help with the shopping. That type of need was apparently beneath his dignity. Thank God we didn't have kids. I would have died of exhaustion."

"He knew you were getting angry."

"You're damn right I was! He got a slave, a mistress, and an extra paycheck in one package. What did I get? A forty-year-old bedwetter."

"It's happened to millions of women, Rhoda. Don't feel bad."

"Look, I've discussed this with therapists and support groups until I was blue in the face. That doesn't mean I've forgiven the shit."

"As far as I can see, Rhoda, you made two mistakes. First, you married a man with not enough money. None of these problems would have occurred if he had been able to support you decently in the first place."

"We're not all as expert as you in snagging sugar daddies, dear."

"You paid the price, all right. The second mistake was that you've been sitting on this and rotating for . . . let me guess . . . six years. What you should have done was replaced the sucker immediately with a better model."

"I told you before, I don't need men any more."

"Ah, where's your sense of humor, Rhoda? So you got a lemon the first time around. Does that mean you're finished for life? Have you ever tried a younger man just for kicks? I mean, twenty years old? A few muscles? Nice smooth ass? A cock that could take on the Statue of Liberty? I bet not. Have you, Harriet?"

"No, dear."

"And you two frauds call yourselves liberated? What the hell's the story here?"

"May I remind you that I am a married woman?"

"Harriet, you're just a talking wall. You've done nothing but criticize spaghetti since 1960. Did you ever notice all those slim Italian waiters who served it to you?"

"My interest was purely professional."

"Sheesh, no wonder nobody believes your columns any more. Oh hello, Fräulein Moser. We were just about to go upstairs. Say, I wonder if I could book the bathroom for a double session tonight. I'm going to color my hair. By tomorrow it's going to be blond again. Thank God I bought some peroxide at the airport. I had a feeling I'd be needing it."

"You need more zen one hour in ze bazroom?"

"Hey, I can't help it if Emwald has no hairdresser."

"Two hours I give you. Zat vill be four Sviss francs."

"Fine. I'll get started right away. Thank God I brought all my disco clothes, too. I had a feeling they'd come in handy. See y'all tomorrow morning. Froy, can I rent a few towels?"

"I vill see. Come vit me." Floyd heard two women, or a paraplegic horse, exit the dining room.

The clumping faded into the bowels of the pension. "I never saw a woman with such a horrifying lack of culture," Harriet said.

"You don't think she was serious about twenty-year-olds, do you?"

"I'm afraid she was entirely serious, dear."

Another pause ensued. Floyd could just see Rhoda contemplating the distant peaks as Harriet studied her teabag. "It could be wicked fun," Rhoda said. Harriet did not obtest.

The approach of Fräulein Moser broke their reverie. "Seven o'clock, ladies. Ze dining room closes for ze evening."

"What are you doing tonight, Harriet?"

"Oh, a little laundry. Mend a blouse."

"When's the bathtub available, Fräulein Moser? Nine o'clock?"

"Yes, but I do not know if zere vill be any more hot vater."

"I'll gozzle her."

"No fighting in my pension. Please bring your dishes to ze back. Good night."

For the second public foray of his students, Chef Eggli had assigned each of them to a table in the hotel dining room and instructed him or her to take care of the guests seated thereat. No formal menu was offered. Diners had a choice of salmon or quail. Wine, soup, the relevant vegetable adjuncts, cheese, and dessert were foreordained: Emphasis would be on clarity of service rather than the negotiation of a dozen Byzantine entrées and spirits.

At eight o'clock, decked in his new gray suit, Count Carnegie seated himself at a corner table which he and Chef Eggli had priorly arranged to be under the aegis of Rhoda. Floyd smiled at the harpist in the opposite corner; tonight she was plucking Satie from oblivion. He glanced around the dining room, reacclimating to the brocade, the chandeliers, the mirrors: It reminded him of that restaurant on Fifty-seventh Street Aunt Margaret had taken him on the nights they went to chamber music concerts. The voices here were not as strident, the tables not as close; women still studied him as they raised wine to their lips.

Rhoda appeared at his elbow and expertly poured a splash of chablis. She was wearing little gold earrings, a tinge of rouge, and a white peasant blouse over black pants. Breeze must have done one hell of a chlorine bleach job last night to startle her classmate out of unisex attire. "Good evening, Count Carnegie," she said.

He looked up at her and almost understood why Louis had hightailed it to his mousy secretary: Rhoda's stare could wither a bull. Something in her eyes almost willed a man to disappoint her. "Hello."

She saw his purple and cobalt shiner but ignored it as one would a huge wart on the tip of a nose. "Tonight we offer our guests a choice of quail or salmon."

When was the last time she had fallen asleep ecstatic? "I leave zat choice to you," Floyd said. "Surprise me."

That surprised her, all right; Rhoda was expecting to hear Count Carnegie order the wrong entrée, quail. "Certainly," she said without the least smile, and returned to the kitchen. Floyd wondered if she was beyond help.

Breeze took this opportunity to detour past Count Carnegie's table with a basket of rolls. Her hair was the color of an oil refinery afire. She really should have waited another few pounds before cramming into her black jumpsuit. "My God, count!" she whispered. "What happened to you?"

"A slight accident."

"Don't tell me. You got into a fight over a woman."

Floyd had been thinking of his mother. "Perhaps a voman vas involved, yes."

"I wouldn't expect anything less of you, count. I bet you're a very romantic person. Was that bouquet you brought me meant for someone else?" Count Carnegie smiled with ineffable sadness and let his black eye speak for him.

Rhoda returned with a bowl of soup. "Excuse me, dear. I believe this is my table."

Ah women, subtle, deadly as night in the tropics. A man would have muttered "Move it, buddy" and illustrated with a quick shove: retaliation guaranteed. Rhoda, on the other hand, made Breeze look crass and herself look magnanimous all in a few economical flicks of the tongue.

"The table is yours. The gentleman isn't," Breeze replied. "*Adiós, count.*" Her yellow hair amplified light from every bulb and candle in the room. As she walked by them, the guests stared at her coiffure as if it might blow away, onto their plates, at any moment.

Rhoda arranged a breadbasket and a dish in front of Floyd. "Cream of sorrel soup," she said. "We made this in class."

"Lovely. Tank you." What the hell was a sorrel? A Swiss squirrel? He ate as deliberately as possible while Rhoda watched impassively from the kitchen doors, debating whether to serve him salmon or quail, which had more bones. Breeze slid by his table a number of times, smiling and half curtseying as Rhoda scowled from a distance.

Floyd watched Chef's seven male students pad around the dining room; he was supposed to be critiquing their service, after all. Each one seemed to be exuding the correct proportions of obsequiousness and hauteur which his clientele had come to expect from a professional waiter. An American male, unless he were an aspiring actor, would have difficulty duplicating that, Floyd thought: Butlering was not in the blood. Eight generations ago, as Europeans ate eels in cream and wrote odes to nightingales, their American peers were panning streams and lynching Cherokees. It was inevitable that their descendents would not consider degustation an art form.

This was all too obvious watching Breeze buffalo through the dining room. The woman was about as suave as crushed garlic. Her unfortunate charges, a pair of elderly Austrians, could do little but frown and stiffen as Breeze first knocked over a glass of wine, then brought them salmon instead of quail, then sneezed into her elbow as she was serving cheese from a tray. Floyd wondered who could have been so naive, or so extravagant, to have shipped her here; the woman would obviously learn nothing. Finally, after Breeze split her pants retrieving a loose strawberry, Eggli had to mollify the Austrians with an impromptu presentation of crêpes suzette. They still did not promise to come back the next time class went public.

Rhoda removed Floyd's salmon plate. "I apologize for the behavior of my classmate," she said. "We are not all like that."

"How unfortunate," Count Carnegie replied. "I do like vimmen with a touch of madness."

"She's hardly mad," Rhoda said. "She's just pathetic."

The moment Rhoda entered the kitchen, Breeze accosted her. Once her pants split, Chef Eggli had forbidden her to appear in the dining room. She was supposed to be scraping dirty dishes in the meantime. "Well, what's he like?"

Rhoda calmly placed a wedge of Roquefort onto a board. "Unusual."

"Unusual what? Queer? What did you talk about?"

In no way was Rhoda about to admit that Breeze had been their most ardent topic of conversation. "Things you wouldn't appreciate."

"Oh come on, that's bullshit!" Chef Eggli wheeled the little cart bearing his crêpe gear into the kitchen. Breeze scurried over to him. "Chef, how did you decide upon the serving arrangement tonight? I mean, how come Rhoda got Count Carnegie while I got those two old farts that smell like Vicks Vaporub?"

"Out of my way," Eggli said, trying to steer the cart past her. "You receive two demerits tonight, although you deserve five. One for ruining the appetites of the people you served and one for turning my dining room into a penny circus."

"I thought Count Carnegie was the only guy who handed out demerits! And what type of review board have you set up?"

Chef Eggli was stunned that Rhoda did not rush to the defense of her compatriot. Instead she left the kitchen, cheese board in hand, smiling nicely to herself. "No review board," he said. "Five demerits and you get a one-way ticket to Montreux."

"That's not fair, chef. I demand that you give me an easier table next time. Like Count Carnegie. Give the old bags to Rhoda. She's just their type."

Harriet entered the kitchen with two dirty plates and placed them in a plastic tub. "My two gentlemen asked me a question, Chef Eggli," she said, removing a mint sorbet from the freezer.

"Yes? About the meal?"

"Not exactly. They wanted to know if Breeze's hair was radioactive."

"What!?" Chef Eggli looked at Breeze a moment, then, without warning, yanked a lock of straw hair. "You comb that rat's nest into a nice neat bun next time or you wash the kitchen floor on hands and knees. You'll never serve Count Carnegie then."

Harriet protested neither Chef's hairpulling nor his humiliating threats against women. Her sudden silence after one week of strident polemics mystified the man. "What? Don't you have anything to say to that?" he shouted in frustration.

"I think a bun would be fine," Harriet said, replacing the sorbet in the freezer. She handed the soiled spoon to Breeze. "Here you go, dear."

Nestor lay in his hospital bed, one leg in a cast, shouting into the telephone at a tardy supplier of Pyrana labels. He had been reading reports, checking advertising copy, and directing employees at the mill for hours already. Unable to sleep, he had called Dingleball at five that morning and informed the disoriented Swiss that Viola was arriving in Montreux the next day with legal papers. Then he had dispatched a nurse to the hospital bookstore and told her to bring him every newspaper in sight: time to study textile wars. Three times he had called the Paterson police, inquiring how their search for a black puppy was proceeding, only to be transferred to a dial tone. Nestor's mood did not improve until Mai Ping dropped off a pair of red silk pajamas, several samples from next spring's collection of lingerie, and a postcard from Breeze the cook, extolling Chef Eggli's fabulous cooking course.

Someone knocked at the door. "What is it," Nestor called irritably. He did not like to be seen in a position of inertia.

In walked Dr. Portia Clemens wearing khakis and thick brown shoes. Instead of flowers she had brought a book. "Good morning," she said. "I understand you had an accident."

"Who told you that? I'll kill her."

"Those are strong words which I'm sure you don't mean," Portia soothed, approaching bedside. "Your ankle must be very painful."

Wincing, Nestor pulled himself up on the pillows so that he was at least eye level with Portia; she was not the type of woman he wanted looking down at him. "Answer the question," he said. "You were not invited here."

Portia, in quest of Nestor's identity and whereabouts, first had walked into the Pyrana boutique on Madison Avenue and bought herself the most utilitarian undershirt she could find. Then she had drawn the salesgirl into an innocuous discussion about "the man in pajamas" who, she soon learned, ran the plant in Paterson. She had also learned he was not married to Viola. Portia had called the mill and asked to speak with Mr. Buffez on a matter of urgent personal business concerning his dog; thinking Smudge had been recovered, the receptionist had directed Dr. Clemens to the hospital.

"I called your office in Paterson," she said. "A woman named Sylvia told me to see you personally."

"Damn that stupid cow, I gave specific orders to keep her mouth shut."

"I told her I was making a follow-up inquiry on your dog."

Nestor chuckled mirthlessly and stared at the bouquet which his employees had sent. "Save your breath. My dog is gone. We'll never see him again."

"No! What happened? Did the stitches suppurate? Why didn't you call me?"

"He ran away."

"Was he on a leash?"

"You know damn well he was in my shirt."

"This is a catastrophe. Thanks to you playing papoose, that dog has no sense of home territory. An animal that size will wither and die within three days if not rescued."

"Case closed then," Nestor said. "There's the door."

Portia realized that she had overplayed her hand. "Chances of such a fate are, of course, minimal." She sighed. "Since I am an optimist, I will give you this book anyway."

"*Your Priceless Mutt,*" Nestor read. "Thank you very much." He placed it beneath the box of cigars which Eugene had given him and stared stonily at Portia for several moments. Since his divorce he distrusted blonds. "Now what do you want? Don't tell me you made a special trip to Paterson just to cheer me up." Nestor was quite sure she had come to scarf up some therapy sessions for Smudge.

Portia had one prop left. She dug in her pocket and picked out the microchip which she had recently removed from the pup's belly. "I believe this electrode belongs to you. It is important evidence should you prosecute."

Prosecute whom? The U.S. Customs Service? "There's no point in that now," Nestor said, dropping it into his pajama pocket. "I have better things to do than whine at slimy lawyers." He rolled his red silk sleeves and picked up the telephone. "Thank you for visiting. I should be getting out of here tomorrow."

Portia did not budge. She had hoped that by this time, Nestor would have furnished her with a complete genetic history of the Buffez family and made an appointment at either the sperm bank or, more economically, her bedroom to assist her quest for motherhood. Now all her ammo was gone and she hadn't even grazed the target. One final, desperate bullet remained. "I owe you a refund, I suppose," Portia said. "You did pay for an introductory therapy session."

"Donate it to the Mad Dog Fund." Nestor punched a few keys on the phone.

"I would prefer to repay you with dinner."

Nestor listened a moment then hung up. "I don't think we understand each other," he said. "If I want to eat dinner with you, I'll ask you to dinner. Since I haven't asked, you can assume that I don't want to."

"Why not?" Portia snapped. "Am I a leper? Do I smell?"

"I wouldn't know."

"Are you involved with someone else?"

"Sylvia," Nestor said into the phone. "Where's Viola? When did she leave? Is she bringing her sketches? Who? Tell that bastard he can shove it. I'll see him at the mill when I damn well feel like it." He hung up after a few more items of business. "Why are you still standing here?" he said to Portia. "Don't you have a clinic to run?"

"You're quite rude, you know."

Nestor held an exiguous pair of panties to the light, studying the raspberries embroidered thereupon. "You and a bunch of misfits picket my store without warning, call me a fascist, annoy my customers, upset my pregnant partner, mutilate my dog, imply he's neurotic, extort information from my secretary, try to con me into dinner, then have the gall to call me rude?"

Portia stood still as a totem pole. "Let me explain," she began.

"Would you get the hell out of here," Nestor shouted, jamming the intercom button next to his bed. "Nurse! Get this pest out of my room! Where's the security system in this stinking hospital? Next thing you know I'll have an insurance salesman in here!"

"Salesperson," Portia corrected automatically, without thinking.

The book of mutts flew by her ear. "Damn you anyhow, I said salesman and I meant salesman," she heard Nestor rant as she retreated down the hall. "If I meant saleswoman I would have said saleswoman! Salesperson! Who would use such a stupid word!" The elevator doors met behind her, silencing Nestor.

Three minutes later the identical elevator opened and out stepped George Hash, face smeared with ointment and bandages. His skin appeared to be simultaneously boiling and gelling. He walked as if one shoe contained a miniscule thumbtack and his right arm hung in a sling. Visitors glanced at him in pity as he walked stiffly by. Hash knocked on Nestor's door.

"Way too late, nurse, she's gone," he snarled. "Praise God I wasn't reporting a fire. I would have been medium rare by now."

Hash opened the door with his good arm and peeped into the room. Cigar in mouth, the patient sat in bed rippling a diaphanous yellow negligee through the air, intently studying its rise and fall upon the draughts. "Who's gone," Hash said.

Startled, Nestor let the negligee, but not his cigar, drop. "If it isn't Major Pizza Face," he muttered in disgust. "Did you find my dog yet?"

"No." Hash walked in and tripped over *Your Priceless Mutt.* "Interesting," he said, gingerly picking it up.

"Just a minute, who invited you in? You're a mess."

"For which I thank you," Hash retorted, seating himself aside Nestor's enormous cast. "Multiple fracture, I understand."

Nestor put the negligee aside and tapped cigar ash into the bedpan. "Couldn't this wait until tomorrow? I'm in the middle of some consumer testing."

"Sorry, no." Hash thumbed through the mutt book. "Where'd this come from?"

"A visitor," Nestor snapped. "Do you mind?"

"To Nestor Buffez," Hash read dreamily from the title page, *"with sincere and lasting admiration, Portia Clemens, D.V.M.* So! You and Clemens are a duo, eh?"

"Give me that." Nestor snatched the book and read the inscription for himself. "Pffffuuuuuii." He tossed it onto the empty chair. This time the spine ripped.

"A fine actor you're not, Buffez," Hash said. Sincere and lasting admiration? How did he reap that from Hoboken's most carnivorous feminist? Did this Satan in red pajamas have two cocks or something? "How long have you and Clemens been seeing each other?"

"I thought you were Customs, not the vice squad."

Hash sighed. "Your devoted admirer is a suspect in an espionage ring which plants microchips on dogs and ships them overseas."

For some time Nestor stared at hin, dumbfounded. "What? Are you calling my dog a spy?"

"Let's just say he was a courier."

"That is totally absurd," Nestor said. "He can't even run."

Hash readjusted his sling, stalling: Nestor's bewilderment looked genuine. "Can we review this from the beginning? Where did this dog come from? Did it just wander in from the streets?"

"My cook found him in the dumpster about a month ago. She was throwing out a ton of brownies she had just burned."

"Why didn't you call the dog catcher or the ASPCA? Isn't that what people usually do in such cases? Honest people anyway?"

"Where are you from? Oz? We're talking about Paterson, New Jersey. When things show up in dumpsters, that means someone trashed them. Period." Nestor mashed the cigar out: He could not blow smoke rings and discuss the departed Smudge with the same breath.

"So you adopted this dog? You just let him run around the mill?"

"Why not? I live there."

"Without rabies shots? Without registration tags?"

"Look, when we found him the poor guy looked as if he had been playing tug of war with a barbed wire. We couldn't see poking any more needles into him until he healed. And forget the rabies. He didn't even have teeth yet."

"All right. Dog is in mill. Then what happened."

"Nothing, until our July Fourth picnic. Smudge got hit with a softball and had to be taken to the clinic."

"Who hit him with the softball?"

"I don't know, I was out getting some beer. Nobody is telling me anyhow. They know I believe in an eye for an eye."

"Do you think it was done on purpose? To set up the connection with Clemens? These things, when well planned, can look very innocent."

Nestor imagined the preposterous. "No," he said finally. "My employees play softball once a year, after they've had a few beers. Most of them strike out. The chance that one of them would hit an object the size of a turtle two hundred yards away, in front of three hundred spectators, is beyond belief."

Hash bought that. "So who brought him to this particular clinic? Quite a coincidence, you must admit."

"I forget."

"You do not forget. I've already told you what a bad actor you are."

"My partner brought the dog in. Big deal, coincidences happen. You start bugging her and I'll tear you apart." Nestor minaciously eyed Hash.

"Okay, Smudge is at the clinic. That would have been the perfect opportunity for your suspect to sew a microchip into him."

"When was the next time you saw Dr. Clemens after that?"

"She and a bunch of mongrels were demonstrating in front of my lingerie shop."

"She just turned up? Out of the blue? To picket what?"

"Underpants. Bras. Contact between the sexes. How the hell should I know? The only way I could pry her away from her bullhorn was to lure her back to the clinic."

"How did you do that?"

"How else, Blister? Smudge! He needed repair work anyhow. His stitches were coming unglued."

Hash was becoming confused: This case had more dangling tentacles than a jellyfish. "Okay, you and the doc are somehow back at the clinic. What happens now?"

"She finds a microchip and acts very surprised and offended."

"How did she just happen to find it?"

"It was working its way out, like a splinter."

"Aha." Hash's epidermis was beginning to flare as his pulse increased. "Where's the microchip now? She didn't replant it on the dog, I hope?"

Something in Nestor rebelled at so easily surrendering the microchip to the man who had not only lamed him but had separated him from Smudge, possibly forever. "She put it in a little dish," Nestor said. "Then I left." That was the truth, after all.

"Did she ever touch the dog again?"

"No. But she came here this morning to get me to bring the dog in for therapy. She was constantly trying to convince me Smudge was becoming psychotic."

So Nestor brought the dog back once a week for therapy and Clemens planted the chip nice and deep next time. One day the mutt vanishes from the Pyrana doghouse, never to be seen again, by Nestor anyway. Chalk up one Cuban, well used, freshly discarded. Hash glanced at the mutt book. "She hates men, you know. That inscription is totally out of character."

"Could have fooled me, Blisterface."

"Major Hash is the name." Hash adjusted a bandage which was sliding off his temple. "How did she react when you told her Smudge had disappeared?"

"She was very upset and accused me of negligence."

"I suppose then she left in a hurry."

"No, then she invited me out to dinner."

"That makes no sense whatsoever."

"Of course it does. The woman is crazy about me."

"You?" Hash guffawed. "Let me tell you something, Clubfoot. She spends all her time agitating in parades and plotting the overthrow of America. The dog doctor bit is just a cover. Two weeks ago, for no reason, she changed a perfectly fine Dalmatian from a male to a female. She tried to do the same thing, without using knives, to a buddy of mine. She's a menace to society."

"Why should she pick on me?" Nestor cried. "Why not the Feinstein Corset Company?"

"That's what we're trying to find out," Hash said. "You have any employees who have been acting strange lately? Any recent employees who are off the wall? There's got to be some link between Pyrana and Dr. Clemens."

Nestor reviewed his personnel. "Only my cook is a total washout. Her application was one fat lie from beginning to end."

"Where is she? Can I ask her a few questions?"

"Not really. She's in Switzerland."

Hash leapt from his chair. "What's going on here? Why does everyone and his dog end up in Switzerland? What's she doing there?"

"She's taking a cooking course."

"I don't understand. You sent a cook to Switzerland? Was this the same cook who found your dog in the dumpster?"

"Yeah."

"Would you consider her personality subversive?"

"I consider her personality a pain in the ass. She's an Indian. Brags that she's related to that guy on the 'Lone Ranger' show. All day long, when she's not wrecking food, she's telling everyone in the cafeteria how liberated she is."

"Back up a minute. Why is she in Switzerland?"

"She couldn't cook. I couldn't fire her. So the accountant sent her there."

"The accountant? What's his connection to Portia Clemens? How long have you known him?"

"Too long," Nestor said. "Look, I don't know about you, but I'm getting a little mixed up. Everything made perfect sense here until you came along and started calling everyone a Communist infiltrator."

"Would you prefer to be a Communist pawn? You're not out of the soup yourself, buddy."

Hash poured himself a glass of water from the pitcher on Nestor's stand, refreshing the tepid bandages on his face, as Nestor picked up the phone. "Police? This is Nestor Buffez. You've been searching for my black dog. Have you come up with anything? Yes, I mind holding!" He did so nevertheless. "All right. Thank you. Keep looking. I'll be waiting by the phone." He sighed forlornly. "Haven't I given you enough clues for one day?" he said to Hash. "Why don't you drop in on Blondie? She seems to know a lot more about this than either of us."

Hash would have preferred to postpone that confrontation a day or two, until the tomatoey flush had faded from his face. "Thanks for your cooperation," he said, getting up.

"You realize one thing, of course."

"What's that."

"Neither of us would be here now if you had just introduced yourself the first time we met."

The door opened and Viola walked in. Maybe it was the prospect of a spending a week in the Alps; maybe she had blown the Porsche over here at one hundred ten miles an hour; maybe Dingleball had just told her that two thousand Christmas robes were in transit; maybe she had finally decided that pregnancy was a blast: She looked lovely. That little silk dress clung to her body like an adoring, fluid skin.

She stopped short and stared at Hash, barely remembering him: His appearance had sadly degenerated since the last time they had met on the mill stoop. So he was a customs agent, eh? She wondered if this man knew Floyd Beck. Of course he would. They were the same age. They had probably joined the Customs Service at the same time. They had the same calm mouths. They both upheld law and order in an anarchic universe: One saw it in the eyes. That had always attracted her and she wanted to get far away from him. The stranger resurrected, albeit peripherally, many torn spectres. "Hello, Nestor," Viola said, approaching the bed. "How are you feeling today?"

"Meet Major Hash," Nestor said. "From Customs. He's the guy who intercepted my pepperoni pizza with his nose the night he got Smudge to run away."

Hash extended his hand. "Hello," he said. Her skin was too cool: He frightened her and it wasn't because of the bandages.

"Viola Flury, my partner," Nestor said.

She smiled perfunctorily at Hash and sat on the bed next to Nestor, taking his hand. Hash could see that the Cuban was beyond crazy about the woman; his face almost changed color when he looked at her. Whether she chose not to respond, or not to respond in the presence of a stranger, Hash could not tell although he would not mind spending the next chunk of his life simply staring at her, trying to figure that riddle out. He wondered what he would do if that blue-white face and wild black hair occupied the same room as he, just beyond reach, at pale sunrise, at noon, at sundown, at midnight, six days per week: No wonder the Cuban was a lunatic. "One more question," Hash said. "Who's the Asian woman in the white Toyota? The one who left your factory late last night?"

"Mai Ping," Nestor said. "She likes to work overtime. I know it's strange."

"What was she doing driving past the pizza parlor?"

"I invited her to join me. She couldn't because she had choir rehearsal. The church is right around the corner."

Hash rose from the chair. "Thanks for your help," he said. "We'll continue another time."

"Do your homework before you bother me again," Nestor called. "And thanks for the broken ankle. I really appreciate it, Blister." The woman watched Hash limp out as if she wanted to make certain that he left. She did not say goodbye.

The door latch clicked and Viola slapped Nestor's hand. "Don't antagonize the man, you idiot."

"Why not? All he has are a few bites and burns. His buddies will probably give him a Purple Heart and a bonus. Meanwhile I'm the schmo in traction."

"Poor baby. Why was he after Smudge?"

"It's too ridiculous to even go into. These people are all paranoids." He pulled his hand away from Viola's. "Tell me something. On July Fourth, why did you take the dog to that particular clinic? Why not the Fort Lee Animal Hospital? Wasn't that closer?"

Viola shrugged. "Richie told me to go there. He said it was open three hundred sixty-five days a year."

"So it was by chance? Totally by chance?"

"You don't think I'd bring a worm in to that woman if I had a choice, do you?"

"No, I guess not. Just wondering." Nestor picked up the raspberry nightie. "You look unusually fetching today. I see the thought of blowing town does wonders for your complexion. How long are you going to be without a chaperone now?"

"Six days."

"And what are you going to do with yourself all that time? Eat fondue?"

"I'll be at the silk convention most of the time. The Lung brothers are coming with all their samples, you know."

"Wear a strapless gown and take them to the casino. There's nothing else to do in Montreux but walk along the lake and feed the swans. When are you seeing Dingleball?"

"Immediately. He swears he's finishing the order as we speak. Just in case he doesn't, I'm hanging around for a few extra days."

"You dropping in on the cooking school? See what that damn squaw is up to?"

"Not if I can help it."

"Why not? Don't you like thermal springs? Mud baths? Raw vegetables?"

"Not if she's anywhere near them. I'm trying to make this a vacation."

He laughed curtly, or maybe pouted out loud. "Flury's last stand."

Hah, that would be the day. She didn't even get winks from the doorman any more. Viola sighed. "Eugene's coming over from Scotland the first of August. I finally convinced him to go on one last fishing trip before he becomes a full-time nanny. We'll visit Italy a week before coming home. Are you going to be all right by yourself?"

"Sure, sure," Nestor said disgustedly. "I'll play solitaire and autograph my cast. There's a pile of paperwork I've been putting off."

"Why don't you take a vacation yourself?"

"Where to? A nursing home? I'll be on crutches until Labor Day."

Viola saw the book on the empty chair. "*Your Priceless Mutt?* What's that?"

"The dog doctor dropped it off this morning."

"That little bitch? How did she find out you were here?" Viola studied Nestor's face. "Why does that woman keep popping up? Are you two a unit or something?"

"Don't tell me you're jealous."

Of course she was jealous. Nestor was a superior lover; he just didn't recognize the distinction between devotion and suffocation. That did not seem anywhere near the vice now that it did five years ago. "She's not your type."

"Thank you very much."

Viola pulled a few reports from her briefcase. "Leases on the London shop. Just so you know what's going on when Morton calls in a panic."

The phone interrupted. Nestor pounced on it. "Hello?" He handed it to Viola. "Eugene."

"Hi." Viola listened a moment. "Wait, that's impossible. I have a million things to wrap up at the office. Can't they come at six? I did so tell you that, at breakfast. No, Eugene, we've got to be at the airport at eight. We're leaving tonight, remember?" As Eugene recited a few paragraphs, the blood beneath his wife's cheeks very subtly crossed from the blue to the red band of the spectrum. "All right. One o'clock," she said, and hung up. "God damn it!"

"What now," Nestor said. "Are you interviewing a witch doctor?"

"A psychologist is coming over with the interior decorator," Viola said. "They're going to spend three hours deciding whether the walls in the nursery should be yellow or blue and whether a red crib is going to make the kid a rapist in fifteen years." She threw the closest missile, Portia's mutt book, at the door. The cover separated completely from the pages. "Don't be surprised if I stay in Switzerland." She began to cry.

"Aw honey," Nestor said, pulling her over. The last time he had seen her cry was five years ago, when Morton told her they were all going to jail.

A nurse looked into the room. "What's going on here?"

"Nothing, dear. My friend dropped a book," Nestor said. "Would you mind bringing us coffee and a few pastries?" Scowling, the nurse left. "Look, V, I'll take care of the office. Buy yourself some great clothes, go home and smile at these clowns, get on the plane, and forget about everything."

Viola wiped her eyes. "He woke me up at four o'clock this morning. He had been working in the laboratory."

"On what?"

"Self-changing diapers."

Nestor's hand continued stroking Viola's hair for several moments. "Now that's a toughie," he said finally. Her hair still smelled of lemon and roses. Nestor wondered if Eugene had ever noticed that. "He's gone totally round the bend lately. Have you ever tested him for premature Alzheimer's disease?"

"That's all I need, two drooling idiots." Viola blew her nose and unwrapped a chocolate from Nestor's bedtable. He would have preferred her to cry on his red pajamas a bit longer, just like old times. "So are your all straight with the customs people now?"

"Not quite. Blister and his buddies will be visiting the plant in a few days."

Then she was getting out of there just in time. "What is going on, Nestor?"

"Forget it," he said. "You have enough on your mind."

Viola stood up. "I have to go." She kissed him goodbye.

"Are you going to relax and forget about Eugene? Look at the mountains and get inspiration for a new collection of underwear?"

"That would be nice." She ate the chocolate. "I'll call you every day. Hope you get Smudge back."

"Sure." Nestor always became surly at farewells.

Viola looked at the dark stains she had made on his pajamas and suddenly did not want to go to Switzerland without her partner. "Maybe we could wait a week and both go."

"Scram," he said. "And don't you dare eat any chocolate over there. It's loaded with caffeine."

Floyd chuckled into his elbow and leaned forward on his kitchen stool. The ladies in Fräulein Moser's dining room had been arguing since sunrise about Count Carnegie's origins. Rhoda thought he was Hungarian. Breeze thought he was Greek. Harriet thought he was a descendent of the Scottish steel magnate. Everyone agreed he was rich.

"What do you think of the black eye and all those stitches? He told me there was a woman involved."

"Did he tell you that, dear, or did you ask him that?"

"I forget. But it looked very dashing. There's something about that guy that says Dangerous When Aroused, don't you think?"

"That hardly distinguishes him from the rest of the swine, Squawfoot."

"You know what I'm talking about. How would Leonard look with a black eye, Harriet?" There was no response. "Pathetic, wouldn't he."

"Most certainly not."

"Sure he would. Black eyes are like black leather pants. They don't suit everyone."

"What's the point of this, Breeze?"

"No point, I just find the count extremely provocative. Sort of Old Worldish. I wish I knew who the woman was. It always helps to see the competition."

"What woman is he talking about? I haven't seen him with a woman yet."

"Don't you get it, Harriet? That's why he has the black eye."

"He does look rather forlorn."

Floyd frowned. What was a single gentleman in a restaurant supposed to do, stick his tongue out and make faces at everyone who passed by?

"I'd like to know when he's coming to class. Isn't he supposed to be passing out demerits and lecturing upon etiquette?"

"Eggli says maybe today. So excuse me, I have to set my hair. I want to be prepared in case he calls on me."

"You're actually going to put electric rollers in that mop? You might start a forest fire."

"I'd rather have a mop than a butch."

"Girls, stop this bickering! Rhoda, whatever happened to all of those Gynamite classes? Don't you remember the Tall, Dark, and Handsome Syndrome?"

"Harriet, you take care of your exposé. I'll take care of the syndromes."

"And I'll take care of Count Carnegie."

Floyd had spent the afternoon playing canasta with Fräulein Moser in lieu of attending Chef Eggli's cooking class. He wanted to keep the ladies waiting a bit longer; besides, he was celebrating his arrival in Switzerland exactly two weeks ago. The silent mountains had pulverized history, fertilized the blood: He felt as if he had spent his entire life here, free as a goat. Without horns squawking at rush hour, without sirens at noon and burglar alarms throughout the night, it was difficult to dice a day into twenty-four headlong hours. Rather, time here was delineated by the ebb and flow of light as the sun, the stars, perhaps the moon, arched across the sky, gracefully eluding each other.

Long ago Floyd had bought postcards at the train station. None had been sent: He could not bring himself to divulge this sweet dream to the outside world. Since his arrival he had not read a newspaper. Therefore, no terrorists had struck Rome, no summits had collapsed, and the Yankees had not lost a game. And if they had, what did it matter to him? Would he brew finer coffee in the morning? Would he float a bit higher in his warm lake? Without the media daily trumpeting the relevance of all global mayhem, life became a much more sensible undertaking. No wonder the Emwalders lived to be one hundred: They didn't concern themselves with events beyond the teats of their cows.

That evening Floyd dressed in his new black suit, slipped out the tunnel, and walked to the Hotel Badhof. Despite his calm, he felt melancholy tonight. The air was a tad too crystalline, the mountains too remote, he too alone. Floyd took his seat in the dining room and moodily contemplated the handwritten menu on his plate. He was not hungry. In the corner the harpist swished through a Chopin medley.

"Good evening, Count Carnegie," said Harriet, bowing from the waist. She had curled her hair and wore a soporific perfume. "You're looking well tonight."

"Tank you."

"Would you care for a drink from the bar?"

Hemlock and soda, maybe. "A bit of mineral vater, please."

Harriet sailed off and Floyd looked around the dining room. The elderly Austrians had come back after all; this time they had a male waiter. Three Japanese and a Swiss sat solemnly toasting each other. Two tables away, a tanned blond contemplated Floyd's black eye as her dinner companion inspected the wine list. Floyd met her stare a moment then turned away: no thanks. She spent too much time sunbathing. It was a subdued crowd tonight. Perhaps like Floyd they had all inhaled the same air, watched the same sunset, and realized that next to these mountains, they were as significant as a pine cone.

Breeze bashed out of the kitchen carrying a large tray and navigated to a distant table. She wore another jumpsuit perhaps two sizes larger than the one which had exploded the other night and her rebellious yellow hair had been pulled into a pony tail garroted by a tremendous white bow.

"Here you are, Count Carnegie," bowed Harriet, setting down the mineral water. "May I bring you an appetizer?"

Floyd glanced at his menu. "Black fruit salat, please."

The moment Harriet left he saw Breeze walking between the tables toward him. The ribbons from her white bow rippled in the air at each step.

"Hey Count," she said, stopping. "How are your stitches tonight?"

"Very well, tank you."

Breeze bent way over the flowers on Floyd's table to get a closer look. She was wearing an expensive pair of false eyelashes. "Your black eye's turning yellow around the edges. She must have really walloped you."

"She did not touch me, I am afraid."

Chef Eggli came bustling over. "Get back to the kitchen," he snapped.

"Ta-ta, Count. If you ever want to talk about it, I'm staying at a little pension on the other mountain. Food's terrible, but the view's nice."

Eggli watched her leave. "She was impossible in class today," he said in the dialect. "Asked me fifty times when you were coming."

"What did the other two say?"

"They told her to shut up. I finally put her in the corner to peel onions." He stared at Floyd's face. "Where did you get that black eye, Anna?"

"I fell down in your cousin's kitchen."

"The ladies seem to think you were fighting over a woman."

Hey ladies, wake up. Men would fight over stock certificates and a mainland invasion but never over women any more: They had better things to do than bloody their noses in defense of items which were no longer considered personal property. "Let them think so."

Eggli smiled nicely at the Austrians. "So when are you coming to class? We can't put this off much longer, you understand."

"I'll be in tomorrow. God knows what I'll talk about."

"Just act supercilious and drink wine. That's what Zimstein did and he was an enormous success." Eggli watched Rhoda serve the three Japanese ice cream parfaits. "These two women act much better now in my class. I do not know why."

"They're cut off from the revolutionaries," Floyd said. "And Blondie is giving them one hell of a counter-brainwashing."

"I do not understand any of this."

"You do not live in America."

Harriet placed the fruit salad in front of Floyd. *"Bon appétit."*

Chef Eggli frowned. "I suggest you study a bit more French before saying that again." He left.

Floyd lifted his spoon. "Delicious."

"I made that in class." Harriet lingered at the table, admiring Count Carnegie's silver-streaked hair. Leonard's hair had not gone silver; it had just gone, period. And he probably would have looked ridiculous with a black eye. "Have you decided what you might like for dinner?"

Breeze whished past with three napkins, en route to a mop-up. Floyd gazed at the white bow bobbing atop her pony tail and momentarily ceased chewing. "I am afrait I am not particularly hungry tonight," he apologized. "Perhaps just this fruit vould be fine."

"Oh no! Try a taste of the grilled chicken. You'll feel much better, I promise."

"If you insist."

What was he looking at like that? Harriet turned around: that damn Indian again. "As you may have guessed, blond is not her real hair color," she said. "And I don't know where she got that bow. Perhaps from Alice in Wonderland. It's all quite embarrassing."

"A most imaginatif voman," Count Carnegie observed. "Very spirited."

"So is a wild horse, Count Carnegie." Harriet retired to the kitchen.

The white bow disappeared behind a chair as Breeze retrieved a gravy boat from the carpet. Mesmerized, Floyd watched the bow soar below the chandelier like a giant albatross and finally veer through the kitchen doors, beyond reach.

This was the second one in a month and it had shocked him as much as the first one he had seen embroidered on those robes back in the Swissair cargo terminal: A white bow meant that Viola wanted to see him. It had meant that seventeen years ago and until they buried him in a coffin inlaid with white bows, one for each April since that first, that was what it would always mean to him. Perhaps had he chosen a more mundane signal like chewing gum or hoop earrings, the sight of a white bow would not startle him so. But how was he to know that bows would go out of fashion for fifteen years?

He had deliberated a long time before daring to suggest such a signal to Viola. All summer after that first year in Carnegie Hall he had plotted how he could meet her alone. Asking her outright would be suicidal. But if he planted a seed and waited . . . she had already come to one concert without Old Richard. Finally in December, realizing that another season was half over, Floyd made a desperate move. He had stood outside the ladies' room at intermission and handed her a small silver box. "Merry Christmas," he had said.

She was still barely talking to him, but he noticed that she was barely talking to Old Richard either. Things were not going well in the forward row. "Thank you."

"Open it." He was standing so close to her that his skin began to cry.

Viola lifted out a long white ribbon. "What is this?"

"You wear that in your hair when you want to meet me at the corner of Park and Eighty-fifth the next morning. In the telephone booth," Floyd said. "Eight o'clock, before school. I wrote it down on the lid so you won't forget."

She laughed at him. "Are we playing cops and robbers?"

He looked at her turquoise eyes. Someday he would like to see them in the sunlight. "No."

She put the box into her purse, half amused, half offended. "Thank you."

Viola wore no bow in January and she missed the February concert. In March she wore a purple hat and her eyes looked as if she had made a solemn pledge to cry through Lent. April she wore the white bow and Floyd met her the next morning at eight o'clock in the telephone booth. He had occupied it since seven-thirty talking in the Swiss dialect to a dead mouthpiece; when he saw her hurrying down Park Avenue in a green rubber raincoat, Floyd lost his voice altogether. Eighteen months palpitating in the dim bowels of Carnegie Hall was one thing; Viola by daylight, unchaperoned, running toward him, was Jesus Christ quite another. For one terrible moment Floyd wished the telephone would suck him into the coin slot and leave him jammed there forever. Then Viola slid open the doors.

"Fancy meeting you here."

Floyd hung up the phone and looked at her stark white face inlaid with eyes like frozen sky. "Hello."

They stood there staring at each other for a ridiculous period of time, ridiculous at least to the woman waiting for the telephone. "Excuse me," she finally interrupted. "Are you two finished?"

"Of course," Floyd said, jerking to life. They left the phone booth. "Have you had breakfast?"

"Yes, and I'm late for school."

Their association began, like most winters, very unevenly. Floyd waited every morning by the telephone booth. She never appeared when it rained, when Old Richard felt like taking a small detour in his limousine, nor the morning after she had lain awake in bed thinking about Floyd. He could always tell when the latter had occurred: She wouldn't speak to him for blocks and would moodily point her nose at the cracks in the sidewalk, looking for lost sleep. It would take two days to pry her open again. Weekends without her were barren and interminable; Floyd noticed that she rarely missed meeting him on Monday morning. They talked about everything but Old Richard and Floyd's parents. He never touched her; perhaps that was how he remained so deliriously happy for five weeks.

Viola wore the white bow again in May, at the last concert of the season. But she did not go to the ladies' room at intermission. She sat stiff as a mannequin in her red seat. Old Richard did not let her out of his sight and when the concert was over he slowly turned around and stared Floyd straight in the eye: Youth, meet Power. Floyd watched Old Richard take Viola's arm and shuffle past the French to the aisle. Youth had lost the first skirmish and she had ever so slightly betrayed him. He should have taken the hint.

"Here's your chicken, Count Carnegie," Harriet said, sliding a plate in front of him. "This should make you feel better."

Floyd blinked and nodded. The blond with the suntan was checking him out again as she daintily wiped her mouth with a napkin. Stash the winks, honey, you don't have black hair and skin the color of water lilies and you would look awful in a white bow. Momentarily forgetting his breeding, Floyd jabbed a fork into the chicken on his plate. Why was he thinking about her so much lately? Was her ghost suddenly getting a charge out of mining his sanity with little white bows? The hell with her ghost! The woman had made her choice. Not once in seventeen years had she tried to find him or explain herself, or beg for another chance. He would never forgive her for that silence, never: She had not slammed the door shut. She had just gone into another room.

Still smiling at him, the tawny blond got up to leave with her companion. Floyd did not respond. Her type wouldn't wait ten minutes for an omelet, much less seventeen years for the second act of a pantomime. She was a lovely pebble on the barren shore of the twentieth century, where clocks had replaced God and nothing was worth waiting for because the Big Bad Bomb might drop at any moment, soiling everyone's quest for self-realization. Life to her was a straight, ascending line rather than a series of massive loops intertwining slowly from birth to death, ending at the same spot if one were very lucky, or very wise.

Harriet returned to the table. "Are you finished, Count Carnegie?"

"Yes, tank you." Floyd folded his napkin. He was tired of being the count. He wanted to be Floyd and he wanted Viola to be sitting across the table so that at least one dark loop would have closed. The tanned woman, while holding her companion's arm, winked at Floyd as she passed his table. All loops, all faith, momentarily wobbled. Was he the only man on earth who breathed from April to April instead of minute to minute? What if all these people were right? What if Now really was God, and Floyd was the deluded, dead-wrong stone? He pushed back his chair, needing the night.

Harriet glanced about the dining room, saw that Breeze and Rhoda were preoccupied, and dropped a little note next to Floyd's hand. "Please don't give me a demerit," she said. "I couldn't think of any other way to contact you." She walked quickly away.

"Dear Count Carnegie," the note said, "I am a well-known food critic, Harriet Swallow. It is very important that I speak with you in private. Please meet me tonight at eleven-thirty in the parking lot of the hotel. Thank you immensely."

Floyd tucked the note into his pocket and left the dining room. He walked down to his warm lake, stripped, and slid into the water, looking at the stars as he floated on his back. For several years, dawdling around Portia, he had ignored that much larger circle describing Viola; he suddenly felt it now, heavier than ever. But was it closing or opening still wider? The moon paused for a cloud, then illuminated the white mountaintops. How long would he be waiting in the dark, dull and thick as the Alps? His life was half over already. If she did not see him once more, if he plodded through the remaining half of his existence with that gigantic loop still gaping, then that blond woman in the Badhof had indeed led a wiser life than he. Floyd paddled slowly back to shore and pulled himself onto the pine needles, listening to an owl question the murmuring wind.

10

"Yep, the count looked down in the dumps last night. Definitely melancholy. Didn't say two words to you, did he, Harriet."

"Your ridiculous hair style seemed to amuse him, I must say."

"Bows are back in fashion, in case you haven't been keeping up lately on what the women of the world are wearing. I hope you don't think your teeny little cherub curls were any less ridiculous than my pony tail. You looked like Napoleon with tits out there."

"Imagine me as you like, dear. At least I didn't douse my customer's fur coat with mushroom gravy."

"At least I got to the main course. You couldn't even sweet-talk your customer into a glass of wine, let alone mushroom gravy. Some waitress you make."

"The word is waitperson, I believe."

"Cut the neuter shit, Rhoda, you're either a waiter or a waitress. There's going to be no doubt about what I am when my turn comes to wait on the count."

"Oh? Are you going to pull out your silver sequin strapless backless tuxedo?"

"Something like that, yes. With matching shoes."

"I'm afraid you're wasting your time, Breeze. Count Carnegie is here to take a break from the absurdity of life."

"And when did he tell you that? When you tried to speak French with him?"

"No, dear. He met me last night after you two had gone home."

Floyd had to jam his hand over his mouth so that the ladies wouldn't hear him laughing in the kitchen. He finally had to stagger under the water pump and flush his mouth with water. Then he rushed back to his post by the sliding door, eager to hear how Harriet would report this touching moonlight rendezvous to her stunned audience.

"He met you?" Floyd could not even tell who had uttered the question. The voice sounded like a talk-ing com-pu-ter.

"Yes. He was waiting for me outside the front steps, near that lovely marble fountain." They had met in the parking lot next to a garbage can.

"This sounds very suspicious, Swallow. Who arranged this meeting?"

"He did, of course. I am not in the business of pursuing men."

"Yeah, yeah, we know, you're a married woman. No offense, but why would a guy like that want to meet you any time, anywhere, for any reason?"

"He wished to discuss philosophy." Wrong. Harriet wished to discuss her cure for black eyes: martinis, ice packs, bed rest.

Breeze and Rhoda mulled this over. "And you consider that a compliment?" Rhoda finally asked.

"A moon, stars, snow on the Alps, a perfect summer night, and all you can get him to do is talk about philosophy? Harriet, you should turn in your bra."

The poor woman had certainly tried. "I am not an animal."

"Sure you are. I'd say you were something on the order of a beaver, or a woodchuck. Sexually speaking, of course."

"My God! Jealousy has certainly brought out the cat in you, Squawfoot! When will you understand that there is more to sexuality than false eyelashes and pony tails the color of chicken fat?"

"So what kind of philosophy did you talk about," Rhoda asked, "Freud? Plato?"

Harriet had delivered an impassioned monolog upon the irrelevance of marriage in general and Leonard in particular. "That is not for me to say. It was a private discussion between like minds."

"Like minds? What's like about your minds except they're both gray?"

"Count Carnegie is a unique and sensitive man. If there were only more like him, women would not be in their present state of agitation."

"You're becoming awfully fuzzy here, Harriet. I don't understand the man's motivation at all. Why does he pick you for a philosophy discussion? Why not me? Why not the squaw? Do you mean to say that you two did nothing but talk for an hour, shake hands, and wish each other a good night?"

Exactly. Around midnight, thinking they were bears, Eggli had turned the floodlights on in the parking lot and come after them with a slingshot. "Something like that," Harriet said cryptically.

"So I guess he didn't invite you up to his room," Breeze said.

"Of course not!" Harriet exploded. "He has more respect for me than that!"

"Well, Rhoda, looks like we're still in the running. Harriet blew it."

"One moment, Tonto. What makes you think I'm in a horse race with you over a man?"

"First of all, you've cut down from three slices of bread in the morning to one. Second, you haven't whined about that dipshit Louis for almost a week. Third, you're wearing rouge."

"The hell I am. It's the clean air and all this mountain climbing."

Breeze sighed patiently. "Rhoda, I own more bottles of rouge than you have hairs on your upper lip. Please don't lie to me about makeup until a cosmetician gives you a few lessons in applying it. Nothing looks worse than a middle-aged bag with cheeks redder than Ronald Reagan's."

Someone's hand slapped someone's flesh: It was probably not applause. Floyd heard several chairs scroop against the floor and steeled himself for the crash of china and cutlery. Instead he heard the crash of a gun in the backyard. Damn! Moser again with the rifle! She must have sneaked it out of the broomcloset last night while he was discussing black eyes and martinis with Leonard's Prize. Should he bolt outside? Stay hidden in the kitchen? Count to ten and call the police?

Instantly all scuffling in the dining room ceased. "What was that," Rhoda muttered. "I'm getting the hell out of here."

"Where are all the men when you need them?" Harriet cried. Floyd heard a frightened pounding upon the sliding doors next to his ears. "Cook! Cook, get out here! Someone's trying to shoot us!"

"Harriet, save your wind. If the bum fights as well as he cooks, we're all dead ducks."

A fourth party in heavy shoes stomped into the dining room. "Fräulein Moser! My God! You're carrying a gun!"

"Of course I am. So vhat?"

"What are you doing with that horrible thing?"

"Zere is a goat vhich robs my chicken coop. I must shoot him."

"No! How can you kill a poor animal?"

"Vhat? He kills my poor chickens."

"Goats do not kill chickens, Fräulein Moser."

"Perhaps it is a vhite volf zen. I do not know. I have missed him anyvay."

"You have wolves? Here? And we walk back from the Hotel Badhof alone at night?"

"Maybe your cook should chaperone us."

"Out of ze qvestion. You leave my cook alone. Gottinhimmel! Vhat have you done to my breakfast table? Bread, coffee all over ze floor!"

"Your shotgun startled us."

"Eh? I zought Americans vere used to guns at all times of day and night. You vimmen must clean zis up immediately. I must charge you two Sviss francs apiece for soiling ze tablecloz."

"Sure, Froy, anything you say. Just put the gun down. When was the last time you had your eyes checked?"

Dr. Portia Clemens had not had a pleasant journey to Switzerland. The plane had dallied on the runway for two hours, braising its contents, before takeoff from JFK. Next to her in Business Class sat an Arab wearing a nauseatingly sweet perfume. The man never stopped leering at his petite blond neighbor, then appeared amused at the philippic this provoked. His unctuous grin only disappeared when Portia told him she intended to make a heavy contribution to the Jewish Defense League; for the remainder of the trip he had tried to smoke cigarettes. Passing Champ through customs consumed three hours as the Swiss authorities triple- and quadruple-checked the dog's immunization papers, then fell into bitter debate over the Dalmatian's gender. Two out of three agents insisted the dog was still a male, his papers had been falsified, and therefore he should not be allowed into the country. Portia finally had to call the American Embassy, an institution she despised, to bail her out. Champ had not assisted her release by snapping viciously at anyone attempting to inspect her genitalia.

Portia soon learned that the Swiss preferred cats to dogs. Despite her insistence that Champ was a priceless biological specimen, unique in all the universe, the Dalmatian was not allowed on the train to Montreux unless she rode in an animal car with three horses. The conductor not only barred Portia from the animal car herself, but tried to collect double fare for hazardous cargo. Tired and extremely irritable, she had finally found her hotel on foot: Cabbies in Montreux did not want a dog shedding all over their spotless seats.

Now there was a slight problem at the hotel. Dr. Clemens very slowly peeled her sunglasses from her freckled nose and stared balefully at the concierge. "What do you mean," she enounced clearly as a ticking time bomb, "no dogs allowed."

"It is against regulations, madame," the man replied, pointing to a small sign behind him. "I am sorry."

"I booked this room weeks ago," Portia said. "My travel agent assured me there would be no problem."

The man shrugged insincerely. He despised Americans: They could never find Switzerland on a map. He handed Portia's confirmation papers back. "Had you used a Swiss travel agent, madame, I am sure you would have been told this."

"Where's the manager?" Portia demanded.

"I am the manager."

"Damn." Portia knew by now that a Swiss male was about as malleable as Stonehenge. "What do you recommend, then? I've just made a long trip and I'm very tired. My dog is tired. We had not expected such a rude welcome."

"You must find another place to stay."

"I understand that!" Portia snapped. "Just tell me where."

The concierge allowed himself a smug smile. "As you know, Montreux is very crowded at the moment. We are hosting both a veterinary convention and a silk convention."

"Where," Portia repeated. "Don't tell me Geneva. There are five conventions going on there. Some friends of mine couldn't find a room within twenty miles."

"You must go to the tourist office at the train station."

All the way up that hill again? Portia redonned her sunglasses. Any moment now she was going to cry. "Please call me a cab."

"I am very sorry, Madame, you will have to walk. The taxi drivers in Montreux are not fond of dogs."

"And I am not fond of Montreux," Portia retorted, clenching her suitcase. She relieved the porter outside of Champ's leash and hiked back up to the train station. Champ was becoming extremely whimpery. The fire hydrants here all smelled like detergent.

A dozen people already queued at the tourist information booth and Portia had to wait a half hour for her turn. To her disgust she saw yet another Swiss male behind the window. "I need a place to stay for five days," she said. "It must accept dogs."

The man flipped through a little book. "This might be difficult."

Portia wondered why she had not listened to Floyd three weeks ago when he told her to leave Champ home and go to Vienna. "Do your best, please."

"Aha! Would you like a little hotel in Reidenbach? Very clean, very quiet."

"How far away is it?"

"Two hours from Montreux."

"You don't understand. I must commute to Montreux every day with this dog. She is an important part of the veterinary convention. You must find me something much closer."

The man exhausted the green pages in his book and started on the blue.

He made a few phone calls, to no avail. Finally he pulled out a tiny yellow pamphlet. "Ah. There is a small pension in Emwald which might suit you. This is a half hour away. However, I must tell you that it is for women only. There is no alcohol and no men allowed."

"Book it immediately!" Portia screeched so loudly that Champ began to bark. "Why didn't anyone tell me about this?"

"There is very little demand for this any more." The man picked up the phone. "Mademoiselle Moser?" he said, then switched to a German dialect. Finally he hung up. "The dog must sleep in the barn," he said. "However, this should be no problem in the summertime."

"Fine, fine, how do I get there?"

"First you must pay my commission, fifteen Swiss francs. The pension costs fifty Swiss francs per night. This will include breakfast and dinner but not hot water. A bath costs two Swiss francs and you must not bring gentleman visitors." The man looked at Champ. "Is that dog a female?"

"Yes, yes! Of course!" Portia cried, paying the man his commission. "How do I get there?" The man directed her to the proper train platform. "Thank you very much."

Portia was exhausted upon her noontime arrival at the pension. Fräulein Moser put Champ into the barn and Portia to bed, explaining the house rules as she led her guest upstairs. "Dinner is at six," Moser said. "You vill eat alone tonight because ze ozzer vimmen vill be at school."

"What sort of school? International diplomacy?"

"A cooking school."

Portia frowned. "I see." She dropped her suitcase at the foot of the bed and looked a moment out the window, making sure that she had a good view of the barn. "I will probably not be able to eat much besides breakfast here. My veterinary convention in Montreux will take all my time."

"Your dog vill behave?"

"My dog will come with me. She is of great interest to science."

"How nice." Fräulein Moser closed the shutters. "You vill not be bringing any men to visit you at zis pension, I hope."

"Of course not! I'm not in the least interested in men!"

"Zat is vhat everyone says to me. I do not believe it any more." Fräulein sighed. "I hope you can sleep. Ze ozzer vimmen sometimes make noise in ze bazroom."

"I have earplugs, thank you," Portia said. "And I intend to use them. Now! May I take a bath?"

"Certainly. Two Sviss francs I charge you."

                         *   *   *

Viola woke in the deep of the night and knew that she was somewhere
else. She never sprawled diagonally across the bed like this any more:
Where was Eugene? And she hadn't slept on her stomach in weeks
. . . no Goldberg belt. The sheets were stiff and so was her neck. Her
stomach somersaulted under her ribs, foraging for food. She did not
recognize the shadows slithering from the window.

Ah, she was lying in a hotel in Montreux, Switzerland. The clocks over
here said four-fifteen. False: It was time for the ten o'clock news and a
cole slaw sandwich. Viola picked up the phone. "Room service? Could
you please bring a glass of milk, a banana, yogurt, cookies, french fries,
peppermint tea, and some carrots to room twenty? No, raw carrots. Thank
you very much."

Ten minutes later a cute little man in a tuxedo wheeled a dinner tray
into the room. "Out on the balcony, please."

He set the table impeccably, leaving one pink rose across Viola's china
plate. *Thank you, Nestor,* she thought: He had chosen the hotel. She
poured some tea, peeled the banana, and watched as the mountains across
Lac Léman gradually distinguished themselves from the lake and the
night, forming a thick, jagged flounce along the horizon. Hmmmm, that
would make a great hem on a black velvet bathrobe. It was unearthly quiet
out on the lake, no birds, no boats, no lovers returning from an illicit swim
. . . maybe the water was polluted as the Hudson; half of Lac Léman, after
all, bordered France. That way both countries could dump sewage into
it and blame the other when the fish choked.

Viola ate a few fries and brought the phone to the balcony. "Hi, Nestor,
how's your ankle?"

"Where are you?" he scolded.

"I am observing sunrise over the Dents du Midi."

"Damn you anyhow! Why aren't you in bed?"

"I slept all afternoon," Viola said, shoveling yogurt into her mouth.
"Maybe that was a mistake. Anyhow, thanks for the hotel. Very quiet.
Cute bellboys. Good french fries. The view is gorgeous."

"What are you trying to do, drive me to suicide?"

"Sorry." Viola licked the spoon. "So how's Paterson?" Nestor made a
noise like a tire kissing a nail. "You got back to the mill all right, I take
it. Did Smudge turn up yet?"

"No. How's that jackass Dingleball?"

"He sent two dozen roses to my room. I'm meeting him for lunch. Says
he's got fifteen thousand robes packed in boxes and we're going to take
a scenic trip in his truck to the airport. He's convinced I'm going to shoot
him, you know."

"Take the Lungs with you. Tell him they're hit men." Nestor waited as his partner's teeth crushed a carrot. "So the convention's going well?"

"Actually, it's a little boring. Montreux's nothing but old geezers walking their dogs up and down the lake. Like a Swiss Miami. And the place is overrun with animals. There's some type of zookeeper's convention going on."

"I told you, why don't you check in on that damn Indian? Take a day trip to the cooking school and surprise the shit out of her."

Viola had not considered it from this angle. "Maybe."

"Are you eating enough? Sleeping enough? Getting enough exercise?"

"Yes, mother." Viola leaned back in her chair. "The tops of the mountains are becoming pink now. They look like nipples."

Nestor tried to picture a ninety-million-ton breast. "Are you speaking maternally or erotically?"

Viola guffawed. "Neither." How depressing. "Well, I'd better go."

"Go where, honey? It's quarter of five in the morning over there."

"I'll take a walk."

"What's the matter with you? Why don't you sleep?"

"Come on, Nestor, this is my last vacation B.C. Before child. Without Eugene. I've got to make the most of it."

"Have fun," he snorted. "Make sure they wear rubbers."

Nestor hadn't worn a rubber in his life. He believed they caused gangrene. "You're pretty hilarious."

"Give my regards to Dingdong."

"Yep." Viola hung up and smushed the banana between her lips as she watched mist consume the helpless lake. The water was smooth and black as ice: It looked like Lake Placid in December. Viola suddenly wanted to put on a pair of skates and race from one end of Lac Léman to the other. How many years had it been since she had felt the wind slice her hair and heard that soft whir of steel upon ice? Or leapt high in the air, spinning like a mad star? Twenty? Viola laughed very softly to herself, aghast and still disbelieving that she had never made it to the Olympics. How had that happened? A figure skater was all she had ever wanted to be . . . before Richard. Now that time had dissolved both of those thorny dreams and replaced them with altered forms of success, Viola could finally look at them side by side, comparing them like two landscapes in someone else's gallery. For years such reflection had been too painful; then she had been too busy; after she had married Eugene, figure skating and Richard became irrelevant as last summer's tan. Now she suddenly found herself alone on a balcony, detached from Eugene, from Pyrana, facing a lake deep and still as her past: Silence begat reckoning.

Viola saw now that she had been much happier skating than she had ever been with Richard, and that she had replaced a pure passion with a hopeless one: Happened every time one bartered the spirit for the flesh, didn't it. What a waste! How many thousands of hours had she twirled on the ice, for nothing? How many thousands of dollars had her parents thrown away on skating lessons? She had bought them a home in Florida and a chalet in Vail and they still kept a picture of Viola, fifteen years old in a purple skating costume, on the mantel, proof that once upon a time their daughter had perfectly pleased them. Would her child do to her what she had done to her parents? How would she feel if she had eaten pot pies and beans for a decade to finance her daughter's training, only to have the kid trash everything for a sixty-year-old banker? Would she want her kid to become Queen of Underpants? Then marry a lunatic inventor who still didn't get their names straight? Christ! No wonder they liked that picture so much!

Viola ate the last french fry, now cold as a smelt, and got dressed. She was going for a walk. It perhaps beat jumping off the balcony. She rolled into a pair of pants which no longer closed at the waist and tripped down to the lobby. The concierge sat at the desk drinking a little pot of coffee and whacking dust off his velvet cap. "Good morning, Miss Flury," he said. "Did you enjoy your breakfast?"

"Yes, thank you. Could you suggest a walking route?"

"Go right, towards Chillon. It is lovely at sunrise."

Viola headed down a promenade bordered with profuse herbage, passing only stray dogwalkers and two fiftyish joggers looking as if the batteries in their pacemakers had just quit. Her mood lifted with the sun. So what if Richard and her ice skates were gone? Had Nestor and Eugene not replaced them, today she would be spoon-feeding an incontinent, senile husband and staring at a wall full of inert trophies. She should consider herself very fortunate indeed. That little fit of depression must have been hormonal. After an hour Viola turned back toward Montreux. Dew and roses saturated the air and the geese honked at the poodles, hopelessly in love. Feel sorry for herself on such a morning? Pfuiii.

In the center of town Viola stopped to buy a newspaper. More and more people were strolling outside now. She walked by a bulletin board and stopped short: No.

In front of her hung a poster of Dr. Portia Clemens proudly displaying a Dalmatian. She was to address the International Veterinary Convention two days hence upon the subject of canine sexuality and exhibit Champ, a revolutionary animal. Tickets could be purchased at the door for ten Swiss francs. Viola read a prodigious list of Portia's accomplishments and had to admire the woman's drive: Each of those initials after her name represented an accumulation of midnights alone with fine print and amphetamined arteries. Floyd must have found that ambition attractive. It was Dr. Clemens's most salient characteristic, besides her anger. Perhaps Floyd had found the anger attractive also. It implied integrity.

Viola studied Portia's photograph. She was certainly a handsome little whippet. Floyd had always had a connoisseur's eye for detail and proportion. Was he still single? Married? Divorced? Portia had purposely not divulged this information to Viola when they had met on July Fourth. Interpretation: She was involved with him, but not yet married to him. Viola stalked away from the poster. The silk and veterinary conventions occurred two blocks from each other; the thought of bumping into Dr. Clemens and that pseudomorphic beast on the shores of Lac Léman just about fried Viola's liver. The lecture was in two days? Terrific. Viola would make sure she was out of town. She'd take the Lung brothers up to the mud spa and see if the Indian had learned to make toast yet.

Floyd pulled himself out of his warm lake, dried and dressed, and walked back to his tunnel behind the Emwald train station. He felt an ill wind creeping up on him but could not pinpoint its source. Isolation? Inertia? Today, again, the mountains oppressed him. They never moved and the snow never melted: Sight of such intransigence year after year could break a man's soul. He was beginning to understand why Caspar had left.

Last night Floyd had dreamed of his father, something he had not done in ages. Perhaps the kielbasa Fräulein Moser bought for dinner had triggered it; perhaps his subconscious was reminding him that he had come here to make Floydwurst and that only a few days remained of his little Swiss escapade. In his dream Caspar stood in the butcher shop tying sausages, whistling to himself, as Floyd sat on a pickle barrel admiring the lightning dance of fingers and string. Then Caspar had looked over and said, "Anna! Where did you get that black eye? Answer me, Anna!" He had tried to explain that his name was Floyd, but no words emerged from his mouth. Sudden dumbness was a very annoying aspect of many of Floyd's dreams, a failure almost as aggravating as a sudden inability to fly when demons were chasing him. Once long ago, when he had awakened croaking from a nightmare, Portia told him that these dreams prefigured impotence. Floyd had immediately disproven that theory. As time went by, however, it appeared that she may have been correct after all. Unlatching the wooden door to his tunnel, Floyd guffawed to himself. Who knows, by now he might be completely useless. He didn't even have the desire to masturbate any more.

Floyd swung open the broomcloset and stepped into Fräulein Moser's kitchen. Their canasta game began in five minutes, just enough time for him to have a beer and a cheese pie. He went to the refrigerator and saw not four but five little pork chops on the top shelf: ho, a new paying guest. He hoped to God it wasn't another screecher.

His three partners were awaiting him in the backyard. "Good afternoon, ladies," Floyd said, laying his customary box of sweets on the table.

"Your eye is not so black today," Moser noticed. "Soon those stitches will be coming out."

Floyd took his seat. "I notice we have a new lady at the pension."

"Yes. She is sleeping from her trip."

He frowned: a bad sign. It implied jet lag. Floyd cut the deck and had no sooner dealt three cards when a dog began barking vociferously from the barn. "What's all that noise?" he asked, looking to the side.

"The new guest brought a dog. A nice white one with spots."

"Aha." Floyd lost his place and had to start dealing all over again. The barking increased. "What could be the problem in there?" he said, laughing shakily.

"I do not know," Fräulein Moser sighed, fanning her cards. "She promised me the dog would behave. Then she put in her earplugs and went to sleep."

They tried to play canasta but the incensed barking from the barn killed all concentration. Finally Floyd threw down his cards: What the hell, this was all too good to be true anyway. "Excuse me," he said. "I'll see what the problem is."

Champ nearly knocked him to the ground the moment he opened the barn door. Portia may have changed the Dalmatian's sex but she had not daintied the dog's tongue, which pumiced Floyd's face relentlessly. "Down, boy," he said, pulling a few ears. "Girl. Whatever you are."

Eventually Floyd emerged from the barn with the Dalmatian on a leash and tethered her to one leg of the card table. "Sit. Good girl." He picked up his cards.

"The dog obeys," Fräulein Moser said. "She likes you."

"She likes my black eye," Floyd said. "Thinks I'm another Dalmatian." He lost the canasta game by eight thousand points. "Fräulein Moser," he said, "how long is this dog's mistress going to be staying here?"

"I am not sure. But she only eats breakfast. Maybe tonight she has dinner. Otherwise she goes into Montreux with her dog and stays all day."

"How did she find this pension?" Maybe one night when Floyd was sleeping she had planted a little homing device in his ear.

"I received a call from the Montreux tourist bureau. Apparently she had a problem with her dog in the hotel."

"I see." They played another few games and Floyd lost every one big. His partner was becoming disgusted. "Well, ladies, I'm afraid I must stop early today," he finally said. "I have some business at the hotel with Urs." He shut Champ back in the barn and returned to the card table. "Which room is the new guest in?"

"Around the other side of the house, with the red flowerbox. So she can watch the barn. Why do you ask?"

"So I can be sure never to walk in front of it."

Surrounded by his students, Chef Eggli stood piping dough from a huge pastry bag onto a cookie sheet as Floyd walked into the kitchen of the Hotel Badhof. The voluptuous aroma of new-baked bread perfused the air. "Ho! Watch out!" Eggli cried, suddenly swinging open the oven behind him. He withdrew a perfect batch of profiteroles and began transfering them to a rack. "Lovely! Here! Try one," he said to the nearest student, who happened to be Rhoda.

"No thank you."

"What?! Don't you like them?"

"She's trying to watch her weight," Breeze said in a loud voice. "Regain an hourglass figure."

"Like hell," Rhoda said. However, she still did not take one.

Chef Eggli offered a roll to Harriet. "What do you think of this?"

Harriet inspected it for several moments. "Very nice."

"Of course it's very nice," Chef snapped exasperatedly. "How does it taste?"

"Give up, chef, she's watching her weight too," Breeze called from the back of the pack. "I know, it's ridiculous. Tell one of the guys to try it."

As he handed the roll to a third consumer, Chef Eggli finally noticed Floyd in the doorway. "Ah! Anna! Zimstein! Carnegie!" he shouted, switching to dialect. "It's about time you showed up for a class!"

"I must have a word with you," Floyd said. The chef came over.

"Hi, Count," Breeze cooed. "You're looking swell today."

"And you also." Floyd bowed to Harriet. "Hello, Frau Svallow." She beamed intimately at him. "And vhere is Fräulein Rhoda?"

"Over here," Rhoda called, clearing an imaginary jungle with her hands. "Behind this goddamn pony tail." She stepped into the open. "Are you going to talk about etiquette today? Some of us are in desperate need of such a lesson."

"Yes, perhaps I have observed enough." Eggli offered Floyd a profiterole. "Tank you. Stupendous." He chewed a moment. "It could perhaps use a bit more pepper."

"Pepper?" Harriet squawked. "In a cream puff?"

Floyd realized that he had a bit of extemporizing to do. "Of course. It is ze great Hungarian secret."

"I told you he was Hungarian," Rhoda muttered to Breeze. "Greek, my ass."

"Listen," Floyd said in dialect to Chef Eggli. "It's time to make a few sausages. We've put this off long enough. I have to leave soon."

"What? Leave? When?" The chef looked pitifully distraught. "You just got here, Anna!" Floyd didn't even bother correcting him. The chef would forever see him as someone else.

"I think the profiteroles are burning, Chef Eggli," a student called.

Cursing in dialect, Eggli tore over to the oven, which spewed a black cloud in his face as he flung open the door. "I have not lost a profiterole in thirty years," he cried, then burned himself. "Go'verdammi! Days like this drive me insane!" He trashed the profiteroles and put his hand under a faucet. "This is all your fault, Anna," he shouted. "How dare you burst in on me like this? I am in no condition to make any sausages with you!" He sloshed brandy into a nearby coffee cup and left the kitchen.

"What were those two talking about," Rhoda asked one of the Swiss students. "Do you understand that language?"

"Ev course I do."

"Well? What were they saying?"

The chef's words made about as much sense to the Swiss as they made to Rhoda, but he was not going to let her know that: Men had to stick together against this feminist putrilage. "None ev your business."

"Thanks a lot, shithead," Rhoda said. "When you come to America, don't ask me for a job." She grabbed the pastry bag and piped some dough onto the baking sheet. "May as well make myself useful here."

"Lovely," observed Count Carnegie, leaning over the table. "A woman's touch is qvite apparent."

"Sure," Rhoda scoffed. "Any of these Swiss turds could do this and you know it."

"Rhoda, where are your manners? You deserve a demerit for that language."

"No demerits," Floyd said. "I do not believe in zem."

"You mean you won't be sending any of us home, count?" Breeze asked.

"Certainly not. I prefer you here."

"Now that's a great line," Rhoda said, refilling the pastry bag. "You're a real charmer, Count Carnegie."

"Rhoda, you are a drag. Count Car was just trying to encourage you. Don't act like he was trying to pick you up or something."

"Pick Fräulein Rhoda up?" Floyd said. "Vhere vould I put her down?"

Harriet bought that one. " 'Pick up' is a vulgar idiomatic expression, Count Carnegie. I am sure you would not want to add it to your English vocabulary."

"It means you go to a bar and try to bring a woman home with you," Breeze said. "Screw her on short notice. Or vice versa. Something like that might have happened to you last night, in fact. When you were talking philosophy with Swallow."

"My God, you are one hell of a bitch!" Harriet shouted. So much blood rushed to her face she nearly had a nosebleed.

"Let's talk about profiteroles," Count suggested.

"Just like a man," Rhoda said, calmly squeezing out a few more pastries. "Always changing the subject when it hits a little too close to home."

Floyd deftly and coldly twisted the pastry bag from her hands; he often used the same technique to disarm criminals. "Let's talk about picking up," he said. "Zis is a point of etiquette after all." He slowly released Rhoda's wrist. "Personally, I despise it."

Breeze recovered first. She hadn't gotten her wrist crushed nor her cheeks scorched. "Why, Count? Don't you consider it a compliment?"

"On the contrary, I consider it an insult."

"That's what you men have been doing to us for years," Rhoda said.

"I have been doing it to nobody ever," Floyd retorted. "Vhere I come from, men pursue vimmen, not ze opposite."

"How boring," Rhoda said.

Someday Floyd would like to meet Louis in a dark alley with a nut-cracker: He had destroyed his wife's faith in white knights forever. From there it was just a short skid to mail-order insemination. "Boring, eh? You have never been pursued properly."

"I have no desire to be pursued. It's a romantic delusion."

"Rhoda, you contain more bullshit than all the beef in Wyoming," Breeze said.

"It puts women in a position of weakness."

"Who told you that, the staff sergeant at your Female Gorilla classes? Pay no attention to her, count, Rhoda's a bit of a sore loser. Her husband stopped pursuing her and started pursuing his secretary."

Floyd tore a profiterole in half, pretended to inspect its interior, then put it down. He sighed. "First I vould send you two dozen yellow roses vit a little card saying 'I adore you.' No name. Every few days I vould send more. Perhaps after a monz, I vould follow you to a mailbox or a bakery and say hello, just so zat you vould see my face. Perhaps after a year I vould introduce myself."

"A year, Count? Isn't that stretching it?" Breeze said. "I mean, time flies, you know?"

"Time means nozing to me. Vimmen grow only more beautiful as zey grow older."

"Did you ever hear of a bell curve, Count Carnegie?" Rhoda said. "The three of us are on the back slope of it."

"Speak for yourself, mush buns. I'm just hitting my prime."

"Ve vould perhaps go to concerts or plays for anozer year," Floyd said. "Perhaps take a trip to Budapest. One night I vould kiss you."

"Where? How? Then what, count? Come on, the suspense is killing me!"

Floyd looked at his watch. He had to get back to the pension and cook dinner. "Enough etiquette for one afternoon. I bore you."

Chef Eggli reeled into the kitchen. His bandaged hand looked like a volleyball fused to his forearm. "Anna! What in God's name are you still doing here?"

"I am trying to raise the *Titanic*."

"What did they say?" Breeze asked a fellow student. "And what language is that anyhow?"

"Zese zings I kennot translate," she was told.

Viola sat on her balcony overlooking Lac Léman and watched a lone swan float by, still as a decoy. Across the lake, in France, late afternoon sun had tinted the Dents du Midi a deep, dense blue and obscured their foundations within a somnolent haze which fused water and sky. Here on the Swiss side of the lake, the haze bathed everything in palest red, lulling the senses like a warm, diluted draught of wine. Silence weighted all.

Viola's ten toes poised on the white table in front of her. She had been swimming in the pool beneath the hotel and was about to take a nap before dinner. It had been a relaxed, almost anticlimactic day: Dingleball had indeed come up with twenty thousand Christmas robes. Beneath that slipshod exterior breathed a patriot who had responded to Nestor's last-ditch challenge that the honor of Switzerland rested with this order. Precisely at noon, Dingleball had reeled into Montreux, loaded Viola and the Lungs into his truck, and driven to the Geneva airport with the entire shipment. The Lungs had taken snapshots of Viola and Dingleball posing at the freight counter amid several boxes marked *Pyrana, Inc.* Looking at those genial portraits, one would never guess the morass of threats, dyspepsia, and phone bills behind them: Dingleball was a wizard, Viola a gem, this entire transaction a beatitude.

So now Viola had some time off. She watched a water skier drone by:

Even the outboard motors were under sedation here. Not a hair was out of place in this entire country. It was somehow unnatural, as if the population, having renounced the opportunity to participate in two messy world conflicts, were trying to redeem some dignity by declaring war upon dust, weeds, and dandruff. And subversive foreigners, of course. Since her arrival in Montreux, Viola had walked to the Château de Chillon three times. When she passed an American, a Frenchman, an Italian, anything but a Swiss, he looked at her eyes; when she passed a Swiss, he looked at her clothes. It was beginning to irritate her.

However, Viola had wanted a change from Paterson and she had certainly gotten one. Back home she would never see such perfect little parks and walks and birdbaths; even the pigeons here used the toilet. Writing of graffiti was apparently punishable by death. All public clocks read within a quarter inch of each other. The flowers were gorgeous and she had not yet heard one transistor radio.

She just couldn't sleep: Inactivity befuddled the biosystem. She had dropped out of the silk convention early. It was nothing but a herd of strangers trying to outdrink and outseduce each other. No thanks: Every man she met looked somehow like a silkworm with ears. Viola had made all necessary social calls on the first day, stunning those who had expected the fulminic Nestor Buffez to make his annual appearance. How did he survive these sordid conventions, she wondered, toweling her hair dry. Nestor didn't drink and he would never touch another business associate, not that he'd be tempted to anyway: The women here all reminded Viola of adding machines in pantyhose. When she got home, she'd ask him if this was what the typical careerwoman looked like nowadays. She hadn't been exposed to them in years; since her marriage to Eugene, Viola had dumped the Travel & Entertainment responsibilities on Nestor while she stuck to design and accounting. She did not remember women having this hard edge back when she was still taking clients to dinner. Careers meant adventure then. Now it seemed most of the adventuresses were divorced, their children were running wild, their alimony hardly covered day care and gasoline, their jobs were a race and they the rats, nobody ever had dinner bought, much less waiting for them, when they slogged home, and meanwhile their ex-husbands were taking cha-cha lessons with the down-stairs neighbor. Oops, backfire: The perfidious phantom Liberation had rolled to the other side of the bed again.

Scratch a feminist, find a disinherited princess. Those two dozen conventioneers in stacked heels and business suits didn't think they were kidding anyone, did they? Each morning they could don those no-non-sense uniforms, slap on a name tag, and pretend they were marching to work. What they were really doing was searching for the Superprince who would make their careers pale by comparison. That's why Viola sold so much underwear. Beneath those prim blouses and tailored skirts pulsed the blood of a woman, forever quick, forever foolish . . . hah, she should know.

Viola stared down at the water: black china. Now it looked like the lake behind Richard's summer house in Putnam County. Richard's lake did not have Alps on the opposite shore, but it was warmer and certainly much more private than this one: He owned it. They used to go up there every weekend from May to October, the first summer anyhow. Viola would swim while Richard read the contents of his suitcases. Many idyllic hours were passed watching the clouds meander overhead. Then Floyd Beck ruined everything.

She finished drying her hair and tossed the towel onto an empty chair, sighing. Floyd himself had not ruined everything. She had, by bringing him to the lake. Even now, when she supposedly had a maturer appreciation of these comedies, Viola still did not know what had impelled her to kill two birds, Floyd and Richard, with one stone. It had seemed a surprise then; it seemed inevitable now.

Richard was away so much the second spring, working on a gargantuan merger. At that time Viola had no idea what this involved; she sure as hell did now. Poor Richard. It must have been grand returning from five twenty-hour days to a rampaging teenager who did not need to catch up on sleep. She actually went to Chicago with him once, when was it, March? Richard disappeared from six in the morning until one in the morning and Viola took all those reuben sandwiches from room service personally. The moment they returned to New York she tied a white ribbon in her hair and started meeting Floyd at the telephone booth.

She sometimes wondered whether she would have worn that white ribbon anyhow, Chicago or no. Probably yes. Floyd had a mesmeric ability to pull faraway objects toward him simply by looking at them. She still saw his eyes at intermissions: No one had ever looked at her like that before or since. They betrayed no adoration, no desire, just a startling, almost omniscient recognition. Viola had seen war coming the moment he introduced himself and she had done nothing to avoid it. She could have stopped going to that particular ladies' room; she could have reported the stranger to Richard; she could have told Floyd she was married to the man sitting next to her. Somehow she never got around to any of this and each month that wordless, patient gravity pulled her a little bit closer to him as Richard flew far away. Those mornings with Floyd at the phone booth had been unreally happy. Viola didn't remember any more what they talked about; she only remembered that, walking next to him, she had felt safe as a little sloop in harbor. With Richard she heaved in a perpetual typhoon.

Richard was an acutely observant man who had not achieved his success by trusting in other human beings. One morning after Viola's strangely hasty departure from breakfast he had Hiram the butler follow her. That evening at dinner Richard gave her a gold bracelet from Cartier's, ran one finger over her cheek, and asked who the young fellow with the black hair was. It was a moment much more dreadful than waiting for her scores at a figure skating competition. "He sits in the row behind us at Carnegie Hall," Viola had said.

Richard would soon verify that. "And what is his interest in you?"

"I have no idea."

"All right, then, what is your interest in him?"

"I see him ten minutes in the morning when he walks me to ballet." Viola did not mention the ten minutes in the afternoon when he walked her back nor the ten hours in between when she thought about him.

"Aha." Richard did not spend that evening with his briefcase.

She did not meet Floyd for a week and at that last May concert at Carnegie Hall she did not go to the ladies' room at intermission. The evening was a horrific out-of-body experience, particularly when Richard turned to the row behind them: She couldn't watch. Viola realized now that that was what had given her away.

Early one Saturday in June Richard had a merger crisis in Chicago. Viola left the house three minutes after him: She didn't care if the butler went along piggyback, she was going to see Floyd. Of course he was sitting on the low brick wall behind the phone booth waiting for her. "Hi," she said, wanting to leap into his arms the way they did in the movies, cover his hand with kisses, somehow finally touch him: It didn't happen.

He stood up. "I guess you didn't get shipped off to summer camp after all."

"Listen," Viola said, "do you have a car?"

If that's what one could call Aunt Margaret's bomb. "Yes."

"Would you like to go on a picnic today?"

For a moment she thought he would say no. "Sure."

"I'll meet you here in one hour."

She had run home, raided the refrigerator, and left a note that she was going on a picnic. Floyd was waiting at the phone booth in a vehicle resembling the issue of a submarine and a wheat thresher. "What is this anyway?" Viola asked, sliding into the front seat. Floyd was wearing dark sunglasses which made him look a little like a greaser. She liked that.

"A Studebaker. It's my aunt's." Floyd shifted into gear and grinned at her. She had never seen his teeth before. "Where to?"

Richard's lake, of course.

Seventeen years and many gray hairs later, Viola laughed out loud, dropping her face into her hands. Little idiot! She had never once considered that Richard might come back from Chicago that same evening. All she cared about was getting Floyd out of Manhattan and into a woods. She couldn't stand to just look at him any more: She had been doing that for two years. It had finally made her crazy.

"I think I should drive," she said when they exited the Taconic Parkway. "I know these roads much better than you do."

Floyd pulled the car over. He didn't seem to mind if she drove. That way he could look at Viola instead of the road. "Where are we going?"

"To a little lake. Did you bring your bathing suit?"

"No." He hadn't brought a fishing rod or water skis either.

Viola blasted the Studebaker off the shoulder back onto the road. Heavy black smoke billowed from the exhaust pipe. "This thing's a little slow on the pickup," she said.

"Why do you drive so fast?" Floyd said after a while.

Because she had no idea what he was thinking. Any moment now he might tell her he wanted to turn back. "Because I'm hungry."

They finally got to Richard's place. A mild sun fanned the breeze and the bugs were not fully awake. Viola led Floyd down a narrow path to a willow draping the east shore. "Whose lake is this?" Floyd asked. "Your friend's?"

Viola snapped a blanket in the air. "Yes."

"Does he know we're here?"

"No."

"Would he care?"

If he really cared, he would have married her. It didn't matter to Viola that they were born forty years apart. "Why should he? I'm not his wife, you know."

"What are you then?"

"I'm his protegée." She had been rehearsing that line for weeks. It didn't roll off the tongue as exquisitely as it looked in print.

Floyd knew better than to ask exactly what Richard was supposed to be nurturing. "How long have you been that?"

"Two years."

"How much longer are you going to be that?"

That was for the patron, not the protegée, to decide. "I don't know." Viola removed a pair of turkey sandwiches from her picnic basket. Richard would kill her when he got home and found all the chutney gone again. Floyd sat on the diagonal corner of the blanket and opened the cooler he had brought. Out came potato salad and strange cheese. "What is that thing?"

"A bockwurst," he said, slicing a white hotdog. "Try it."

"Where'd you get that?"

"From a butcher downtown." He brought out some thick black rolls. "You eat it with this."

He held a piece to her mouth. She took a big bite, managing to nip two fingers with her teeth: contact. Floyd didn't like that at all. His eyes opened wide and he yanked his fingers away. Then he retreated to the far corner of the blanket, looking for ants in his potato salad. "Not bad," she chomped. It would take an hour to swallow this. She wanted to crawl all over him.

"My father made better bockwurst than these," Floyd said eventually.

"He made bockwurst?" Men did not enter kitchens in those days unless to raid the refrigerator.

"He was a butcher. All of his recipes are in a book."

"You mean like secret formulas?"

"Yes. Nobody knows about the book but me."

She put the turkey sandwiches away and ate a strawberry which Hiram had probably betrothed to a shortcake. "Could I see it someday?"

Again Floyd didn't answer right away and Viola assumed she had overstepped the brink of propriety: Silence was one person's ecstasy, another's dismay. "Sure," he said.

They finished lunch and hiked to a faraway fire tower. Floyd touched Viola's hand once assisting her over a fallen tree; otherwise he kept his distance. That unbalanced her because she had never yet been wrong about a man. They climbed to the top of the fire tower and watched the sun flare just above the horizon, striating light over the hills, gilding a small airplane. Only two people lived on this magnificent green earth.

Floyd leaned over a corner rail. "Where's your lake."

"Behind that hill." Another millimeter and their shoulders would touch. She could feel him breathing.

He stepped away. "What time do you have to be home?"

"Whenever I get back." And it wasn't her home.

"Don't you have a curfew?"

She could just picture Richard trying to ground her or take away her allowance. "No, do you?"

"Midnight."

Then they had to leave here by ten, just when the best stars were coming out. Viola started down the winding stairs. "Let's get going, then."

They got back to the lake with just enough light to finish off the sausages and open some beer. She had brought that, of course. "How about a jigsaw puzzle," Viola said.

"You have one here?"

"No, it's in the house."

Floyd looked at her the way Richard had after that last concert at Carnegie Hall. "I don't want to go into the house."

"Want to go swimming?"

"I didn't bring a bathing suit."

He was suddenly much too quiet. "What's the matter?"

"I have a strange feeling."

"About what?"

"I don't know."

"Does beer make you dizzy or something?"

"No."

The hell with him: She had some lightning to work off. Viola ran to the boathouse, changed into a bathing suit, and ran back to the willow tree, dropping a pair of trunks in Floyd's lap. "Here's a suit and there's the lake," she said, then tore into the water.

It was not as cold as she had expected. Viola swam ferociously towards the other side, splashing as much as possible to scare the turtles away. One never knew what sort of monsters departed their underwater lairs once the water became black as the night. Halfway there, Floyd caught up with her. She had no idea he was a swimmer; he had always seemed more of an outfielder. "Race you," he said, and slithered off.

Viola nearly drowned: He only had a bathing suit on. Nothing remained between his skin and hers but the water. She fought to keep up with him but it was no contest. Floyd had longer arms, bigger feet, less hair, and no breasts to create drag.

He was waiting for her, half submerged, on the opposite shore. "Nice try."

"Where did you learn to swim," she snapped. Richard had not won a single race against her all last summer.

"Here and there." Floyd looked over. "Little out of breath, aren't you."

"No." They sat in the water like two albino bullfrogs as a few bugs circumvolated their heads. Something splashed nearby, either preying or fleeing. She felt dizzy from the beer and the swim and from Floyd never touching her. In her experience men made their intentions known rather immediately and ladies had the honor of sloughing them aside. "What are you thinking about," she finally said.

"You."

Well? Good? Bad? Ugly? "What about me?"

To her dismay he slid into the water again and paddled slowly away. "Come on, Viola. We'll go back side stroke." There was nothing she could do about that. In those days, women never threw themselves at men: Men still bought the milk shakes. She floated after him.

They were almost to the other shore when Floyd turned on his back. "Do you know anything about stars," he said.

Sure. She had about as much chance of touching one as she did of touching Floyd. Viola went belly up. "I can find the Big Dipper. There."

Floyd caught her wrist as it fell back into the water. His hand locked hers for a moment; then his thumb started crawling slowly as a starfish along her skin. She froze, instantly dead; then she sank. The lake filled her nose. Sputtering, Viola pulled herself to the sandy shore by the willow tree.

He had to touch her then because she was coughing like a tubercular. Floyd thumped her back until it appeared that a call to the first aid squad would be unnecessary. "I'm sorry," he said finally. "Didn't mean to drown you." Viola did not move and he was suddenly holding her. Floyd felt very different than Richard, much harder but much softer, much cooler, much sweeter. He had probably never touched a woman before.

Floyd pushed her wet hair aside and kissed her shoulder. She realized she was not the object of a man's desire but an awesome mystery: Viola didn't know how to react to that so she sat still as a stump in the water. That was no mouth on her skin. That was a creature from the bottom of the lake who had learned to draw some magical current from the water lilies and was now softly transferring it into her. It would take all night, she would die, but she would awaken a lily herself and bob on the dark lake, beneath that slender moon, forever.

Suddenly Floyd pulled his head up. "What's that," he said. "Shhhhh." She heard the water and the wind. Then she heard the car and turned to stone.

"Viola," Richard called. "Where are you?"

"Get out of the water," Floyd whispered, dropping his arms. "Tell him you're here."

Was he kidding? She wanted to swim to Canada! "I can't," she wailed.

Floyd pushed her away and sank into the water seconds before the floodlights from Richard's house lit up the lake. To anyone of lame imagination it appeared that Viola was chasing fireflies and Floyd was disporting amid the algae. "Viola," Richard called from the deck, "what are you doing down there?"

"What does it look like," she retorted. "I'm having a picnic."

Richard immediately descended to lakeside and saw Floyd's clothes piled aside four bottles of his imported beer. "And who might this gentleman be?" he addressed his lake rather than Viola. "Would you mind introducing yourself?"

Floyd stepped out of the water and stood next to Richard's protegée. "Floyd Beck," he said. "You must be Richard."

"That is correct." He turned to Viola. "I rather expected to find you here, my dear. Alone." Viola resisted looking at him. "Where might I find your pile of your clothes? Beneath Mr. Beck's?"

"In the boathouse."

"Aha." Richard inspected Floyd's trunks. "You really should have given him Hiram's suit, Viola. I'd say that Mr. Beck is one size larger than I am. At the moment, anyway." The three of them stared at Floyd's erection.

"Very funny, Richard," Viola finally said.

Richard lifted the lid of Viola's, or rather, his, picnic basket. "Did you and Mr. Beck leave me any chutney, darling?"

"No."

Richard pulled out a bottle of beer. "Still cool. Thank God for small miracles." He offered it to Floyd, who refused. "Is that by chance your car in my driveway?"

"Will you stop this?" Viola cried. "Of course it is!"

Richard leveled Floyd with that same look of contempt and amusement he had used in Carnegie Hall. "Would you mind picking up your clothes, getting into your car, and driving away?"

Floyd looked at Viola. "Are you coming back with me?"

She had not been expecting that so she said nothing. Richard chuckled affably. "Of course she isn't, Mr. Beck! We're staying here for the weekend."

"I didn't ask you, grandpa," Floyd said. Again he looked at Viola. "Are you coming?"

Viola had been living with Richard long enough to realize that once she crawled into that Studebaker, she would never be allowed back in his house, or his lake, or his bed, again. The bed she could live without. She just wasn't quite ready to exchange everything else for a beautiful lad who had accompanied her on one picnic. "I can't, Floyd," she said. She'd straighten this all out Monday morning at the telephone booth.

"Well then! I suppose it's good night," Richard said, putting his arm around Viola's shoulder. "You're sure you know how to get out of here or should I lead you to the highway?"

"Save your gas." Floyd picked up his clothes. His legs cast long shadows into the lake. "Goodbye, Viola." She watched his pale skin recede into the trees.

"By the way, keep the bathing suit," Richard called.

Viola tore the beer bottle from Richard's hand and flung it at the willow tree, smashing it to smithereens. "I hate you," she said.

"That was quite foolish, pet," Richard replied. "It's going to take you all morning to clean that glass up." He walked into the house and shut the lights off. Viola heard Floyd's car pull away and started to cry. Richard came out a while later with a large towel and took her inside.

She had gone to the phone booth every morning for a month but Floyd never came back. She called his apartment; his aunt always answered and always said he was out. Viola did not stoop so far as to haunt his front steps. For him, it was finished. Richard never quite forgave her for that picnic. However, he did finally ask her to marry him. Viola told him she'd have to think about it; she was going away to school in the fall and wanted to see if absence made the heart grow fonder.

She never found the answer to that question and she never spoke to Floyd Beck again. Each time she went to a chamber music concert or saw a white sausage, she thought of him and ached: There had been something extraterrestrial there. She could tell herself oh, the boy had haunted her for two years, he was remote and gorgeous as a black panther, she had used him only to hurt Richard . . . then she remembered that lake, and knew she had not yet resolved Floyd Beck.

Her phone rang. Viola left the balcony and went inside. "Hello."

"Hi, darling! How's everything? Did I wake you up?" It was Eugene, the halfway point between Floyd and Richard, calling from Scotland.

"No, I was just sitting on my balcony watching the sun go down."

"How do you feel? How's the convention?"

"Fine. Dingdong delivered the robes yesterday, right on schedule. It was ridiculously easy."

"That's wonderful. Somehow I knew he would. Now you have some time to relax, eh?"

"The Lungs and I will take a few side trips. An opera in Geneva. Drive to a sanatorium in the mountains. Tour the local vineyards."

Eugene delicately cleared his throat. "Wine? Are you going to be drinking wine? I thought we had discussed that."

"No, Eugene, I'm not going to be drinking wine." Viola sighed resignedly.

"Are you feeling strong? Sending good vibrations downstream?"

"Yes. The air is wonderful here. I'm not sick at all."

"Do you know what today is?"

"Wednesday."

"It's exactly twenty-five weeks til D-Day."

"Now that's fascinating." She looked down at her belly. In another month it would become obvious that a fetus, and not the detritus of three dozen fudge cakes, dwelt therein. "So tell me about your fishing trip. Are your new flies working? How's Murdoch?" That was the guide.

"He's fine. Taking us way upstream tomorrow and I won't be near a phone at all. I suppose we won't be in touch until I see you in Rome." Eugene sounded anxious. "Are you taking your vitamins and everything on that list? Are you sleeping enough? Is the Goldberg belt working on European current? How's your jet lag? I hope the baby doesn't get confused."

"Darling, everything will be all right! I'm doing nothing but eating, walking, and sitting in my hotel." And wondering how the hell she ever got there, of course. This was her last shot at philosophy for the next twenty years.

"I miss you so much, sweetheart. I wish I were in Switzerland."

"You'll see me in a week! Go have a good time with your friends!"

"I can't. We're not on the same wave length any more."

Eugene had probably been driving them insane with baby talk. "Darling, do me a favor. Forget about me completely. Forget about the baby. Go catch the biggest fish of your life." Viola almost laughed at her own pep talk: That's what she'd like to do herself.

"All right," he said halfheartedly. "I love you."

"I love you too."

"Know what the best thing about this trip is?"

No Goldberg belt. "What?"

"We can have that amniocentesis when you get back. Then we can really get cracking with the names."

Major George Hash stood in the Customs locker room at JFK Airport inspecting his scalded face. In another day or two the blisters would pass for a fierce sunburn and he could return to The Outpost without looking like a forty-year-old with acne or, worse, the epidermal manifestations of AIDS. He had not realized that pizza could be such a deadly weapon; next time he followed a dangerous suspect into Little Italy, he'd remember that.

Despite the efforts of a squad of free-lance dogcatchers, Smudge the mutt had not been located. Hash doubted he'd ever find him; word on the streets was that Smudge would be terminated the moment that goon from the CIA caught him. Nestor Buffez's loquacity had thus guaranteed his pet's vanishment. Served him right, Hash thought, daubing antiseptic cream on his chin. Some clouds indeed had a silver lining. He left the locker room.

McPhee was in the office transferring paperwork from the right to the left baskets on his desk. Next week he would actually read some of it. "Morning," he said, blearily glancing up. His mouth dropped. "What the hell happened to you?"

"Burned myself," Hash said, nonchalantly pouring some coffee. "All in the line of duty."

"Did someone try to torch you? I told you never to go to Paterson without backup!" McPhee came over to the coffee machine and examined Hash's face, wincing. "I guess that's the end of the Aqua Velva man for a while."

Hash's red cheeks acquired a purplish tint. Saying nothing, he went to his desk and picked up the phone. "Hello? I'd like to speak with Dr. Clemens, please. Is that so? When did she leave? Would you happen to know where she's staying? I'll be going over there myself. Yes, of course. This is Dr. McPhee, from Flushing." McPhee looked darkly over at Hash; he did not like his name dragged into perverted cases. "Thank you very much."

McPhee sat stiffly on the desk. He was trimming the post-Frisk hangovers down to five a week now. "What's going on."

"The dog doctor has fled the country," Hash said. "She's going to make her delivery in Switzerland at a veterinary convention. The Dalmatian's with her. It's the perfect arrangement, of course. She'll be surrounded by people, going out to dinner, taking that dog everywhere. I've got to stop her."

McPhee said nothing for quite a while. "I thought you suspected the Cuban."

"He's more or less proven his innocence. He's in the hospital with a broken ankle."

"What about his partner?"

Hash hesitated. "Instinct tells me no."

"Instinct has burned a few holes in your face recently." McPhee sighed. "I don't know, Hash. This whole case is very strange. You seem to have developed a fixation on this pipsqueak feminist. It's unlike you."

"Wrong. Look at the facts. I get a telex from Berlin. My informant tells me to look for corsets. I find one of these courier dogs with Nestor Buffez. He leads me to Portia Clemens. She goes to Switzerland with a slashed-up Dalmatian just when things get a little dicey. This is not a strange case. You just have no imagination."

"How'd you get burned," McPhee said.

"I got hit with a pizza. Chasing the Cuban."

"How'd he break his ankle?"

"He slid into a pinball machine."

"So where's the dog? The microchip? Your only evidence, I might add?"

"The dog's disappeared. The microchip's with Portia."

McPhee looked startled. "Who told you that?"

"Nestor. She obviously got the chip back and planted it on the Dalmatian."

"Why did she even bother planting it on the mutt in the first place, then?"

"Don't you get it, McPhee? She knew I was on to her ever since July Fourth. She had to find a holding tank until she took off. The Cuban's just a dupe."

For a long while McPhee looked into the customs terminal. An agent was leading away a black woman in a silver jumpsuit. "You're right. I have no imagination."

"I need a week off, McPhee. I've got to get over there."

"You're on a wild goose chase. But I told you that from the beginning."

"I'll pay for the plane ticket. You pay for the hotel. Trust me."

Frisk entered the office. "See that chick in silver, Albert? I just nailed her."

"For what," McPhee said tonelessly.

"She had a pet tarantula in her carry-on." Frisk noticed Hash. "If it isn't the local babysitter. What happened to you, Uncle Hash? Did one of those red-hot numbers sit on your face?"

"Very funny."

She picked up a donut. "Hey, guess who called me last night. Floyd."

"From where," Hash said.

"From vacation."

"Well? What did he say? What's he doing?"

"Swimming. Playing cards. Climbing mountains."

"In Florida?"

"I'm only telling you what the man told me, Albert."

"He was speaking figuratively," Hash said. "Beck does that all the time. So how did he sound? Good? Better?"

"Better than what? He always sounds fine when he's talking to me."
Frisk left.

Hash watched her walk back to her station, wondering how many hands
a man must have to really do her justice. "So McPhee," he said. "If I can
get a standby tonight, I'm out of here. I'll be back in three days. You won't
even know I'm gone."

McPhee continued staring out the window at Frisk. "I know when
anyone's gone," he said.

11

Floyd awoke the moment footsteps sounded overhead: Portia. His sub-conscious recognized the compact, light tread and for a moment had him believe he was back in Hoboken, waiting for his alarm to officially roust him from bed. He looked at the ceiling of his neat Swiss room, following her path. Fräulein Moser had put her directly over him; they slept only ten feet apart, Portia on top, of course. She had just blown two Swiss francs in the shower. Now she was making her bed. Now she walked over to the little table by the window and was yanking underpants out of her suitcase. The bras she had left home. Whoa, dropped a shoe, jet lag. They were heavy monsters, all right. Over to the closet, pulling on a business suit, probably the beige linen model with the straight skirt. Floyd shut his eyes: yep, the blue blouse with little trumpets all over it. She always wore that when she was trying to make a solid first impression.

The baker was coming up the path. Dressing quickly, Floyd met him at the kitchen door. He threw the bread on the table and pumped water into the heavy kettle. Fräulein Moser had neglected to tell him how many extra coffee beans to use this morning for the new guest, therefore he'd use the same number of beans but increase the water. She'd appreciate that. Floyd boiled the milk, poured it into a pitcher, sliced the bread, dolloped some jam into a dish, and shoved everything onto the counter. It was exactly six o'clock.

A while later Portia entered the dining room. Sitting behind the little sliding door, Floyd heard her remove the pitchers and breadbasket to her table. Now she was lifting the lid off the thermos and sniffing the coffee. Didn't like what she smelled but poured herself a cup anyway. She stirred the coffee and milk for a long time, as if she were busy reading—aha, the train timetable. The stirring stopped. Now she was actually going to drink the stuff. He held his breath, waiting.

"Oiiiiiff." Bingo! She hated it! Floyd grinned as if he had just won a prize. Upon such small victories were egos furbished. Now she was poking around the breadbasket looking for the heel of the loaf. This was Portia's favorite piece so Floyd made sure he had not included it.

Last night she had slept ten feet away from him and now she ate ten feet away from him. He felt suddenly angry, realizing that even when they had slept and eaten together, the walls had always been there. But she had let him know that the day they first met on the sidewalk outside her clinic. "I'm unlisted," Portia had distinctly said. Did he buy that? Of course not. In each of her walls, he thought he saw a door. Once again he had paid the price of not taking a woman at her word. "I don't know who you are, but you're beginning to bother me," had been Viola's introductory sentence. He had misinterpreted that also. A costly error.

Floyd leaned his cheek on a fist, eavesdropping on Portia's silence. He wondered if she had gotten herself impregnated yet. Probably not. Since asking him to inseminate her, she had not ovulated again. Unless, of course, she had found an immediate replacement, determined to conceive a child on Independence Day. That would have made great copy for her Female Awareness constituents but Floyd doubted it. When she left him that afternoon, Portia had a distinct Dr. Clemens the Veterinarian air. She had probably worked until midnight rearranging Champ's nipples.

So she had made it to the convention after all: Hash couldn't bring himself to sabotage the dog's papers. Portia would soon deliver her speech to a packed house. Today she would parade Champ around the premises, whipping up controversy. Floyd felt sorry for her having to commute all the way into Montreux with a dog and jet lag. But the lady was tough; if anyone could do it, she could. He imagined her speech which, he was sure, William and her shock troops had helped to write. Tomorrow afternoon, eh? Maybe he'd drop by if Fräulein had no canasta game planned.

Heavier footsteps thumped into the dining room. "Good morning, Fräulein Clemens."

"Good morning, Ms. Moser. Would you mind calling me Ms. Clemens? Or just Portia? Thank you."

"I see you are up qvite early."

"Yes, I must catch the six-thirty train."

"Did you sleep vell?"

"Very well, thank you."

"And how do you like your room?"

Portia poured herself another cup of coffee, deliberating. Floyd shook his head: better sit down, Fräulein. "It is for the most part not bad."

"Not bad? Vhat do you mean?"

"I must tell you that the wallpaper is quite offensive."

"My vallpaper? How? It is a bootiful design. Small flowers and ribbons."

"This reinforces a false image of femininity. It portrays women as weak and narcissistic sexual objects. Such subliminal messages are totally unacceptable in today's society."

"How can vallpaper do zis?"

"And the problem is compounded by the little lamp by the bed."

"Is it broken?"

"You must get rid of that fluffy lampshade, Ms. Moser. I want a light, not a ballerina."

"I am sorry, but you must use zis one. I cannot be rearranging my pension for ladies who vish to pretend zey are alvays in America."

"My goodness, you Swiss are opinionated."

"Zank you."

"Well, I must be going. Do not expect me back in time for dinner. Perhaps you might deduct that from my bill."

"I am sorry, zis is not possibell. You must remember zat I charge you nozing for your dog."

"That's very generous of you."

"I zink so also. Did you have a shower zis morning? Yes? Zat vill be two Sviss francs. So. I must go. I vish you a good day in Montreux."

Shortly thereafter, Portia brought her dishes to the counter and left the dining room. Floyd slid open the door. Upon Portia's saucer lay a little note. "To whom it may concern: This coffee is vile," she had written. "Please do not boil it tomorrow morning. Also, please serve the heels of the bread. I prefer these to the middle pieces. Thank you very much. Your guest, Dr. Portia Clemens, DVM."

Never say die, Portia. She had written the note with the fountain pen he had given her for Valentine's Day. Floyd threw the paper away and leafed through his father's book of recipes as he waited for Fräulein Moser's three remaining guests to come to breakfast. In the next few days Eggli and he were finally going to make the Floydwurst and suddenly Floyd was not looking forward to the experience. This morning he had felt a distinct dread upon waking up which was only partially caused by Portia padding overhead. A dip in barometric pressure, perhaps? The foehn? Knowing that he had only a few more days here? It had to be the sausages. Floyd was not at all sure now that he wanted to tamper with Caspar's butcher shop. It belonged in a sweet bygone dream. Resurrecting a recipe so many years later under the harsh lights of Eggli's kitchen was a very perilous dip into that vault of perfect memories, of which he had so few already: Reality had a way of cinderizing legends.

Two chairs drew eight more lines into Fräulein Moser's wooden floor. "Where's Tonto?" Floyd heard Rhoda say.

"Putting on her war paint. She's supposed to be serving Count Carnegie tonight."

"Oh God, I can't stand it. The man will be sick."

"I think not. He seems to find her amusing. Likes her spirit, he says."

"Europeans have always idealized the American Indian."

"No, Europeans have always idealized women." Harriet sighed. "Men are so different over here."

"They're exactly the same everywhere. Don't get carried away because of one Romeo with a black eye."

"Rhoda, sometimes you depress me."

"Good morning, ladies."

"My God! Where did you get that outfit?"

"What's the matter, can't you deal with a little pizzazz?"

"Let me guess. Pocahontas in a space suit."

"Very clever, Rhoda. This happens to be the dress I got married to Stanley in. Number Two. I notice that's quite a low-cut blouse you've got on."

"It's going to be a hot day."

"Anything you say, dear. Hey, it's late. I didn't think it would take this long to put a few corn rows in my hair. We'd better get going."

"You don't think I'm going to be seen on the streets with you in that outfit, do you?"

"Rhoda, you really disappoint me. Haven't you been listening to your leaders these past few years? Haven't they been telling you to dress the way you feel and not the way designers in Rome and Paris would have you feel?"

"It does seem a bit hypocritical, dear."

"Get off my case, Harriet." Rhoda's chair scraped the floor. She left.

"What's gotten into her lately?"

"She has a crush on Count Carnegie. It's obvious a mile away."

"Poor thing. She doesn't have a chance."

Harriet's cup plinked upon its saucer. "I'm afraid none of us do, dear."

"Is that so? We'll see tonight."

After the women had gone, Floyd finally wrote postcards to Frisk, Hash, and McPhee although they'd probably see his cheerful face well before receiving them. Unless his plane crashed, of course: Whew, he was in a poor mood today. It had to be Portia and that damn dog invading his Paradise. Floyd walked to his warm lake but did not swim: too hot, unusually so. He felt like sleeping but Fräulein Moser was counting on him for a few rounds of canasta.

"You seem not yourself today," she commented after two slapstick games. Moser would have fared better playing with Champ as a partner.

"I'm sorry," Floyd said. "It's difficult to concentrate. Maybe it's the heat."

Moser looked upward. "We shall have a big storm then everything shall be fine again." She glanced at her cards. "I tell you what. I give you the night off."

"Who's going to make dinner?"

"The three Americans are at cooking school. Miss Clemens is in Montreux. We shall have a new guest, but she will sleep." Floyd frowned. "She comes all the way from India."

"What about your dinner?" Floyd asked.

"Perhaps I go to the Hotel Badhof. I would like to see once what these women and my cousin Urs do over there for three weeks."

Floyd looked at his cards: blah. "Perhaps you would like to eat with me."

"You would buy me dinner?"

"Of course."

Fräulein Moser popped one last chocolate into her mouth. "That sounds very nice."

The skies blackened terribly and wanted to cry but somehow could not, so they stung the mountains with lightning instead. Thus the card game, which transpired upon a metal table, ended earlier than usual. Floyd tried to nap and Fräulein Moser took a ten-franc bath in anticipation of her first dinner date in three decades. There was not a drop of hot water left when Floyd stepped into the shower. Just as well, he needed a stimulant. He had been watching the lightning attack the mountains and was semi-hypnotized, full of heavy air, as if he had witnessed a far-off Armageddon.

Fräulein Moser awaited him in her drawing room at exactly seven o'clock wearing a black dress of timeless design and a heavy brooch at her throat. Floyd had never seen her bun this latitudinous; it was almost the size of a second head. She had powdered her nose and about her shoulders rested the remains of a half dozen mink. Sight of her knitting placidly upon the couch stopped Floyd dead on the threshold: Something had whooshed by him again. Aunt Margaret? Were they going to a concert? "You look lovely, Fräulein Moser," Floyd said, presenting her with a small rose corsage. He had gotten it at the little flower shop in Emwald during her bath.

"And you look very nice in your suit," she said. "Very nice indeed."

"Remember to call me Count Carnegie," Floyd told her. "And tell no one that I stay at your pension."

"Someone would ask such a question?"

"Perhaps." He extended his arm. "Off we go."

Having failed to indent the mountains, the storm had fled, ripping gray from the sky and exposing a limpid blue expanse in its place. Cool, fresh air eddied between the Alps. As she shut her front door, Moser sniffed the evening. "Soon it will be fall." She outpaced Floyd all the way to the Hotel Badhof, remarking several times how hungry she was.

The dinner guests peered at Count Carnegie and his dowager companion, wondering what their relationship might be, as the maître d' led them to the table next to the harpist. Tonight she was playing Bach. "Last time I was here the walls were green," Fräulein Moser said, removing her pieces of mink.

Breeze rushed over to the table immediately. Her silver outfit clashed with everything in sight, with her blond hair most of all. "Jesus Christ, Froy, how did you pull this off? What are you doing here with the count? Gee, corsages and everything."

Floyd switched to English. "I see zat you two have met."

"Of course we've met. She tries to poison me every morning and three nights a week. I live in her pension."

"Zat is a very colorful outfit you are vearing tonight."

"Thank you. It's an Indian costume, updated. Bet you didn't know I was an Indian, did you, Count. Perhaps you'd be interested in hearing my family history tonight. It's much more entertaining than talking philosophy with Harriet."

"I might like to hear zis also."

"No you wouldn't, Froy. It's full of sex and violence."

"*Gottinhimmel!* You Americans are all alike!"

Floyd had better pacify her. "Two gin-and-tonics, please."

"For Froy? I can't believe it!"

"Just bring zem," Floyd said. Breeze flashed to the bar. "Ignore what that woman says," he told Fräulein Moser. "The chemicals she uses in her hair have penetrated her brain."

Urs Eggli flitted to the table in his spotless white apron, hat, pants, and shirt. In another culture his costume could have been a bride's. "Erna, how nice to see you." He looked coldly at Floyd. "Hello, Anna." Behind them the harpist began a gigue from one of the Bach partitas.

Floyd sighed. "Wrong again."

"Urs, you know very well this is Count Carnegie," Moser said. "You brought him here yourself."

"I certainly did not. He phoned me in the middle of the night and said he had to see me. Now he wants me to make sausages with him." Chef Eggli watched one of his students ignite a flambé. "Well done," he called.

Then his face darkened. "I refuse to have anything to do with that bastard Caspar."

"You never will," Floyd said. "Caspar's dead."

Eggli looked coolly down at Floyd. "So is Anna." He studied the face which was so like hers. "Be glad you were not a woman," he said. "I would have murdered you."

"Urs! How can you say such things!" The chef walked away. "Excuse my cousin, he sometimes has relapses," Fräulein Moser explained. "I do not understand why he just does not forget about this. Anna was in love with Caspar all along. No one but Urs was surprised when they ran away. For years he told everyone that she would come back to Emwald someday." She shrugged. "Instead he got you. I am afraid he has ruined his life."

Ruined? Did a monk ruin his life in a monastery? "Some men are meant for only one woman," Floyd said. "They are like a tree which can only grow in one type of earth. They would probably not die if they were planted elsewhere, but they would not bear much fruit. So I would not say they were ruined. They were just misplaced."

"I find this attitude very impractical."

If Fräulein had ever met her Caspar, her sympathies would extend beyond canasta and chocolates. "You are not a tree."

Breeze slid to the table with two highballs. "Sorry this took so long, gang. The bartender insisted on shaving the ice." The tiers of fringe on her silver outfit swayed in unison as she moved. "So! For dinner tonight we're serving a salmon pâté, veal in cognac, and gooseberry pie."

"No potatoes?"

"Of course potatoes, Froy. They're a side dish. Don't plan on getting more than three or four little ones. So Count, are you interested in a little American history?"

Five thousand scions of American history filed past him every day at JFK airport. Their stories were more or less the same. "Ve vill see."

Rhoda strolled to the table in a V-neck blouse which exposed fifty percent of her torso. "Good evening, Fräulein Moser, Count Carnegie. Come to check us out, have you?"

"Yes, I am interested to see vhat you are cooking over here."

"Believe me, we're not going to serve you what you serve us." Breeze looked at Floyd. "Froy's got the world's worst chef at her pension. He makes coffee taste like gall-bladder soup. I don't know why you keep the guy, Froy, really. Unless he's your lover or something."

"Vhat!? How dare you say zese zings!"

Floyd stood up. "Apologize immediately to Fräulein Moser."

Breeze threw up her hands. "Sorry, sorry, Froy. Guess I struck a nerve."

"That's your forte, Tonto," Rhoda said in disgust. "Perhaps you two would enjoy your dinner more if I waited on you instead."

"Flash the cleavage at your own table, Rhoda. I can handle this."

"My table has not arrived yet. They're driving up from Montreux."

"Oh boy, you're going to be the first thing they see here?"

"Unless you blind them first."

"Ahem," Floyd said. "Fräulein Moser is extremely hungry tonight."

"Sorry, Froy, two salmon pâtés coming up."

Rhoda's shapely bosom had been brought into relief by her two-week crash diet. Against his will Floyd found his eyes drawn to it. He had not touched a woman in months and his hormones were suddenly mutinous. Obviously Rhoda was taunting him for overlooking her; Floyd did not want her to know how well she was doing. "If you vould excuse us," he announced. "Fräulein Moser and I have much to talk about."

"Of course." Her breasts bowed and left.

Moser watched Rhoda's buttocks ripple into the kitchen. "The last time I came to eat here, all of the students wore formal black suits," she said. "I see that Urs has let certain disciplines slip shamelessly."

"Before the first buffet the ladies told him those uniforms were demeaning and made them feel like servants. They threatened to sue him."

"But I thought women in your country wanted to dress like men."

"Sometimes they do, sometimes they don't."

"Why can't they make up their minds?"

Harriet strode by in a leopard-print jumpsuit. "Because they're women, of course."

Breeze returned. "How you holding up, Froy? I see you demolished all the rolls. Ready for another G & T?" She placed a slab of pâté on the table. "You are going to love this. It contains salmon, cream, eggs, fine spices, butter . . . all kinds of things you never serve in your pension. And you eat it with a little of this special mayonnaise." She spattered a large spoonful atop Fräulein's portion and stood expectantly to the side. "Okay, try it."

Moser remembered a specious compliment she had recently received. "Not bad."

Breeze presented Count Carnegie with his salmon and reached into a pocket beneath the fringe of her outfit. "I thought these might interest you, Count," she said, placing a pile of photographs upon the table. "Whet your appetite for my life story."

"And vhat are zese?"

"They're the last roll of film I shot, Froy. I suppose you can see them too. I thought Count would be alone tonight, to tell the truth."

Floyd put down his fork. All this quicksilver was giving him a dazzling headache. He should never have had that gin and tonic. "Vould you mind bringing us a good bottle of vine, Fräulein Breeze? Ask Chef Eggli for his recommendation."

Harriet Swallow passed their table wheeling a little trolley. "Hello, Count Carnegie. Congratulations, Fräulein Moser."

Floyd's dinner companion finished the last of her salmon. "Why do these women all make such insinuations?" she asked. "It insults me."

He watched Harriet stop at a nearby table, rattle a few pans, ignite a flambé, and announce "Veal in cognac" to her charges. "It shouldn't. They are insulting me."

Fräulein Moser wiped her mouth on a napkin and reached for the photographs. "Is that so? I thought they were all rather taken with you."

"They think they're not supposed to be. I might seduce them."

"If they don't want that, why are they fighting over you?"

"Simple biology, Fräulein Moser, no matter what their instructors say."

"But will you seduce them?"

"Of course not! That would wreck all my fun." He couldn't see himself in bed with any of them.

The harpist in the corner began an arrangement of the Third *Brandenburg* Concerto as Fräulein Moser browsed through the photographs beside her plate. Floyd watched Chef Eggli's students weave amid the tables, deftly serving and clearing dishes. Except for Breeze, their improvement over the past three weeks had been remarkable. Soon the class, and he, would disband from this elegant pink dining room and return to the technological wilderness beyond. In four days, at exactly this time, he'd be standing in an airless terminal sifting through the luggage of innumerable conniving rogues. Floyd much preferred to play the delphic, immaculate Count Carnegie and spend the rest of his life here playing canasta, waking up to a primeval sunrise, and swimming in his secret, warm lake, waiting, waiting . . . when he first came to Emwald, Floyd had a premonition he was on the edge of something monumental: roots, Beckian skeletons, spiritual revelation. In three weeks his most galvanic adventure had been a black eye, or perhaps meeting Champ in Moser's barn. Tomorrow or the next day, Eggli and he would make a few sausages, wave hello to Caspar—then Floyd would go home. Somehow, somewhere, a piece was missing, a loop was still open. It did not feel right.

Floyd heard a strange swishing and rattling to his left. Breeze arrived at the table lugging a silver wine bucket and two glasses which had miraculously remained unshattered. "Sorry this took so long," she said. "It was a bitch filling this thing up." She pulled a bottle from the icy water.

"Eggli says you'll like this." After an inelegant display of her corkscrew expertise, Breeze poured the wine.

"Lovely," Floyd pronounced, toweling bits of cork from his tongue. "Our compliments to Chef Eggli."

Moser held a snapshot up. "Vhat is zis, please? A castle?"

Breeze leaned back to look, poising two dishes on her forearm. Floyd braced himself for the crash of china. "No, Froy, that's where I work."

"Vhere is zis mansion? In Newport, Rhode Island?"

"Nah, nah, Paterson. That's a city in New Jersey."

Floyd sat very still, feeling his throat rust. "Look," said Fräulein Moser, showing him the picture. "Vhat a nice building. Like a Sviss castle."

He looked at it only because a lady had asked him to. Then he looked away, at the harpist, at the chandelier, anything. "Hhhh."

Moser passed to the next shot. "And vhat is zis? Baseball?"

"Those are a few shots of the company picnic. July Fourth, just before I came over here. That's my boss giving out baseball caps."

"He is Japanese? He vears a yellow kimono?"

"No, he's Cuban and he wears pajamas. Doesn't like regular clothes."

Aware of Breeze's candor, Fräulein Moser did not pursue this volatile topic. "Py-rana," she read off the cap. "He has a dog?"

"Yeah, that's Smudge. I found him in the garbage."

"Very cute. Look, Carnegie."

Floyd swallowed a mouthful of wine. Then he was force-fed Nestor. Immediately he knew Viola had slept with those ten-thousand-volt eyes. That must mean she was finally through with Old Richard. "Charming. Could ve please get on viz dinner?" He suddenly felt as if the pâté in his stomach had metamorphosed back to a huge, writhing salmon. So Portia wasn't bad enough: Now Viola had invaded Emwald. No wonder he had felt sick all day. He would never look at Breeze the same way again. She came into daily, casual contact with the woman who had altered the course of his life. In three weeks she had not once mentioned her employer in Floyd's hearing. Damn her! She knew so much and it meant nothing to her!

"Look at this one," Fräulein Moser said, lifting another snapshot. "I have never seen so many hotdogs in my life. Everyone is eating them."

Sighing, Floyd poured more wine. "I've seen hotdogs before." He bored his eyes at the harpist, then out the window.

"This Cuban has a beautiful wife."

"Let me see that," Floyd said, snatching the picture away. It was a close-up of Nestor, Viola, the dog, and some man cut off at the ear. Nestor and Viola were seated at a picnic table, shoulders touching, glaring at each other as Smudge sniffed the hotdog upon Nestor's paper plate. Breeze had taken the photo right after Viola had gotten back from the clinic with Smudge in bandages; Nestor was furious that she had not kept a closer eye on his pet while he was off getting beer. They looked about ready to sock each other. "What makes you think this is his wife."

"She wears a ring, of course. And they sit so close."

Viola had tucked most of her black hair under the baseball cap, revealing the neck he remembered so well: That was the last part of her his lips had touched. She had remained partial to heavy gold jewelry and her skin was still that bluish white which even now made his blood whirl. Upon her cheek rested the same black mole which he had kissed only in dreams. He stared at her mouth, her eyes, searching for regret, for wisdom: haughtier than ever.

He flung the picture down. "Would you mind putting those damn things away? I do not find them at all interesting."

"What was that you said, count?" Breeze asked, shimmying out of nowhere with a trolley. "Maybe you could give me a few language lessons after I tell you my life story. No one here understands a word of that stuff."

His skull was going to explode: mnemonic overload. Floyd took a deep breath as the dining room blurred in front of him. How did he land in this particular dream? Emwald was just another lovely, dead-end tendril of that picnic.

The silver fringe on Breeze's outfit rustled as she lifted the lid from a warming pan. "Veal in cognac," she said. "Which I shall flambé at your table. Chef Eggli insists we all get this technique down before going home." She lit a match and laughed nervously. "I've never done this before, you realize, so it might take a few tries. I keep getting the steps mixed up."

Moser looked at Floyd. "Perhaps ve can skip zis part."

Breeze threw the match into the veal. Nothing happened. "Aha! I forgot the sauce," she said, picking the match out of the meat. "Wait a minute. Now I have to heat up the booze." She poked another match at the wick beneath a small copper ladle. "Should have done this in the kitchen, sorry. Ouch!" she cried, flinging the match into the wine bucket.

Glancing in resignation at Fräulein Moser, Floyd looked over the dining room. Breeze had become the center of attention, as usual. After the fourth match, people started to titter: This performance was definitely going to earn her a round of applause. He noticed movement in the entryway and saw three Asians and a woman with gorgeous black hair standing with the host. Then Breeze stood up, blocking his line of sight.

"Almost ready, gang," she said. "This sauce is getting very hot. Okay! Bombs away!" She poured it over the veal and stood back to light a match.

On the periphery of his vision Floyd followed the bundle of newcomers as they broke into single file and headed to their table: whoa: freeze frame: replay the body in royal blue. He knew that walk. A cold, lascivious finger slowly climbed his back, frosting vertebrae. Floyd sat up straight as an icicle, moving only his eyes, following the woman. She was the shadow of a shadow, one in his brain, one in his blood, no, God yes: shadows fused and became flesh for the second time in his life: Viola.

Breeze threw her last match at the meat, shielding her eyes as it erupted into flame. "Veal in cognac," she shouted in triumph. "Crap! Don't ask me to do that again!" The surrounding tables applauded. "Thank you, everyone." Breeze looked at Count Carnegie. "Well, aren't you impressed? Didn't I do well? What's the matter with you?"

Floyd neither answered nor removed his eyes from the woman seated facing him three tables away. She wore diamonds in her hair now and her eyebrows seemed to be ever so subtly thinner, like the next phase of two tiny, black moons. Her face looked older, but softer; more skin, less bone. More mouth. More Viola. He wondered if her shoulders still smelled of roses and cream, and if she was happy. He hoped not. How dare she come here to his monastery, giggling with three Chinese.

"Vhen does zis fire go out?" Fräulein Moser asked. "Soon it vill burn ze meat."

"Relax, Froy, everything's under control," Breeze said testily, having expected a bit more appreciation than this. "I know what I'm doing." She lifted the lid of a chafing dish and dropped it back with a clatter. "Damn, that's hot."

Three tables away Viola conferred with Rhoda as the Chinese stared wide-eyed at Breeze's silver outfit. Nothing on "Star Trek" even came close to this. No one noticed the two somber figures seated behind the sparkling fringe. Seeing that mischievous face, Floyd knew why Viola had come here. He smiled wanly: She was going to get one hell of a dose of her own medicine. He wondered when her husband would turn up.

Breeze lifted the lid from the dish of potatoes. "Smell that, Froy. Great stuff," she said, ladling them onto a plate. "How many for you, Count? Count? Yoohoo! What the hell's so interesting over there? Did Rhoda lose a boob in someone's gooseberry pie?" Breeze leaned over the veal in cognac, staring into the dim dining room. Then Viola innocently waved hello at her. "Holy Mother of God and jumpin' Jesus Christ!" Breeze screamed, dropping the potatoes. "It's my boss!"

The fringe on Breeze's silver outfit started to smolder and sporadically catch fire; luckily the manufacturer, cognizant of the lifestyle of women who would buy such clothing, had used flame-retardant fabric. Stunned by the appearance of her employer, Breeze did not even move away from the flame for another five seconds, unaware of the damage such immotion caused. Customs Inspector Beck, however, reacted quickly: textbook fire drill. He yanked the bottle of wine from its bucket and in the next motion doused Breeze with the ice water therein. Then he threw her over a shoulder and carried her into the kitchen as the dining room watched in dismay.

Floyd hiked Breeze into the kitchen sink and ascertained that her dress had indeed sputtered out. Chef Eggli dashed over from the pastry counter, where he had been daubing rosettes of whipped cream upon gooseberries. "What's going on here?" he shouted in dialect. "What did this damn billy goat do now?"

"Thought she was a veal in cognac," Floyd said. "Just send a sanitation crew into the dining room. There's a bit of a mess out there." Cursing, the chef strode through the swinging doors.

Her slight immolation unhinged Breeze less than her trip across the carpet upon the shoulder of Count Carnegie. No man had swept her away in his arms since Stanley, her second husband, had levitated her over the threshold on their wedding night; swashbuckling gestures had gone out of vogue soon after women began sleeping with men on their first date. "Count," she said, "you were too much. That was like *Gone With the Wind* and *From Here to Eternity* rolled into one."

Floyd began to tremble, remembering what was in the dining room. He went to Chef Eggli's private stock of brandy hidden in a cannister marked Soap. "Ladies first," he said, watching her drink. "Gentlemen second."

Harriet and Rhoda rushed into the kitchen. "Are you all right?"

"I'm fine," Breeze said, getting out of the sink.

"Not you, jerkoff," Rhoda growled.

He looked at the three women clustered around him. One wore a leopard-print jumpsuit; another wore a décolleté down to her nipples; the third wore a silver hallucination, all in pursuit of a man who would remain forever pure, forever beyond them, like a Jesus Christ with testosterone. Was Floyd's folly any different? "I am fine," he said. "How is poor Fräulein Moser?"

"She's eating potatoes as if nothing happened," Harriet said.

Rhoda looked Breeze up and down. Fire had balded most of the fringe previously rooted upon her outfit. "Nice going, Tonto. You made an imbecile of yourself again."

"Let's see what you'd do if your boss showed up out of thin air. Spooked the shit out of me, waving like that."

"She was probably waving goodbye to all the money she spent sending you here," Harriet said. "Unless she was waving to Count Carnegie, of course."

"Give me a break. She's got enough lovers already."

Floyd replaced Chef Eggli's brandy above the sink. Such comments still cut him terribly. "Perhaps you had better go home, dear. You have had enough excitement for one night." He did not want Breeze in the dining room buffering her employer from him. Viola did not deserve such mercy.

"But what about your dinner, Count? You're still on the main course!"

"Never mind," Floyd said. "As soon as Fräulein Moser finishes her pie, ve vill leave."

Chef Eggli returned to the kitchen dragging the watersoaked remains of Breeze's dinner trolley. "Look at this mess," he fumed. "I should expel you here and now."

"Mistakes can happen," Count Carnegie said. "Such an unusual dress ruined. Let the poor voman go home to bed."

"Alone? After all that's happened between us?"

Floyd toweled his suit off and gave Breeze the cannister marked Soap. "Zis should help." He walked toward the door. "Good night, ladies."

He felt her eyes clamp onto him the moment he stepped into the dining room. Floyd walked very deliberately back to Fräulein Moser, allowing Viola a maximum dose of disbelief and uncertainty. He knew the black eye threw her: It could be taken for a large, winy birthmark now. She had never seen him in a tuxedo. He had grown another few inches. And he was the last person she expected to run into up here. He could feel a huge vortex of air and fire, Viola at its center, swirl slowly around the dining room, trying to pull him in. No, Viola. This time you could do a little waiting.

The harpist began picking at a few of the *Goldberg* Variations. Floyd slid into his chair and stared her full in the face. Then she knew. So many phantoms whooshed past him that his hair stood on end. Gigantic loops and tiny loops finally closed and a myriad more loops began their course as nothing more than flecks upon his soul. He did not know if he would ever live to see their completion. "Excuse me," he said. "I'll be right back. I must pay my respects to someone I know."

Fräulein's fork bisected the last of her potatoes. "Certainly."

Floyd walked to her table and looked down at her face a moment. It had not really changed. "Hello, Viola."

"Hi." More an audible tremor than a word. She gave him her hand and he kissed it because he was a count and he had to know if her skin still smelled of roses and warm cream. His nose touched a daunting diamond ring: rocks in the garden. "This is quite a surprise," she finally said. Viola never would have admitted that seventeen years ago.

"Yes." Floyd bowed to the three Chinese. "Good evening."

Viola introduced the Lung brothers to Mr. Beck. So she had not forgotten his name after all. He had killed many bottles of scotch wondering about that.

"Are you staying at the Badhof or just passing through," Floyd asked.

"We're staying tonight," Viola said.

"Perhaps I might ring you later." He'd ring her, all right, with both arms and both legs. Then he'd wring her. Her husband could watch.

She dropped her eyes to the bouquet on the table: The Lungs might be Chinese but they were not blind. "Yes."

Floyd returned to Fräulein Moser and sat at her right, not left, elbow. He could not tolerate another minute in the dining room lest he sat with his back to Viola. "The other seat's wet," he explained.

"You know those three men?" she asked, making no connection at all between the woman in blue, the woman in the photographs, and Floyd. That was not the way her mind worked.

Harriet came to the table. "Me again. I'll be filling in for the Indian."

"Is she burned?" Moser asked.

"No, just a mess." Harriet removed the remaining dishes. "Two gooseberry pies? Coffee? How about it, Count Carnegie? You've had a rough night."

He could feel Viola's eyes boring like twin wood screws into his back: This night hadn't even begun to get rough. "Tank you." God Almighty! Were they condemned always to be seated in the same room staring at the back of each other's head?

"Carnegie," Moser said. "You look very tired. Eggli and this Indian have upset you." She peered at his face. "Did you hit your eye again carrying that woman out of here? It's very black again."

Just a bit of blood bashing the capillaries, Fräulein. Every muscle was agonizing towards the right, wanting to turn him around so that he was facing her again. Thank God for Moser: Without her here, he would have yanked Viola out of that seat and marched her—where? Out to the woodshed for a spanking? Over to the pension for tea? Wherever it was, Floyd was not going to do much talking. His head already contained a seventeen-year-long monolog and he was sick to death of words, words, words, each adding another link to a chain which grew longer and longer but was ultimately welded to Viola, so that he was not really freeing himself with these patient, reasonable sentences, but drifting further and further asea, destined to rot in a remote doldrums, tugging weakly on a submerged anchor. Whatever words came tonight would be from her mouth, not his. He would find out where she had finally gone to college; what she had studied; the fate of Old Richard . . . no, he couldn't bear to listen to this. Why tear open all his old wounds? This spin around the carousel she was legally married.

"Gooseberry pie," Harriet announced, sliding two dishes to the table.

Fräulein Moser inspected her portion, obviously disappointed at its size. No wonder no man had ever asked for her hand. "You have some vhipped cream?"

"Yes dear, right here," Harriet said, placing a little dish to the side. "For that I charge you two Swiss francs." She winked at Floyd. "An inside joke, Count Carnegie."

Rhoda appeared at his elbow with two brandies on a tray. Her breasts hung exactly at eye level; if Floyd stuck out his tongue, he could lick one. Rhoda didn't realize that in the last fifteen minutes everything had reversed again and that she could be standing there naked and Count Carnegie would take no more notice of her than he would of the draperies. "How's everything here? Have you two recovered from the excitement?"

"Ve are just about to go home," Floyd said.

"These are sent compliments of my table." Rhoda set the snifters down. "They thank you for getting rid of the Indian."

"I do not drink brandy," Fräulein Moser announced.

"I do," Floyd said. He lifted a glass, turned, and toasted Viola, not smiling. Her white face stunned his blood. The three Chinese nodded hospitably back at him. "After ve leave, please bring zem ze same. Vish zem a good night's sleep."

"I'll do that." Rhoda left.

Later, in the lobby, Floyd turned to Fräulein Moser. "Breeze will probably be sitting in the drawing room in a black lace nightgown waiting for me to drop you off. The lady with the dog might be back from Montreux also. I don't want to see either of them."

"This would be terrible. I walk home myself."

"Of course you won't. I'm going to put you in a cab."

"But that will cost twelve Swiss francs."

Floyd didn't care if it cost twelve million Swiss francs. He was not going to leave the hotel. "I don't want you walking at this time of night," he said.

"There are no muggers in Switzerland," Moser said. "I'll walk."

Finally he understood the problem. "Of course I'm paying for the taxi."

Minutes later she was being chauffeured down the steep gravel drive. Floyd watched until the taillights had disappeared into the pines, then went to the shadowy veranda of the Hotel Badhof. From here he could see through the sheer curtains into the dining room: How strange that only a few panes of glass now separated him from the woman who had possessed him for seventeen years. There she sat, beautiful, chimerical as ever, surrounded by men. Rhoda was serving them dessert and Viola was laughing at something one of the Mr. Lungs had said, damn her. Behind them the harpist caressed her instrument; a couple touched glasses and kissed each other. Now Rhoda returned with four brandies and made a little announcement. Her pale cleavage mesmerized the Chinese. Viola regarded her very coolly, as if Rhoda were offering a free trip to Reno. She took the brandy, but did not drink.

Floyd walked to the other side of the veranda and leaned far over the side, gauging the ravine below. If he leapt off the edge, he would probably not hit the ground for five seconds: That distance would fairly well guarantee results. But he was not going to jump tonight. He was never going to jump while that woman in the dining room still lived. Floyd watched the moon lie patiently in the black sky as tiny clouds flurried across it. Millions of miles away a sun which no one saw made that moon glow; so it was with him. He returned to the windows. They had finally finished. Viola stood up and he nearly broke through the glass he wanted her that much. Purest lust: The moment he saw her his mind had disengaged from this thing with hands and feet and had floated off into the mountains, whispering as it left him that such a night would never come again, and that under such circumstances a mind was the last thing a man had use for anyway, because then the pain would kill him.

A few more clouds traversed the moon before Floyd returned to the lobby. "I would like to call Miss Flury," he said to the clerk in dialect, wondering whether this was even her name any more.

"Room twelve," the man said, handing over the phone with a well-rehearsed disinterest. Floyd knew the fellow would be eavesdropping with all his might.

"Hello." Her voice sounded almost falsetto. Nervous.

"It's me," Floyd said. "The guy in the phone booth." The hôtelier noiselessly slid a message into a guest's mail slot, thinking he had heard incorrectly. Viola still did not say anything; perhaps her husband was sleeping two feet away. "Are you free?"

Of course she wasn't free. She would never be free. "Yes," Viola said.

"Would you like to meet me for a drink?"

"Could we get out of the hotel?"

She didn't want her husband stomping down to the bar and yanking her by the ear upstairs. Something like that had already happened last time Floyd had met her for a nightcap. "We could go for a walk."

Hesitation. "Fine. Where are you?"

In whichever room, or lake, or life, you have just vacated, my dear. "In the lobby."

"I'll be down in ten minutes."

Floyd hung up and looked at the hôtelier. "Would you have a room free tonight?" he said, switching to perfect dialect.

"A small one, yes. Would you have any identification?"

Floyd picked up the phone again. "Connect me to the kitchen, please." He got Chef Eggli. "It's Carnegie. I'll be staying at the Badhof tonight. No, not with the Indian, for God's sake. I'll explain everything later. Could you please tell the hôtelier who I am?" He handed the phone over.

Eggli had a few words with the fellow. "Everything is straight," he said shortly, giving Floyd a keyring, still unsure whether to disapprove of Floyd because he was an American, or approve of Floyd because he was a Swiss.

"Thank you. I will be needing a large picnic blanket."

Viola came to the lobby wearing canary yellow pajamas, a heavy red sweater, and purple sneakers: She still didn't wear pastels and she still didn't exercise discretion. She still turned his lungs to stone. "You're going for a walk in that?" she asked, looking at his tuxedo.

"It's a long way home," he said, and strode outside.

She trotted to catch up to him. "Where are we going?"

"Downhill." Again he left Viola behind.

"Floyd," she called. He stopped dead. "Wait." She took his arm. Her skin looked like a piece of the moon. "I can't go that fast."

"Please don't touch me," he said.

She shrank immediately away, saying nothing until they reached the edge of the forest. "Looks dark in there."

"There's a path leading to a lake."

Still she hesitated; that was unlike her. "I might fall."

And muss those cute little pajamas she had borrowed from her husband? God forbid. "Here," said Floyd, extending his hand. "You won't fall." He walked so fast now that he almost dragged her to the lake. Finally they got to the little clearing Floyd visited every day. He threw the blanket on the pine needles and went to the edge of the water, looking at the monstrous eruption of earth and rock rising from the other side. He wanted to fly to the ice on top of that mountain and numb the places where she had touched his skin, before the fire spread totally out of control. He couldn't do that of course, so Floyd removed his shoes, rolled up his cuffs, and stuck his feet in the lake. At least he didn't have to look at her then. "So," he said finally, "what have you been up to?"

He heard no answer for such a long time that he finally turned around. Viola was sitting in the middle of the blanket watching him. "Richard died," she said.

No more would that bastard offer Floyd an escort back to the highway. That man had lost her forever and Floyd had not even had the courtesy to return his bathing suit. He regretted that now. "I'm sorry." He wondered if the last image Richard perceived had been of his little lake, or the *Wall Street Journal,* or Viola undulating beneath him.

"He had a heart attack," Viola said. "I was away at school."

She had probably just come out of Utopian Literature II and been taken aside by the dean, who had informed her that—what? Her career as a protégée was over? "Did he ever marry you," Floyd asked.

"No."

Then he deserved to die. "He was too old for you anyhow."

"He was perfect for me, thank you."

Floyd turned around. "Really? How many times did he take you to the movies on a Saturday afternoon and try to slide his arm around your shoulder? Did he take you to the senior prom? What did he buy you for Christmas, a Beatles album? Did he ever get all dressed up and nervous when he had to meet your parents? When he took you to bed, were his hands shaking so badly that he could hardly take his own socks off?"

"He's dead," she cried. Her voice wobbled through three octaves. "What more do you want?"

This lake was too hot. Floyd pulled his feet out of it and walked to the edge of the forest and back, describing a huge circle around Viola as if the blanket she sat on was a pool of boiling quicksand. He went to a pine tree and leaned his head against it so that his skin was touching something, anything, alive; Floyd had to struggle not to put his arms around the tree and kiss its bark in a desperate attempt to transfer some of this insanity from his blood to another object. He sighed into the trunk: Resin, dirt, brandy fumed into his nostrils.

When the roaring had quieted to a black whirlpool, he pulled away from the tree. Tossing his coat on Viola's blanket, Floyd returned to the water. The moon opalesced his white shirtsleeves. "Then what did you do," he said.

"I went home for three years." Lucky girl. Her parents had forgiven her. "Then I moved back to New York."

"Why."

"Richard left me his brownstone."

Floyd wondered if he had left her the summer house, too. "What did you do there?"

"Read books and went to museums. He left me quite a bit of money also."

So while Floyd was killing mosquitos and whatnot in Vietnam, Viola was dawdling through the Guggenheim. That was just terrific. He wondered how many old men she had picked up there. "Then what."

"I met Nestor Buffez."

"At the Guggenheim?" That goon's natural habitat was a lifeguard stand.

"At a benefit for the ballet." Romantic. "We went into business together making lingerie."

Just their speed. "I know. You make the newspapers now and then." Floyd slowly dribbled some water over his face. "When did you get married?"

"Two years ago."

Floyd unbuttoned his shirt and leaned back into the pine needles. He was looking at the stars. "Forgive me if my questions end there."

Viola stared at his chest, wondering how many women had run their fingers through that hair and called him darling, and to how many he had responded. "That woman at dinner," Viola said. "Was she your Aunt Margaret?"

"My aunt died five years ago." They were getting old, weren't they. The previous generations were all dead. "Fräulein Moser is a friend of the family," Floyd said. "I've been staying at her pension for a few weeks. Vacation."

"You work for Customs, don't you." His white shirt momentarily halted its shallow rise and fall above his stomach. "Dr. Clemens told me."

"That's right."

"I always thought you would end up in some sort of law-enforcement agency."

"Why."

"You always had a very strong sense of right and wrong."

"Black and white," Floyd said. "Big difference."

He had shut his eyes. She wanted to crawl over and touch his mouth and tell him she was sorry for everything. But she didn't dare; if he still thought in black and white, he would push her away and despise her even more. How was it possible that they had never even kissed each other? That would have blurred the black and white a bit. Viola unfolded her legs. "It's so quiet here," she said. "No birds. No fish jumping in the lake."

"It's not really a lake. It's a hot spring."

Viola walked to the edge and stuck her hand in: warm as a bathtub.
She debated a moment then took her purple sneakers off, dropped to the
bank, and rolled up her pajama bottoms. Her feet hardly made a noise as
they broke the surface of the water. "Did you get into NYU?"

"Yes. Then I got drafted."

"You went to Vietnam?"

Floyd sat up immediately. "You don't think I'd try to get out of it,
would you?"

She wanted to shrink to the size of an acorn, roll to the bottom of the
lake, and quietly rot. "Of course not."

He lay on his back again, shielding his eyes with his forearms, as if the
moon were too bright. His shirt lay completely open. Viola wanted to rub
her cheeks in that hair and see if any of this was real. "Where'd you get
the black eye," she said.

The mouth beneath the arms smiled. "I fell in Fräulein Moser's
kitchen."

"Why did that waitress refer to you as Count Carnegie?"

His arms dropped and he turned his head. "It's a long story, Viola. Let's
not get into it."

This time she had to get up. Viola went back to the blanket and played
with a sock. "Are you married?"

"No."

"Have you ever been married?"

"No."

"Are you seeing anyone?"

"Not now."

"Were you seeing anyone?"

A meteorite drew a tiny scratch against the sky before night swallowed
it. "Portia Clemens," he said. "But I suppose my heart wasn't really in
it."

Viola sounded as if she were trying to do deep breathing exercises. Then
she ran up to Floyd and hurled a purple sneaker at him. It whapped him
in the chest and bounced into the water. "God damn you!" she shouted.
"How dare you disappear like that! Do you have any idea what you've
done?"

He bolted upright just in time to get the second sneaker square in the
back. Then Viola tried to throw a sock at him. She was about to fire the
sneaker again when Floyd caught her wrists. "Don't you dare touch me
now," she shrieked, yanking away.

Ah, if only all criminals were this easy to fell. Floyd carted her three
steps to the left and had her down on the blanket before the third "I hate
you." She was crying so violently he thought she'd choke herself but that

didn't stop him: He had to taste her neck again, resuming where he had left off wasn't it really only moments ago, and this time he'd make it to her mouth and her ears and every last piece of her because there had been no gray hairs and black eyes the last night they had done this, and there was no telling when they might ever meet again this side of dust. The moment his lips touched her skin she gulped as if he were drawing blood: God, he hoped so. He tasted roses and that perfect warm cream mixed with tears and the last vapors of an extravagant perfume. Their arms locked each other so tightly that neither could tell who was trying to kill what any more. They rolled over and over onto the pine needles like a heavy log uprooted from the top of the mountain; a few more turns and they'd be in the lake.

Finally they thudded into a tree and just lay there like two terrified mice, quivering into each other. Viola was still crying beneath him and that broke his heart. He smoothed the hair off her pale face, the only black and white he had ever believed in. The rest was only gray fog and fading twilight. "Shhhh," he whispered. "It's not too late."

Viola turned her face to the side: He finally kissed the black mole on her cheek. "I'm pregnant," she said.

He became quiet as the mountains. Then he rolled off of her and lay on the ground alongside. After a while he stood up, dropping his white shirt to the pine needles close to her head. A zipper, a rustle, then she heard him wade into the water. He swam away.

Viola finally realized that the fork in the road had not been between Richard and figure skating at all, but between Richard and Floyd, and that tonight she was back at the original split with that beautiful boy who had loved her longer than Nestor, Eugene, and Richard combined, yet had remained the only stone unturned. Omission had created this night. Not many mortals had the chance to retrace their steps and feebly redeem themselves. Viola looked across the water: Add a few willows, a few lilies, remove a few mountains, and they were back to when they had last been happy.

She took her pajamas off and slid into the lake after him. Floyd was already halfway to the other side, floating on his back like an iceberg wanting to be melted. He heard a splash and righted himself. When he saw her white arms coming toward him he thought of diving to the bottom, because once he touched her, it would be all over, pregnant, married, mother of ten, he didn't give a damn any more: This loop was finally going to close on both of them.

He treaded water until she was next to him. "You left me again, Bozo," she said.

Floyd swam behind her and slipped an arm beneath her chin, pulling her in to his chest: the warmest apparition he had ever touched. Everywhere he drew his hand he found one curve rolling into the next, like waves in a tropical ocean. Quiet now, a baby slept beneath one of them. "Viola," was all he could say: The mountains in all their awesome, eternal splendor couldn't come close to the beauty of a woman. He towed her slowly in to the shallows, grazing her slippery skin with his legs and his penis. There would be no Richard this time to remark upon bathing suits, nor erections. His hand touched the warm clay bottom. Floyd rolled onto his back. "Land or water," he said.

"Water," she said, and splashed down on his mouth.

He had had appendicitis and migraines, he had been trashed by fiancées, he had buried two parents and an aunt. None of this was excruciating as not burying himself in that beauty named Viola, then doing so, then not coming once he had. A seventeen-year drought would have to continue a few more moments; he was competing with God only knew how many lovers. There was no hell like riding herd on the jagged edge of orgasm waiting for that gorgeous flesh to come tumbling down on him. Stars blazed purple and red and he thought each time the end had come before the water, maybe her eyes, reined him back for yet another plummet on that narrow, white-hot roller coaster. Thank God he had not tried this when he was seventeen! It would have been all over in thirty seconds! She would have laughed in his face and gone back to Old Richard forever. His hands slithered down her back and around that twin hill with the velvet well between. She kept shifting its pitch, pulling him toward the moon, pointing him toward Polaris, until the whole universe began to melt around the axis he had staked inside of her. "Viola," he said finally, voice rickety as an antique rocker, "that is unbearable."

She put her hands behind his neck and pulled him to a sitting position. Water ran down their elbows, dribbling softly back into the lake, as her mouth devoured him: no more intermissions. Below the warm water she began to tremble.

Even in the bleakest years he had known that someday she would be clinging to him like a frightened child and he had habitually pictured himself nudging her away saying "It's too late for that, my dear" and walking off, gravid with dignity. Now Floyd tipped her head back: When he saw tears in those eyes which had enthralled his youth and transfixed his manhood he knew that she had loved him all along and that no multitude of husbands or children would ever change that. He kissed her neck, breathed the roses, and was avenged. Then he looked at the snow-topped mountains behind the lake: avalanche.

* * *

Major George Hash stepped to the hotel desk and dropped his suitcase, smiling suavely at the brunette checking in next to him. "I would like to telephone Dr. Portia Clemens," he said. "Could you please tell me which room she's in?"

The clerk glanced through the guest list. "Sorry. Her name is not here."

"That's impossible. I know she had a reservation. She arrived two days ago."

The man observed Hash as if he were just another tomcat with a rude sunburn. "And what is your name, please?" Equally as smugly, Hash displayed his credentials and waited for the desired effect. "You are a special investigator?"

Hash flipped his I.D. case shut. "Any information you might have would be appreciated. She is a petite blond, here attending the veterinary convention."

"Aha, now I seem to remember. She brought a dog."

"Correct."

"We unfortunately do not accept pets at this hotel. She had to go elsewhere."

Hash smiled to himself, imagining Portia's fond adieu. "Did she leave a forwarding address?"

The clerk checked his memos. "Yes, yes. She is staying at a pension in Emwald. This is a tiny village in the mountains about a half hour away. Here is the number. That is the owner."

"Thank you very much." Hash walked to a phone in the lobby, admiring the calves of a woman depressing an overstuffed chair. He dialed the number and waited through a dozen rings. He was just about to hang up when someone finally answered. "Hello? I would like to speak with Dr. Portia Clemens please."

"She is not here. She vent to Montreux for ze day."

"I would like to book at room at your pension for a few days."

"Excuse me, are you a man?"

"Yes, of course."

"Zen zis is not possibell. My pension is for vimmen only. Only my chef he is a man and he does not have anyzing to do viz ze vimmen."

The place sounded fundamentally bogus. He had better check it out. "This reservation is not for me," Hash said. "It is for Miss"—he scanned the lobby for inspiration—"Leggo."

"Who is zis voman?"

"An Indian," Hash said. "She is writing an important scientific paper upon altitude."

"An American Indian?" Moser's voice sounded suddenly cold. "I am afraid zere is no more room for such Indians in my pension."

"No, no!" Hash cried. "An Indian from India! A very cultured person." Moser hesitated. "She is quiet as a mouse and hardly eats anything."

"Vell, all right."

"She'll be arriving this afternoon," Hash said. "You might want to put her in the room next to Dr. Clemens. These women would probably have much in common." By Fräulein Moser's renewed silence Hash realized he had made a mistake. "Although Miss Leggo is much more polite."

"All right, I expect her, but not betveen two and four. I play canasta."

"Certainly. Thank you very much." Hash hung up and returned to the hotel desk. "I need a sari," he said. "An Indian woman's costume."

The clerk crinkled his eyebrows. "You must go back to Geneva for such things."

Hash drove his rented Audi back to Geneva and found a shop behind the Red Cross world headquarters. From there he went directly to Emwald, changing into costume in a clump of bushes behind the train station. Hash had already used this disguise in pursuit of a Bombay opium king and quickly had himself wrapped to the eyeballs in gray chintz. It irritated his burnt face, but he didn't plan to stay in costume long. He walked up to the pension, rehearsing falsetto, and yanked the cowbell outside Fräulein Moser's front door. Eventually a short, stout woman with a large bun appeared. "Hello," he said in a high voice, what the hell, if Mama Juana could do it, so could he. "I am Miss Leggo. I believe you are expecting me."

Fräulein Moser inspected the new arrival from head to foot. Everything seemed to pass muster except the red sneakers. "Yes, come in. I take you upstairs."

"Thank you."

She put Hash into a clean little room and hastily recited the house rules. "Now if you vill excuse me, I must go. I vill be going out to dinner tonight at ze Hotel Badhof. It is very famous and expensive."

Hash bowed. "How wonderful. I will take a short nap. Then I will begin conducting my experiments."

"You vill not disturb my ozer guests?"

"No, no, not one word. In fact I will pretend that I do not speak English. It is the only way I can get any work done. Otherwise everyone pesters me with questions. I hope you will understand."

"Of course."

Hash unlaced one sneaker. "When will Dr. Clemens be returning, do you think?"

"Perhaps at ten o'clock."

"Well then, I will be taking a little nap. Have a very nice dinner." Hash closed the door, tore off his steaming veils, and fell asleep.

Several hours later his alarm sounded. Hash heard someone moving in the drawing room beneath him. He tiptoed into the bathroom, salved his cheeks, donned a sari, and went downstairs. To his surprise he saw not Portia on the couch, but a flamboyant blond giving herself a manicure. She wore the most provocative black peignoir he had ever seen. It was intentionally difficult to tell where the lace ended and the nipples began. Hash had to force himself to look away.

She glanced up as he came in. "Hi. You must be new here." He nodded and sat at a far table, pretending to read an Indian newspaper which he had picked up in Geneva: Details made the disguise. "Have a nice trip?"

Hash cleared his throat. "Neh Engesh," he said in a weak voice.

"Too bad." Breeze resumed her manicure.

Several minutes later they heard a dog barking in the backyard. Then someone fiddled with the front door. Breeze jumped off the couch, realigning areolas and black lace, and rushed to the hall. Hash heard the door swing open, then silence.

"Well," said Portia, "this is quite a reception."

"Who are you," the blond replied.

"My name is Dr. Portia Clemens. I am a guest at this pension."

The door creaked open. "I'm Breeze. Ditto."

The two women entered the drawing room. Portia was wearing a conservative business suit which juxtaposed oddly with Breeze's negligee. It was hard to believe they were both blonds. "Hello," Portia said to Hash.

"She doesn't speak English," Breeze said. "Have a seat. It's boring enough around this place."

Portia sat on a rocking chair and removed her hiking shoes. "I must say it's one hell of a climb here after a long day."

"Where were you?"

"In Montreux at an international veterinary convention. I will be delivering an important speech there in conjunction with my Dalmatian."

"Oh, so you're not a real doctor."

"Of course I'm a real doctor," Portia snapped.

"Sorry, sorry," Breeze said, opening a bottle of nail polish. "So where are you from?"

"Hoboken, New Jersey. You've probably never heard of it."

"Of course I have. I work in Paterson."

Portia dropped her other shoe to the floor. "Is that so? What's your field?"

"Food." Breeze told Portia about Chef Eggli's cooking school. "I got sent home early from the Badhof tonight. Started a little fire in the dining room. But it really wasn't my fault. My boss Viola turned up out of the clear blue. She startled the shit out of me, know what I mean? She's supposed to be back home working, not farting around the mountains with a bunch of Chinamen."

"Chinese, you mean. What does your employer do?"

"She makes lingerie. The company name is Pyrana. Maybe you've heard of it."

Hash nearly lost his veils. Viola? What could she be doing here . . . besides meeting Portia? His eyes slid over to the doctor, watching how she would handle this.

Portia sat very still for a moment. "Vaguely," she replied in a tight, clipped voice: A lie detector would have sizzled over that answer. She pretended to fluff the pillow behind her. "I think I have heard of the other fellow who works there. Nestor someone or other?"

"Oh, Nestor Buffez. Yeah. The other boss." Breeze blew on her newly painted fingernails. "Now there's one guy I'd like to be shipwrecked with."

Portia studied the wooden plates enlivening Fräulein Moser's walls. Hash could just about hear her brain whirring. "Oh? I thought he was spoken for."

"Unofficially, yes. He's madly in love with Viola." Breeze sighed. "She's expecting a baby, you know. Everyone in the plant is sure it's his."

"Isn't Viola married?"

"So what, honey? These are modern times. They're together all day and all night. They go out of town every other week. Viola's husband shows up once a year at the company picnic looking like the butt end of a telescope." Breeze dropped the nail polish into a cosmetic bag. "Don't get me wrong, he's a nice guy. But Nestor's a knockout. Until that dog came along, Viola was the center of his existence."

"Dog?" Portia tittered artificially. "He has a dog?"

"Yeah. I found a cute little pup in the dumpster one day. Nestor adopted him and more or less transferred his affections. When he latches on to something, boy, you know it. That's one damn lucky pooch, believe me. I wouldn't mind being under Nestor's pajamas all day."

"Does anyone else go near the pup?" Portia asked.

"Are you kidding? Nestor would kill him."

"Has anyone ever come looking for the dog?"

Breeze looked quizzically at Portia. "What do you mean?"

Portia shrugged. "You didn't exactly get the animal from a licensed breeder."

"I think some schmuck came around one day but Nestor took care of him."

Portia went to the bookcase and loosened an old volume of poetry. "Would you happen to know where the dog is now?"

"Lady, I've been here for three weeks. I assume it's still under Nestor's pajamas. Why are you asking all these questions, anyway?"

Portia took the book to her chair. "I am a veterinarian, after all."

"Aha." Breeze removed a compact from the cosmetic bag and began powdering her face. Then she took out two cases of eyeshadow. "Hey doc, which do you think is more dramatic? Cossack Blue or Wild Ivy? I'll go for the Ivy. Brings out the green in my contact lenses."

In silence Portia watched Breeze apply copious layers of eye makeup. "Are you expecting someone?" she asked finally, barely masking the irritation in her voice.

"As a matter of fact, yes," Breeze said. "Count Carnegie. He should be here any minute. He took Froy to dinner."

"You're doing this for a man?"

Breeze guffawed. "I wouldn't do this for a woman, dear." She looked at Portia. "Why? Any objections? Don't tell me you're one of those."

"I am not a lesbian."

"I meant feminist," Breeze replied. "I've had enough of them these last few weeks to drive me out of my mind. So! Do you have a boyfriend, doc?"

"No, I do not. My work takes priority in my life."

"That's a big mistake, but you'll find that out soon enough." Breeze finished putting on her lipstick and stood up. "What do you think?" She swirled the negligee through the air. "This is one of the hottest numbers Viola ever designed. She did it after she and Nestor got back from a week in Paris."

Hash nearly rushed over from his corner and tore it off. "I think you will have achieved the desired effect," Portia said coldly. "This Count Carnegie, if he is a typical man, will rape you immediately."

"Now we're talking," Breeze said, rubbing her hands.

A car pulled up outside. "Here they are!" Breeze shouted, rushing to the door. Hash and Portia heard it fly open. "Hi there," she cooed.

The voice of Fräulein Moser finally cut the silence. "Vhat is zis, Miss Breezi? It is not enough zat you almost burn me up tonight? Now you valk around my pension vit no clothes on?"

"Where's Count Carnegie, Froy? I thought he would drop you off like a gentleman."

"He put me in a taxi like a chentleman! Go immediately to your room before my neighbors see zis shameless clozing! I have never in my life had such a person in my pension!"

"Simmer down, Froy. Be glad you're not upstairs when Swallow and Rhoda are parading around in their underwear. That's truly obscene."

Footsteps ascended the staircase. Then Fräulein Moser, flushed, walked into the drawing room, scowling at the Indian wrapped head to toe in gray robes and at Dr. Clemens in her business suit and athletic socks. Both of them looked up innocently from their reading material and nodded at her. "And vhat are you two vaiting for?" she snapped. "Count Carnegie also?"

"Certainly not," said Portia, rising. "Goodnight, Ms. Moser."

Hash slowly got off his chair, allowing Portia a good head start. "I think I will take a bath and go to bed," he chirped. "Good night."

Fräulein Moser sighed. "Remember to pay me two Sviss francs in ze morning." She went to her room and shut the door.

12

Before he opened his eyes Floyd sensed that this morning was different. Dreams never left him in such soft bliss. Then he realized he was lying next to Viola and they were breathing exactly in consonance: contagious serenity. He petted the mass of hair strewing the pillow next to his, following the strands of white threading the black. He had never seen that mole high on her shoulder. His pulse picked up and their aspiration slipped out of sync. Floyd wanted her again. Already too late: Judging by the depth of pink in the dawn, he knew he'd have to return immediately to the pension to make breakfast. Floyd kissed the white neck so beguilingly close to his mouth, appalled that he had even allowed himself to sleep.

Viola rolled to her back and saw him. Finally she smiled. "You snore," she said.

"So do you, grandma." She bit his arm: Floyd was strangely reminded of Hash and his wounded biceps. He sighed. "I have to go." Deathly words.

"Now? Where?"

"Back to Fräulein Moser's pension. I'm cooking for her. It's breakfast time."

"You cook?"

"Let's say I boil coffee and hack bread into pieces."

"When are you coming back?"

"How soon are you going to ditch the Chinese?"

Viola was going to ship the Lungs back to Montreux and stay another day at the Badhof. Then she had to meet her husband in Rome. "As soon as they finish breakfast." She slid a hand over his stomach: A tiny, sweet wind puffed from beneath the sheets.

"Keep that up and no one's going to get any breakfast today."

She kicked off the blankets. "Scram."

305

Floyd slipped through his tunnel back to the pension just in time to meet the baker, who stared a moment at his tuxedo before handing over the bread. On the kitchen table Fräulein Moser had left a note instructing him to add twenty extra coffee beans to the grinder since two new guests would be eating breakfast. He was also to telephone Chef Eggli at his earliest convenience. After putting the kettle on the stove Floyd went back to his room to change. Overhead he could hear Portia gasping in march time: morning exercises. Pedestrian traffic upstairs was unusually thick.

To his surprise, the three gastronomes arrived at breakfast first. "Step on it, you guys," Floyd heard Rhoda call as she collected the bread and coffee from the counter. "Eggli wants us at the hotel by seven."

"I have always loved field trips," Harriet said. "This is going to be very exciting. It's a perfect day to drive to Ticino."

"This is a bit of a surprise, isn't it? I thought we were going to be frosting cakes today."

"Dear, Chef Eggli can decide whatever schedule he pleases. He did make the announcement before we all went home last night. It's your own fault you missed it."

"New blouse, eh, Rhoda," Breeze remarked with her mouth full. "You're really going in for the low necklines lately, aren't you."

"I don't notice much of a back on that little sundress."

"That's the point of a sundress. Gad, this coffee's terrible today. That moron back there must piss into it."

Floyd heard the quick, purposeful footsteps of Portia. "Good morning, sisters."

There was a short silence. "Oh, hi doc," Breeze said. "Pull up a chair. I guess you haven't met my two schoolmates yet. Harriet and Rhoda. This is Dr. Porsche, girls. Like the car."

"Portia," Dr. Clemens corrected. "Like *The Merchant of Venice*."

"Whatever you say. Bread? Some great coffee? Sorry we seem to be in a rush here, but Chef Eggli is taking the class to Ticino. We're going to be buying sausage fixings today. Tomorrow we're going to be butchers."

Floyd almost dropped his coffee cup. Eggli was taking the whole class on this excursion? Today? Without consulting him?

"I've always wondered how to make hotdogs," Rhoda said.

"It's quite revolting," Portia told her. "I used to know a fellow who was obsessed with them. The ingredients would turn your stomach. Pig snouts. Suet. Intestines. As a veterinarian, I find this obscene."

Floyd was tempted to tear back the sliding doors and discharge Fräulein Moser's rifle at Dr. Clemens. However, since this would have delayed his reunion with Viola, he remained silent.

"That is perhaps a prejudiced opinion," Harriet said. "One must retain an open mind. As a food critic, I have found that most anything, properly prepared, can be delicious and nourishing."

"I'll make sure we don't buy any dog parts, doc," Breeze said.

"That is not the least amusing."

There was a short silence as another guest shuffled into the kitchen. The ladies all exchanged salutations. "That's a very handsome sari," Floyd heard Harriet say.

"Give up, Swallow, she doesn't speak English."

"It's still a handsome sari, dear. Quite elaborate. The poor woman must be stifling."

"Male-dominated society has placed entirely too much emphasis on the frivolous aspect of clothing," Portia said. "Thank God women in America have learned to dress sensibly. Clothes should be primarily utilitarian."

"Sorry, doc. You won't ever catch me in a suit like the one you've got on. That goes beyond utilitarian into the downright homely. You look terrible in shoulder pads that size. Makes you look like a midget trying out for the Jets."

"Look at that, Tonto, you've made the Indian choke and she doesn't even understand English. Go slap her on the back, for Christ's sake. Say you're sorry."

"Speaking of clothing, you ladies seem to be quite elegantly dressed," Portia said presently. "Will you be visiting a four-star restaurant in Ticino for dinner?"

No one replied immediately. "We normally dress this way," Harriet finally said.

"You do? Here in the mountains? Whatever for?" Then Portia burst out laughing. Floyd was shocked: He hadn't heard her laugh like that since she got a huge federal grant to hypnotize poodles. "Don't tell me it's this Count Carlisle fellow!"

"Count Carnegie is the name," Harriet said. "How do you know about him?"

"His name came up last night in the drawing room," Portia said. "Breeze was hoping he would be dropping Ms. Moser off after dinner."

"Waiting in ambush, eh, Tonto?"

"Cool it, he didn't show. Shipped her home in a cab."

"I find it hard to believe that in this day and age, females still dress to please a man," Portia said. "Such attitudes have already kept women in the gutter for centuries. Look at that poor wretch in the sari, for example."

"Are you implying that we're abasing ourselves, doctor?" Rhoda asked coolly.

"Have you ever been to a cosmetic factory?" Portia continued. "Do you have any idea what goes into a pot of rouge? It makes whatever you grind into a sausage look like milk and honey."

"We don't eat rouge, dear," Harriet said.

"Why don't men wear makeup?" Portia asked. "Have you ever thought about that?"

"They don't need it," Breeze said. "They're naturally beautiful."

"And we're not?"

"Let's put it this way, doc. You've got a decent enough bone structure. But you'd look a thousand times better with a little mascara and something to tone down those bags under the eyes. Do you really enjoy facing the world looking like that? Isn't life ugly enough?"

"I am quite comfortable with my looks, thank you," Portia replied. "I wouldn't have anything to do with a man who expected me to paint myself simply to boost his male vanity."

"Vanity has nothing to do with this," Rhoda said. "It's a matter of esthetics."

"The man is divine," Harriet said. "You'd understand once you met him."

"Harriet, she wouldn't appreciate him."

Portia sighed. "Whoever this creature is, he has bamboozled the three of you. You're all in desperate need of a few Female Awareness sessions."

"Rhoda and Harriet have been going to them for years."

"What?! You have? And you've learned nothing?!"

"Let's just say they've forgotten the parts which had no basis in reality."

"I'm ashamed of you two," Portia said. "Abandoning the cause like that."

"What cause, dear?"

"The cause of women! Of liberation! Freedom!"

First Breeze, then the other two, began to giggle. "Doc, you are a real hoot," Breeze said. "Straight out of 'The Twilight Zone.' "

Portia became incensed. "Don't you understand? Men are the weak sex!"

"Of course they are, dear. What difference does that make?"

"All the difference in the world! You must rid yourself of all dependency on them. I have and I've never felt better in my life. There's absolutely nothing a woman needs a man for any more."

"Let me get this straight," Rhoda said. "You've sworn off sex? Even with twenty-year-olds?"

"Absolutely. Except for procreative purposes."

A ruminative silence settled upon the dining room. "You'd make a terrific Catholic," Breeze said. "Have you ever thought of joining the church?"

Floyd heard a chair skid backwards. "I've had about enough guff from you three this morning," Portia said. "This conversation will definitely continue later. Excuse me, I must feed my dog and catch a train."

"Doc, just to show there are no hard feelings, I'm going to lend you my shampoo tonight," Breeze called after her. "It's specially made for blonds. Washes out the brown, washes in the gold."

Portia did not reply. Floyd soon heard footsteps above the kitchen.

"Now that is what I would term hard-core," Harriet remarked.

"And I thought you guys were bad," Breeze said. "Whew! She must have had some kinky relationship with her father."

"I wonder if she ever had a guy really screw her brains out," Rhoda said.

Three times, Floyd thought from the kitchen. She had been plastered for each. He would never understand Portia. She had so many fine qualities and yet, without that critical mortar of mercy, she was a ton of bricks stacked uselessly on the ground. Even had he stayed with her another fifty years, Floyd would never have patched that original gap in the DNA.

"Good morning," Fräulein Moser announced.

"Hi, Froy, how did you sleep after that wild night at the Badhof?"

"Not very vell."

"Are you aware that we will be going on a field trip today? We will not be back until late tonight. So please tell your cook not to make dinner."

"Vhere vill you eat?"

"Chef Eggli is taking us to a restaurant in Ascona."

"I see."

"Hey, let's get going, it's late. Ta ta, Froy, have a nice day."

After the noise faded Floyd heard Moser take a seat. "Good morning, Miss Leggo."

"Hello," someone bleated. What a strange voice, Floyd thought. It sounded like a transvestite with tonsillitis. And now it spoke English?

"Vill you be vorking on your experiments of altitude today?"

"Yes. In Montreux. I do not think I will be back for dinner."

"Very vell. But you must pay for dinner neverzeless."

"Of course. Here are two francs for my shower last night." Floyd wished there were a peephole in the cabinet so that he could take a look at the originator of these strange squeaks. They made him somehow uneasy. "I must be going. Good day."

"Goodbye. Do not come back too late. I must lock ze doors."

Fräulein Moser came to the kitchen after she had finished breakfast. She looked unrefreshed. "Good morning. Did you get my little note?" she said in dialect.

"I did, thank you. I'll call Urs right away."

"I expect you will not be able to play canasta this afternoon if you go with the class to Ticino."

"No, I will definitely not be at the pension this afternoon. Nor this evening, I am afraid."

Moser sighed. "No one will be eating here again tonight. All right. I will go into Geneva and do some shopping. I lock the pension up and take the next train."

Floyd had a brief phone conversation with Eggli in which he explained that Count Carnegie could not possibly go on this particular field trip due to prior commitments of great importance. Eggli could not comprehend why, after three weeks of whining and prodding, Floyd was not more interested in procuring the materials necessary to make his sausages. "Does this have something to do with that room you took last night, Anna?" he asked.

"I'll explain everything later," Floyd said.

Chef Eggli cursed and hung up.

One minute after Hash drove his rented Audi out of Emwald, he pulled to the side of the road, tore off his sari, and threw it in the trunk. It was the most godawful cumbersome contraption this side of a straitjacket and he was quite sure by now that the whole costume routine had been unnecessary: Nothing at all pertaining to microchips was going on in that pension unless Portia and those three women were the world's most cynical and accomplished actresses. He probably would have been better off staying in Montreux and snooping around the convention for shady veterinarians. Despite the sartorial aggravations, Hash did enjoy sleeping next to Portia, albeit a wall separated their loins. And he still did not hold everyone in the pension entirely above suspicion. That Fräulein would dynamite the Alps for two Swiss francs.

Hash was already at the station in Montreux when Portia and Champ detrained. Tomorrow was the doctor's grand speech; Hash had no idea what she had planned for herself today. He followed her to the convention center, watching her toss off a few hellos then proceed to the lecture hall, Champ in tow. They would obviously not be separated. Hash took a seat several rows behind Portia and sat through three arcane disquisitions upon the tails of dogs, the hooves of horses, and feline hairballs as Portia took copious notes and Champ slept in the aisle at her feet. After the last speech, Portia took Champ outside for a short walk, fed her from a paper bag, and ate a cheese pie with a fellow veterinarian whom she met on the promenade. The fellow looked innocent to the point of imbecility. Then they returned to the lecture hall. Hash did not understand how she could prefer another trio of speeches to the sun shining so perfectly upon Lac Léman.

Just as the third lecturer ascended the podium, Portia handed Champ's leash to her colleague and left the lecture hall. What?! She was actually leaving the dog behind? Hash was torn between remaining with Champ or tailing Portia. Finally he followed her out into the gorgeous sunshine. Portia hurried two blocks up the street and bought a ticket to the International Silk Convention. She wandered into the hall and around the booths, not too subtly searching for someone. She suddenly stopped in her tracks and talked for a moment to a trio of Asians wearing yellow baseball caps. Then she left.

Portia slipped back into her seat beside her doelike associate at the peroration of a lecture concerning reptile psychoses. This time she didn't take any notes at all but stared into the curtains above the stage, fidgeting with Champ's leash. The moment the lecture ended Portia congratulated the speakers and excused herself. She walked Champ at a brisk pace all the way to the Château de Chillon, then, to Hash's stupefaction, ran into the three Asians again at an ice cream stand. For almost half an hour the four of them sat on a park bench entertaining Champ with balls and dog biscuits. Then she bowed politely and went back to the station.

After the train pulled away, Hash drove his Audi back to Emwald. He was in his room at the pension well before Dr. Clemens traipsed upstairs. She banged a bit around her suitcase before locking herself into the bathroom.

Portia sank into the bathtub and closed her eyes: What a wretched day this had been. She hadn't slept a wink last night. After her conversation with that awful blond in the drawing room, all she could think about was Nestor Buffez with Flury in Paris, in bed . . . the woman was married, for Christ's sake! All she did all day was sketch underpants! So she was six feet tall, riveting as Carmen, big deal. Portia still didn't understand the fascination. Even the iceberg Floyd had blanched at the mere mention of the name Viola Flury. It was ludicrous that a woman of Portia's attainments had placed second to a commercial artist not once, but probably twice.

Then, after her insomniac night, the last thing Portia needed was breakfast with those three jeering magpies. What the hell had gotten into them up here? She had never been treated so disrespectfully by man nor beast in her life. Even that pathetic Major Hash's attempts at harassment were mothballs compared to the barrage of abuse she had received this morning. It had gotten the whole day off to a sour, treasonous start. That Hindu slave in the corner had not cheered her up, either.

A field trip for sausages! Criminy! Instead of concentrating on her upcoming speech, Portia had been jolted into thinking of Floyd the entire trip into Montreux. Now that she had put him out to sea, Portia missed his judicious eye, his suspicion of change, his loyalty—the very qualities she had found so onerous before. What could he be doing in Florida? He hated the heat. Had he already found another woman? What a slap in the face; she had assumed he would remain in deep mourning for at least another month. Portia sank even deeper into the bathwater. She had made a huge mistake with Floyd. Before shedding him, she should have made sure she was pregnant. He would never need know and she would have saved herself a thousand bucks, to say nothing of that humiliation on his deck July Fourth.

Then this damn pension fiasco! She would never stay at a Swiss hotel again. Portia was going to write a severe letter to someone about that insufferable troll behind the desk in Montreux. She never would have come to this convention had she known she and Champ would be sleeping forty kilometers away. The dog was unused to barns and had always been mildly claustrophobic; after a half hour in a darkened baggage car, Champ emerged scatterbrained as a Chihuahua. Weeks of obedience training now tottered on the brink of total amnesia. About all Portia could do was take the animal on long, brisk walks and hope she would calm down in time for tomorrow's lecture.

The convention, to top everything off, was an agonizing bore. Everyone here agreed with everything she said. What the hell did it matter, though? Even had she run across a dynamite personality, Portia's networking opportunities would have been constrained by the Montreux-Emwald train schedule: By the time she arrived at the convention, every rental car between Geneva and Paris had already been reserved. Portia hadn't thought she'd be needing one, of course.

In desperation this afternoon she had gone to the silk convention on the outside chance that Nestor Buffez, broken ankle or no, would be there. The closest she had gotten to that hunk of Cuba was three Chinese wearing Pyrana baseball caps, who informed her that Nestor had indeed stayed home and Viola had come to Montreux in his place, as Portia had suspected: The woman had turned up at the Hotel Badhof last night without him, after all. That loutish blond was still reeling from the shock.

Only after she had returned to the lecture hall did Portia realize that Nestor's absence had dispirited her beyond mere procreative considerations. She had an enormous, illogical, adolescent crush on the man. Why,

why, why, she had screamed at herself throughout that final lecture, imagining the reaction of her Female Awareness group to their leader's tergiversation. Not one word of that speech about reptiles had registered on her brain and even after an exhausting trek to the Château de Chillon and back, all Portia could come up with in her own defense was the word *pheromone*. Apparently the Cuban triggered some animal rush beyond her control, like a triple-dense Floyd with a *soupçon* of violence. They did look vaguely similar . . . and neither wanted anything to do with her.

At the terminus of her walk she had again run into the three Chinese, by far the most charming creatures she had encountered in Switzerland. Portia had sat on a park bench asking them stupid questions about Beijing and, of course, Nestor Buffez. They hadn't been able to furnish much information upon the latter but had many kind things to say about the beautiful, ravishing Mademoiselle Flury. Portia would have truncated the conversation within five minutes had not Champ appeared to be benefiting from a spell in the sun.

She had caught the last train to Emwald and found the pension empty as a cocoon in midsummer. Fräulein Moser had padlocked the barn, forcing Portia to put Champ into the chicken coop for the evening; the dog only settled down after a sedative and ten minutes of hypnotic petting. A little note on the bannister informed Portia and Miss Leggo that Moser had gone into Geneva and that no supper would be served tonight. Fine meals could be had at the Hotel Badhof instead.

The only civilized response to all this aggravation was a hot bath. As the water gradually cooled to body temperature, Portia decided to take Fräulein Moser's advice and eat at the hotel. She desperately needed a martini. Stage fright: Tomorrow she would be reading the most important professional paper of her life and she somehow was not getting properly geared up for the occasion. Sleepless nights followed by train rides through the clouds with a finicky dog had sieved all concentration. Portia had to forget about this cartoon Nestor and pull herself together. After a few cocktails and a decent meal, she'd be much better capable of giving her speech that final Clemens polish.

Portia dressed in her best business suit and hiking boots. Before leaving the pension she checked in on Champ, snoozing tranquilly aside the chickens: The sedative would not wear off for another few hours. She walked briskly to the Hotel Badhof, inhaling deeply of the pellucid air. Despite its present population, Emwald was much more beautiful than Montreux. One could do some serious self-analysis in the shadow of these mountains; perhaps next year she would book Fräulein's pension for a month and bring the entire Female Awareness group over.

"One for dinner," Portia announced to the host. "I would like a quiet table where I could work undisturbed. No, not that one! Don't try to hide me in the corner, thank you. Yes, that would be better."

The maître d' led Portia to the table of her choice along the far wall, half into the draperies, whence she immediately ordered a martini and withdrew the text of tomorrow's speech from her briefcase.

"What is the menu tonight," she asked when her drink arrived.

"Normally we would have a buffet served by the students of Chef Eggli," the waiter replied. "However, they have gone into Ticino for the day."

"Yes, I already know that," Portia said irritably. "I would like some fish."

They finally agreed on steamed trout. Gradually, as Portia proofread her speech, the adjacent tables became occupied. Two martinis later, she lay down the last page: magnificent, seminal material, in need of minor corrections before she could truly call it perfect. Portia raised her glass. "Congratulations, doctor," she toasted herself.

Choke: Floyd. Portia nearly swallowed her pearl onion as she saw him in the doorway with the maître d' and—no, God damn her! Portia had never seen Floyd laugh in public in her life and there he was, joking with the staff as if he owned the place. Not twice, but three times, he kissed Viola: Newlyweds could not have exuded a more voluptuous, innocent joy than those two. They didn't care who saw them. Portia watched as the host led them to a table near the harpist. Floyd did not once take his eyes off Viola: Portia was quite sure that, in all the years Floyd had followed her to a table at Disraeli's, his eyes had never smoldered like that at her behind. Rage and frustration swept her. How dare he devour the woman so shamelessly after all Portia's hours patiently convincing him of the error of such ways?

Portia read the opening of her speech five times over. Had she scissored the paragraph into three hundred separate words and randomly plucked them from a teacup, the sentences would have made about as much sense. Sighing, she shoved the speech back into her briefcase and stared darkly at the Alps. Portia could only engorge her steamed trout with the assistance of a half bottle of expensive Riesling. Each time she peeked to the left, Floyd was either kissing Viola's hand or whispering in her ear or, most infuriating of all, simply looking in her eyes and saying nothing: Two more obvious lovers would be hard to find among the ranks of Caucasian heterosexuals. Portia was highly insulted that Floyd had not exhibited such passion towards her. It might have saved their relationship. She laughed bitterly, finishing the last of her trout. She had no idea the man was so pathetically susceptible to ruffles and skirts. He had never gotten over that maiden Aunt Margaret after all.

With utmost deliberation, Portia forced herself to swallow a dish of summer berries. She settled the bill, pushed her chair back, and turned left. "Hello, Floyd," she said.

Floyd barely removed Viola's hand from his lips. He didn't appear in the least fazed at seeing his former girlfriend. "Hi, Portia."

She looked at Viola. "It's a small world," she said, not smiling. Never would she have anything in common with a woman who wore diamonds in her hair.

"It's a great world," Viola replied.

"Where'd you get the stitches, Floyd," Portia said. "Wrestling alligators in Florida? Jealous husbands?"

He pulled out a chair. "Won't you join us in a bottle of champagne?"

"Impossible. I have work to do." She waited, but neither Floyd nor Viola asked what that work might be. "I'm here for the veterinary conference, as you recall. We discussed this a few weeks ago."

"I remember well."

Portia blushed. "What brings you here? A customs violation?"

That familiar smile tweaked his mouth. "Exactly."

She had always detested these stupid word games which fooled nobody. Portia turned to Viola, who was still holding Floyd's hand. "And what brings you here? Don't tell me the silk convention in Montreux."

"Yes. Originally." Viola's finger slid ever so subtly, so intimately, over Floyd's. That drove Portia beyond the edge.

"I understand you and Mr. Buffez are expecting a baby," she said. "Congratulations."

Viola's finger froze: touché. "Who told you that, Dr. Clemens?"

"Your employee Breeze. She's staying in the same pension as I."

"How interesting." Viola looked at Floyd for such a long time that Portia almost believed they had both turned to marble.

"Are you all right," he whispered to her as if Portia were not even there.

Floyd had never whispered like that to her, never, never. Portia knew it was time to go. "Goodnight," she said. "Sleep well."

Portia hurried down the front steps of the Hotel Badhof, not even noticing George Hash, who stood on the veranda in precisely the spot Floyd had occupied the previous evening, and in about the same state of incomprehension. He had been sitting there drinking beer for two hours, glancing every so often into the dining room at Portia, who seemed to be devouring more wine than trout. Considering the morrow, Hash thought her behavior somewhat irregular. Perhaps she was having qualms of conscience about having given away all those military secrets. Hash had often returned to his contemplation of the moon; he had never enjoyed watching a lady get drunk unless he had a chance of reaping the benefits thereof. When Portia stood up to leave, however, her stance caught his practiced eye: direction, purpose . . . impossible, that was not Floyd, was it? He was supposed to be fishing in Florida, for God's sake! It was! After a few moments Portia stepped away, revealing Viola Flury. Hash thought his ribcage had turned to glass and shattered. He stood outside in the shadows watching as Floyd and Viola quickly paid their check and left the dining room. They walked through the lobby and disappeared into the elevator. Hash waited ten minutes, fifteen minutes, and they did not emerge, nor did he hear activity in the parking lot. After half an hour he sprinted after Portia.

Dr. Clemens had returned to the empty pension, flung herself across her bed, and sobbed as if she had just lost a litter of greyhounds. This had been the worst day of her life! She was a total failure! No one appreciated her! After all these years of toil, she had ended up with nothing more than a denatured Dalmatian while Viola had scooped Floyd *and* Nestor. Was there no justice? Viola represented everything she had been campaigning against for years. She dressed like a tsarina; she had made a fortune manufacturing objects which could only perpetuate the enslavement of women; her life revolved around men; if she had gone to one feminist meeting in her life, Portia would personally buy out the boutique on Madison Avenue. Yet somehow this woman had acquired a husband, a lover, a business, a fortune, and now a baby. One case like that canceled out everything Portia had fought for; even more frightening, Viola's child would inherit the same horrific values. Where the hell was Portia's baby?

The door to her bedroom opened and Hash quietly slipped inside. Portia's face was buried in her pillow and her jacket lay crumpled on the floor, atop her hiking boots. That miniature rump, as always, made his fingers writhe. Hash cleared his throat. "Okay, Clemens," he said. "Where's the microchip."

She whirled around, her face an impacted, teary mess. "What the hell are you doing here?"

Hash rushed to the bed and clamped his hand over her mouth. "Not so loud, please. You'll wake up the chickens."

Portia realized that this would also involve waking up Champ. She tore her mouth away. "How did you get in here," she spat.

"I'm the Indian," Hash said. "The one in the sari."

Portia slowly comprehended that Hash spoke the truth. "I suppose I should be flattered by your devotion. What do you want."

Hash allowed an inch of airspace to trickle between her back and his chest. "The three of you are in it together, aren't you," he said.

"What are you talking about."

"You, Floyd, Viola Flury. The three of you are running this little operation."

"Don't talk to me about the two of them," Portia snapped. Her breath smelled of wine and berries.

Hash had to slap his hand over her mouth again. "Quiet, I told you. Last time." He pushed her away. "I'm finally seeing how you pulled it off," he said. "You pretend to give Beck the shaft. He pretends to have a mental breakdown so that no one suspects he's the plant in Customs. Meanwhile you stash a decoy with Flury so you can throw the scent off that Dalmatian in the barn. Then you all meet over here to deliver the microchip to those three Chinese."

"You're out of your mind," Portia snapped. "I know nothing about a microchip."

Hash took a stab in the dark. "That's not what Nestor Buffez tells me."

Portia turned her head so sharply her neck snapped. Perfidious bastard! Had he been using her all along just to get that thing out of his damn mutt? Of course. He worked for Flury. "Oh? Did he tell you what was in his pajama pocket?"

"He's got the chip?" Hash cried.

"You stupid idiot! Anyone with half a brain could see that!"

Hash got off the bed and paced the room. Someone very, very clever had led him on not one, but two wild goose chases. "How did you get involved in this?"

"Involved in what? Can you at least tell me what's going on?"

"No." Hash sat on the foot of the bed. "We already know how you met Floyd."

"Do not talk about Floyd." Portia's voice teetered on the hysterical.

"Control yourself," Hash snapped. "How did you meet Viola?"

"She brought that black dog into the clinic on July Fourth. Someone had hit it with a softball."

"And you believed that story?"

"Of course! There was no reason not to!"

"Did the dog look in any way suspicious?"

"He had a lacerated stomach. Flury told me it had been in a fight."

"And you believed that?"

"Don't give me this shit, Mr. Hash. Of course I believed her. What she told me was entirely plausible."

Hash sighed: Civilians were so gullible. "When was your next contact with her?"

"At a demonstration outside her boutique in New York."

"Why would you demonstrate outside her boutique, for Christ's sake?"

"Because the products that woman manufactures are detrimental to society. It is our duty to protest such obscene sexism."

"That's not what I meant. Why did you picket her boutique in particular? Why not the lingerie counter at Bonwit Teller?"

Portia thought a moment. "A woman in my Female Awareness group had seen her on *OmniFem.*"

"What's that? A drug?"

"A television program devoted to women. Flury avoided every opportunity to discuss serious issues with Gloria Budd, the interviewer. It was very disturbing."

"So you challenged her at this demonstration?"

"Yes. She pretended to be shocked."

"Nothing is by chance. You might please remember the name of the woman who convinced your group to stage that particular demonstration."

"Certainly. It was your wife Pearl."

Pearl!? Hash walked to the window, stunned. The vipers were getting closer and closer to his bosom. "All right," he said after a while. "Then what."

"Flury called Nestor to come break up the demonstration. He had the black dog with him and in most uncivil terms accused me of malpractice because the stitches on the pup's stomach were not healing properly. We went back to my clinic. Whereupon I discovered the microchip." Portia sighed: What a fool she had been.

"Was he surprised?"

"Of course! Yes, yes, I believed him! Sorry!"

"What was his explanation of this?"

"He said that a hit man from the Customs Service had been following him with the intention of kidnapping his dog." She looked over. "It seemed reasonable. I know the types of escapades you and Floyd used to pull."

Hash cleared his throat. "Didn't you consider, at any time, this man's attachment to this dog a bit . . . excessive?"

"No! I resent that! You have no idea how people can love their pets!" Portia snorted. "That's one reason Pearl left you."

"Let's not get bogged down with side shows," Hash said, holding up a hand. "When did you next meet Nestor?"

"In the hospital. I gave him the microchip."

"I thought he left it at your clinic."

"He did. Then I brought it back."

Hmmmm. "Why didn't you bring this matter to the proper authorities? Never mind, stupid question." Hash drummed his fingers upon Portia's ruffly white bedstand. "Okay, you gave Nestor his chip back like a good girl. Then you and Champ went to Switzerland."

"Yes. A veterinary convention."

Hash already knew how she had ended up in Emwald. "What were you doing at the silk convention? Looking for sick worms?"

Portia gazed sullenly at her big toe. "That's personal."

"Fine, great. Then you twice made contact with the Chinese."

"You've been following me, you schmuck!"

"It was no thrill, darling. So what did you and the boys talk about on that park bench for an hour this afternoon?"

"Panda bears!"

Hash sighed. Her story made more or less sense until the very end. "So why were you meeting Floyd Beck and Viola Flury at the Hotel Badhof?"

Portia became infuriated. "I was not meeting them! I had no idea they would be there. I have no idea how they got there. I have no idea what they're doing there." A strange cackling broke from her mouth. "Besides screwing each other's brains out."

"Did Floyd or Viola know you were coming here?"

"I told that bastard I was possibly going to be in Montreux."

"And when was this?"

"July Fourth, the day he supposedly left for a vacation in Florida."

"What did he say?"

"As usual, he tried to dissuade me from coming. Floyd is an extremely negative person. He probably knew this would only guarantee my arrival."

Hash thought back to July Fourth. "Did you tell Floyd you had seen me that morning at the Cliffside Park parade?"

"Of course. And I told him about our little run-in on Forty-second Street."

Hash had told him about neither: Floyd must have known immediately what was going on in Hash's mind. Half an hour before his plane took off, he had called Hash and told him to stomp on Champ's quarantine, knowing full well that Hash would get sucked into this up to his naive, horny eyeballs. Portia and hound leave country; Hash leaves country. Nestor is left wide open to deliver microchip. Ah, Beck was a genius.

Chickens began mildly squawking in the coop. Portia rushed to the window. "They're going to wake Champ up," she said. "I've got to get over there soon."

The door slammed downstairs. Portia and Hash heard the voices of three ladies returning from a sausage excursion in Ticino. Hash glanced out the window and saw Fräulein Moser, laden with packages, pass beneath a street lamp. "The gang's all here," he muttered, extinguishing the frilly white light on Portia's bedstand. He sat on the bed close to her. "Viola Flury," he whispered. "What does she have to do with this?"

As Hash's eyes gradually accustomed to the dark he could see Portia toying with her straw belt. "I think she and Floyd used to be lovers," she said finally. "I suspect they never stopped being lovers."

"Even when he was with you?" Hash said in surprise.

"Don't get me started on this. I've had an extremely bad day."

"Keep the voice down," Hash hissed. "So you didn't meet them here intentionally?"

"Cripes, are you thick," Portia cried, getting off the bed. "No!"

"Were they surprised to see you then? Shocked? Embarrassed?"

"Nothing of the sort. Floyd seemed almost to be expecting me, now that I think about it." The cawing from the coop intensified. "Can we wrap this up," Portia said.

Money? Revenge? Blackmail? Hash sighed; he would never comprehend Beck. He should have guessed from those evenings at The Outpost that Beck's personality contained critical flaws. "What the hell was Beck doing at the Badhof," Hash asked, suddenly remembering all those suits and the tuxedo he had seen hanging in Floyd's living room. "Taking mud baths? Meeting the Chinese?"

"They were all there last night," Portia said. "Tonight it was just Floyd and Flury."

"Why didn't they just hole up in Montreux?"

"Because everyone at the silk convention would recognize her, you idiot."

Hash looked almost relieved. "Now that makes perfect sense. Beck is very clever."

Portia suddenly slapped his burnt face. "You goddamn men are all alike."

She was losing it again. Hash put his hand over her mouth and pulled her close to his chest. "Cool the tantrum. It's a little late for jealousy."

The door to Portia's room swung open and there stood Breeze in her backless sundress. In her hand she held a bottle of shampoo. "You there, doc?" Hash and Portia froze on the bed. Humming, Breeze walked into Portia's room and turned on the fluffy little nightlamp. "Jumpin' Jesus Mary and Joseph!" she shouted. "What's going on here?"

Hash released Portia immediately. "There has been a slight misunderstanding."

"You can say that again, buster! This is a pension for ladies only!" Then a huge smile lifted Breeze's cheeks. "Well, well, Dr. Feminist. Is this what you call doing without men? Where'd you pick this guy up? In the doghouse?"

"How dare you enter my room," Portia snapped, sliding off the bed.

"I told you this morning I would lend you my special shampoo," Breeze said. "Here. Although I see you get results without using it."

Portia looked out the window. "What in God's name is going on in that chicken coop? I have a dog in there trying to sleep."

"Your dog wasn't sleeping when I looked in there. He was whining and trying to eat his leash."

"It's a she," Portia retorted. "And what the hell were you doing in the chicken coop?"

"We brought a load of air-dried beef back from Ticino. Eggli told us to hang it in the barn overnight to cure a little more. I guess Froy locked the doors when she left for Geneva this morning."

The chickens were screeching garishly. Then a dog started to howl.

"You put that beef into the chicken coop with my dog?"

"What's the problem? She won't suffocate. I left the door wide open."

"Get out of my way!" Portia knocked Breeze aside and tore down the steps.

"It's locked," Breeze called into the hallway. "Froy said everyone was home for the night."

The front door rattled violently. "Where's the key," Portia shrieked from downstairs.

"Froy's got it," Breeze said. "Use your head, doc."

Attired in an ancient nightshirt, Harriet tumbled into the hall. "My God! A man!"

"Brilliant, Swallow. Go to the head of the class."

"What's going on here," Rhoda said, emerging naked from the bathroom. "Aiii!"

"She's very shy about those spare tires," Breeze said. "You must excuse her."

Harriet frowned at Hash. "Who are you?" she demanded. "Fräulein Moser's cook?"

"Swallow, don't be so huffy. I bet Dr. Porsche doesn't even know his name yet." Breeze peered down the stairs. "Doc, quit breaking dishes! Froy's not in the kitchen! Her room's out back!" She looked at Hash. "Did you slip something into her drink, cutie? She's going berserk down there."

One, two, three rifle shots stung the night. Hash blazed down the stairs towards Fräulein Moser's room. "I must say," Breeze remarked to Harriet, "it's certainly nice to have a man around the house." She looked toward the bathroom. "You can come out now, Rhoda."

Hash ripped into Moser's room. She was leaning out her window, about to unload another clip. He roughly yanked the rifle up just as she fired: No stars fell. Moser was tossed aside as her rifle fell out the window. "Who are you?" she cried in dialect. "How did you get into my pension?"

Hash leapt out the window and raced toward the coop, there to discover four chickens lying dead, or very bloody and exhausted, in their cages. Champ sprawled whimpering across the floor, jaws full of beef, belly full of buckshot. The surviving chickens were trying to fly away with their cages.

Hash dropped to the sawdust. "Champ," he whispered. "Hey girl." The dog did not respond.

Portia arrived with pieces of Fräulein's blue windowsill in her blouse and instantly became a veterinarian. "This dog is going to die," she told Hash without emotion, as if the Dalmatian belonged to him. "She'll bleed to death before morning."

"She will not," Hash said. "Get her in my car. Out front."

The two of them lifted Champ onto a blanket and slung her into the rear seat of Hash's Audi. By the time Fräulein Moser got her front door unlocked, Dr. Clemens, that strange man, and the Dalmatian had long since departed. Moser stood for a long moment staring at her dead chickens, her live chickens, and a mound of beef composting in the corner, wondering whom to charge for what. She was very grateful that Chef Eggli's cooking class would be ending the next day.

Viola stood on her balcony breathing the night. Floyd came up behind her and rested his chin on her shoulder. His arms circled her stomach and they stood very still, listening to the pines. Tonight it would probably be easier not to look at each other. "What are you thinking," he said.

Oh, that tomorrow she'd be meeting Eugene in Rome and putzing around Italy for a week; that Nestor had probably been calling her in Montreux once an hour since Thursday; that she never wanted to leave this room; that in seventeen years she had crawled too far from that original fork in the road to ever go back. "That I love you," Viola said. "And we should probably never see each other again."

No response necessary. They were twins separated at birth, soon to be separated again. They had the same wrinkles on the forehead, the same trick knees, the same melancholy on a Sunday afternoon. Viola ran two fingers through Floyd's hair; white had overtaken the black at exactly the same place on their temples. She had not seen them accumulate one by one, nor would she ever share the myriad of banal crises which had nurtured them. When, if, they ever met again, would their hair be completely white, their health brittle as ivy in the snow? She wondered why she had known this man, if she could never have him. Perhaps Floyd was a divine slap on the hands to teach her that only God had everything. Clever. Viola wished she held a stone so that she could throw it at the moon. *Send me to hell then, Old Man. I'm keeping him.* How generous of her to volunteer Floyd for another seventeen years in limbo. "Damn."

"That white bow on your bathrobe," he said. "Were you thinking of me when you drew it?"

"I thought of you when it was finished."

"When I saw that," Floyd said, "I knew it would just be a matter of time."

She had never had his extraordinary faith in the future. "How did you see that robe? It's not in any of the stores."

"I inspected the first box that came into the States." She could feel his heart thrumming her shoulderblades. "Your partner refused to leave the cargo terminal until we had released it."

"Good old Nestor," Viola said. Floyd stared at the blackness between two stars: from here an inch, in reality a million light years. "We've been through a lot together."

That said it all, didn't it. Thirty hours, be they incandescent as the sun, couldn't begin to evaporate years spent with another man. This morning he and Viola had taken a long walk through the forest. They had gone swimming in the lake and found the purple sneaker which had ricocheted into the water last night. They had driven Viola's rented car to the next village for lunch, then spent the afternoon in bed. Had they a week together, they would maybe have gotten around to broaching Nestor, husbands, babies—objects dully omnipresent yet irrelevant, like cruise missiles. Viola never mentioned the word *husband;* "we" was as close as she got to that fact of life. Floyd knew she was trying to protect him and he didn't press her. If this little island of time was all they'd ever have together, then he and Viola would be its sole inhabitants.

His hands drifted down the front of her body. Thank God he had met her now; in another month that belly, so obviously another man's inheritance, would have pained him too much to touch. Maybe. He realized that after tonight, he would have to let her go: Nothing extinguished an old flame like motherhood. Ah, lucky Viola. All the misplaced love and longing could be rechanneled into its most perfect receptacle. What was he supposed to do, become a godfather? Compound the error with a family of his own?

"I'm sorry about this baby," Viola said. "It complicates everything."

"It simplifies everything."

"Really?" She turned around. "Will it make me forget last night in the lake? Would wheeling a carriage along Park Avenue stop that ache each time I pass the phone booth where we used to meet?"

"Forget about me," he said. "It's the only solution."

Ah, the old black-and-white routine again. Why was amputation still the only cure for this disease? "I despise that solution." Where the hell was an ashtray when she needed it? It was either that, or she, off the balcony.

Floyd broke away. "Would you prefer to start meeting at the phone booth again? We could wheel the carriage up and down Park Avenue and pretend the baby's ours."

"If you hadn't been such a damn proud fool this baby might have been ours," Viola snapped. A bird twitted from the forest, stopping her. For a long while she listened to its solitary melody; Eugene would know if that were a nightingale or a whippoorwill. From the other side of the balcony, Floyd watched mother moon bathe daughter Viola's unhappy face as he waited, as always, in the shadows. Finally she turned her head. "I will never divorce my husband," she said softly. "I'm going to have a baby. I will never stop loving you." She smiled ruefully: joke on her. "So much for women's liberation."

Floyd closed his eyes. Whenever he looked at her the old longing washed him away. So they were finally back to where this loop had begun many years ago, weren't they. He was still adoring her from the next row and she still belonged to another man. All they had ever had, would ever have together, were intense intermissions.

Three shots, twelve echoes, rang through the valley. The bird ceased singing. "What was that?" Viola said.

"Firecrackers. August First is Swiss Independence Day." Floyd came to her side of the railing. "It's late," he said. "We should be in bed."

Fog stifled the mountains, leaching the dawn monochromatic gray. Floyd hurried down the steep drive of the Badhof, allowing gravity to pull him away from Viola. He couldn't do it himself; thank God the hotel didn't lie in a valley and the pension on a mountain. When he drifted awake this morning Viola was already waiting for him, breathing lightly on his face. The man who began his day next to those blue eyes was King of the World: Floyd pulled her immediately over, knowing that his reign was at an end. As the clockface ticked doggedly towards five-thirty, he took one last lingering ride through his domain, memorizing the colors and scents which he would probably never know again.

Finally she slid out of bed; the sheets died immediately. Viola pulled on a blue robe with fishing flies embroidered over it and handed him his clothing piece by piece, watching as he dressed. Then she put her hand on the doorknob. "When will I see you again?" Floyd asked.

"August fifth, Swissair from Rome," she said. "Midday. Will you be working?"

"Go to the lanes on the right," Floyd said.

"I won't be alone," she said.

"I don't care." He ran the back of his hand along the black mole on her cheek. "I love you." Then he left.

Floyd crept through the tunnel to the pension, met the baker, boiled the coffee, and waited for the women to arrive; he needed the company of their voices to fill the ravine inside of him. Today he did not hear Portia's footsteps over the kitchen. She wasn't going to sleep through her own speech, was she? Nor did he hear water running for anyone's shower. Six-thirty, seven, still no one came to breakfast, not even Fräulein Moser or the Indian with the odd voice. Floyd wondered if the ladies had returned from Ticino yesterday at all. Finally at eight o'clock, he took a shower and shaved, thinking ahead to today's sausage class, to his trip back home, maybe a canasta game, anything but Viola. He didn't think he could go back to the lake again.

By now she should be driving to Montreux at her typical pace, speed limit plus thirty percent. At the hotel desk she'd collect a mound of phone messages from Nestor; within a minute of entering her room, she'd be on the phone with him. Floyd wondered if the man would notice any change in her voice and if he'd be glad she took a day off in the mountains. She'd rejoin the Lungs at the silk convention, fib a bit, then take a late flight to Rome. Adieu, warm lake: She'd be sleeping with her husband tomorrow night.

Finally, as he sat listlessly combing his hair, Floyd heard activity in the room overhead. That was not Portia, though, unless she had gained a hundred pounds and flat feet overnight. Sounded like Fräulein Moser opening windows. Portia must have checked out of the pension at four this morning in order to be in Montreux well before speech time. No doubt she'd be joining William in Geneva afterward for a little celebration . . . God knew she hadn't wanted any champagne last night. A door slammed, someone shuffled to the bathroom: The damsels were slowly emerging from hibernation upstairs. Floyd wondered what hour they had finally returned from their field trip.

Looking as if she had spent the night in the chicken coop, Fräulein

Moser appeared in the kitchen. Her bun perched more over her left ear than the nape of her neck. "Are you all right?" Floyd asked, pulling out a chair. "Let me make you some tea. Where was everyone this morning?"

Fräulein Moser sniffed a piece of bread before putting it down again. He had never seen her refuse food before. "This was the most terrible night since the war," she said. "The police from Montreux came at three o'clock in the morning and kept us up until five asking many frightening questions. We all thought we would go to jail." She decided to nibble a piece of bread after all. "You were not here, I think."

"I was at the Hotel Badhof," Floyd said. "Visiting with my friend from the restaurant. What happened here? Did the Indian start another fire?"

"No, no. By mistake I shot that woman's dog."

"You shot Champ!? My God, Fräulein Moser! Do you have any idea what you've done?"

"I do now," she said. "That horrible woman is going to sue me for fifty million Swiss francs." Her face grayed. "My life savings will be gone."

"Don't worry about a thing," Floyd said, patting her arm. "I will take care of everything. Believe me." He set down her tea. "How did you shoot that dog?"

"There was a terrible noise in the coop when I returned from Geneva last night. I thought it was the neighbor's goat attacking my hens again."

"What was the dog doing in the coop? Why wasn't it in the barn?"

"I locked the barn when I left that morning for Geneva. It is a habit." Fräulein Moser dropped two large teaspoons of sugar into her tea. "But there is something much, much worse which happened."

"You shot Dr. Clemens too?"

"There was a man in my pension. He was upstairs in the room with this doctor with all the lights out. After I took my shots he ran into my bedroom without knocking and threw my gun away. Then he jumped out the window." Fräulein Moser's voice shook. "It was terrible. Then Fräulein Clemens ran into my bedroom and jumped out the window after him. Half her clothes were off. The two of them got into a car and disappeared."

"What happened to the dog?"

"They took the dog with them. Unfortunately it died on the way to Montreux. The police told me." Moser sighed. "It seems very unfair that I must pay fifty million Swiss francs for a new dog. I am sure I can buy her another one for five hundred."

Fräulein would never understand the fair market value of mental anguish. "Listen," Floyd said, "she's not going to sue you. First of all, you're not a man. Secondly, no Swiss court would even listen to such a case. Every farmer in the country would scream."

"She wants me to be extradited to America."

"The Swiss don't extradite criminals who stash billions of dollars in numbered bank accounts. Do you think they're going to extradite a sixty-year-old woman who mistook a dog for a goat?"

She considered this in the calm light of day. "Yes, I suppose you're right. But it was still horrible. I am never going to let such a person into my pension again."

Fräulein had better turn in her bun, then. Floyd stood up: sausage time. "What you need is a game of canasta this afternoon. What do you say? I'll meet you here at two o'clock, after class."

"Yes, after I clean my chicken coop. It is a terrible mess." She left the kitchen.

Floyd took a long walk, but not to his lake, then dressed carefully in his new black suit; today was Count Carnegie's last appearance in class. Overhead he heard Fräulein Moser tromping around Portia's vacated room, removing all washables. The rest would have to be fumigated. Poor Portia had paid quite a price for getting herself inseminated last night. Where had she found the fellow so fast? Hitchhiking back to the pension? Alone, she had left Floyd and Viola around ten o'clock; those three shots had cut through the valley an hour later. He wondered whether Portia had even gotten the show underway before Fräulein's small disturbance. If she still had half her clothes on when she dove through Moser's window, no; once Portia undressed for the evening, she remained that way.

As Floyd walked into the kitchen of the Hotel Badhof, Chef Eggli and his class were just finishing their preparations for the Floydwurst. On the table lay neat little piles of pork butts, hearts and snouts, delicate spices, beef, and a box of casings, all of which class had purchased yesterday on their field trip. "This is really pretty disgusting, Chef," Breeze said. "I don't know if I can go through with this."

"Do not be such a cultural snob!" the chef shouted. Floyd watched him almost hit her with Caspar's book of recipes. "The nutritional value of a snout is hardly less than that of a hamburger."

"What if the pig had a cold when it died?"

"Only you would think of something like that," Rhoda said.

Chef Eggli stared at the table. "Where's the Büntnerfleische we bought yesterday? Did you forget it in Fräulein Moser's barn?"

After a few moments Harriet cleared her throat. "There has been an unfortunate accident, Chef Eggli," she said. "A dog has eaten it."

"What? How is this possible? Fräulein Moser owns no dogs!"

"It's a long story," Breeze said. "Let's forget it. Froy shot the dog for his bad manners anyway."

"Who cares about the dog? I need that Büntnerfleische for tonight!"

Chef was planning to serve a genuine Alpine supper. "It cost a small fortune, damn you!" This time he did slap Breeze with the recipe book. Two pages flapped to the floor. "Would you care to reimburse me for it? How about another demerit?"

"Good afternoon," Floyd said, quickly stepping to the table. He retrieved the fallen pages and pointedly handed them back to Chef Eggli. "I zink you have dropped somezing very valuable."

"Perhaps valuable to you, Anna," the chef said, switching to dialect. "To me it's just shit that I promised to make for your son."

"What did he say, Count," Breeze asked, tugging his sleeve. "Come on, translate."

"He said this is going to be an in—" Floyd's eyes fell on the front of her tee-shirt—"interesting lesson."

"What's the matter, don't you like my tee-shirt? Everyone in the company got one at last year's picnic." *Pyrana, Inc.*, the letters spelled.

"It's lovely, dear," Harriet said. "Yours should perhaps have been given to someone a size three."

Stifling in here: Floyd removed his coat. Pink on black had always been one of Viola's favorite combinations. "So," he said, rolling up his sleeves, "here ve go."

"You're going to help us make sausages?" Rhoda asked.

"Vhy not? Such things have always intrigued me." He looked at the ingredients lying on the table. "Zis looks like a particularly delicious combination."

"What's this going to be called anyhow," Breeze asked Chef Eggli. "Snoutdogs?"

"Floydwurst."

"Floyd? Wurst? That's pretty lame, Chef."

"Shut up! I have still not forgiven you for that Büntnerfleische!" Across the table Floyd could smell the brandy on the chef's breath. "All right. Men, begin carefully measuring all the spices. Ladies, you wash out the snouts and intestines."

"Didn't you mean the other way around," Rhoda suggested.

"Absolutely not! For three weeks you've been telling me there is no difference between the sexes!"

"Great going, Rhoda. Hope you're happy." Breeze carried the casings to the sink. That way she wouldn't have to deal with the snouts. "Let's get on with it, girls."

"These sausages are going to taste awful, Anna," Chef Eggli said to Floyd in dialect. "This is one of the most miserable recipes I have ever read. That son of a bitch Caspar was never anything but a hack."

"You're mistaken," Floyd said. The chef was maddened with jealousy. His father wouldn't bestow his son's name on any sausage less than sublime.

"We shall see." Chef Eggli looked impatiently toward the sinks. "Hurry it up, ladies," he called. "We have plenty of work yet today."

"Cut us a break," Rhoda snorted. "These snouts are a godawful mess. Who the hell is going to eat this stuff anyway? I thought this was a health resort."

"Don't mind her, Count," Breeze called, carrying the intestines back to the table. "Rhoda did not get enough beauty sleep last night. We had a little excitement at the pension. There was a shooting and the police came." She carefully lay the casings down.

"The Swiss police came to your pension?" Eggli asked.

"Yeah, the dog doctor had an unauthorized visitor in her room. Cute guy with a big moustache. A few skin problems, but you can't get too picky in these mountains. I walked in on them by mistake. They were sitting on her bed in the dark. 'There has been a slight misunderstanding,' he says to me."

"He was English?"

"He was American."

Floyd slowly put his recipe book down. "Vhat happened next?"

"Well, we stood there looking at each other and all of a sudden Froy's gun went off. This guy tore downstairs faster than a jackrabbit."

"He ran away?"

"No, just the opposite. He went straight for Froy's gun. Then he jumped out of her window and ran into the barn. He took Doc and the dog into Montreux. Laid a patch about three miles long in reverse getting down Froy's hill." Seeing that her tale held Chef's entire class spellbound, Breeze sighed and fell silent. It was a tactic she had learned many years ago in singles bars.

"Well? Well?" Chef Eggli cried. "What happened next? Don't keep us in suspense!"

"I really need a drink to continue this," she said. "I could be persuaded to take a rain check on that, though. Perhaps Count Carnegie would do the honors tonight."

Rhoda unceremoniously dumped ten pork snouts on the table. "The police from Montreux came at three in the morning," she said. "They thought we were a smuggling ring. The dog lady must have fed them one incredible story about the pension."

"What sort of smuggling?" Chef asked. "Diamonds? Gold? Impressionist paintings?"

"They kept talking about dogs and microchips," Harriet said, dropping another load of snouts on the table. "It was terribly confusing. Ms. Clemens wanted to sue Fräulein Moser for fifty million francs damages."

"I thought they'd throw us in jail," Breeze said. "Sheesh, my boss would never send over bail money. He'd rather use it to go to Hawaii with his wife."

Count Carnegie looked at his watch. "Could ve please make a few sausages? I have unfortunately a very important appointment at two o'clock."

Chef Eggli peered suspiciously at Floyd. "And what might that be, Anna? Are you expecting company?" he said in dialect. "Not Caspar, for example? You're not eloping this afternoon, are you?"

"Will you stop this ridiculous fantasizing," Floyd snapped. His nerves were frayed enough without Eggli reminding him how it felt to be left behind.

Harriet laid a hand on Floyd's arm. "I understand how difficult these time constraints must be for you, Count Carnegie. I have to deal with deadlines myself every day in my profession."

"Was Chef talking about deadlines," Breeze asked another pupil.

"Ev course not."

Floyd spied an apron and tied it over his white shirt. "My apologies to ze class," he said. "Zis has been an unusually difficult day for me."

Chef Eggli clapped his hands. "All right! Put those snouts through the meat grinder," he instructed Harriet. He peered at the yellowed recipe in his hand. "Five kilos of ground beef into the tub. Who has the juniper berries? The marjoram? The garlic? Salt? Who has the diced sheep hearts? Fine, fine, throw them in also." Chef scratched his head. "What a terrible combination." He looked at Floyd. "You're in for a bad shock, Anna," he said in dialect. "I think Caspar was trying to poison his son with this. He must not have liked the boy very much. Perhaps he suspected he was mine."

"Here are the snouts, Chef Eggli," Harriet said, wiping her brow. "Whew! When are you going to get an electric grinder?"

"Just add them to the tub," he said, elbow deep in the mush. "Well, Carnegie? Did we forget anything? Have we followed this recipe precisely?"

Floyd checked the ingredients. "I believe so."

"Excellent! We begin stuffing then. Are those casings good and wet?"

"They're pretty gross, Chef," Breeze said, handing one end over. "This thing looks like a huge rubber."

"Intestines were the original condoms, dear," Harriet said.

Chef Eggli mounted the meat into an upright metal cylinder with a crank on one side and a nozzle on the other. He rolled and secured one end of the casings to the nozzle as class watched in silence. "That's quite erotic, Chef," Breeze said finally.

"Will you stop these asinine comments," Rhoda snapped. "Is there ever anything on your mind besides sex?"

"How can I help it, Rhoda? Sausages are very phallic objects. I haven't had a man in weeks. Deprivation like this is very bad for my hormonal balance." Breeze looked frankly at Count Carnegie. "I sometimes think I'm a man in a woman's body. I have very strong sexual desires."

"So do dogs and fish, my dear," Count Carnegie replied, nudging Chef Eggli away from the sausage machine. He began cranking the handle. Very slowly, meat emerged from the nozzle and impleted the limp casing. "Zis is a bit tricky," he said to the class. "You must go at just the right speed or you vill get air bubbles in ze sausages." He was feeling very strangely displaced in time and body. Part of him was back in his father's butcher shop, most of him was still inside Viola, and the rest of him was witnessing a tortuous live birth.

"How did you know that, Count," Rhoda asked.

"His father was an amateur cook," Chef Eggli said. "He enjoyed making sausages when he got in from the polo matches."

"Polo? In Hungary?" Harriet said.

"No more questions about the count's personal life!" Chef Eggli snapped. "It is filled with separation and death." Silence stilled the cooking class. The three women fell in love with Floyd all over again: Tragedy was a potent aphrodisiac.

"Just think, Harriet," Breeze observed as the mixture gradually swelled the casing. "This is what goes on in your intestinal tract every day."

"What do we do next, Chef Eggli," Harriet asked.

"We tie these into sausages, then we smoke them," he said. "They will just be ready by dinner tonight."

Floyd kept cranking until all the meat had been extruded from the sausage maker. He lifted the lid and Chef Eggli spooned in another load of meat from the tub. Then he resumed slowly turning the handle.

Unbeknown to Chef Eggli's cooking class, George Hash had been standing at the door of the kitchen observing them for the past several minutes. He had just spent all night in Montreux with Portia and the Swiss authorities, who insisted that Champ must either be cremated or buried immediately according to health regulations. At midnight the Swedish president of the veterinary convention was informed of the unforeseen change in tomorrow's lecture schedule. He rushed to the police station demanding a full explanation of this terrible accident. An attaché from the American Embassy finally had to be summoned when Portia threatened to call the *Herald Tribune* and amplify Champ's demise into an international incident that could damage the Swiss hotel industry. When Portia began raving about a smuggling conspiracy and implied that Fräulein Moser might be a hired assassin, the police from Montreux were dispatched to the pension to confiscate her gun and have a few words with the witnesses. Then Portia's friend William and a dozen participants from the International Women's Conference in Geneva arrived to lend Dr. Clemens moral support by accusing the police of crimes against women. In the heat of the moment Portia accused Hash of raping her because, had he not been interrogating her at the pension, she perhaps could have rescued Champ from the chicken coop in time. Hash had to call McPhee in New York to exonerate himself, an experience he found quite embarrassing. Finally around six, when it became obvious that Champ would be incinerated despite the efforts of herself, Hash, William, the U.S. consul, and fifteen women, Portia decided to leave the country. The moment the police brought back all of her belongings from the pension, Portia left for the airport in Geneva, promising to call the New York *Times* the moment her plane arrived at JFK Airport. She never even thanked Hash for the ambulance ride to Montreux.

Seething, excruciatingly tired, Hash had driven straight to the Hotel Badhof and asked for Floyd Beck, who was not a registered guest. He flashed his identification at the clerk and described a tall man with a black eye who had been at dinner last night with a beautiful woman. Aha, that was Count Carnegie, he was told. Sometimes the count visited Chef Eggli in his kitchen downstairs. Of course Hash would be shown the way.

Now Hash stared at Floyd all dressed up in a fine white shirt, silk tie, and apron, calmly cranking sausages out of a machine as a mesmerized group looked on. Finally he understood everything. The dogs, the microchips were all just diversions.

Hash strolled silently behind Floyd. "So," he said, "are we adding emeralds to this batch?"

Floyd turned quickly around. Hash looked a wreck. His eyes were red and watery. His shirt was covered with blood. His face looked as if he had been bathing it in Agent Orange. "Good afternoon." He spoke with a strange accent which Hash had not heard before and he didn't seem at all surprised to see him.

"Hey, look who's here! Dr. Porsche's lover!" Breeze said. "You sure left in a hurry last night, cutie. Missed a great pajama party at the pension."

Hash ignored her. Now he was staring at Floyd's waning black eye.

Again he modified his theory. "You've got a chip in there, don't you," he said to Floyd. "Beneath the stitches. That shiner is a fake."

"The hell it is," Rhoda said. "You should have seen it a week ago." She was still peeved that Hash had seen her naked last night.

"Who is this man, Anna?" Chef Eggli asked ominously in dialect.

Floyd did not remove his eyes from Hash: That wild stare reminded him of many a rabid dog he had brought to Portia's clinic. "An old friend of mine," he said in dialect. "I think he needs help."

"Where is she," Hash said.

"Hot damn!" Breeze exclaimed. "I told you there was a woman involved in this, Swallow! So that's why I never got anywhere!"

"Anna," Eggli warned. "Tell that man to go away and leave us alone."

Hash tottered into the wooden table. "The two of you almost got away from me this time," he said weakly.

Two of them? What was he talking about? "You're delirious," Floyd said, placing a hand on Hash's blistery forehead. "You have a fever. I'm putting you to bed." He removed his apron. "I'll be right back," he told Chef Eggli, slinging Hash's arm over his shoulder. "What the hell's going on," he whispered to Hash the moment they were out of earshot of the class. "What are you doing here?"

"No, what are *you* doing here? How do you dare call yourself a friend of mine and pull a stunt like this? Didn't you inherit enough money from your aunt to keep you satisfied? Florida! What's the phony accent for? Are you running these microchips to the Chinese?"

"What Chinese? I'm here to make sausages!"

Chef Eggli suddenly realized that Anna was leaving the room with another man. He pulled a heavy skillet from the overhead rack and ran after Floyd and Hash. "No you don't, Caspar," he shouted, smacking Hash on the head as they were almost to the door. "You did it once, but you're not going to do it twice, you bastard!"

Hash dropped to the floor. "Are you out of your mind?" Floyd shouted at the chef. "This man's a United States law officer!"

"I don't care what he is, Anna," Eggli said. "You are not leaving with him. You belong here with me."

"Someone get over here fast," Floyd ordered, switching to English. He almost lost his accent entirely.

Breeze shot over. "What can I do, Count?"

"Help me get zis man away from Eggli before he kills him."

The chef started to cry. "Please don't leave, Anna. I beg you."

"What's he saying? He's sorry he hurt the guy?" Breeze asked.

Hash moaned from the floor and tried to sit up, rubbing his head. Floyd

sighed. "I need one more assistant from class, please," he called. This time
the tall Danish student responded. "Tell the hôtelier to find zis man a
room," he said. "Put it on my account." He watched Breeze and the Dane
help Hash to his feet. "Keep him entertained," he told them. "I vill call
later zis afternoon."

After they left he turned to Eggli. "See, I'm still here. Don't cry."

"It's all right, Chef Eggli," Harriet called from the table. "We know
you didn't mean to hurt him. Come on back. We'll finish making these
sausages."

Sniffling, the chef returned to the table. Rhoda looked quizzically at
Count Carnegie. "Did you know that guy?" she said.

"Yes," Floyd said, "he is one of ze finest special agents in ze U.S.
Treasury Department. Ve have sometimes vorked togezer on special
cases." He lifted the handle of the sausage press. "It appears ve vill be
vorking togezer again."

"Do you mean to say you're a spy? Like James Bond?" Harriet asked.

"No more questions," Chef Eggli interrupted, tying the sausage. Once
he saw that Anna would remain, his recovery was instantaneous. "This is
classified information. Count Carnegie has enough on his mind."

Eventually the Danish student reappeared in the kitchen; Breeze had
decided to remain upstairs with the patient. Saying very little, Floyd
stayed until Chef Eggli's class had deposited the last of the sausages in
the smoker according to Caspar's directions. Then he excused himself.
Before returning to the pension for a farewell canasta game with Fräulein
Moser, Floyd stopped by the doctor in Emwald and had his stitches
removed.

It was another keenly beautiful day, his last here. At the door of the
pension, Floyd turned and looked at the mountains: Even if he lived
among them the rest of his life, they would never cease to awe him. They
were eternal, omnipotent parents, sheltering the tiny, confused humans
who scurried in their shadows. They transcended time. Who or what,
besides God, could claim to do that? He watched a cloud graze a blue peak
far in the distance, continue on, and knew the answer: Viola could. She
had already obliterated seventeen years. She could do that twice, maybe
three times more before the mountains outlived him. Floyd knew he
would see her again; until that time, he would live quietly as an abbot,
consoled that she watched the same sunsets, the same autumns, and that
the next slow, gigantic loop now encircled them both.

Floyd went to the backyard, where the three women waited for him.
"So! Did you finally make your sausages today?" Fräulein Moser asked as
she opened the box of chocolates he had brought.

"Yes. But we will not eat them until tonight."

Moser dealt the cards. "These few weeks have gone so quickly. It is hard to believe that you will be leaving tomorrow. I shall be quite sad."

Everyone who left this place was going to be quite sad. So was everyone who remained behind. If only humans were as dense as the mountains. Floyd patted her hand. "I'll be back."

Floyd met Hash at the Hotel Badhof at eight o'clock for dinner. The host led them to a quiet table next to the harpist, who was back to Debussy tonight. They ordered two beers from Chef Eggli, who had decided to wait on them personally, still dubious that Floyd and Hash were not going to run away together.

"So," Hash said after a long silence, "what brings you here? You tell me first."

"I came to make a sausage from my father's recipe book." Floyd said. "Eggli helped me. He was an old friend of my father's. Mother's."

Hash frowned. "So why did you tell me you were going to Florida?"

"It was a personal thing. Like a funeral."

"After all we've been through you couldn't tell me?"

"Sorry. I was not very sociable three weeks ago."

Eggli came to the table with two bowls. "Cold potato soup. Remember, I am watching you, Anna." He bowed and left.

"A strange man," Hash said. "He never even apologized for hitting me."

"He thought you were someone else."

Breeze, in a red sheath, stopped at the table. A host of rhinestone barrettes struggled to rein her hair within five inches of her scalp. Around her neck was a colorful scarf that seemed familiar to Floyd. He stared at it a moment, then greeted her. "Hello, Count," she said. "Well, George, an afternoon in bed has certainly done wonders for your complexion." She winked and left.

Hash blushed terribly. Floyd looked at him. "You didn't, did you," he said.

"I had no choice! When I woke up she had half my clothes off. And all of hers."

Floyd dipped a spoon into his soup. "What happened to your face, anyway."

"Wait a minute, finish your story. So you've been here doing nothing but making sausages for three weeks."

"Yep."

"Aren't you forgetting something? A little interlude with Viola Flury, maybe?"

Of course Portia had told him. "She was here checking in on the Indian. Breeze. Your nurse. She works for Viola."

"I noticed her shirt," Hash said. "When she finally put it back on." He swallowed some soup. "You believe in such coincidences?"

If one just stepped back far enough in distance or in time, it was obvious that coincidences were like isolated brooklets, all part of the vast oceans, flowing, evaporating, raining upon themselves without end. "We knew each other years ago."

Chef Eggli removed their soup plates. "The worst is yet to come," he said in dialect. "Remember that, Anna."

"Two more beers, please," Hash said.

"So you've been here alone for three weeks making sausages with that madman. You run into Viola by chance. Portia happens to see you two. And here we are."

"Correct."

"Why are people calling you Count Carnegie? What's with this bogus accent?"

Why did everyone feel this was something odd? Count Carnegie was Floyd's most perfect, inevitable incarnation. "I'm filling in for Eggli's editorial assistant. He ate a few poisonous mushrooms a while ago and couldn't come to class."

"And these ladies have no idea who you really are?"

"No, and I intend to keep it that way." Floyd glanced at Hash. "Please indulge my little conceit. I'm trying to neuter Portia a little. Even the score."

"Go for it."

Chef Eggli set two plates of sauerkraut, pork chops, apples, and Floyd-wurst on the table. "There you are, Anna," he said. "I hope you're happy." He stood by, looking at the two men. "Well, go ahead and eat it!"

"What's he saying," Hash asked.

"He wants us to try the sausage."

"Why? Is it special?"

"It's called Floydwurst."

"Is it from the book of recipes I saw you reading that morning?"

Floyd nodded. "My father invented it for my eighth birthday. This is what I came over here to make."

"Hey, that's great," Hash said. "You're immortal." He cut himself a wide wedge and popped it in his mouth. Finally he swallowed. "Very interesting." Hash drained his beer. "Very unusual." Now he understood why Floyd didn't want to tell him about it.

Floyd sliced off a piece and inspected it a moment. The sausage was a dark, angry red oppilated with gelatinous white globules. It looked like a lifesize model of a cholesterol-choked artery. Floyd put it in his mouth and started to chew: tough as tripe. It tasted sweet and yet acrid, like Lestoil with a tinge of garlic.

"Pretty terrible, isn't it," Chef Eggli said. "I told you so."

"You came all the way over here to make this?" Hash asked.

"You came all the way over here to chase Portia. What's the difference?" He looked at Chef Eggli and raised his glass. "Here's to Caspar."

"What for? Inventing a wretched hotdog?"

"Bringing his son to Switzerland," Floyd said.

Breeze stopped by the table with a pot of mustard. "This might help those sausages, gentlemen," she said. "Everyone's been asking for it." Again Floyd stared at her fuschia-and-green scarf. He had seen it before.

"Thank you, sweetie," Hash said. As Rhoda passed the table, his eyes fused to her low-cut blouse. "Where'd all these gorgeous women come from?" he said. "This is unbelievable."

"Ask Count Carnegie," Chef Eggli replied, and left.

"So," Floyd said, slicing a pork chop. "What brings you here?"

Hash described in detail what had happened to him over the past weeks, from the telex from Berlin to his informant's information to his involvement with Nestor, Smudge, Champ, bubbling pizzas, and of course, Portia.

"What's on this microchip anyway?" Floyd asked.

"No idea."

"Where is it now?"

"I think Nestor has it."

"First you suspect Nestor. Then Portia. Then Viola and me?" Floyd's pulse swayed as he pronounced that beautiful name. She was in an airplane now, on her way to Rome, her husband, her alter life.

"Why not? You disappeared and turned up at just the right moments."

"What was my motive?"

"I hadn't figured that out yet. With you, it's always tough." Hash finished his pork chop, napkined his mouth, and set down his fork. He had not made another stab at the Floydwurst. "This has to be an inside job," he said.

Breeze, and the scarf, walked by their table again. Floyd slowly smiled. "You're getting warm, Georgie."

"What? You know who's been running me around in circles like this?"

Floyd put a second morsel of sausage into his mouth and chewed pensively, wondering what Caspar could have been thinking when he invented this. Maybe Floydwurst was to be used as prandial punishment whenever his son misbehaved. Maybe Caspar was still perfecting his recipe when the final gong sounded. Hell, maybe Caspar thought it tasted great. No matter. The Floydwurst had completed a great, mysterious loop named Viola and brought an aging orphan one day of perfect happiness. Caspar could rest now: He had given his son immortality enough.

Floyd motioned Breeze to the table. "Vhere did you get zis lovely scarf, may I ask?"

"This?" Breeze ran a hand over it. "I'm a little embarrassed to tell you, Count."

"Go ahead," Hash said. "We're very open-minded here."

"Okay, in the dumpster. Remember that pooch you were asking me about, Georgie? I found it wrapped in this scarf." Unknotting it from her neck, Breeze displayed it to Floyd and Hash. "Pretty, huh. I knew it would match this dress perfectly. So I had it cleaned and there you are. I hate nice clothes to go to waste."

"Look familiar?" Floyd said to Hash, pushing his plate away. He had not finished the sausage either.

Hash studied it for just a moment. "Frisk," he whispered. "Damn."

Eggli came over. "What is this, a striptease," he asked Breeze. "Get back to your table this minute." He looked at the two dishes in front of Floyd and Hash. "Had enough sausages, gentlemen?"

"Yes," Floyd said. "You may take them away now."

Chef Eggli smiled. "Thank you, Anna."

After dinner, Floyd and Hash went to the veranda for a nightcap. For a long while they stared at the stars, saying nothing: a habit acquired in Hoboken. They were thinking about women. "So," Hash said finally, "what are you going to do about Viola?"

Live. Hope. "Wait." Floyd swallowed some brandy. "I'm good at that." By now she was in Rome, in bed but not asleep. "What are you going to do about Portia?"

"Forget her, she's a terminal case. There are much more deserving women around."

"Yoo hoo! Georgie!" Breeze tripped onto the veranda and sat on the arm of Hash's chair. Moonlight turned her blond hair into a phosphorescent, man-eating coral. "I got out of class as soon as I could. How's your concussion, baby cakes?" She swept a hand over Hash's bandage. "Ouch! Feel that lump! You need ice on that pronto."

Count Carnegie raised a hand. "Don't let me keep you here."

"Well, it is a little sore," Hash said.

Rhoda and Harriet came to the balcony. Count Carnegie had invited them for a farewell drink. "Rather suspected you'd be out here, Tonto," Rhoda said. "You've never dried dishes that fast in your life."

"Have a seat, girls," Breeze replied, getting up. "We were just about to leave." She looked at Floyd. "Well, Count, I suppose this is goodbye. You know I adore you madly. You have my address and phone should you ever visit New Jersey."

"Tank you. It vas a pleasure to know you." Floyd stood up and kissed her hand as Hash's face condensed into a familiar jealous frown.

Halfway across the balcony, Breeze stopped. "I'll never forget the night you carried me out of the dining room," she called. "It was fantastic." Hash took her arm and brought her inside.

Harriet sighed. "I suppose you're out of the hot water, Count Carnegie. For tonight, anyway."

"My colleague is accustomed to hazardous duty." Floyd ordered a round of brandy. "But I zink he has finally met his match."

Rhoda looked at the quiet mountains. "What a beautiful night," she said. "I will certainly miss Emwald."

"Vhat vill you be doing vhen you leave, Fräulein Rhoda?"

"Go back to work, of course."

"Are you going to find yourself a tventy-year-old man?" Floyd asked. She looked at him, startled. "It should not be difficult for such a handsome voman as you."

"How'd you know about that?"

"Oh, a little bird told me."

"Named Breeze?"

Floyd raised his glass. "Success to you." He looked at Harriet. "And vhat about you, Frau Svallow? Have you finished your exposé upon cooking schools?"

Now Harriet's mouth fell open. "My goodness, Count Carnegie! You really are a spy!"

"Zese are dangerous times. A man must keep himself informed."

"Well, Harriet, have you finished it?" Rhoda asked. "You haven't mentioned that thing in weeks."

Harriet's finger twiddled a curl above her forehead. "It got off to a great start, then bogged down. By the time we got back from class at night, I was just too tired to write." She sighed. "Let's face it, I just couldn't do it to Eggli. I'm going to tell my editor there was no case here."

"Ach," Floyd said, "I am going to miss you two ladies. You have been an enormous . . . consolation to me."

"Sounds as if you've lost someone, Count Carnegie."

The moon didn't get lost; it just slipped below the horizon. "Only for ze moment."

13

Eugene had been anxiously awaiting her at the Rome airport. As she walked off the ramp into the reception area Viola stared at her husband a moment as if he were a total stranger holding a little card which said "Viola Flury" and now she must follow him outside. Then he threw his arms around her. "Darling!" He kissed her face in a dozen places. "How I missed you. I am never taking a fishing trip again." Eugene stepped back. "Look at you, you're getting so big! There are really two of you now!"

"Eugene, I've only been gone six days."

"It felt like six centuries. God, you're beautiful. Everyone's staring at you."

"Everyone's staring at you, silly. Come on, we're blocking the aisle."

They walked to the baggage claim. "How was Switzerland?"

Well, dearest and only husband, it goes like this. Seventeen years ago, when I was just a kid, I met a boy named Floyd Beck in the shadows of Carnegie Hall. Fusion was instantaneous, but only Floyd recognized that; at the time I was hemorrhaging with a man at once father, lover, Merlin, North Star . . . you know my weakness for men who do a convincing imitation of God. They're the only ones who have ever challenged me. Well, before we even got to kiss one another, this fellow Beck and I had an abrupt sayonara. I never forgot him, though. The first few years I missed him terribly. He was like a low-frequency hum, felt but not seen, always there, never there. Drove me mad. Finally, when Nestor and Pyrana began to boil, the hum almost faded away, or I went deaf, I don't know. Those were hectic times. Then that quiet boy came back again, no longer as a flat hum, but as a graceful, silent loop, like the orbit of a planet around the sun. He'd disappear for months and then pow! perihelion: In the middle of a perfect spring night I'd feel his arms around me as if we had been in that lake only yesterday. Aprils were always bad: I first met him at a phone booth, alone, in April. Even after I married you, lovely man, there were two Aprils. I had resigned myself to these seasonal loops of regret: my punishment for making that boy walk the gangplank so many years ago. The planets were against us then. Two weeks ago Nestor broke his ankle and I went to the Hotel Badhof. Guess who was there, seventeen years older and still the most beautiful, blackest sun I had ever known. That was Floyd: That was fusion. It was an inevitable event of nature and had nothing to do with being married to you. His molecules and mine had begun to consume each other too many years ago. Do I love him? Ha, do I love my own blood? It's been in my veins forever. "Switzerland was full of mountains," Viola said.

Eugene and she had spent a quiet week eating pasta and puttering through Roman ruins. Her husband loved archaeology almost as much as he did fishing. Once, almost, he had broken his vows of sexual abstinence; Viola had kissed him on the forehead and asked him to fetch the Goldberg belt. She wouldn't yet have been able to make love with Eugene without wishing he were someone else.

Now they were flying home. "Seat belt on, dear?" he asked, leaning over.

"Yes." Viola peered down at the clouds. Maine lay beneath them. "Hope Nestor doesn't run into too much traffic coming to the airport."

"He shouldn't at this time of day," Eugene said. "It was very nice of him to meet us."

"I think he's bored stiff," Viola said. "And of course he has to show off Smudge." The pup had been recovered a few days ago, by customs agents. Nestor was beside himself.

"How's he going to drive with that cast?" Eugene asked. "Not fast, I hope. All that plaster will give him a heavy foot."

"Mai Ping is driving. Nestor's become quite fond of her."

Eugene kissed Viola's hand. "Don't tell me he's finally getting over you."

"Babies change things, darling." Some things, anyway. Viola closed her eyes, feigning sleep. She'd be seeing Floyd within the hour.

Albert McPhee looked up from his desk at the U.S. Customs and Immigration office as Floyd and Hash walked in together. "Well, look who's back! Wyatt Earp and Sir Lancelot!" He shook their hands. "You look great, Beck. But where's your tan? That a black eye?" He inspected Hash. "You look worse every time I lay eyes on you. What's that bandage on your head now?"

"I got hit with a frying pan."

Floyd took a seat and crossed his arms. "You're looking good, McPhee." Unusually so, he thought. "What's new around here?"

"Not much. So, Hash! How was your little trip? I got quite a kick out of that call from the Montreux police station. The Dalmatian got shot, eh?"

Hash poured himself a cup of coffee and sat on the desk next to Floyd. "McPhee," he said, "if I had two good arms, I'd beat the shit out of you. You were running this operation in rings around me all the time, weren't you?"

The supervisor slowly smiled. "Be a sport. Who was I to stand in the way of romance? You went after that vet like a mutt after a bitch in heat."

"There's one thing we don't understand," Floyd said. "Why did you drop that little black dog off at the Pyrana plant in the first place?"

McPhee bit into his donut. "You boys impress me," he said. "How did you know that?"

"You wrapped the pup in Frisk's scarf," Hash said. "The one you gave her for Valentine's Day."

To their surprise, instead of blush or denial, McPhee burst out laughing. "Aha! The cook did keep it then!" When Floyd and Hash did not join him in laughter, McPhee sighed. "Okay. I suppose you've earned an explanation. About two years ago, the people at Agriculture got wind of the Chinese trying to implant microchips in a pair of woodchucks going from the Bronx Zoo to the Beijing Zoo. The U.S. and China were working up to a cultural exchange at the time."

"How come I didn't know about this?" Hash interrupted.

"You were getting divorced, sonny boy. You were a mess."

"What was on the microchips?" Floyd asked.

"Drug formulas. You've heard of Zygotia Labs in Brooklyn? They've been experimenting for years with synthetic sperm."

Floyd and Hash looked at McPhee a long moment before deciding he really wasn't kidding. "Give me a break," Floyd said finally. "Isn't frozen sperm good enough?"

"Of course not. Synthetic sperm would be like having a wig made to order. The woman fills in a little card with eye color, brain power, gender, all that. Then she gets a little suppository. No sex, no messy paternity suits, no AIDS. Great for all those liberated women with no husbands."

"That's disgusting."

"Don't tell that to the people at Zygotia. They think they can patent it in a few years."

"So why do the Chinese want the formula? Or what's been done on it so far?"

"They might want a generation of only men. Or only women. Outlaw sex. How the hell do I know? Maybe they're going to send a bunch of people into space. Population control has always been the national pastime."

"Enough halfassed theory," Hash said impatiently. "So you penetrate the original woodchuck ring. I assume the Chinese had agents at Zygotia and at the Bronx Zoo. Then what?"

"We got together with the Defense and Commerce departments and decided to start feeding them mildly bogus formulas. It was the least we could do for our friends at Zygotia. They've invested millions in this."

"What do they call this stupendous drug?" Floyd asked.

"CurSex. Curtail sex. Curse sex. Don't ask me."

"Why didn't you just blow the whole operation out of the water?"

"Because we've been getting great microchips in return, for keeping our traps shut."

"Really! What's on them? The formula for synthetic ovaries?"

"Missile systems. Telemetry. Much more practical stuff. The Chinese are no slouches. Invented firecrackers, you know."

"What makes you think they're any less bogus than the formulas you're sending them?"

"Hey," McPhee said, "that's not my job. I'm just the middleman."

Hash's fingers nudged his newest bandage. "So you were the middleman in Customs and Agriculture," he said, wincing.

"Yep. The zoo connection ran out of woodchucks and muskrats about a year ago, and the Chinese came up with the idea of shipping the chips in and out in dogs. They were anonymous and people took them everywhere. We found a great veterinarian in Harlem. He'd get a load of mutts, pugs, poodles, and implant the chips. We'd drop them off, the Chinese would pick them up, babysit them until the stitches healed, then out they went. Everything was fine until that stupid pug scratched its butt and Hash got his first telex from Berlin."

"So why Pyrana?" Floyd repeated. "Wasn't that a little risky?"

"Beck, that was the fifth dog we unloaded there. That dumpster was perfect. Nobody bothered it. We dropped the pooch off when we were delivering milk to the cafeteria. The Chinese had an agent working as a cutter. She just went out back and picked the dog up before going home for lunch."

"Then Breeze intercepted one of your pups in the dumpster."

"Yep. That was a bad day. We had no idea Nestor would become so attached to it." McPhee looked at Hash. "Then your stupid informant told you to go looking for drugs in corsets. He was trying to tell you dogs with *CurSex.*"

Hash shrugged. "What can I tell you? At least he got Paterson right."

"So you go to the Feinstein Corset Company and take a walk next door to Pyrana," McPhee said. "Finding Nestor out there was an unbelievable stroke of luck."

"It was not," Hash said. "I cased that joint for a solid half hour. My nose told me something was off the second I saw that guy in pajamas."

"I almost had to tell you everything then and there. But you spared me. You saw Floyd's girlfriend at a July Fourth parade and suddenly decided that she was your villain."

"She's not my girlfriend," Floyd said.

"Will you shut up," Hash snapped. "Go on, McPhee, I'm listening."

"You followed her to the clinic a few days later and saw her there with Nestor. From what our informant Mai Ping reported to us, he was just there getting the dog checked out. It had gotten hit with a softball at the company picnic the week earlier. You immediately jumped to the conclusion that Nestor and Clemens were in cahoots."

"Why the hell didn't you try to stop me?"

"I did more than once, if you recall. You didn't want to hear about it. And this was a top-secret operation. The less you knew, the better."

Hash scowled. "Thanks to you, I have second-degree burns all over my face."

"Hey, pal, I didn't tell you to follow Nestor into a pizza parlor. By that time you were so far gone, all the blonds in Sweden couldn't have stopped you. Next day you visited Nestor in the hospital, reconvinced yourself that the Dog Woman was behind everything, and took off in hot pursuit."

Hash slumped morosely in his chair. "Shit."

"What happened after Hash went to Switzerland?" Floyd asked.

"Back up a day. The Chinese agent scooped the mutt fifteen steps out of the pizza parlor."

"While I was lying on the floor in agony? Was Mai Ping the chick in the white Toyota?" Hash demanded. "I knew she couldn't be going to choir practice. The church around the corner is a condo now."

"She's a great agent. She hardly let that dog out of her sight. She worked overtime at Pyrana. She took the mutt out to the treadmill every day, waiting for the opportunity to kidnap it back or replace it with another one. She was even prepared to seduce Nestor Buffez. Of course, after the riot in the pizza parlor, such steps were unnecessary."

"So you got the mutt back," Hash said. "But without the microchip."

"That's right." McPhee sighed. "Apparently Clemens had removed it already. That was a nasty surprise."

"Serves you right, schmuck," Hash muttered.

McPhee smiled broadly. For some reason he was enjoying this. "Obviously the chip had to be with either Nestor or Portia. Just on the slim chance it was with Portia, I figured I'd let you tail her to Switzerland. You offered to pay the air fare, after all."

"That was big of you."

"Two days after you left, I took a little ride to the Pyrana plant with Smudge. Nestor was hobbling around on crutches screaming at the employees. Obviously distressed. I took him aside and said that we had recovered the mutt, but without any chip in his tummy and that a trade was a trade. He went to his office and returned a minute later with the chip. He got his mutt back and I drove away with the next installment of CurSex."

Floyd and Hash looked at McPhee for some time. "I still don't believe you didn't let me in on the deal," Hash said.

Why should he? Hash had been winging Frisk jokes past McPhee for over a year now. Life presented so little opportunity for good, clean revenge.

Inspector Frisk sailed into the office. Her pants, if possible, had shrunk another size. Perhaps she was testing seams for the navy. If the thread held up under this pressure, it could anchor a nuclear submarine. "Hey! Welcome home, boys," she said, walking behind McPhee, pulling his ear: They were lovers again. Floyd and Hash exchanged much white of eye. "Having fun, Albert?"

"They found your scarf," McPhee said.

"My Valentine scarf? Where was it?"

"On an Indian in Switzerland," Hash said. "I wouldn't plan on getting it back if I were you."

"I left it in the front seat of his car," Frisk said. "Albert says he appropriated it for a national emergency. Is that true?" She looked at Floyd. "Hi, handsome. Swell black eye you got there. Make your sausages? How'd the cooking go?" Hash she ignored.

"No one died," Floyd replied.

Frisk looked into the terminal. "Plane's landed. Come on, Beck, let's nail 'em." She tweaked McPhee's nose. "Later."

"Am I missing something," Hash said to the supervisor after she had gone. "Last time I checked in, you and Frisk were playing North and South Pole."

Grinning stupidly, as if he had just won the lottery, McPhee scratched his chin. "You know what she did three days ago? Took all my clothes and books and everything else that was lying around her apartment and returned them."

"A fine idea," Hash said. "Beck and I have done the same to the low-lifes who deserted us." Just before going to Switzerland, in fact, Hash had taken Frisk aside and told her to purge her apartment of every iota belonging to McPhee. Then he had offered to take her to The Outpost for further catharsis.

"It was two o'clock in the morning. She rang my doorbell. The wife answered and found a huge box with all my underwear and personal belongings right there on the stoop."

"Way to go, Friskie," Hash said. "I hope your wife went after you with a rolling pin."

"My wife went after the lawyer the next morning," McPhee said. "I suppose I owe it all to you, Hash, thanks. I understand you were the fellow who put her up to this. Tell me you'll be our best man. We're getting married the second the ink dries on the divorce papers."

Hash looked over at Floyd. If it weren't for Breeze, his batting average over the last six months would be lower than the dollar-to-yen exchange rate. "What would you call the opposite of a Midas touch?"

Not answering, Floyd walked to the window and stood looking quietly into the terminal. The Swissair flight had landed. "McPhee," he said. "When did you last see Nestor?"

"Two days ago."

"He never went to Europe, then?"

"Not that I know of. Why?"

Floyd smiled to himself: This skit would have a great punchline. "Nothing. I'll take the lane on the right." He started to leave.

"Wait, how was your vacation?" McPhee called.

"Ask Hash." Floyd walked into the terminal.

She was in the crowd around the luggage wheel; he could feel her gently drawing him in, like an ocean reclaiming the ebb tide. He wanted to keep walking past his inspection station right into the throng, wandering among this forest of disheveled, talking trees until he stood next to her and took her hand. If Nestor was not her husband, who was? That tall fellow in the white suit? Adonis there in the designer tennis shorts? Oh God! Did it matter what the extra baggage looked like? Where was that pale face that belonged to him? Floyd saw nothing but tee-shirts and sneakers.

A well-kept woman carrying only an alligator purse arrived at his station first, probably visiting the States for lunch. Then a couple from Cleveland passed by with a suitcase full of brown cuckoo clocks. More baggage, more nods and smiles, chocolate, cheese, watches: inexhaustible as the warm springs beneath his secret lake. As each passenger appeared in front of him, Floyd forced his eyes to concentrate solely upon an unknown face and a white customs declaration. He did not want to see her slowly edging closer to him from the periphery of his vision: He wanted nothing—then Viola like a splash of cold water, like sudden death.

"Hello," said a pleasant old man, extending two passports. Floyd took them, and saw Viola. "My wife and I are traveling together."

Eugene Phillips was born in New York City, October 1924, sixty-three years ago. She had found another Richard, this time a benevolent one. Someday Floyd would like to ask her why such a beautiful woman, who could have any man on earth, would choose to marry someone who would probably never live to see his child graduate from college. Was time that irrelevant to her, too? He opened Viola's passport, pretended to study the picture, then looked at her face. They both knew they were going to wait another ten, twenty years. In her hair was a white ribbon.

"Do you have anything else to declare?" Floyd asked, perusing Eugene's customs form.

"No, sir. Just the fishing rod and the hobby horse." Eugene beamed, the proudest soul alive. "My wife and I are expecting a baby."

Floyd understood why she had married him: Eugene had no idea he was supposed to be a crotchety old man. Somehow, against all odds, his genes had failed to manufacture that little bitterness switch. Was that mutation hereditary? If so, the man had an obligation to reproduce himself; the species needed him. Floyd folded the passports and handed them back to Eugene. "Congratulations," he said.

"Thank you." Eugene took Viola's arm. "Let's go, darling." Without Viola, no matter what the configuration of his DNA, Eugene would die. That would not be right. His wife smiled, or subtly lifted her lips, in Floyd's direction. Then they left.

A woman about Floyd's age filled the vacancy at his station. She looked as if she had just given herself a haircut with an airplane knife. A mile of adhesive tape trussed her mortally swollen suitcase. "Please don't make me open this. I'll never get it shut again."

Floyd looked at her customs declaration. "How long were you in Geneva," he asked.

"One week, for a conference on women's rights."

"How was it?"

The woman shrugged. "I think I'm getting too old for this."

He initialed the form and handed it back. "Never say you're too old for anything."

Several hours later, when the terminal had emptied again, Frisk walked over to Floyd's station, whistling lightly. If she wasn't pregnant by Christmas, McPhee should trade in his testicles. "Hey, I've got something for you," she said, handing over a gift box. "You won this. Confiscator-of-the-Month for June. Congratulations."

Floyd pulled the ribbon. In the box lay one of Viola's pink-on-black teddies of Manhattan. A few weeks ago he had removed something like this, and a couple hundred thousand bucks, from a visiting tourist. "I notice you liked that when I held it over my shirt in the office," Frisk said. "I don't know what size you'd ever need, but you can exchange it. The lady said just bring it back to the boutique on Madison Avenue any time."

"Thanks." He'd keep it in his top drawer, to look at whenever the winters got too long. On the way out Floyd checked in at the office but Hash and McPhee were long gone, perhaps for beer and an armistice. Floyd walked to his Falcon, rolled down a window, and started the tired engine. Immediately the radio jolted to life, spilling voluptuous waltzes from *Der Rosenkavalier* over the seat. Floyd listened until they had ended, knowing that someday he and Viola would finally dance. She would never have worn the white ribbon otherwise.

Floyd suddenly decided that tomorrow he was going to buy a new car, one which did not remind him of dead dogs. How about cats for a change? Jaguar: black, like her hair, like their lake, like the fewer and fewer nights he would spend waiting for that perfect shadow redolent of roses and warm cream. He rolled the Falcon out of the lot, toward home. Yes, a Jaguar would be fine. Count Carnegie would appreciate that.